D

"Would you like to dance?" He nodded in the direction of the dance floor.

"You don't dance," Lizzie said. "You never did."

"I think I can manage this one." He tugged on her hand and pulled her gently into his arms. "I'll try not to step on your toes."

She laughed, and wrapped her arms around his neck, aligning herself against him, her head fitting nicely against his shoulder. He let out a long sigh as his body recognized hers and flowed to close the gap between them. The actual song made no impression on him because he was too busy enjoying having Lizzie in his arms. She felt right there—as if su puzzle made s

"Thi

"Mm kissed the top y there all nigh . .

Books by Kate Pearce

The House of Pleasure Series
SIMPLY SEXUAL
SIMPLY SINFUL
SIMPLY SHAMELESS
SIMPLY WICKED
SIMPLY INSATIABLE
SIMPLY FORBIDDEN
SIMPLY CARNAL
SIMPLY VORACIOUS
SIMPLY SCANDALOUS
SIMPLY PLEASURE (e-novella)
SIMPLY IRRESISTIBLE (e-novella)

The Sinners Club Series
THE SINNERS CLUB
TEMPTING A SINNER
MASTERING A SINNER
THE FIRST SINNERS (e-novella)

Single Titles
RAW DESIRE

The Morgan Brothers Ranch
THE RELUCTANT COWBOY
THE MAVERICK COWBOY
THE LAST GOOD COWBOY
THE BAD BOY COWBOY
THE BILLIONAIRE BULL RIDER
THE RANCHER

The Millers of Morgantown
THE SECOND CHANCE RANCHER
THE RANCHER'S REDEMPTION

Anthologies
SOME LIKE IT ROUGH
LORDS OF PASSION
HAPPY IS THE BRIDE
A SEASON TO CELEBRATE
MARRYING MY COWBOY

Published by Kensington Publishing Corporation

THE RANCHER'S REDEMPTION

KATE PEARCE

ZEBRA BOOKS
KENSINGTON PUBLISHING CORP.
www.kensingtonbooks.com

ZEBRA BOOKS are published by

Kensington Publishing Corp.
119 West 40th Street
New York, NY 10018

First Printing: December 2019
ISBN-13: 978-1-4201-4824-4
ISBN-10: 1-4201-4824-9

ISBN-13: 978-1-4201-4827-5 (eBook)
ISBN-10: 1-4201-4827-3 (eBook)

10 9 8 7 6 5 4 3 2 1

Printed in the United States of America

Many thanks to Jerri Drennen for reading and proofreading, and to Melissa Blue for making me a better writer in so many ways. Continued thanks to Meg Scales for all things ranch-related.

Chapter One

Morgantown
Morgan Valley, California

Roman ran up the path and knocked hard on the front door. When Gabby unlocked the child gate and bent to give him a hug, the excitement on his face made both women smile.

"Hey." Gabby let Roman wiggle past her into the house. "Is everything good?"

"Seems to be," Lizzie said. "I washed Doofus the Dinosaur."

"Thanks." Gabby made an amused face. "Roman and Gus found a muddy spot in the yard where one of the sprinklers was leaking. By the time I cleaned them up, I had no time for the stuffed toy."

"It's all good." Lizzie nodded. "I'll pick him up at the usual time."

Gabby lowered her voice. "Coretta was looking over the fence again, yesterday."

Lizzie tensed. "Did she say anything?"

"Nope, but I think she might have been taking pictures."

Gabby hesitated. "If you like, I can call Nate Turner and see if there's anything we can do about it."

"I think that would just make everything worse." Lizzie sighed. "I'm going to have to try and talk to her again." She checked the time on her phone and looked at the house next door. The drapes and blinds were closed against the morning sun, giving the place a bland, shuttered look. "I can't have her scaring Roman."

"She's usually up and about by nine," Gabby said. "Should I text you if I see her?"

"Would you?" Lizzie smiled at her friend. "I'd really appreciate it."

Deep in thought, Lizzie went back onto Main Street and walked toward Yvonne's café where the owner had been at work since four baking bread and creating fabulous confections. Lizzie loved her boss and enjoyed her job, although when it was tourist season, it could get extremely busy. Sometimes she didn't sit down for hours.

It was good that her commute was so short. When Ted Baker had converted the top floor of his mechanics shop into an apartment, she'd jumped at the chance to rent it from him. Ro's day care was right around the corner, and everything in Morgantown was within easy walking distance.

Using her key, she entered the rear of the shop, hung her coat in the back, and went through into the huge industrial-sized kitchen.

"Hey!" Yvonne Payet called out to her. "How are you this fine morning?"

"I'm good." Lizzie fixed on a bright smile. "I might have to pop out today to deal with something for Roman. Is that okay?"

"As long as someone can cover you from the kitchen,

then of course it is." Yvonne gave her a quizzical look as Lizzie washed her hands and put on her apron. "Is everything all right?"

"It will be," Lizzie reassured her boss. Gabby was the only person in town who knew the full story about Roman's parentage, and Lizzie preferred to keep it that way. Yvonne had never asked who the father of her son was or made a big deal out of it, for which Lizzie was eternally grateful.

"Roman's not sick, is he?" Yvonne placed a tray of choux buns out on the stainless-steel work surface and picked up a piping bag of crème pâtissière.

"No, he's doing great." Lizzie delved into the pocket of her apron and drew out her notepad and pen. "What are the specials today?"

Two hours later, when the early morning commuters and townsfolk had come and gone, and the tourists hadn't yet arrived, Lizzie took the opportunity to check her phone. There was a text from Gabby saying that Coretta was up and hanging out washing in her yard.

After checking with Yvonne, Lizzie left the almost-empty café, and made her way back to Gabby's, smiling as she heard the kids shrieking in the backyard. The sun was shining and Gabby's garden was in full bloom. Bypassing the house, Lizzie marched determinedly up the path and knocked on Coretta's door. It took quite a while before it opened. Lizzie had to act quickly when Coretta realized who it was and tried to slam it shut again.

"I need to talk to you," Lizzie said politely.

"I have nothing to say," Coretta replied through the narrow gap in the door.

"If you won't speak to me I'm going to ask the sheriff

whether it's legal for you to be taking pictures of my child without my permission."

"He's not just your child."

"I am well aware of that." Lizzie held on to her patience. "If you want to meet Roman, that's *great.* I've offered to introduce you to him several times, but you've brushed me off. I think it would be good for him to know he has a relative right here in Morgantown."

"After what you did to poor Ray?" Coretta sniffed. "I don't believe that for a second."

"What *I* did?" Lizzie blew out a calming breath. "Okay, if you want to have a relationship with your great-great-nephew, then come and find me at the coffee shop and we can discuss it. If you *don't* want to do that, please stop spying on him. It's creepy, and wrong, and if you keep it up, I'll talk to Nate about how to stop you."

Coretta put all her weight behind the door and finally succeeded in shutting it in Lizzie's face.

"So much for being nice," Lizzie muttered. She didn't get it. If Coretta wanted to get to know Roman, she was all for it. Just because Ray had behaved like a complete jerk didn't mean that the rest of his family had to be jerks, too.

Except that they all *had* been jerks to her and worse . . . cutting her off, refusing to give her the chance to talk to them, totally believing whatever bullshit story Ray had cooked up to explain leaving her high and dry. She wasn't the same person now. Having a child had helped her grow up fast. She would do anything to protect her son from harm.

Aware from the twitch of the faded curtains that Coretta was now spying on *her,* Lizzie turned around, and went back toward the café. She'd check in with Gabby at the end of the day. If Coretta still didn't get it, she would speak to

Nate. Maybe if the sheriff had a word with the old woman, she'd finally listen.

Lizzie was almost at the door of the café before it occurred to her to wonder why Coretta was taking photos, and if she was sharing them. Did anyone on Ray's side of the family care about the little boy they'd never bothered to meet, or was Coretta just taking them for herself?

Stifling a sigh, Lizzie went into the kitchen, washed her hands, and went back out to the front of the shop where Yvonne was busy serving a customer. Her boss saw her and smiled.

"That was quick!"

"Thanks for holding the fort for me." Lizzie tied on her apron. "Has it been busy?"

"Not really. Just Jackson Lymond buying pastries for Daisy." Yvonne sighed. "They are so in *love*. . . ."

Lizzie couldn't help but smile when she thought about the couple who often had lunch at the café, and had no problem airing their grievances in front of an audience. Daisy Miller deserved the best, and Jackson seemed determined to prove she'd found the right man.

Yvonne signed off the cash register and lingered by the glass display cases, straightening up the regimented rows of pastries and cakes with the eagle eye of a French patisserie owner.

"I wanted to ask if you'd take charge this coming Saturday?" Yvonne finally turned to Lizzie.

"If I can get someone to take care of Roman, sure." Lizzie never minded extra hours. "Are you off somewhere?"

"Well, yes, and no." Yvonne made a face. "Rio wants to look at some land in Morgan Valley."

"That's good, isn't it?" Lizzie asked cautiously. "That

he wants to make his home here with you where your business is?"

"Yes, but I don't fancy clomping around acres of nothing in the scorching sun. All I want is a decent view, a big kitchen, and a short commute into town."

"Have you considered the Cortez ranch?" Lizzie asked. "It's close by."

"I forgot that was for sale." Yvonne looked interested. "I'll have to tell Rio and see if it's big enough."

"Big enough for what?" Lizzie signed into the register.

"His bull-breeding schemes." Yvonne rolled her eyes. "Don't ask."

Lizzie held back a chuckle as Yvonne went back into the kitchen. Her boss was engaged to a former world champion bull rider so his interest in raising bulls was not way out of field. He also had a role in an international company founded by his billionaire father. He could probably afford to live in a palace, or buy up a small country. . . .

Lizzie looked up as the door opened and Nate Turner came in. He was the only representative of the law in Morgantown, and had a quiet, laid-back manner that suited the town he'd grown up in.

"Hey, how are you?" Nate asked as he approached the counter. "I wanted to talk to Yvonne about some catering for my wedding. Is she here?"

"She is. Do you want to go through?" Lizzie pointed at the kitchen door. "And when you're done, would you mind stopping by, and having a chat with me?"

"Damn." Adam Miller winced as he hit his thumb with the hammer. He took off his glove using his teeth and studied his throbbing digit.

He was fixing the chicken coop to the side of the main

ranch house. He'd noticed a couple of escapees the previous night and had discovered a hole in the wire where one of the posts had split. Like all easy jobs it had taken him far longer than he anticipated, and now the sun was blazing down on his head, and he needed a cold drink.

He replaced his glove, unrolled the new piece of wire mesh netting, and cut it to size before attaching it firmly between the two new posts he'd just hammered into the ground. Several of the chickens watched from the shade of the coop, but they were too hot to attempt an escape, which suited him just fine. He didn't have the energy to chase chickens.

Gathering up his supplies, he walked back to the barn and replaced everything in its correct space. With a big family sharing all the tools, he didn't want to be the one who messed up the system. One of the barn dogs came dancing up and he bent down to pet it, grimacing as his bones creaked. Jeez . . . he was getting old. Thirty-five next birthday, and almost fourteen years since his wife Louisa had died.

He made a mental note to visit her grave and spend a few hours with her parents at the Cortez ranch that weekend. He hadn't been over for a while. His in-laws were planning on moving to Sacramento to take advantage of the expert healthcare necessary for Carlos's particular type of cancer. Adam couldn't blame them. He wasn't sure what he was going to do when his last link with Louisa left the valley.

He entered the rear of the sprawling ranch house his grandfather had rebuilt in the 1940s after the original home burned down. It was large enough to house his father and his five siblings, which some days he appreciated, and some days not so much. He took off his boots and washed his hands before walking through into the country kitchen.

His brother Kaiden had designed the light and airy space and custom made all the cabinetry.

Adam drank two glasses of water straight from the faucet and then moved on to the fresh lemonade in the refrigerator. It got blazing hot during the summer in Morgan Valley and every rancher worried about drought and fire. He considered walking through to the farm office but decided to stay in the coolness of the kitchen. He had his schedule on his cell so he didn't need to use the ancient computer.

For once, everyone was out, and the house settled quietly around him, the only sounds the whirring of the refrigerator and the ticking of the kitchen clock. He checked his phone and found a text from Ines, his mother-in-law, which made him frown. His afternoon was clear, which meant he could go and pay the Cortezes an early visit.

His stomach growled and he headed for the pantry. He'd make himself a sandwich, leave a note to tell his father he'd be back for dinner, and be at the Cortez ranch in half an hour.

"It's so nice to see you, Adam." Ines Cortez patted his hand and poured him another glass of iced tea. "Carlos hasn't been getting out much, and you've cheered him up."

"How's he really feeling?" Adam lowered his voice, aware that his father-in-law was sitting outside on the porch, and the door was open. He'd spent half an hour visiting with Carlos, and had only come inside when his companion started to doze off.

Ines grimaced. "He's very tired. These long trips to the hospital aren't helping. The sooner we move to Sacramento, the better." She hesitated. "Do you know a guy called Rio Martinez?"

"Yeah, he's engaged to Yvonne who runs the café. Why?"

"He called me today, said he'd heard the ranch was for sale, and wanted to know if he could come visit."

"I haven't heard anything bad about him," Adam said cautiously. "He'd also be good for the cash, seeing as his father is some kind of billionaire."

Ines nodded. "That's good to know. I'll call him back and ask if he can come up this weekend." She looked around the old-fashioned kitchen. "Not that's there's much to see. We're barely functioning as a ranch right now."

"I can always come over and help out. You know that," Adam reminded her.

"You've got enough to do." Ines smiled at him, the worry on her face easing slightly. "Jeff will be coming after me if I keep you from doing your job."

"He has plenty of alternatives," Adam said. He'd noticed the gradual decline in the number of cattle and the unplowed fields. He'd decided not to mention them because the couple had enough to deal with.

"Nonsense. Jeff relies on you. He told me so himself." Ines surreptitiously checked the time. "I hate to cut your visit short, but I have to fetch Carlos's prescriptions from Dr. Tio's office."

"I could get them for you," Adam suggested as he rose from the table. "I have to go into town anyway. I can drop them back on my way home."

"Would you?" Ines cast a worried glance at the door. "I don't like to leave Carlos by himself."

"It's not a problem." Adam took the list from her and stowed it safely in his jacket pocket. "I'll be back as soon as I can."

"God bless you, Adam." She hugged him tight, "You are such a comfort to us."

He kissed the top of her head, said good-bye to Carlos who was dozing in the sunlight, and got back in his truck.

Now that he really looked at the place, he could see the heart had gone out of it. The decline had started when Louisa, their only child, had died so young, and had only accelerated when Carlos became ill.

He wished he had the money to buy it himself, but it wasn't possible. He'd told Carlos not to worry about leaving him the place in his will—that he should take the money *now* and use it to get well. It had been a hard thing to do, as if he was giving up on his last promise to Louisa, but Carlos had to come first. Things were changing. He didn't like it much, but there wasn't anything he could do.

He drove into town through bare hills covered in yellow grass while dust clouds swirled across the road and the sun blazed down. Every breath felt like it scorched his throat, and his eyes were dry and scratchy. He sighed as he approached Main Street and came to a complete stop. Two tour buses were taking up the width of the street and they didn't look like they were going anywhere anytime soon.

One change he could agree on was the current push to get the historic street closed to traffic. He took a quick right turn onto Front Street, which would take him around the back of the town and deliver him at the other end of Main Street where Dr. Tio's medical center was situated.

The sunlight was so blinding that he almost missed the figure on the side of the street attempting to flag him down. After a quick glance in his rearview mirror, he stopped, backed up, and let down his window.

"Lizzie?"

"Adam!" She ran toward him, her face so anguished that he scrambled to get out of the cab to reach her. "*Help* me!"

"What's up?"

"It's Roman. He's unconscious! I need to get him to Dr. Tio's."

"Where is he?"

She ran toward Gabby Kennedy's house and he followed her through the front door, momentarily blinking at the sudden darkness as she kept going straight out into the yard.

Gabby was holding the boy in her lap. "I think he was stung."

"Okay." Adam gathered the boy up in his arms and checked his airway and breathing. Roman's face and lips were already swelling up. "You call ahead, Gabby. Lizzie and I will take him."

"Already done." Gabby looked like she was about to burst into tears. "I'm so *sorry,* Lizzie."

Adam ran back to the truck. Lizzie climbed into the passenger seat, and he handed her the boy.

"Hold on to him. I'm going to go as fast as I can."

"Thank you." Lizzie's voice was barely audible as she cradled her son's head. "Neither Gabby nor I have a car here, so I didn't know what to do. I was just about to pick him up and start running."

"It's all good," Adam reassured her, his gaze everywhere as he tore down the narrow street, hazard lights blinking. *Where was Nate Turner when you needed him?* "We'll be there in a minute."

He swung into the parking lot behind Dr. Tio's medical center, getting as close to the door as possible, shut off the engine, and ran around to help Lizzie get down.

Dr. Tio appeared at the rear door of the twenty-four-hour medical center, his cell phone clamped to his ear and waved at them. "Bring him right in."

Adam took the boy from Lizzie and went through the door, aware that Roman's breathing had deteriorated, and that the swelling was getting worse.

"Set him down here." Dr. Tio immediately started checking Roman's pulse as the nurse took his temperature and blood pressure readings. "Was it a bee sting?"

"Yes." Lizzie nodded. "I think so. I'd just gone to pick him up, and he was playing in the yard. When I went out to get him, I heard him cry out, and he just dropped to his knees."

Adam instinctively grabbed Lizzie's hand as she faltered through her explanation, her voice shaking.

"I don't suppose you got the bee, did you?" Dr. Tio asked as he stripped Roman down to his dinosaur print boxers.

"No. Does it matter?" Lizzie bit her lip.

"Not really." Dr. Tio placed an oxygen mask over Roman's mouth. "I'm going to give him a shot of epinephrine. Would you two mind stepping back a bit so Adrianna and I can work?"

Chapter Two

Lizzie found herself crowded back against the considerable bulk of Adam Miller, his big hands steady on her shoulders as Dr. Tio cared for Roman. Even though, at six-foot-four he was about a foot taller than her, she was glad of his support. Her own legs were shaking like Jell-O. Seeing her son drop to the ground had frozen her to the core—until panic set in, and she'd ended up flagging down the only man in Morgantown who consistently tried to avoid her.

Dr. Tio looked back at her and smiled. "He's responding well to the epinephrine, and he's about to wake up. Do you want to come up here and reassure him that everything's going to be okay?"

Nodding like a fool, Lizzie went toward Roman, and tried to smile as he focused on her.

"Mommy?"

She patted his hand. "It's okay, baby. You got stung. Dr. Tio is taking care of you. I'm going to stick around until he says it's okay for me to take you home."

"Okay." Roman closed his eyes again. "I'm sleepy."

Her anxious gaze flew to the doctor.

"It's all right if he wants to sleep," Dr. Tio said. "Adrianna is going to stay and monitor him until he's ready to go home." He smiled at Lizzie. "Why don't you go through to the front and sort out the paperwork? I'll call you back in once Roman is settled."

"Thank you, Doctor," Lizzie said fervently. "Thank you so much."

"You did the hardest part—getting him here so fast—so thank you." Dr. Tio smiled at her and held the door open.

She went out into the hallway and had to steady herself against the wall as a wave of swirling black dots descended over her vision. A hand slid under her elbow.

"Hang in there, Lizzie. Come and sit down."

She allowed Adam to take charge as he led her into a small waiting room at the side of the twenty-four-hour care unit. He unceremoniously eased her into a chair and shoved her head down between her knees.

"Breathe."

She gulped in some air and eventually straightened up, her gaze settling on his unsmiling face as he sat opposite her. Oh God, he looked pissed, but when did he ever look pleased to see her? He was a big guy who never had to raise his voice to be heard because his mere presence was so intimidating. She set aside the past and focused on what he had done for her and Roman.

"Thank you for everything."

"You're welcome." He nodded to her. "I'm glad I could help."

"You were . . . amazing," Lizzie said fervently.

"I was just in the right place at the right time." He shrugged his broad shoulders. "It was stop and help you, or run you over."

Lizzie opened her mouth to reply, and then studied him. "Was that a joke?"

"Might have been."

"Well, whatever, I really appreciate what you did,"

Lizzie said firmly. "I'm sure you have things to do so I'll thank you again."

He raised an eyebrow, got to his feet, and headed out toward the main office of the doctor's practice. When the door shut behind him, Lizzie let out a shaky breath. He was just so big and unapproachable that he made her act like an idiot. He always had even when they were kids. As a scared newcomer to the town and school, it had taken her a while to realize that behind his impenetrable front, he was the kindest, sweetest, guy you would ever meet. Not that there was much evidence of that these days. After Louisa died. the joy had drained right out of him, and from what she'd seen in the intervening years, it had never returned.

She went to take out her phone to call Gabby and realized it wasn't in her pocket. With a silent wail, she searched around the floor, peeked into Roman's room, but couldn't see it anywhere. She reluctantly concluded she'd have to retrace her steps to Adam's truck.

Of course, when she got to the parking lot, Adam was already standing by the passenger side of his truck. He saw her and silently held up her phone.

"Thank you," Lizzie said for what felt like the twenty millionth time. "It must have fallen out of my pocket when I got in the truck."

"You're welcome."

"I'm not normally this klutzy," Lizzie blurted out.

"That's not what I remember," Adam said as he relocked the truck. "You were always losing stuff when we were at school."

"I've *changed*." For some reason, Lizzie wasn't prepared to let it go. "I have a *child* now. I'm a responsible adult."

He nodded and started back toward the building.

"Where are you *going?*" Lizzie asked.

He swung around and looked down at her from his considerable height. "I offered to pick up Carlos's prescriptions for Ines. I'm just going to turn them in at the pharmacy and wait."

He didn't say *if that's okay by you,* but Lizzie heard it regardless.

"How are they doing?" Lizzie asked.

"Not great." He half turned away. "You should visit them."

"I do." Lizzie said the words quietly to herself once he'd moved out of earshot. He'd done her a huge favor today. She really didn't want to get into an argument with him about her best friend Louisa's parents. They had been very good to her after Roman was born, and her son loved going up to the ranch to see them.

Clutching her phone to her chest, she went back into Dr. Tio's, and set about texting Gabby to let her know that Roman was going to be okay. She also texted Yvonne to give her a heads-up about maybe not being in the café tomorrow. Both women replied and offered their help, which made her want to cry again. Despite having to bring Roman up by herself, she'd never felt alone in Morgantown.

After an interminable hour, Dr. Tio agreed that she could take Roman home. They lived right across the street from the medical center. If there were any problems Lizzie could get him back in a flash. He gave her a lot of information about anaphylactic shock, and a prescription to fill at the pharmacy for EpiPens, which she would need to have around Roman twenty-four seven.

He'd already sent the prescription through to his pharmacist so while Roman was being checked out, she went to pick it up.

"Hey."

Adam Miller was just coming out as she went in, a bag

of prescriptions in his hand. He must have been there for ages. He paused to hold the door open for her.

"How's Roman doing?"

She didn't think he'd ever used her kid's name before, or suggested he knew she even had a son. In such a compact town, it was hard to avoid people, but he'd done a pretty good job of it until now, hiding up at the family ranch, rarely going to church, and only speaking to her when it was absolutely necessary.

"Ro's doing good." She gestured at the pharmacist. "I've got to pick up some EpiPens for him."

"Makes sense." He lingered by the door, his expression grave. "Do you need a ride back home?"

Surprised, she looked up and met his gray-eyed stare. When was the last time they had actually looked each other right in the eye? She had a terrible feeling she knew exactly when, and tried not to think about it.

"Not really. I, I mean *we,* live right here—over Ted Baker's mechanics shop."

"Yeah, I know."

"How do you know?" Lizzie inquired suspiciously.

"It's a small town." He looked over at the gas station and then back at Lizzie. "It's still a long way to carry him."

"I wasn't going to—" She stopped, and let out a long weary breath, her shoulders dropping. They'd been friends once. He was as stubborn as she was, and she wasn't going to argue when she really needed his help. "Okay, thank you. I'd appreciate it."

He nodded. "I'll meet you in the waiting room."

Adam wanted to kick himself for offering to help Lizzie again, but she'd looked so . . . defeated, and worn down that he hadn't been able to stop himself. He was already late getting home. Another ten minutes carrying the boy over to her place wouldn't make much difference. He called Ines and said he'd be with her in the next hour, and texted Kaiden to start dinner.

The door into the waiting room opened, and an older woman came in and scanned the room. Adam automatically got to his feet as she faced him.

"Where is she?"

"If you can tell me who you are looking for, I might be able to help you," the receptionist pointed out brightly.

"Lizzie Taylor."

"And if she was here, who wishes to speak to her?"

"Coretta Smith."

Just as Adam was about to intervene, Dr. Tio emerged from the inner sanctuary of the office carrying Roman wrapped in a blanket.

"Ah, here you are." He smiled at Adam and then down at the boy. "Your taxi home has arrived."

Roman giggled as Dr. Tio passed him over to Adam, and then went quiet as he studied Adam's unfamiliar face. He had Lizzie's blue eyes and sweet smile, but not her reddish hair. His was brown and curly.

"Hey, I'm a friend of your mother's," Adam said gruffly.

Lizzie came up beside Adam and put a hand on his arm. "This is Mr. Miller, Roman. He's the one who helped bring you to Dr. Tio's."

"In his truck?"

"Yes."

"Cool." Roman settled himself more firmly in Adam's arms. "Can we go home now?"

"Sure." Lizzie ran ahead of Adam and held the outside door open. "Thanks again, Dr. Tio."

"You're welcome."

Adam ducked his head slightly to make sure his Stetson cleared the doorframe, and stepped out into the warm evening air, the boy safe in his arms.

"Lizzie Taylor!"

He'd forgotten about Coretta Smith, whom he remembered lived next door to Gabby. Maybe she'd seen the accident and wanted to make sure the little boy was okay.

Beside him, Lizzie stiffened and turned around to the older woman.

"What do you want?"

Coretta stuck out a finger. "You're not fit to have charge of that precious angel!"

"He was stung by a bee," Lizzie said tiredly. "I—"

"And if you'd been taking care of him like a good mother should in his own home rather than leaving him with strangers this would never had happened!"

"That's not true—if he's allergic to bee stings it could've happened anywhere." Lizzie turned to Adam. "Let's keep moving. I don't want Roman to have to listen to this."

"You're a bad mother, and I'm going to make sure everyone knows about it!"

Coretta continued to shout even as Lizzie and Adam crossed the road beside the pizza parlor and headed for Ted's place. Adam only realized how badly Lizzie was shaking when she couldn't get the key into the downstairs door lock.

"Pizza?" Roman asked hopefully.

"Let's just get you settled into bed first, okay, buddy?" Adam murmured.

Lizzie finally managed the lock, and Adam followed her up the stairs and into her apartment. He paused on the threshold and silently appreciated the warm colors and inviting spaces she'd created out of the uninspiring square box. She'd always been good at that.

"Nice place."

"Thanks." She rushed ahead of him opening doors. "This is Roman's bedroom."

He carefully placed the boy on the bed and unwrapped him from the blanket.

"You're home, buddy."

"Say thank you, Roman." Lizzie closed the drapes and snapped on the light beside the bed. "Mr. Miller's been very kind to us today."

"Thank you, Mr. Miller." Roman smiled up at Adam.

"You can call me Adam. Mr. Miller sounds like my dad."

"I don't have a dad," Roman said and then yawned really hard. "Mom said he's missing out."

"She's right." Adam got off the bed and walked toward the door. "Nice to meet you, Roman. Stay away from any bees, okay?"

He followed Lizzie out to the kitchen-diner and stood awkwardly as she fluttered about putting on lamps and fixing the window shades. He sunk his fingers into the throw on the back of the couch and appreciated the softness. There was little of that in his life now; only his affection for his sister allowed him to express any warmth for anyone.

"I'd better go," Adam said, shifting from one foot to the other. The whole scenario was making him anxious.

Lizzie came toward him and offered another exhausted smile. She'd gotten very thin after she'd had the baby, all sharp angles like a baby stork. He'd been worried about her for a while, but she looked much more like her old self now.

"I know I keep saying it, Adam, but thank you."

"You're welcome." He hesitated. "Is there something

going on between you and Coretta? She sure seemed mad at you."

"She—" Lizzie sighed and shoved a hand through her hair. "I'll deal with it. There's nothing for you to worry about."

"I wasn't worrying."

"Of course you weren't. Why would you?" She straightened up, all the softness disappearing from her face, and went over to the door. "Thanks for helping me out today."

For some reason, he was reluctant to leave. It was the first decent conversation he'd had with her for years, and he'd missed her. They'd been best friends at school before he'd fallen in love with *her* best friend, Louisa, and everything had changed.

Adam took a step toward her. "Lizzie . . ."

"Mom!"

They both turned to see Roman standing in the hall doorway, his eyes filled with tears.

"What's wrong?" Lizzie rushed over to pick him up. "Do you feel sick? Do you want me to call Dr. Tio?"

"I've lost Doofus!" Roman began to bawl.

"No, you haven't. You just left him at Gabby's" Lizzie patted his back. "You can get him tomorrow. It's okay, it's okay."

"But I need him *now,*" Roman choked out through tears.

Uncomfortable with the kid's tears, Adam's roving gaze fixed on a photo on the wall of Lizzie and Louisa, their arms locked around each other as they grinned at the camera. He remembered the moment so well, it hurt. They'd been teasing him and laughing so hard he'd had trouble taking the picture. He abruptly averted his gaze.

"Look, I'd better go."

"Sure." Lizzie didn't turn around as she rocked her son.

She probably thought he was terrified of kids. "Take care now, Adam."

He headed down the stairs, his steps slowing as he reached the street. He felt unsettled, like he'd been drawn into something, and couldn't set himself free again. Seeing Lizzie . . . seeing how she loved her son had reminded him of everything he'd lost when Louisa died.

He'd never hold a child like that; he'd never have to worry about anything hurting him. He winced, the sound of Roman's crying filling his ears as he walked back to his truck and got inside. After checking the time, he determined he might as well make one or two more stops before he finally made it home.

Lizzie finally persuaded a sobbing Roman to get back into bed, but only after she'd allowed him to put every single stuffed toy he owned in the bed as a substitute for Doofus. There was barely room left for him, but he didn't seem to mind. As he'd stopped crying, Lizzie was fine with it.

She went back into the living room and collapsed on the couch. What an awful day. For the first time in a long while she wished she had someone there to hold her, to offer support, and tell her that everything would be okay. She could call her parents in Vegas, but then they'd be worried, and she didn't want to do that to them.

She'd dealt with worse; a crying baby with colic while she had the flu and had to get the tax forms out for her clients for the end of the year came to mind.

The sharp ring of her downstairs doorbell made her jump. Had Coretta followed her home, or was it one of her friends come to commiserate with her? Lizzie got to her feet and peered out of the window, frowning as Dell Turner waved cheerfully back at her.

She went down to open the door and smiled at Dell. He wore a green and gold cap with GINA'S on it, and held out a flat pizza box.

"Hey, Ms. Lizzie. Your pizza's here."

She frowned. "I didn't order pizza."

"I know." He didn't seem fazed by her weird attitude as he handed over the box then fumbled in his backpack. "Don't worry, I chose your favorite toppings. He said to give you this as well."

Dell gently set Doofus down on top of the pizza box. "Here you go."

Lizzie stared at the dinosaur. "Who did this?"

"Adam Miller," Dell said. "He also paid the tip. Have a great night, Ms. Lizzie."

She walked back up the stairs, her mind grappling with what had just happened. She put the pizza on the countertop and went through to Roman's bedroom where he'd already fallen asleep surrounded by his toys. When she slipped Doofus under his arm, he smiled, rubbed his cheek against the dinosaur, and gave a satisfied sigh that went straight to Lizzie's heart.

Her stomach rumbled as she approached the pizza box. She hadn't eaten since midday. What would she have done if Adam had brought the pizza back himself? Sat here with him at the counter? Tried to repair the damage of over a decade of hurt?

She took out a slice of pizza and inhaled the sweetness of pineapple. Maybe it was better that he hadn't come back. He'd looked out of place in her apartment—too big, too masculine, and yet somehow she'd liked the contrast between his frowning presence, and her obvious femininity.

Did he ever smile? She couldn't imagine him sitting on her couch, much less moving fifteen frilly pillows off the bed. . . .

Lizzie almost choked on her pizza. Too much of Adam Miller in one day was hard for a girl to take. She'd eat her pizza, make sure Roman was sleeping peacefully, and see how he felt in the morning before she made any definite plans for the following day.

Chapter Three

"I had a letter from your mother this morning."

Adam and his siblings looked up from their dinner, shared a surprised glance, and all stared at their father.

"And?" Kaiden asked.

"She's coming to visit in two weeks."

Adam put down his fork. "Where's she going to stay?"

"You don't want her here at the ranch?" His father raised an eyebrow. "I suppose she could stay at the Hayes Hotel in town."

"It might be better if she stayed there," Daisy, the only girl in the family, commented. "We might not get on with her. It would be awful if we were stuck with her here for a week."

Adam and Daisy were the only two of Leanne's children who weren't keen on the idea of their mother coming back into their lives after more than a twenty-year absence. Daisy had only been five when her mother left, and barely remembered her having been brought up by Auntie Rae, their dad's sister. Adam had been old enough to witness the fights, and had no desire to see them reenacted.

The middle siblings, Ben and Kaiden, Danny and Evan were happy to see their mother, which made no sense to Adam, but he wasn't going to say that out loud. When they met Leanne, they'd have the chance to make up their own minds about her. She might have changed. Twenty plus years was a long time. . . .

"I'll write back and tell her to book a room at the hotel." His father was speaking again, and Adam paid attention. "I must say I'm looking forward to seeing her after all these years."

Adam had no idea why. One of his last memories of his parents was his father literally throwing Leanne's clothes and belongings out the front door while she cursed at him and ran around trying to gather everything up. Adam had tried to help, begged her not to leave, but she'd been too intent on fighting with her soon-to-be ex-husband to pay any attention to a twelve-year-old.

Adam shoved that memory away, stood up, and started gathering the plates. "Anyone want dessert?"

"Stupid question," Ben said. "When has anyone ever said no?"

"Well, there was that one time when you and Evan were trying that Sparta diet," Kaiden reminded his brother. "And all you wanted to eat was meat and more meat."

Ben groaned. "Don't remind me." He patted his stomach. "I'd rather have my sanity, and a few more pounds on my bones."

"Me, too," Evan said. "It's not even like there's anywhere around here where you can take your shirt off and dazzle the ladies with your abs anyway. It's either freezing cold, or so hot you'll burn."

Adam took the apple crumble out of the oven and placed it on the table with a jug of whipped cream, and a carton of ice cream. He liked to cook after a hard day working on the ranch. He found it soothing.

"Dig in."

He didn't need to repeat himself as his family fell on the

dessert like vultures, arguing over who got the bigger serving, and why someone had taken all the whipped cream. Usual family stuff and he loved it. If he hadn't had their support when Louisa had died, he wouldn't have stayed sane.

"Rio Martinez is looking at the Cortez ranch," Adam said as he helped himself to what was left of the crumble.

"Yeah?" Kaiden studied him closely. His eyes were brown like their mother's, and not the steely gray Adam had inherited from his father. "Are you okay with that?"

Adam shrugged. "I told Ines that Rio was a good man with deep pockets."

"Which is true." Daisy nodded. "I suppose it would be ideal for him and Yvonne if they want to be close to town. It's got to be better than a housing developer coming in and destroying it."

"Yeah." Adam kept his gaze on his plate, aware that his siblings weren't sure how to deal with him offering up information about the Cortez family. They'd gotten used to walking on eggshells about anything connected to Louisa. That was his fault. "Carlos wanted me to have the place, but I told him I'd rather he sold up, got the money, and received the treatment he needs right now."

Daisy reached out and touched his hand. "That must have been hard for you." She sighed. "I wish I had the money to help them out, but—"

"It's all good," Adam cut her off. Although Daisy ran the flower shop in Morgantown, she was also involved in a Silicon Valley startup, which if successful would make her a millionaire one day. At the moment, all her money was tied up with the company and its investors. "I don't want your money."

"I'd like some of it." Their dad scraped out the bowl and drowned the remnants in cream, obviously forgetting

Dr. Tio's advice to moderate his fat intake. "I'd *love* to be a kept man."

Daisy's face fell, and this time it was Adam who reached for her hand. "I'm sure that if Daisy makes it big, she'll throw a huge pile of cash your way, Dad, but for now we're doing fine just the way we are."

"*Sure* we are—but—"

Ben grabbed the empty bowl and a handful of glasses. "How about we clean up? There's a game on."

Grateful to his brother for intervening, Adam started helping clear the table. Their dad wasn't one to mince words. He believed in speaking his mind whenever he found the opportunity. Sometimes his honesty was hard to take even when he was right. Daisy felt bad about having all her money rolled up in the tech company. It wasn't helpful to pick at her about it.

In fact, when he'd first found out Carlos was thinking of getting rid of the ranch, he'd asked Daisy whether she had the ability to buy it for him. Even thinking about that low point in his life made him feel ashamed. He had no right to criticize his father for asking the same thing.

As he stacked the dishwasher, Adam wondered how Lizzie was doing. His stupid, impulsive gesture of retrieving the toy, and getting her pizza, seemed crazy now. She hadn't called to say thank you even though she must have known it was from him.

Like she'd call him. She probably didn't even have his number. He'd told her to keep the hell away from him, and she'd kept her promise for almost fourteen years.

He passed a plate to Daisy who had stayed in the kitchen when the rest of them had disappeared into the TV room. She rarely cooked, but she was always willing to make up for it by cleaning up at the end of the meal.

"Are you really not happy about Leanne coming here?" Adam asked her.

She made a face. "I'm trying not to think about it too much. I don't know what she wants from me."

"Maybe she just wants to get to know us." Adam tried to convince himself that was the truth.

"Why now? Why wait over twenty years?" Daisy demanded.

"I hear you." Adam added more hot water to the sink. "I'm interested to hear what she's got to say for herself, but I'm not expecting much."

"I'm glad you feel like that, too." Daisy looked over at him. "The rest of them, including Dad, seem to think it's a great idea."

"I know." He dunked another set of plates into the water to rinse them off. "I don't get it."

She sighed. "Well, apart from Dad, you and I are known as the most stubborn people in the family, so maybe it's us."

"Maybe it is." He considered that. "Maybe we need to try and become more flexible."

"Jackson keeps telling me that one day I need to meet her and make up my mind as an adult." She grimaced. "Like I can forget that she walked out when I was five. I cried myself to sleep for months."

Adam remembered crying himself a few times, but he wasn't going to tell Daisy that.

"She can't hurt us anymore," Adam reminded his sister. "We don't have to give her that power."

"I know." She grinned at him. "You sound just like Jackson."

"Seeing as you think he's good enough to marry, I'll take that as a compliment."

"You should."

He was closer to Daisy than anyone else in the family

and her approval meant a lot to him. He continued cleaning the pans as she chatted away about her floral business, his mind straying back to Lizzie even as he tried to concentrate on his sister.

"Did you go to Yvonne's today?" Adam asked, surprising himself.

"Yes, I had lunch with Nancy there. Why?"

"Was Lizzie around?"

Daisy paused to consider. "No, she wasn't. Yvonne said she'd stayed home with Roman."

"Makes sense." Adam carried on rinsing the plates like a man who asked questions about random women all the time. "He had a bit of a shock yesterday."

She put down her tea towel. "How do you know about that?"

"I drove them to Dr. Tio's." He shrugged. "I just happened to be passing Gabby's when everything went down."

"*You* did." She was staring at him now. "But you never even talk to Lizzie."

"I talk to her," he protested. "I see her all the time in the café."

"You order food. It's not the same thing at all."

"What did you expect me to do?" Adam demanded. "Drive past and ignore her?"

"No, of course not." Daisy was still studying him way too intently. "What you did was awesome. Why don't you call Lizzie and check on Roman yourself?"

Adam took a step back and almost tripped over the lowered dishwasher door. "I don't have her number."

"I'm sure I can find it for you," Daisy said.

"Like she'll want people bothering her when she's got a sick kid." Adam tried to sound like he didn't care either way. He was annoyed with himself for even starting the stupid conversation. "I'll see her in the café over the next few days."

"If she comes back."

Adam frowned. "Did Yvonne suggest otherwise?"

"See?" Daisy pointed at him. "You *do* care."

"I—I—" Adam slammed the door of the dishwasher shut with unnecessary force. "Give it a rest, Daisy, okay?"

"Sure." She paused to flick his ass with the tea towel. "Why don't you have lunch with me tomorrow at Yvonne's so you've got an excuse to check in?"

"Daisy . . ." Adam tried his best big brother voice, but apparently it no longer worked, as his sister winked at him and waltzed away.

Well, he'd walked right into that one by opening his big mouth and asking about Lizzie. Adam wiped down the countertop one final time and folded up the dishcloth. But he did feel invested in finding out what had happened to the kid—the kid who had no father—which was another mystery he'd often wondered about. The trouble was, he'd forfeited all rights to ask Lizzie anything even as a friend.

Maybe he would go into town tomorrow. He had to visit the feed store anyway. . . .

Lizzie settled Roman at the table in the kitchen with a freshly made batch of play dough, food coloring, a carton of juice, and his favorite sandwich. It was a bright sunny afternoon and Yvonne had gone out with Rio to look at property while Lizzie managed the café.

"I'll be out front if you need anything, Ro. Maria's going to be here in a minute to play with you, okay?"

"Maria?" Roman looked thrilled. "*My* Maria?"

"Yes."

Blue Morgan's teenage daughter, Maria, was in town for

the afternoon, and she loved keeping an eye on Roman. There were also two members of the kitchen staff still on duty who were happy to provide adult supervision. Yvonne was due back just before closing time and would help with the clear-up.

Lizzie put on her apron and went through to the front of the café where Angelo was already helping customers. Maria came through the front door with her grandma Ruth and waved at Lizzie.

"Hi! Where's my little buddy?"

"He's in the back." Lizzie hugged Maria who was now taller than her grandmother. She had her father's bright blue eyes and her deceased mother's olive complexion and black hair. "Have fun and let me know if you have any problems."

Ruth Morgan smiled at Lizzie. "Thank you for giving Maria something to do for an afternoon."

"I would've thought there were plenty of jobs for her up at the ranch," Lizzie said.

"Yes, there are, but apparently they are all 'boring'." Ruth rolled her eyes. "Although, she does babysit Chase William. She's very good with him."

"I'm delighted she's happy to spend time with Roman." Lizzie signed into the cash register. "Can I get you anything while you're here?"

"A dozen cakes would be nice." Ruth peered at the glass case. "Two of each, please. Then I don't have to worry about baking a dessert for tonight."

After seeing Ruth to the door, Lizzie got busy taking orders and popping back into the kitchen to check up on Roman and Maria. They were having a great time and hardly noticed her attempts to interact with them. By three o'clock, the rush had died down, and Lizzie took a moment to have her own lunch.

She looked up as the door opened to see Daisy Miller coming in followed by the much larger bulk of her oldest brother. Lizzie shot to her feet and swallowed her mouthful of sandwich so fast she choked on it.

"Hold on."

The next moment, Adam was slapping her between the shoulder blades while a sliver of cucumber shot out of her nose. She wheezed out a breath and groped for the edge of the table, her eyes full of tears.

"Thanks," she croaked.

"You're welcome."

No wonder he thought she was a klutz. Every time he came near her she was doing something dumb.

He looked down at her, his expression shielded by the brim of his Stetson. "Are you okay?"

She nodded and offered him a smile. "I'm good, thanks!"

Daisy touched her shoulder. "You sure?"

"Yes. Can I get you something to eat or drink? Yvonne's off looking at property with Rio today so I'm in charge." Lizzie fumbled for her pad and pen. "The specials are still available, and up on the board."

"We'll both have coffee." Daisy turned to her brother. "Do you want anything else, Adam?"

"No, I'm good."

Lizzie nodded. "Then take a seat and I'll bring your drinks over."

"Adam was wondering how Roman was doing," Daisy said brightly. "He was going to call you, but he didn't have your number. Did you, bro?"

"I—" Adam looked at Lizzie over the top of Daisy's head. "I didn't say any of that, but—"

"Of course you didn't. Why would you possibly be interested in knowing my number?" Lizzie raised her chin. "Roman's fine now. Thanks again for all you did."

"It was nothing. I—"

Lizzie didn't let him finish, but turned on her heel and stalked back behind the counter. Her indignation kept her moving right through to the kitchen where Maria and Roman were still having a great time making dinosaurs out of the soft dough.

Daisy was a sweetheart, but Lizzie had no idea why she'd dropped her poor brother in it by pretending he'd cared enough to want to call her. He'd barely spoken to her for fourteen years and had looked profoundly uncomfortable the entire time he'd been with her the previous day. Why would he be interested now?

"Hey, Angelo?" She called out to her fellow employee as he came into the kitchen carrying a load of dirty plates. "Do you have a sec to get Daisy and her brother some coffee? I've got to go and get some napkins from out back."

"Sure!" He grinned at her. "No problem."

She got the key for the supply closet and went through to the back of the café where there was an exit door, a sink, and a line of cupboards. She opened up the second door and surveyed the packed supplies. The napkins were of course just out of her reach. She jumped up and down experimentally to see if she could reach them.

"Hey."

She clutched at her chest as Adam appeared at the kitchen door. Of course he had to be the one to see her looking stupid again.

"What on earth are you doing here?" Lizzie asked.

He leaned against the doorframe as if reluctant to come any farther. "I wanted to apologize for how I sounded out there."

"You sounded just the same as usual," Lizzie retorted. "But since you're here and you're tall, can you reach a packet of those napkins down for me?"

He silently complied and she shut the doors and locked them. "You can go now. Thanks for the pizza, by the way."

He grimaced. "Look, I really did want to know how your son was doing."

"He's doing great. I've ordered him some EpiPens, and we're all going to learn how to use them."

It wasn't like her to be terse, but Adam Miller suddenly deciding to chat with her after fourteen years of near silence was somewhat disconcerting.

She grabbed the napkins out of his hands. "I'd better be getting back."

He still didn't budge. Unless she wanted to run out the back door, rush around the building, and reenter at the front, he was blocking her exit. For a moment she seriously considered it, but she was done being the one who backed down.

"Excuse me." She attempted to get past and deliberately elbowed him in the side, which hurt her elbow, and did absolutely nothing to make him move.

"Lizzie . . ."

His deep voice did something to her; it always had—something she'd had to hide when he'd taken one look at her best friend when they were all sixteen, and instantly fallen in love. Up until then, he'd been *her* friend. She'd built some silly adolescent dreams around him that had all come crashing down. Luckily, she'd never told him any of it. Seeing him with Louisa had shown her the difference between like and love. And, as she'd loved them both, she'd learned to be happy for them.

"I know you're busy right now, but could I possibly come and see you after work one night?" Adam asked.

"What?" Shock made her stop and stare right up into his eyes. "Why?"

He shrugged. "I'd like to talk to you."

"Really." She didn't know how to process that, how to deal with his sudden reversal. It made no sense and he was making her feel way too many things all at once. "Maybe I don't want to talk to you."

He stepped back and she breathed more easily.

He held out a card. "This is my cell number. I don't have yours. If you ever do want to talk, call me, okay?"

"Fine." She took the card. "I've got to go."

She practically sprinted through the kitchen, glad that Roman was too busy to notice her weird behavior. What was up with Adam Miller? She slowed down as she went through into the coffee shop. She didn't want the customers to think the place was on fire. Daisy beckoned her over and Lizzie reluctantly complied.

"Is everything okay?" Daisy asked. "I think Adam was mad at me for suggesting he wanted to talk to you."

"You think?" Lizzie sighed. "I know you want us to get along, Daisy, but—"

"You're right. I'm sorry." Daisy bit her lip. "I was just so pleased when he was concerned about you. It's the first time he's ever been like that about someone outside the family since Louisa died."

"It's all good." Lizzie took a quick glance behind her, but there was no sign of Adam emerging from the kitchen. Perhaps he'd left.

She went back to the counter and served another couple of customers, and then, unable to resist any longer, took a sneaky look into the kitchen, and discovered Adam sitting with Maria and Roman apparently making dinosaurs. She still wasn't sure what was going on, but he was definitely behaving oddly. She poured him a fresh cup of coffee and took it through, setting it at his elbow as far away from Roman as she could manage.

"Here you go."

He looked up at her, his work-roughened fingers now streaked with green food coloring. "Thanks."

She lingered for another second and came to a decision. "If you like, you can come and see me tonight at seven after Roman's gone to bed."

"That would be great." He nodded slowly, the surprise in his gray eyes a mirror of hers. "I'll be there."

She scribbled her cell phone number down on a piece of paper Roman had drawn a picture on, and slid it over to Adam.

"My cell number. Let me know if you change your mind."

He took the paper, put it in his pocket. She went back into the café. If Daisy wanted to know where her brother was, Lizzie would direct her to the kitchen.

Chapter Four

Lizzie checked on Roman for about the fortieth time, but he was sleeping soundly. She'd almost have welcomed him deciding to stay up and chat so that she wouldn't have to spend time fretting about exactly why she'd caved and invited Adam Miller to her apartment. Seeing him sitting there, patiently making dinosaurs with her son, had done something to her resolve.

She'd changed out of her day dress into sweats and a T-shirt, and had not bothered to reapply her makeup. He'd have to take her just as she was. She had coffee brewing and cookies from Yvonne's if he was hungry. Thinking of her boss, Lizzie smiled. Yvonne and Rio had looked at the Cortez ranch and two other vacant properties within Morgan Valley. They'd still been amicably arguing things through while they helped Lizzie close the shop for the night.

Knowing her boss's laid-back fiancé, she guessed Rio would be happy to let Yvonne have her way as long as he got enough land for his new project. His deep love and respect for Yvonne was obvious in every single thing he did. Lizzie could only dream of finding a man like that. Not that she wanted one; she had enough to deal with in her life right now bringing up Roman.

Her front door buzzed, and smoothing her wayward hair, she went down the stairs to let Adam in.

"Hey." He touched the brim of his Stetson. He wore a dark blue denim shirt over a gray T-shirt and his usual jeans and cowboy boots. It was too warm for a jacket. "Thanks for seeing me."

"Come on up."

Lizzie took a quick glance around to see if anyone was out and about, but except for the bright lights of the pizza restaurant, the street was deserted. She hadn't taken Roman to Gabby's since the incident with the bee, and had so far avoided another confrontation with Coretta. The fact that the woman had followed her to the doctor's and shouted at her in the street in front of Adam had been mortifying and slightly worrying.

"Is Roman in bed?" Adam asked as he entered the kitchen-diner and turned back to Lizzie.

"Yes."

"I found this at home and wondered if he'd like it." He took a piece of rock out of his pocket and placed it on the countertop. "It's a fossil. I picked it up near Morgan Creek when I was a kid."

"Oh my gosh, that's so cool." Lizzie crowded up against him to look down at the clear imprint of some kind of fly thing engraved on the flat surface of the rock. "He'll love it."

"I was using it as a paperweight." He shifted slightly away, making her aware of the loss of his warmth and the hint of sandalwood that hung around him. "I'd almost forgotten I had it."

"Hey! I remember when you found it!" Lizzie said excitedly. "I was *there*. You were so keen to get to it that you rushed past me, creating a wave. I slipped on the rocks and ended up sitting in the creek!"

"I don't remember that, but it sounds like something I'd do." He considered her carefully. "Maybe you deserve to have it after all."

Lizzie went around to the other side of the counter and got out some mugs. It was weird to be reminiscing with him after all this time. "Would you like coffee?"

"Sure. Black for me, please."

"At least that hasn't changed," Lizzie said as she poured the coffee and added cream to hers. "Go sit down, and I'll bring it over."

He sat on her small couch, taking up way more than half of it, and rearranged the pillows until he could sit back more comfortably. He took off his hat and placed it carefully on the side table. He still didn't look at ease, but then how could he? He wasn't hiding up at his ranch and was in unfamiliar territory now.

"Thanks." He took the mug and cradled it between his large hands. "It was good of you to let me come over after all this time."

Lizzie sipped her coffee and didn't say anything, far more interested in what he had to say than her own blathering.

"My mom's coming for a visit," Adam said.

This was so out of left field that Lizzie just stared at him. "Leanne?"

"Yeah." He studied his coffee with way too much interest. "Apparently, she wants to see us all and have 'closure' or something."

"That's . . ."

"Weird. I know." He still wouldn't look at her. "I'm not that keen on seeing her myself, but Dad and my brothers are all okay about it."

"I don't really remember much about her," Lizzie

confessed. "I saw her at school a couple of times picking you up. I never really had a conversation with her."

"Neither did I." He sighed. "I was twelve. She was my mom, it never occurred to me that she'd be going anywhere, or that I needed to get to know her before she left."

"Maybe this is a chance for you to remedy that?" Lizzie suggested. She got up to fetch the plate of cookies she'd left on the counter, and placed them on the coffee table in front of Adam. "You're both adults now."

"Yeah, I suppose that's one way of looking at it." Adam shifted restlessly in his seat. "I'm not sure why I just laid that on you."

"It's okay. Family can be complicated sometimes."

Lizzie took a cookie just to have something to do with her hands. This wasn't how she'd envisioned their evening together, but she was loath to shut him up when he obviously needed to get stuff off his chest.

"Is she going to stay at the ranch?" Lizzie finally asked as he remained silent.

"No, Daisy wasn't keen on the idea. She's going to stay at the Hayes." Adam took a cookie and dunked the whole thing in his coffee before eating it in one bite.

Lizzie waited, but he seemed to have clammed up again. Maybe saying that many words to her in one go had exhausted him.

"Is that why you decided to come and talk to me?" She tried to coax him along.

He raised an eyebrow. "Come again?"

"Did you want 'closure' with me, too? Because I'm quite happy to finally have a discussion about what happened between us."

"You mentioned something about Rio and Yvonne visiting the Cortez ranch," Adam said abruptly.

"Yes, I did." She was all at sea again. "What about it?"

"Did Yvonne say anything to you about the place?" Adam asked. "Do you think she and Rio might buy it?"

Lizzie set her mug down on the table with deliberate precision. "You came here to ask me about a private conversation that I *might* have had with my boss, which has absolutely nothing to do with you?"

"It does have something to do with me. Ines and Carlos are my in-laws," Adam protested. "I'm just trying to look out for their interests."

Lizzie stood and just remembered to keep her voice low so that she wouldn't wake Roman. "Then talk to them or talk to Yvonne. Don't expect me to be your snitch!"

"I'm just asking . . ."

She shook her head. "You haven't bothered to talk to me for years, and now the moment you think I can be of use to you, here you are, without a word of apology or anything!"

Picking up his hat, she threw it at him. "Go away, Adam."

He caught his Stetson and jammed it on his head. "Lizzie . . ."

"Don't you dare Lizzie me." She walked across to the door and held it open. "Go. Away."

She marched down the stairs and unlatched the lower door, enjoying the breeze that hit her flushed face.

He finally reached her, but he didn't go past. In the narrow hallway, he was much too close.

"What do you want me to say about what happened back then? That I'm still disgusted with myself? That I know what I did was unforgivable?"

She looked up into his anguished eyes and spoke as clearly and calmly as she could. "What you did? What we did *together* was a perfectly natural reaction to losing someone we both loved."

"It was a betrayal and you damn well know it."

"A betrayal of *what,* Adam?" Lizzie asked. "Louisa was dead. You weren't cheating on her. We weren't hurting her. We were just grieving her loss."

"By jumping into bed together?"

"There wasn't even a bed." She cupped his rigid jaw. "There was just you, hurting so badly that we were all afraid for you, and a moment of me giving you the comfort you needed."

"I shouldn't have—"

"You were *grieving."* She made him look her in the eye. "You needed—"

"I needed *Louisa,* not you."

"Do you think I don't know that?" Lizzie said softly. "We comforted each other in the most natural way possible. That's not a sin. Louisa—"

He jerked his head away from her touch. "Louisa told me that you always had a thing for me."

"Ex-Excuse me?" Lizzie stammered. "Are you trying to say that I *came onto you* just after my best friend in the world had died?" She stepped back, her hand coming up of its own accord, swinging to slap his face. "You complete *bastard!*"

She ran back up the stairs, locking the door behind her. She went into her bedroom where she buried her face in her pillow and cried her heart out. That's why he hadn't spoken to her for so many years? He thought she'd been trying to become the second Mrs. Adam Miller rather than just reacting to his raw pain, and trying to make it better for both of them?

After what felt like hours, she rolled over onto her back and stared up at the ceiling. When Roman's father had walked out, she'd promised herself to always face up to things even if they reflected badly on her. Was it possible that Adam was right? That some small part of her had wanted what her friend had?

"No." Lizzie spoke the word aloud. "He's wrong. That's not how it was at all."

She'd found him in the rain kneeling by Louisa's grave, his father's gun by his side, and persuaded him to take shelter with her. She'd held him and rocked him, and reassured him that everything would be okay, even when she knew that for him it never would be again. When he'd kissed her and pressed close, she'd invited him inside her, so full of grief that giving herself to him, sharing the moment, and reaffirming life had seemed somehow inevitable.

She hadn't lured him into her arms; she'd tried to help him. Now that she was older, she might think that her twenty-year-old self had acted too emotionally and without considering the consequences, but at the time? She'd instinctively offered the most natural thing she had to give, and she wouldn't regret that

But, because of that impulse, in the end, she'd lost not only Louisa, but Adam Miller, too.

Adam spent a restless night, berating himself yet again for what he'd done and said to Lizzie. Her face when he'd suggested she had a thing for him . . . The utter betrayal in her eyes had shaken him to his core and made him feel ashamed. He was so used to internalizing his grief for Louisa that letting it out, lashing out, had been a weird kind of relief. But hurting Lizzie . . . That was unacceptable.

Knowing he had to apologize, and aware that she'd

probably never allow him in her apartment again, he considered how best to reach her. The café was probably his safest bet. She couldn't walk out on him there, but it was also a public place. Maybe he deserved to be told off in front of the whole town.

He parked his truck near the post office and checked the ranch mailbox before going into Yvonne's. There was no sign of Lizzie, but the owner was busy placing cakes and pastries in the glass-fronted cabinet.

"Hey." Adam went right up to the counter. "Is Lizzie around?"

"She is, but she's not in a very good mood today." Yvonne studied him closely. "Is it possible you have something to do with that?"

"Yes." He met her eyes. "I need five minutes to apologize to her."

"Then good luck." She waved him through to the kitchen. "If she doesn't want to talk to you then you must leave immediately."

"I will. I promise."

Stiffening his spine, he went through into the immaculate kitchen where Lizzie was counting croissants into large boxes. She looked up as he came through the door, and all the emotion drained from her face. He could tell that she'd been crying, and his heart twisted with guilt.

He stopped just inside the door and took off his hat.

"Will you just let me apologize, and then I'll leave you in peace?"

She glanced around at her coworkers who were all doing a terrible job pretending they weren't listening, and nodded. She stalked to the back of the kitchen, head held high, and went out the back door into the sunshine.

Adam followed, making sure the door remained unlatched, and faced her.

"I'm sorry. I didn't mean to imply that anything that happened between us that night was your fault."

She folded her arms across her chest. "Yes, you did."

"I *meant* that I knew you liked me enough to feel sorry for me. I was the one who made the first move and took *advantage* of that. That's totally on me."

"I did have a crush on you, once. After you fell in love with Louisa I was happy that we were all still friends."

"It was still my fault." He rubbed a hand over his unshaven jaw. "Will you *please* forgive me? I really mean it."

She regarded him for a long moment, her face expressionless. "Okay."

He expected to feel relieved, but he didn't. Everything in his world was changing, and the safe spaces he'd created for himself were disappearing faster than he could ever have imagined. "Are you sure?"

"It's fine." She nodded stiffly. "I have to get back now."

"Look, now that we've established that I'm a fool who should've apologized to you all those years ago, and not let it come between us, can we really put it behind us, and be friends again?"

She bit her lip and looked away from him. "I don't know."

"Can you at least think about it?" Adam wasn't sure why he was practically begging her to make things right for them, but he needed to say it. She'd been his best friend before he'd fallen for Louisa and he'd let her down. "I'd appreciate it."

She finally looked up at him. "I shouldn't have slapped you."

"Yeah, you should." He touched his cheek. "I was an insensitive jerk. I deserved it."

"Maybe you did, but I'm still not proud of myself." Lizzie glanced back toward the kitchen. "I really do have to go."

"Okay, as long as we're good now?" he asked. "Maybe I can come in one day, and we can have coffee together or something?"

"Sure." She nodded. "Good-bye, Adam."

He stayed where she'd left him, his gaze on the back door of the café as it dawned on him that she had no intention of ever letting him get close to her again. The fact that it bothered him was a surprise because what had he expected? He'd not only trodden all over her emotions during their initial encounter, but now he'd done it again.

He rubbed his hand over the back of his neck. He sucked at anything emotional. Maybe Lizzie was right and he should just stick his head back in the sand and shut the hell up. He certainly wasn't making anything better.

One thing he did know was that Louisa would've been furious with him for turning against their best friend. All those years he and Lizzie could've grieved together, destroyed by one stupid, desperate act of two people barely out of their teens. An act he'd turned into yet another cudgel to beat himself up with and blame Lizzie for. Was he some kind of fricking martyr? Did he enjoy wallowing in his own pain?

Adam cursed under his breath and walked back onto Main Street where he'd parked his truck. Maybe that was the real reason why he'd stayed away from Lizzie—because she'd be quick to point out his bullshit arguments. He slowed as he approached the vehicle where Coretta Smith was taking a picture of his license plate number.

"Can I help you with something?" He raised his voice above the sound of the traffic, making her jump and turn to face him.

"There's nothing I need to say to you, young man."

"Then why are you taking pictures of my truck?"

"Evidence."

He blinked at her. "Evidence of what?"

"Do you think I don't know what you're doing with Lizzie Taylor? I saw your truck parked outside her apartment last night."

"I still don't see what any of it has to do with you, ma'am."

"Because of the *child*." She glared at him. "Lizzie's a bad mother. *Someone* ought to be reporting her to the authorities."

"And that someone is you?"

"Who else has a better right?"

"I'm not following here," Adam said. "Would you like to come down to Nate Turner's place of work so we can continue our discussion? I'm fairly sure there are laws about stalking and prank calls."

Coretta stuffed her phone in her bag. "You can do what you want. I have to get home and make sure that poor child is not being neglected at Gabby's house."

Before Adam could speak again, she crossed the street and set off toward her house. He frowned after her and then made a reluctant decision.

Yvonne greeted his reappearance in her café with a raised eyebrow. "*You* again?"

Lizzie had just come out of the kitchen and almost backed up when she saw him. He spoke directly to her.

"I just caught Coretta taking pictures of my truck."

"Oh, God, no . . ." Lizzie sighed. "She's getting completely out of hand. How on earth did she justify that?"

Adam lowered his voice and moved closer. "I think we should talk to Nate."

"I have spoken to him."

"Officially?" Adam asked.

"No, I just told him that she was taking photos of Roman over the fence. He said he'd have a quiet word with her."

Adam looked over at Yvonne. "Are you okay if we go down to Nate's office right now?"

"Go ahead. It's not busy." Yvonne waved a hand at them. "You need to do something, Lizzie. This is not right."

The last person Lizzie wanted to be walking beside right now was Adam Miller. She'd rather be at home, curled up in bed eating ice cream and having a good cry. But, as a working mother, and an adult, that option was apparently no longer available to her.

"Coretta said that she had to protect the boy," Adam said. "I asked her why, and she said she had the right."

Lizzie concentrated on crossing the street. "She's Roman's great-great-aunt."

Adam stopped walking and looked down at her. She could see the wheels turning in his head. "Ray Smith is Roman's father?"

"Yes." There was no point in denying it. She'd have to tell Nate anyway. "He used to come and stay with Coretta for the summer."

"I remember. He was a really good baseball player."

"He went to college on a scholarship and played professionally for a while before he got injured," Lizzie said as they started walking again. "He's a sports journalist and media commentator now."

He glanced down at her. "How come I've never seen him with you and Roman?"

"Because he bolted when I told him I was pregnant."

"What an asshole."

"Correct." Lizzie pushed open the door into the sheriff's office and appreciated the coolness of the air-conditioning. There were two desks, an office behind them, and two small holding cells.

Betty, the woman who managed the office, looked up with a smile. "How can I help you, folks?"

"Is Nate in?"

"Yes, he is. Would you like to speak to him?" She pushed back her chair, went through to the back, and hollered at the sheriff so loudly she might as well have stayed at her desk.

Nate came out wincing, a finger in his ear, and beckoned Lizzie and Adam to come through.

He took his seat behind his desk and looked expectantly up at them. "What's going on?"

Lizzie let Adam explain about Coretta photographing his license plate and her threats to call social services on Lizzie. He also suggested that Coretta thought they were seeing each other, which might have been hysterically funny if she wasn't stressing out.

"And she's also been taking pictures of Roman?" Nate was writing notes. "I have to ask this, but is there any reason why she should be worried about the child's safety?"

"Of course there isn't," Lizzie said. "You know Gabby's a fantastic day care provider. Coretta just hates me because her great-nephew has somehow convinced his family that I'm the bad guy."

"In what way?" Nate looked up, pen poised over the paper.

"Ray Smith is Roman's father," Lizzie reluctantly

explained. "He's never seen his own child or paid me a dime in child support. Coretta's his great-great-aunt."

Beside her, Adam frowned and shifted in his seat.

"So, Coretta has some family connection to your son," Nate said.

"Yes. I've offered her the opportunity to meet Roman properly, but she refuses to do that." Lizzie pushed her wayward hair away from her face. "I'm worried that she's sending all this 'evidence' to Ray's family to make me look bad."

"Sure sounds like it," Adam murmured beside her. "But seeing as they had no interest in supporting the kid, what will it matter?"

"I don't know," Lizzie said despairingly. "I just want her to stop."

"I'll go talk to her in an official capacity and give her a warning," Nate said. "You could try and get a restraining order against her, but it's going to be hard to enforce when she lives next door to your day care provider." He paused. "Is there any chance you could find someone else to mind Roman?"

"In Morgantown? Not likely." Lizzie grimaced. "And Roman loves going there." She rose to her feet. "Thanks for listening, Nate, and for taking it seriously. I appreciate it."

He stood, too. "That's what I'm here for." He put on his hat. "I'll go right now. I'll give you an update this evening."

Lizzie followed Adam out into the sunshine and headed back to Yvonne's. She was so deep in thought that she didn't notice he was following her until they reached the front door.

He held it open for her. "Are you okay?"

"Just peachy." She couldn't even muster a smile. "I'm sorry you ended up involved in all this."

"It's all good."

"No, it is not, Adam. It's not good. If Coretta contacts Ray . . ."

"He won't do anything. You know that."

"I hope you're right." She eased past him, aware that being close to him right now was still too hard for her. "Have a great day."

Chapter Five

Adam parked his truck and stayed in the driver's seat staring out at Gabby's house. He'd spent the rest of the weekend worrying about Lizzie. Even his family had noticed, and asked why he was so distracted. He hadn't told them anything. It wasn't his story to tell.

He knew Lizzie was due to pick Roman up from Gabby's right about now. It was the first time she was likely to encounter Coretta since Nate had called on her. Adam wanted to make sure everything went okay. It was none of his business, but he couldn't seem to stay away.

A tap on his side window made him jump. He turned to see Lizzie staring at him. Her reddish brown hair was drawn back from her face in a high ponytail and she wore a soft floaty dress that made her eyes look even bluer.

He reluctantly lowered the window and met her inquiring gaze.

"What exactly are you doing here, Adam?"

"Yeah, I know it's weird." He winced. "You're going to think I'm stalking you."

She pointed at the passenger side and walked around as he unlocked the door for her. She stepped up into the truck, bringing the beguiling scent of coffee and sugar in with her.

The moment she settled herself, he started talking. "I was worried about Coretta. I thought I should be here in case she came at you."

"Why?" She crossed her arms over her chest and regarded him steadily. "I'm quite capable of taking care of myself."

"I know that," he struggled to explain. "I just feel . . . responsible somehow."

"Because Ray Smith walked out on me?"

He allowed himself to get distracted, which was easy when he had no real answer for her question. "How did you ever get involved with him anyway?"

"Not that it's any of your business, but he was always a charmer, and I was stupid enough to let him charm the pants off me. Which still doesn't have anything to do with why I am currently sitting in your truck with you."

"I suppose I felt I'd like to help you out with this," Adam said slowly, feeling his way through his complicated emotions, which were somewhat rusty with lack of use. "I've let you down so many times that maybe this time I can make amends."

"By doing what exactly? Threatening an old lady?"

"By just being here." He grimaced. "I don't want your son to have to deal with all that hostility. If she wants to go off at you maybe I can help keep him out of it."

"That's . . . very thoughtful of you."

He nodded awkwardly, tried to remember the last time he'd reached out to someone outside his immediate family, and came up with nothing.

"Roman's a good kid and you're a great mother," Adam said firmly.

She cupped his chin, tears glinting in her eyes. "Thank you for that."

Her emotions made him uncomfortable again, and he

turned away to contemplate the street. "You're welcome. Do you want me to leave?"

He wasn't sure whether he wanted her to say yes or no, which surprised him. He usually bolted when anyone got upset around him because he had nothing left to give them.

"Now that you are here, I'm okay if you stay." She hesitated. "I *am* worried about what Coretta will do next. As only Gabby, you, and Nate know who Roman's father is, I could do with some backup."

"Okay, and how about I take you both out for pizza afterward?" Adam couldn't quite believe he was still flapping his gums. Even his own family wouldn't recognize him right now. "Make sure she doesn't follow you home."

"That's very kind of you." Lizzie was looking at him as if she'd never met him before either. "Let's see what mood Roman is in before we make that decision, okay?"

"Sure." He made sure the ignition was turned off and got out of the truck to open the door for Lizzie. "How's he been?"

"Fine." She sighed. "But every time he sees a boo he flips out."

"Sensible kid." Adam followed her up the path to Gabby's, keeping a close eye on Coretta's front door, but there was no sign of movement.

Gabby opened the door and let them through the child gate. Her house was a comfortable, bright space with a big kitchen that led out into the yard. The refrigerator was covered in pictures done by the kids—at least half of which were dinosaurs. The kitchen table bore evidence of the afternoon's work, weaving bookmarks with paper strips and pots of glue.

Adam glanced through into the yard where Roman and two other little boys were running around with their arms out like fighter planes, screeching at the top of their lungs.

It reminded him of growing up with four brothers and made him wonder where all that fun and energy had gone in his life.

"He ate all his lunch and he had a good nap." Gabby was talking to Lizzie as she found Roman's little backpack and handed it over. "I haven't seen 'her' at all today."

"Well, thank goodness for that," Lizzie said. "Maybe she's finally gotten the message to leave us alone."

"She's been behaving oddly for a while now." Gabby frowned. "I'm wondering whether she's suffering from some kind of dementia and that her obsession with you and Roman is just part of it. Does she have family living around here?"

"Not that I know of," Lizzie replied. "Not that any of them would talk to me even if they did."

Roman came rushing in and went straight into his mother's arms. "I saw a caterpillar! It was green and red!"

"How cool is that!" Lizzie patted his dark, curly hair. "Are you ready to come home now?" She glanced over at Adam. "We've been invited out for pizza at Gina's."

Roman's attention immediately pivoted to Adam. "How did the bug get squashed?"

Adam blinked at him. "What?"

"In the stone."

"Oh, the fossil!" Adam said. "Well, it's a bit more complicated than that."

Lizzie watched as Roman took Adam's hand and danced alongside him on the sidewalk, peppering him with questions about the fossil. She walked behind them, Roman's backpack slung over her shoulder, and just enjoyed the moment. If someone had told her six months ago that Adam Miller would've emerged as her somewhat grumpy champion, she would've died laughing. But here he was, his concern for her obvious. She didn't really know how to deal with it, or him.

The beguiling smell of pizza reached them long before they saw the shop. Roman pulled on Adam's hand, trying to make him speed up. As the man was built like a mountain and had the stubbornness to go with it, Lizzie already knew it wasn't going to make any difference.

They ordered and sat outside in the sunlight while Roman unpacked all his dinosaurs from his backpack and gave Adam a lecture about each one. Adam was both remarkably patient and attentive to her son, reminding Lizzie of when they were at school and he'd helped her with her math homework.

She wiggled her toes. It was nice to be sitting down and not doing the serving. She didn't often have pizza because it was too expensive, and she could get leftover food from the café. Twice in one week was a luxury indeed.

Adam turned to her. "You should bring Roman out to the ranch."

"He'd probably enjoy that," Lizzie agreed. "You like horses, don't you, Ro?"

"Yes, but I don't like Uncle Carlos's horse," Roman said. "He has big teeth and likes to eat my hair."

"Uncle Carlos?" Adam asked, his gray gaze now directed at Lizzie.

"And Auntie Ines," Roman carried on talking. "She makes cake."

"You've taken him up to the Cortez ranch?"

"Yes. Carlos and Ines were very kind to me after Roman was born." Lizzie fanned herself with the pizza menu. "We go and check in on them quite regularly."

"That's good of you."

"Louisa was my best friend. I spent a lot of time at her house when we were growing up. Her parents were always very good to me."

Gina arrived with the pizza and they all dug in. It was still hot. Quite a few of Lizzie's neighbors came by to get pizza rather than cook. She introduced Adam to Sonali Patel, who helped out in the Red Dragon kitchen, and Perpetua Grande, who was a new nurse at Dr. Tio's place.

It was surprising he'd never bothered to really interact with these people before, preferring to keep to the ranch and his immediate family. The Adam she'd known before Louisa's death had been outgoing and full of energy. This one was almost too self-contained, too careful with the words he allowed out of his mouth, and hard to understand.

But he'd tried to stand up for her—offered her his help—and she still had no idea why.

Eventually, after Roman practiced burping, much to his own hilarity, they walked back toward her apartment. Adam paused as they reached the door.

"I'd better be getting back."

Lizzie smiled up at him as she unlocked the door. "Thanks for looking out for us."

He shrugged, the faintest of smiles enlivening his rather harsh face. "It's about time I stepped up."

Without thinking, Lizzie went on tiptoe to brush a swift kiss on his stubbled cheek. "Thanks again."

Even as Adam reached out to steady Lizzie, or maybe to draw her closer, he wasn't sure *what* he intended, Roman pushed between them and took Adam's hand.

"Come on." He tugged hard, his intention to drag Adam up the stairs obvious.

"I'm not sure—" Adam hesitated.

"*Please?*" Roman looked up at him. "It's a very special thing."

Behind him, Lizzie chuckled. "It's okay. Go ahead, but you must be quick. It's bedtime, and Adam has to get home."

"Okay."

Adam allowed himself to be towed up the stairs and eventually into Roman's bedroom where the little boy disappeared under his bed.

"Are you all right in there?" Adam asked as he crouched beside Roman's feet.

"Here." Roman wriggled back out with a little wooden box, dust bunnies in his hair, and offered it to Adam. "Special things."

Adam sat on the bed and studied the fossil he'd given the boy, along with a couple of photos of a very young Ray Smith, and a nugget of fool's gold.

"Wow."

Roman crowded close to his side and took out the gold. "See this?"

"It's awesome." Adam nodded. "You'll have to come up to our ranch and see if you can find any more in Morgan Creek."

"More gold?" Roman asked. "Yes, please." He shut the box and slid it back under the bed. He yawned. "I'm going potty, and then I'm going to bed."

"Okay." Adam drew the drapes and turned on the small lamp next to the bed. The boy was back way too fast for a proper cleanup, but Adam didn't say anything.

"I'll get your mom," Adam said.

"'Night, Adam." Roman got into bed, wearing just his T. rex boxers, pressed his cheek into his dinosaur's side, and closed his eyes.

Adam went back through to the kitchen where Lizzie

was standing with her back to the door, one hand pressed to her mouth. Something about her rigid stillness set off every alarm in his body.

"Is everything okay?"

She shook her head. He closed the door and came around to look at her.

"What's up?"

She handed him the letter, her hand shaking. He bent his head to read before looking back up at her.

"Child protection services want to visit to ascertain the health and welfare of your *child?*"

"Coretta must have . . ." She gulped in a breath and started to cry. "Oh, Adam . . ."

The next second she flung herself against his chest and started to sob. He didn't know where to put his hands, what to say, or what to do. He awkwardly patted her back.

"It's okay. They'll take one look at you and Roman together and know someone was pulling some first-class bullshit."

She cried even harder and somehow, despite himself, his hand slowly rose to curve around her skull, his fingers threading through her hair as he breathed her in. How long had it been since he'd held someone like this? Comforted someone? Wanted to make everything better for them?

He leaned in closer, his lips brushing the top of her hair like she was giving him life, one arm now anchored around her waist, holding her from knee to shoulder. She fitted perfectly against him, her head just reaching his shoulder; her face was buried in the crook of his neck like she belonged there.

Which she most certainly did not.

He gently eased back, aware that he didn't want to, and forced his hard-earned common sense to reassert itself.

"Sorry." She moved away, too, making him immediately

want her right back where she'd been. "You're probably sick and tired of me crying all over you."

"Nope."

He watched her wipe her tears and blow her nose, saw her superhuman effort to regain control of herself, and admired her so much.

"I can't let Roman see me like this." She blew her nose again. "Is he getting ready for bed?"

"Yeah, he's already tucked himself in," Adam said. "I told him you'd be in to see him in a moment."

Her attempt at a smile tore at his heart. "Maybe he'll be too sleepy to notice I've been crying. I'll go and check up on him."

She went out, leaving Adam alone and wondering what to do next. He should leave. If he stayed, he'd be opening himself up to her, making her think she could depend on him, and that wasn't fair. He wasn't good with emotions anymore. They made him feel inadequate.

He had his hand on the front door latch when she returned and caught him trying to escape. He turned to face her, wondering if he looked as guilty as he felt.

"Let me know what happens with CPS, okay?"

"I will." She'd wrapped one arm around her waist as if she was physically holding herself together. "I'm glad I spoke to Nate. At least we have an official record of everything Coretta's been doing to us."

"Yeah." He gestured at the table where her cell phone sat. "Call me if you need anything. I really mean it." He hesitated. "If Roman wants to come up to the ranch, I'd be happy to take him off your hands for a day."

"Thank you." Her gaze fastened on the letter and she visibly swallowed. "I'm sure everything's going to be just fine."

He nodded, and went down the stairs, deliberately

concentrating on his steps rather than the fact that for the first time in over a decade he'd reacted to a woman, that his body was waking up, and that he didn't seem to have any control over anything anymore.

When he reached the safety of his truck he sat for a while in the gathering darkness, trying to get a handle on how he felt before he went home. The thought that anyone would target Lizzie as a bad mother was appalling. He'd known her all his life, and she was one of the kindest, most genuine people he'd ever met.

He gripped the top of the steering wheel with both hands and rested his chin on them. If Louisa were still alive she'd have made sure Adam was right there supporting Lizzie, who had no one else in town to help her. But what would Louisa make of him suddenly thinking about Lizzie at all? And he couldn't stop thinking about her, and not just in a protective way. . . .

Adam turned on the ignition and put on his seat belt. Things were changing way too fast for him. His little sister was contemplating marriage, and his mom was coming back after skipping out on them all those years ago. It wasn't surprising he was feeling unsettled. Maybe he should focus on one thing at a time. Help Lizzie with Roman and any potential fallout from Coretta's report to CPS. He was one hundred percent certain that Louisa would have no issue with that.

As soon as Adam left, Lizzie opened up her laptop and googled everything she could find about how CPS worked. From what she could tell, if she was honest and open with them, she should have nothing to worry about.

"Yeah, right," Lizzie murmured.

She contemplated her phone. Should she tell her friends what was going on? She knew they'd be supportive, but the mere thought of them knowing someone had called CPS on her was embarrassing. Part of her wanted to storm around to Coretta's house and ask the older woman exactly what she was doing, but she suspected that wouldn't help matters at all. . . .

At least Adam had offered his support.

She closed her eyes, briefly reliving the moment when he'd let her lean into him and given her comfort. She'd felt safe and protected, and for one crazy second had imagined what it would be like to have that all the time. She'd never had that—never had anyone to help her protect Roman and keep him safe.

Not that Adam could do much right now. But just knowing he was around, and that she could call him if she needed something was far more reassuring than she could ever have imagined.

Chapter Six

"Is everything okay, Lizzie?"

Lizzie turned as Yvonne followed her into the kitchen. "Yes! Why?"

"You just gave January the wrong lunch."

Lizzie scrabbled in her apron pocket for her order pad. "Did I?" She scanned her notes. "She ordered a tuna sandwich, right?"

"Yes, and you gave her the vegetarian one meant for Jenna," Yvonne said. "It's okay. I switched them around. Angelo's got the tuna one coming right up."

"I'm sorry," Lizzie apologized. "It's not like me to mess up so much."

"No, it's not." Yvonne perched on the corner of the steel worktable. "Is Roman all right?"

"He's fine." Lizzie found a smile somewhere. "I'm really sorry, Yvonne. I've got a lot on my mind, but it's not okay for me to bring it to work."

Her cell buzzed and she jumped like she'd been shot. She forced herself to stay focused on her boss.

Yvonne gestured at her apron. "Maybe you should take that."

"No, I'm good. Really, I—"

"The lunchtime rush is over. Check your phone, and if you need to go somewhere just let me know, okay?"

"You really are the most amazing boss," Lizzie said.

Yvonne's grin was a welcome relief. "I'm the best boss in Morgantown; everyone knows that."

"And I appreciate that you are willing to put up with me right now." Lizzie paused for breath. "I promise things will get better soon."

"I hope they will, because I might need you to take on more hours soon." Yvonne washed her hands. "We can talk about it when you're ready. Now go and check your phone."

Lizzie took out her cell and read the text from Gabby. She'd had to tell her friend that she'd had a letter from CPS and that Gabby might be getting a call in the very near future to check on Roman.

Thought you should know I just had a visit from CPS. I told them all about Coretta and they met Roman. They've already left so there's no need for you to rush over.

Lizzie scrolled through until she found Gabby's number. She walked out to the back of the building and into the parking lot to get some privacy.

"Hey!" Gabby answered on the first ring. "Seriously, don't worry. It went really well. The woman was supernice and was great with Roman. She only stayed about half an hour. I got the distinct impression that she realized there was nothing to be concerned about."

"Thank goodness." Lizzie leaned back against the wall and closed her eyes. "Maybe once they get back to Coretta that will be the end of it."

"I should think so," Gabby agreed. "Coretta hasn't

been home the last couple of days. She's probably been lying low."

"That wouldn't surprise me." Lizzie sighed. "Why she just can't meet Roman and get it all out in the open, I don't know."

"Don't feel like you have to rush over and collect Roman," Gabby said. "He's having a lovely time building Lego castles for his dinosaurs, so I'll see you at the normal time, okay?"

"Okay. Thanks so much, Gabby."

Lizzie put her cell away in her apron pocket and took a moment to gather herself before heading back into the fray. Roman was okay. CPS hadn't immediately taken him away, and by the sound of it, wouldn't be following up on the report. On an impulse, she took her phone out again, her fingers flying over the keys.

CPS visited Roman at Gabby's. Apparently all went okay.

She waited as the little bubbles in the corner of the texting box appeared and Adam replied.

That's great. Good to hear it.

And then a moment later another text appeared.

Thanks for letting me know.

You're welcome and thanks for everything.

She paused and then added xx. If he was here now, standing in front of her with his usual stern expression, she'd kiss him right on his hard, beautifully shaped mouth. He'd probably kill her, but it would be worth it.

"Adam?"

Adam jerked his attention away from his phone, his gaze lingering on the kisses Lizzie had texted him. She probably did that on all her messages. . . .

"Yo! Bro!" This time Ben shouted at him. "Are you coming?"

Adam put his cell away and forced himself to pay attention to his brother. They were out on the ranch in a distant field rounding up some cattle, and he needed to be on task.

Ben rode over, his hat down low over his eyes against the glare of the sun, and reined in his horse.

"What's up with you?"

"Nothing." Adam met his brother's direct stare with one of his own.

"You're like totally distracted." He gestured at Adam's pocket. "You're constantly checking your cell."

"Sorry." Adam gathered his reins. "What do you want me to do?"

"Don't you know? Aren't you supposed to be the boss or something?" Ben rolled his eyes. "We're *supposed* to be clearing this part of the ranch of cattle so we can do the count later in the month."

"I know *that*. I meant what specific thing right now?" Adam responded. "It's not like we're dealing with a stampede or anything. We're just pushing them toward the ranch."

"Which is hard for me to do by myself while you're on your phone," Ben repeated patiently.

"I'm good now." Adam settled himself in the saddle. "Sorry."

Ben still wasn't moving or looking like he'd finished yacking.

"Does this have something to do with Lizzie Taylor?" Ben asked.

"Does what?"

"Your obsessive interest in your cell phone."

Adam went still. "That's a hell of a question."

"I saw you in town with her yesterday," Ben said casually. "I was at the feed store and then I went to get gas at Ted's. You were walking along the street with Lizzie and some kid was hanging off your arm. I literally pinched myself to make sure I wasn't hallucinating."

"That's Lizzie's boy. His name is Roman."

"You looked"—Ben paused and rubbed his hand over his bearded jaw—"like you were having a good time."

"What's wrong with that?" Adam asked, aware that he probably sounded defensive. "He's a nice kid."

"Because that's not like you."

"To have a good time?"

"Yeah." Ben nodded. "That."

"Thanks for nothing." Adam gave his brother a killer stare. "I'm sorry I dared step out of line and enjoy myself."

"It was great to see you like that," Ben protested. "You haven't looked that happy since Louisa died."

A pang of guilt squeezed around Adam's heart. He stared past his brother out over the Sierra Nevadas and reminded himself how insignificant his tiny life and troubles were.

"I helped get Roman to the doctor the other day," he said abruptly. "I was just checking up on him."

"So Daisy said." Ben hesitated. "It's okay, you know."

"What is?"

"For you to spend time with Lizzie."

Adam briefly considered strangling his brother and riding off into the sunset, and reluctantly concluded that Ben would just get up and follow him. Ben was quieter than Kaiden and his other siblings, but remarkably tenacious once he got an idea in his head.

"I'm not 'spending time' with her," Adam repeated doggedly, aware that he wasn't being honest with himself, and unable to decide why. Was he afraid to admit he was interested in what Lizzie was up to? Or was it simply that it still felt like too much of a betrayal of Louisa? "And don't go around telling the rest of the family anything different, okay?"

"Too late for that." Ben grinned at him. "I already dropped you in it last night at dinner when you were still in town with Lizzie."

"I was *not*—"

"Okay, whatever, if you say so." Ben glanced over his shoulder. "Shall we get some work done?"

Relieved that his brother had finally shut up, and anxious to move on, Adam nodded. He whistled to his dogs and they all headed toward the small group of cattle at the bottom of the field. If his whole family were on alert for him mentioning Lizzie, he'd better shut the hell up and ride it out.

"Please come on up." Lizzie held the door open and invited the woman from CPS inside. She'd had a call at work requesting the meeting and had decided to get it over and done with as soon as she could. "I rent this place from Ted Baker who owns the gas station and mechanics shop. It was only recently converted into living accommodations.

It's a really great location for me to get to work and for Roman's day care provider."

Yeah, she was in full-blown chatter mode. Fear did weird things to people, and she was never going to be the hero who kept silent. She was definitely a babbler who'd betray her own mother. She'd spent the whole of the previous night rehearsing what to say when she was interviewed, and now felt like a complete fake.

"It's lovely." Patty Young looked around the kitchen-diner. "It's so light."

"Do you want to see Roman's bedroom? He has his own room next to the bathroom." Lizzie gestured toward the connecting hallway.

Patty politely peeked into each room, and then returned to the kitchen and set her briefcase on the table. She took out a small laptop and opened it up.

"I just need to ask you a few questions, and then I'll be on my way. Is that okay?"

"Sure!" Lizzie sat opposite her and tried to look as honest and open as she could. "What can I help you with?"

"Is your full name Elizabeth Jane Taylor?"

"Yes, and I still can't believe my parents called me that. I'm not exactly brunette mega film star material, am I?" Lizzie mentally told herself to shut up as Patty kept typing.

Patty went through a lot of the basics, and just as Lizzie was starting to relax asked, "Is it true that Roman's been taken to the twenty-four-hour emergency care facility three times already this year?"

Lizzie frantically tried to remember. "Well, there was the bee sting; that was the latest. Then the time he fell out of a tree, and I was worried he had a concussion—he didn't. And he jumped into a patch of poison ivy up on the

Cortez ranch, so we had to get that treated. All normal boy stuff really."

"Do you ever leave Roman unattended in your apartment when you go to work?"

"No, I only work if I can get a sitter," Lizzie said firmly.

Patty looked up. "You don't take him to work with you?"

"Only if I'm meeting a babysitter there." Lizzie paused. "Why? Did someone say I did those things?"

Patty didn't answer as she continued to type. "Am I correct that you don't allow the father of your child any contact with his son?"

"Er, seeing as he ran out on me when I was pregnant, I think it's the other way around," Lizzie replied. "I've encouraged Roman's only relative in this town to get to know him, but she's chosen not to. I have no idea why."

"Okay, thanks for that." Patty typed away, which seeing as her nails were long and beautifully manicured was quite an achievement. She finally finished and smiled at Lizzie. "I think we're good. Roman is a very nice little boy."

Lizzie smiled. "He's awesome."

Patty put her laptop away in her bag and stood up, smoothing down her skirt. "Thanks for letting me speak to you."

"You're welcome." Lizzie paused by the front door as Patty came up to her. "Will you let me know what happens next, or is that confidential?"

"If we need to speak to you again, I'll be in touch," Patty said, firmly shutting the door on Lizzie's fishing expedition. "Have a great day."

Lizzie followed Patty down the stairs and locked the outside door behind them. She was due back at the café, having used her lunch hour for the interview. She felt slightly better having met Patty. She had a sense that there was very little else she could do except hope, and wait for the matter to be resolved.

As she approached Yvonne's she was struck by a pang of guilt about how busy the place was. She normally ate later to manage the rush, but Patty had asked to meet her at twelve, and Lizzie hadn't wanted to argue. She hurried through the café and into the kitchen, washed her hands, put on her apron, and went right back out there to help Yvonne and Angelo.

The next couple of hours rushed by until she finally looked up and noticed the crowd had disappeared. She made herself a cup of hazelnut coffee and leaned against the corner of the counter catching her breath.

"Hey, Lizzie." Daisy came in with her boyfriend, Jackson. "Can we have one coffee to go—that's for Jackson." She beamed fondly up at him "And two for the table? Ben's just parking his truck." She perused the sadly depleted offerings in the glass case. "And a slice of carrot cake for me, too, please."

"Coming up." Lizzie made Jackson's coffee and handed it to him with the lid already on. "Black, no cream or sugar, right?"

"Yup. Thanks." Jackson handed over his debit card. "Put it all on my account."

Lizzie handed him back his card and he went to kiss Daisy good-bye, which seemed to take a ridiculously long time.

Ben Miller came in the door and walked up to the counter. "Hey, Lizzie. What's up?"

"Nothing much." She pointed at the table where Daisy was sitting. "Your sister's waiting for you over there. I'll bring your coffee."

"Thanks." Ben made a revolted face as Jackson gave

Daisy one last lingering kiss. "Dude, enough. You're only going back to your own ranch, not off on a world tour."

Lizzie concealed a smile as she plated up the cake and put the two coffees on the tray beside it.

Jackson departed, looking very smug. Ben took off his Stetson and placed it on the vacant chair beside him. Lizzie delivered the coffees and was just about to turn away from the table, when Daisy spoke up.

"Have you got a minute?"

"Sure." Lizzie did a quick sweep of the café, but everything was under control. "What's up?"

"Ben and I were wondering if you'd like to bring Roman up to the ranch for Sunday lunch this weekend."

Lizzie blinked at her. "I beg your pardon?"

"Adam said Roman was very interested in fossils and fool's gold, and that he would probably enjoy coming out to our place."

"*Adam* said that?" Lizzie asked doubtfully. "Like, out loud?"

"Yeah, we couldn't believe it, either, but he's definitely been thinking about you and Roman a lot," Ben chimed in. "It would be nice to see him crack a smile occasionally, and you two seem to make that happen."

"Does Adam know you've asked us?" Lizzie countered.

Daisy and Ben exchanged a guilty look. "He'll know when you get there."

"I'd have to check if it was okay with him first," Lizzie said firmly. The thought of having a reason to contact Adam was way too exciting.

"Sure! Ask away." Ben added sugar to his coffee. "We'd love to see you both."

After they left, Lizzie checked in with Gabby who had offered to hang on to Roman for another hour so that Lizzie could make up her time. It was always quieter around five as the tourists left, and the townsfolk transferred their allegiance to the Red Dragon, which offered good bar food and, more importantly, beer.

Yvonne was sitting in the kitchen, her tablet in her hand, making up her list of tasks for the following day. She got up at four to make the bread and pastries and was usually asleep by nine at the latest. She glanced up as Lizzie entered.

"Can you make me some coffee, and I'll join you out front in a minute?"

"Sure."

For one terrible moment, Lizzie wondered if Yvonne was going to fire her before she remembered that her boss had said she wanted to talk about something café related.

There was no one new in the café so Lizzie made the coffee and sat at the table closest to the counter, so that she could leap up to serve any new arrivals.

Yvonne came through with her list and settled herself at the table, pouring herself a cup of coffee from the carafe before slowly exhaling.

"That's better. Today was busy."

"And I'm sorry I wasn't here to—"

"It's okay." Yvonne studied Lizzie over the rim of her cup. "There is no need to keep apologizing. We were fine. Your family comes first; you know that."

"I *think* everything's been resolved now," Lizzie said cautiously. "So, there shouldn't be any more problems."

"Good, because I want to make some changes to my work hours. I need you to think about your future commitment to the café."

"As in?"

"When Rio and I are married and based here, I don't want to be working fourteen-hour days," Yvonne said.

"And I might be pursuing that TV reality show deal, but don't tell anyone I said that."

"Okay. Makes sense." Lizzie nodded.

"I still want to bake and I'm happy to keep getting up at four to make that happen. What I don't want to be doing is managing the café and waiting on people, which is where you come in." Yvonne smiled encouragingly. "I want to create a position as manager. I'm hoping you'll step up and take it on."

"Me?" Lizzie asked.

"Yes, you've been with me from the start. You know how I like things done, and I trust you." Yvonne reached over and took Lizzie's hand. "I'd pay you more and you'd have fixed hours, which we can talk about if you decide you might like the job." She paused. "Nothing is going to happen until Rio and I decide on a property and get it into shape, so there's no need to make an immediate decision."

"Okay, thanks." Lizzie wasn't sure what to say. She sure hadn't been living up to her perfect employee status over the past week or so. "I'd certainly like to think about it."

"Good." Yvonne sat back and smiled. "Now, how is that lovely son of yours, and why did Adam Miller come into my café and insist he had to apologize to you?"

"Roman's fine," Lizzie said. "He's definitely allergic to bees, which means we'll be carrying EpiPens for the foreseeable future."

Yvonne shuddered. "I'm not sure I could stab anyone with one of those things. I'd probably do it wrong."

"Gabby and I are going to attend a class Dr. Tio holds at the health center to show us how to do it properly."

"Good for you. And Adam Miller?" Yvonne wasn't going to be put off.

"He . . . apologized. End of story."

"For what?" Yvonne asked.

“Something that happened a long time ago,” Lizzie said. “He’s been very kind to Roman.”

Yvonne sighed. “You’re not going to tell me, are you?”

“Nothing to tell.” Lizzie lied merrily through her teeth. “He helped me out, I thanked him, we had a fight, and now we’re all good again.”

“How good?”

Lizzie eyed her boss. “God, you’re so persistent.”

Yvonne shrugged in a very French way. “Well, somebody has to be. The whole town wants to know what’s going on between you two. I’m the first person everyone asks, and I need up-to-date information.”

“Nothing is going on. We’re just friends,” Lizzie repeated patiently. “Adam’s not the kind of person who gets involved with anyone.”

“I know, which is why him being seen with you is such a big deal.” Yvonne tilted her head to one side and fluttered her eyelashes. “*Please* tell me what’s going on? Pretty please?”

Lizzie picked up her mug as the front door opened. “Oh, dear, have to rush. Enjoy your coffee and feverish fantasizing.”

Yvonne chuckled. “You know I’ll just keep asking.”

“And I’ll just keep on denying it,” Lizzie said sweetly.

Lizzie dealt with the customers, her mind busy on what Yvonne had said about becoming the manager of the café, but also about Adam. If people in Morgantown were starting to notice his change in behavior, and he got wind of it, he’d probably hightail it back to his ranch, and never set foot in town again.

Chapter Seven

By the time Sunday arrived, Adam was getting sick of the speculative glances his siblings kept casting his way *and* their stupid jokes. When Lizzie texted him to say she and Roman had been invited for lunch, and was it okay with him, he'd had a long struggle with his conscience. He wanted to see her, but he also didn't want to create any gossip within his family, especially as his mother was due to arrive for her visit next week.

But they were already meddling and getting things all bent out of shape. It finally occurred to Adam that if they got to see him and Lizzie in the same room, and realized there was nothing going on, they might back off. He also wanted to share the wonders of the ranch with Roman whom he was certain would appreciate having the run of the place after being stuck in an apartment with no yard.

Adam checked the two chickens roasting in the oven and turned his attention to the potatoes and vegetables that would go with them. Ben and Kaiden had offered to cook, but he'd rather keep busy, and not let himself worry about whether Lizzie would turn up or not. She was due to hitch a ride from his dad who had gone to church and would bring them home with him afterward.

Since his wife's death, Adam wasn't a great believer in

God, and rarely attended church, even when most of his siblings made the effort. He preferred to stay home and offer them a great lunch when they returned.

With one eye on the clock, he started to peel a small mountain of potatoes, tossing them into a bowl of water when they were done. He had carrots and green beans to deal with next, and gravy to make. He'd already made a plan for the duration of Lizzie's visit. He would focus his attention on Roman and let the rest of his family entertain Lizzie.

When he'd ventured a mild complaint to Daisy about being railroaded into having Lizzie over, she'd reminded him that he'd once invited Jackson to dinner and not even told her about it, and something about karma biting him in the ass. He'd left it at that.

"Adam!"

He straightened up as Roman came running into the kitchen, a big grin on his face, and launched himself at Adam.

"We came in the big truck and Mr. Miller said a lot of bad words!"

"He would." Adam picked the kid up because he seemed to expect it, and balanced him on his hip. "Don't listen to him, okay? He's not a good role model."

Roman squinted at him before wiggling to let Adam know he wanted to get down. "Can we go to the creek?"

"How about we do that after lunch?" Adam suggested. "I bet you're hungry."

"No." Roman looked back toward the door where Lizzie was now standing. Her reddish hair curled around her shoulders and she wore jeans, a T-shirt, and one of those soft fluffy wrap things women loved that seemed to serve no real purpose. It looked good on her. Adam couldn't help giving her a slow smile.

"Hey."

She came toward him, her expression a little uncertain as if she wasn't sure of her welcome. She'd always been like that. As an only child, her parents had been such a complete couple that they'd never seemed to have much time for her. He suspected that was why she'd enjoyed visiting Louisa's parents, because they made everyone feel part of the family.

"Hey." Lizzie put some flowers and a box of chocolates down on the kitchen table. "Thanks so much for inviting Roman to the ranch."

"I think that was mainly Daisy's idea," Adam replied, aware that she seemed just as keen as he was to pretend it was all for the kid. "But he sure is welcome."

She came closer, and he caught a hint of the coffee and lavender that followed her everywhere. She lowered her voice. "Are you sure you're okay with this?"

"Why wouldn't I be?" He raised an intimidating eyebrow. "It must be hard not having any outdoor space. Kids need to run around. Roman's more than welcome to do that here."

"He'll run all day." Her smile was rueful. "The major problem will be trying to catch him."

"There are enough of us here to hunt him down. Ben's the best tracker in the valley."

"So I hear. He's going to work with BB Morgan on that new dude ranch survival course thing, isn't he?" She turned to where Roman was currently questioning Daisy about something dinosaur related. "I wish kids came installed with a tracking device. It would make life a lot easier."

He chuckled and too late he remembered his resolve not

to get chatting, and stepped back. "I'd better check how the food is doing."

"You *cook?*" Lizzie asked.

"Yeah."

She pressed a hand to her chest and gazed up at him. "That's . . . amazing."

"Yeah?" He had to get away from her right now before he did something really stupid like bend down and kiss her slightly parted lips.

"How about you get Daisy to give you and Roman a tour of the house while I get lunch finished?" Adam suggested.

"That sounds awesome." She smiled at him again, and he fought the urge to smile back. So much for showing his family that he didn't give two hoots about her. They were all probably enjoying watching him act like a complete pushover.

Seeing Adam in the middle of his family kitchen, sleeves rolled up to display his muscled forearms, and slightly flushed from cooking, was doing all kinds of terrible things to Lizzie's libido. A man who looked like that, was incredibly competent at his ranch job, and could cook? They were probably as rare as unicorns.

He'd even smiled at her, although it hadn't lasted long, and he was now back in his *get away from me, woman,* mode. Which was a shame because seeing him at home surrounded by his family meant that even here he apparently struggled to relax.

She dutifully went off and admired the ranch. Her whole apartment would probably fit in the newly restored kitchen. The rest of it was a warren of unexpected rooms and add-ons that made no sense but didn't detract from the overall feeling that the ranch was a very happy and well-loved place.

"This is Adam's room."

Daisy paused to open the door, inviting Lizzie inside. She lingered on the threshold. His room was incredibly neat with a large double bed, which he probably needed, covered in a patchwork quilt. The only photo was of him and Louisa on their wedding day, both looking incredibly young, and so in love that Lizzie had to look away. How did Adam keep on going when he'd lost so much?

"Come *on,* Mom." Roman nudged her hip. "Daisy says there's a swing."

She followed Roman out into the fenced yard where she could easily imagine a horde of young Millers horsing around. There was a slide set, a climbing frame, and a swing, which Roman was heading for at a fast clip.

"Hold on there, youngster!" Ben dashed past Lizzie, his long strides eating up the ground. "Let me help you up."

Ben grinned at Lizzie as he settled Roman on the wooden seat. "I tested everything out yesterday, which was kind of fun, so don't worry about anything breaking." He gestured toward the house. "Why don't you go inside and see if Adam needs any help in the kitchen? I'll hang out here with Roman."

With a strong feeling that she was being manipulated, Lizzie went back in and immediately lost her bearings. Faced with a whole lot of doors, she turned a slow circle only to bump right up against Adam when he suddenly appeared behind her.

"Sorry." She rocked as he steadied her with one hand on her elbow. "I got confused about which way to go."

"It's a confusing house." He gestured at his T-shirt.

"I just spilled gravy all over myself so I came to change. If you hang here a minute, I'll take you back to the kitchen."

"Sure."

He walked past her into his bedroom, stripping off his unbuttoned shirt as he went, and then removed his T-shirt, giving her a perfect view of his broad shoulders and muscled back. Lizzie tried not to react to the sight of such work-hardened, masculine beauty, but it was hard not to sigh.

"Did you say something?" Adam turned around as he took a clean T-shirt out of the drawer.

As the front view was even more spectacular than the back, she just shook her head, aware that speech was now beyond her and that drooling was probably not allowed. He had very little body fat, well-defined abs, and the physique of a man who worked hard for a living, and Lizzie was all for it.

He took out a shirt from his closet and put it on over his new T-shirt, before checking his appearance in the small mirror on the wall.

"Ready to go?"

Lizzie stepped back to allow him to move past her, and meekly followed him back to the kitchen.

"What can I do to help?" Lizzie asked.

He pointed to the large pine table set off to one side of the kitchen. "Can you set the table? I put everything out."

"Sure." Glad for something to do that didn't involve staring at him and wishing he'd kept his shirt off, Lizzie got started. "Do you have water glasses somewhere?"

"In the top cupboard to the right of the stove." Adam bent to check the oven, giving Lizzie a nice view of his jeans-clad ass. For some reason, the Fates seemed to want her to notice everything good about him today.

She went over to fetch the glasses, standing on tiptoe to reach the correct shelf.

"This kitchen was built for giants," Lizzie grumbled.

"Daisy says the same thing, but she's all for it because it means she doesn't have to cook much." Adam reached over her head and brought the glasses down for her. "Here you go."

"Thanks." She peered at the pans of vegetables. "It all looks really good."

"It will be. Roast chicken is my specialty." He returned his attention to the stove. "Do you want to tell everyone to wash up and get ready to eat?"

"Sure!" Lizzie agreed and then looked around. "I don't know where anyone is."

Adam pointed at the kitchen door where an old-fashioned metal triangle hung. "Use that. They'll hear you."

The food was excellent and the company even better. To Lizzie's relief, Roman behaved himself and ate well, chattering away to all the Millers as if he'd known them forever. Seeing her son in the middle of such a large family made her feel nostalgic for something she'd never had, and that Roman had never been given a chance to experience.

At the end of the meal, Kaiden cleared his throat and looked over at Adam. "Seeing as you cooked, we'll clean up. Why don't you take Roman and Lizzie out to the barn to see the horses, and maybe take them out for a ride down to the creek?"

"Yes, please!" Roman shouted and rushed over to grab Adam's hand. "Come *on*."

Adam allowed Roman to drag him toward the door and Lizzie followed. It was still warm outside, the sky a cloudless blue with only a slight breeze to disturb the stillness of the long, yellowing grass. For every step Adam took, Roman took five, which included a hop and a skip in an attempt to keep up. It was a long time since she'd been to the Miller ranch, yet not much had changed here—except her and Adam.

She went down the slight incline, which took her to the large, new barn overlooking the foothills of the Sierras, and stopped to admire the view. Adam was pointing out things to Roman, who was now perched high on his shoulder.

"You see that fence way down there?" Adam asked.

"No."

"Well, it's there, and that's the boundary of our land in this direction. On the other side, we bump up against the Lymonds and a tiny bit of the Gardins."

"Where's the horses?" Roman demanded.

"Don't be rude, Ro," Lizzie admonished him. "Adam's trying to tell you something."

"It's all good." Adam started walking again, ducking down as he entered the open end of the barn so that the kid wouldn't knock his head off. "Is this enough horses for you, Roman?"

"Yes! Let me down." Roman scrambled to the floor.

Adam caught hold of him by the back of his overalls and crouched beside him. "Don't go into any of the stalls or open the doors, okay?"

"I know." Roman nodded obediently. "Uncle Carlos told me. Just pat their noses and give them apples."

Adam reached into the pocket of his shirt. "I got you some carrot sticks. Will they do? One each, okay?"

He straightened up as Roman skipped over to the right-hand side of the barn and studied the first horse intently.

"It's okay. We haven't got any biters." He glanced down at Lizzie who was anxiously watching her son's progress. "He's quite safe. There's a gate at the other end and nowhere else to go. Has he ridden before?"

"A little. Just around the paddock at the Cortez place with Carlos leading him." Lizzie sighed. "Not for a while, though."

"And how about you?"

She looked up at him. "Not for ages."

"Then I'll put you on Auntie Rae's horse. She only rides when she comes out here for Christmas, and Peg never gives her any trouble." He kept an eye on Roman as the boy offered the horse a carrot flat on his palm in the approved manner. "Roman can sit in front of me, if that's okay?"

"Perfect." She smiled up at him and he couldn't look away. "Thanks for such a lovely day. After all that nonsense with Coretta and CPS, it's nice to get away."

"Have you seen Coretta?"

"Nope. Her house was all closed up." Lizzie walked farther down the barn, patting the noses on any of the horses who looked out over their doors. "I wonder if she reported me and then left to avoid any friction?"

"Probably." Adam paused. "I still don't get why she's so against you."

"Well, I don't think she's well, so her obsession with me might be due to that. And Ray wasn't good at facing up to the consequences of his actions. He probably told her some kind of story to make me look bad, and him the poor, injured party."

"Did you care for him?" Adam couldn't believe he'd blurted that out.

She sighed and pushed a strand of hair behind her ear. "He was young and kind of charming, and so *into* me. It had been so long since I'd had that kind of attention, I fell for him without really thinking it through. I guess I was lonely." She half smiled. "That makes me sound lame, but it's the truth."

"He duped you."

"I let him." She met his gaze squarely. "I wasn't a child. I was almost thirty. I also let him into my bed *way* too quickly. And before you ask, I didn't mean to get pregnant. I changed my brand of birth control and about the same time I had the flu, which apparently doubly screwed everything up."

"Damn . . ." Adam shook his head.

"Ray decided I'd done it deliberately to entrap him." Lizzie's mouth twisted. "Which was weird because after that one night, I'd already decided I'd made a terrible mistake. When I told him I had no intention of asking him to marry me, he took me at my word and ran for the hills."

"Without making provisions for his child?" Adam asked. "What kind of a man does that?"

"My mom said I should have gotten a lawyer and gone after him, but I didn't want to."

"Why not?"

"Because I made the decision to sleep with him and keep the baby." She grimaced. "And, if I'm honest, I didn't want to have anything more to do with him."

"I hear you." Adam slowly exhaled, his gaze on Roman who was still happily feeding the horses carrots. "Ray's definitely the one who's missing out."

"He was way too self-centered to care about another human being, let alone his own child. His entire focus was on becoming a professional athlete. He was terrified I would try and bring him down somehow."

"I remember he always thought he was something special," Adam commented. "And he did make it into the major leagues before he got injured."

"That's right, and now he's doing sports commentary in

the Bay Area and I get to see his face every other night on the local news." Lizzie made a face. "He's very good at it, too."

He cupped her chin. "You deserve better."

"I know." She slightly turned her head until the corner of her mouth touched his thumb. "And now I've got Roman to think of, and he deserves the very best."

Was that an oblique way of telling him to back off, or was she just sharing with him as a friend? Adam wasn't sure.

"Can you grab hold of Roman while I get my horse saddled up?"

"Sure! Which one is yours?" Lizzie asked.

He walked down to the end of the barn and pointed through the open top of the door. "This one."

Lizzie scooped Roman up and brought him over to the stall. "This is Adam's horse. You're going to ride on his back."

"What's his name?" Roman asked.

Adam paused. "He doesn't have one."

"He *must* have a name, mustn't he, Mom?"

"What do you think he should be called then?" Adam asked.

Roman contemplated the big, black and white horse; his lower lip stuck out. "Spot."

"Really?" Adam couldn't help but glance at Lizzie who was shaking with laughter. "Don't you think he's a bit big for that name?"

"No." Roman made a clucking noise. "Come on, Spot. Let's go!"

On the ride back from the creek, Roman fell asleep, his whole body relaxed against Adam's chest, his right hand curled around the glittery rock he'd discovered in the stream.

Adam tried to remember the last time he'd spent such a peaceful day with someone other than his family. Despite Roman being a ball of energy, he'd enjoyed it. He couldn't imagine how Lizzie dealt with the kid twenty-four seven.

Lizzie rode alongside him, her seat relaxed, her gaze everywhere as they passed through a knot of trees under dappled leaves and headed for the steep upward slope. Was it because he'd known her for so long that he felt so calm in her company? If so, what a fool he'd been to waste so many years regretting that one night he'd lost himself in grief. He'd been determined to make her pay for it as well, and had lost one of his best friends.

She caught his glance and looked back at him. "Thanks again for a lovely day."

"I've enjoyed it," Adam admitted. "I don't value my home as much as I should. Seeing Roman appreciate it kind of reminded me of that."

"It's a wonderful place." Her voice was quiet.

It occurred to him that in the early days of their friendship she'd been the glue that had held the fierier Louisa and him together. They'd often turned to her to sort out their arguments until she'd laughingly bowed out and told them to fix their own shit. Had she been lonely then? Watching her two best friends fall in love, leaving her on the outside again? He'd never gotten that vibe off her. She'd loved them both too much.

And he'd taken his friendship away after Louisa's death, leaving her alone and vulnerable to idiots like Ray Smith. . . .

"Is he still asleep?" Lizzie asked.

"Yeah." Adam glanced down at his snoring passenger. "Do you want me to wake him, or shall I put him straight in my truck so we can take him home?"

"If your dad moved the car seat into your truck then let's

just put him in it." Lizzie yawned. "Wow, too much fresh air. We can leave the door open and keep an eye on him while we deal with the horses."

When they reached the barn, Ben and Danny were already out doing the evening chores. Ben came over and took Roman from Adam's arms.

"Finally wore him out, did you?"

"Just about." Adam dismounted. "Did Dad move the car seat?"

"It's in your truck. Do you want me to put Junior in it?"

Adam nodded. "I'll just put Spot away, and I'll be right back."

"Spot?" Ben looked up at Adam's majestic seventeen hands high gelding. "Since when—?"

Lizzie pointed at Roman and Ben started to laugh.

"Just for that"—Adam took the boy back—"you can put Spot and Peg away, and I'll drive Lizzie and Roman home."

Lizzie sat back and closed her eyes as Adam drove down from the ranch, and out onto the county road that led back to Morgantown. She'd had a lovely day and had deliberately shut out everything else that was going on in her life to enjoy it to the fullest. Seeing Adam with Roman, his patience under a barrage of questions, and his kindness had reminded her of the qualities she'd loved in her old school friend. He rode like he was part of the horse, his big body so relaxed in the saddle that he hardly seemed to direct the horse, although she knew that was an illusion.

"Good abs," she murmured.

"What's that?" Adam asked.

Lizzie felt herself blushing. "Nothing." She yawned as they approached the edge of the small town. "I think we'll both sleep well tonight."

Adam didn't answer, his attention on weaving his big truck through the narrower roads behind Main Street. They went past Gabby's, and Lizzie noticed that the lights in Coretta's house next door were on, and that there was an unfamiliar car parked outside.

"Coretta's back," Lizzie commented.

"Let me know if she causes you any trouble, and I'll be right there," Adam said grimly.

"I'm hoping there won't be any." Lizzie turned to check Roman who was still sleeping. "I'd like things to get back to normal now, please."

"Me, too."

Lizzie bit her lip and stared straight ahead. "I bet."

He'd been quiet all the way home, and she sensed he was withdrawing from her. She knew how he felt. Seeing him again—spending time with him—had reminded her of everything she'd lost. Underneath that somewhat humorless exterior, he was still the Adam she'd known at school: funny, kind, gentle. . . . Part of her wanted to find that man and coax him out of his self-imposed shell. It was also a scary prospect because she feared she'd like him way too much, and then where would their friendship be?

"You don't have to come in." Lizzie stated as he drew up in front of her apartment.

He frowned. "Roman's asleep. I'll carry him up for you."

Knowing that waking her son would mean he'd be up all night, Lizzie gave up her feeble protest. She unbuckled Roman from his car seat, handed him over to Adam and took the seat out of the truck. She let Adam in the lower door and followed him upstairs into Roman's bedroom where he gently laid her son on his bed. He smoothed the boy's hair before he straightened, and turned to Lizzie who was watching him from the door.

"He's a great kid."

"Thanks."

She went back into the kitchen and undid the straps of her backpack, trying not to make Adam feel like he had to stay a moment longer than necessary.

He paused by the counter. "You should bring him out again."

"I'm sure he'd love that." She wouldn't look at him, she couldn't. "Maybe you can pick him up and take him out there one day?"

"I'd rather you came with him."

"You're probably sick to death of me." She found a smile. "I'm not sure I'll have the time anyway, but thanks for the offer."

He went still. "When I agreed that I'd like my life to get back to normal, I didn't mean I wanted to get rid of you and Roman."

"Okay."

His voice deepened and he took a step toward her. "Lizzie . . ."

"What?" She turned to face him and found she was stuck in the corner between the two countertops with nowhere to go. Just as she looked up, he leaned forward, hands planted on either side of her. His mouth brushed hers, making everything inside her go quiet and still.

"I mean it."

"Okay." He was so close that she literally breathed her answer against his lips.

"I like to see you. . . ." He angled his head, catching all of her mouth this time, and she let him kiss her because she didn't have the strength or the desire to push him away.

He slid his hand around the back of her neck and kissed her properly, deeply, *perfectly,* and she kissed him back.

He took his time learning her, each flick of his tongue and press of his lips, a slow exploration that made her feel like a precious artifact.

Eventually, he drew back. "Did I do that right?"

She nodded, her brain too addled to form actual words.

"I'm out of practice." He grimaced, and dropped one last kiss on her nose. "Thanks again for a great day. I'll speak to you soon."

The next thing she knew, he was leaving. It was only after the door slammed shut behind him that she realized she was still holding Roman's drinking cup in one of her clenched hands. Adam had taken her completely by surprise, and now she didn't know what to think. She pressed her fingers to her lips, tasting him again, and went to put Roman to bed in something of a daze.

Chapter Eight

He'd kissed Lizzie Taylor. Adam let out a breath and tried to focus on the accounts his father had given him earlier to transcribe the records online. He'd kissed her more than once, and not in just a friendly way, but in a deep and personal way that had made him rock hard and ready for more. The shock of that had sent him running down the stairs like a speeding bronco.

He'd made no attempt to explain himself, and five days later he still didn't know what he was going to say when he did. *I kissed you because I didn't feel like I had any other choice? I kissed you because I had one of the best days of my life since Louisa died?* Both of those reasons were totally about him and Lizzie probably wouldn't appreciate either of them.

He glanced down at his cell. She hadn't contacted him either. Maybe that was a clear message of its own. . . .

"Adam?" Daisy came in and sat on the corner of the desk. "Are you going to pick Leanne up from the airport? Dad's saying he's going to do it."

"He can if he wants." Adam shrugged. "He might stand a better chance of recognizing her than I will."

"But he's a terrible driver, and he's never been to the

airport before. If he and Leanne get into a fight on the way back, he might drive himself off the road while he's arguing with her."

"You have a point." Adam considered her comment. "Maybe I'll offer to go."

"Would you?" Daisy smiled at him. "I don't particularly want her to come here, but I don't want Dad driving them both off a cliff, either."

"Fair enough. Are you off to work?"

"Yes, and then I'm having dinner with Jackson in town."

"Cool." Adam squinted at their dad's terrible handwriting. "I'll probably still be here when you get back, trying to make sense of these figures. I wish Dad would get into the age of technology."

"I bought him a tablet and installed all the software he needed to link directly to the farm account online," Daisy said. "I can't do much more than that." She picked up a stray pen and put it back in the pot. "Maybe you should take a break and come and have dinner with me and Jackson. You could ask Lizzie to join us."

Adam sat back in his chair and looked up at his diminutive sister. "Stop."

"Stop what?"

"Fishing. Lizzie and I are just friends."

She sighed. "When she and Roman came out here you looked so . . . *happy*. We all noticed it—even Dad."

"It was a nice thing to do for the kid." Adam crossed his arms and sat back until the chair creaked. "He doesn't get to run around much in an apartment in town."

"It *was* a nice thing," she agreed. "But I saw the way you looked at Lizzie."

"Daisy." Adam met her gaze. "Lizzie and I were really

good friends at school. I deliberately ended that friendship after Louisa died, and I'm trying to get it back. Can we leave it at that?"

"You and I are quite alike," Daisy said conversationally.

"Yeah, so what?"

"We're both really stubborn, and we tend to hang on to things for way too long."

Adam raised an eyebrow. "What's that supposed to mean?"

"I think you know." She hesitated. "I was so hung up on my first love that I almost blew my chances of having a relationship with Jackson."

"I'm not you, Daisy." Adam paused. "And, I'm not trying to be rude here, but your brief college romance is hardly in the same league as my marriage, is it?"

Daisy rolled her eyes and slid off the desk. "There's no need to get all defensive, bro. I'm just asking you to think before you rule something out entirely."

"Thanks for the advice." Adam returned his gaze to the screen of his laptop. "Now scoot."

She was still laughing as she walked away. He was still unable to find the humor in anything she'd said. He *was* stubborn. Louisa had been the same way. Their short marriage had been full of stormy disagreements, and a fair amount of sulking, usually followed by joyous reconciliations, and mind-blowing sex. They'd been teenagers for most of it.

The last year had been the most difficult with Louisa not willing to embrace the treatment options Adam insisted would save her, even when he knew that because of the type of cancer she had there was little hope. His wife had been a great believer in fate and had accepted hers long before Adam had come to terms with any of it.

He stretched out his legs and leaned back, making the chair groan again as he stared up at the ceiling. At twenty-one, Louisa had found a grace and strength Adam feared he would never have. She'd died as she'd lived, with her gaze direct, her conscience clear, and her courage evident. He'd gone to pieces, ended up seeking consolation from their mutual best friend and destroyed another lifetime relationship.

He tried not to think about the night Lizzie had found him weeping beside his wife's grave. He'd been really close to doing something so stupid and selfish, that she'd literally saved his life. Holding her, *being* with her in that anguished moment, had given him a new chance. He'd never had the guts to tell her that. He'd just hidden himself from her in his ongoing shame.

"Pathetic," Adam muttered to himself. "Daisy's right. I am way too stubborn."

He sat back up, grabbed his phone, scrolled through to his text messages, and started typing.

> Would you like to have dinner with me, Daisy, and Jackson tonight at the Red Dragon? (If you can get a sitter for Roman.) If so, I'll see you in there around six.

He checked the time and realized Lizzie might not have access to her cell until she took a break. While he waited to hear from her, he'd better get a move on and straighten up the accounts.

Lizzie stared at Adam's text message for way too long. Just seeing it pop up had made her heart skitter like a mad thing. She reminded herself that she wasn't twenty anymore, and that as a mature women she didn't have to get all stupid over a boy—although Adam was hardly one. He was more of a big, hot, smoldering hunk of grumpiness.

"You okay?" Yvonne asked.

"Yes." Lizzie smiled at her boss and put her phone away. "I just got an invite to the Red Dragon tonight."

"From Adam Miller?"

"Possibly," Lizzie acknowledged. "But it's far too late to arrange a babysitter for Roman anyway."

"I'll babysit."

Lizzie blinked at Yvonne. "What?"

Yvonne shrugged. "I'll do it. I've got to stay in and set up my schedule for next month before Rio gets back and demands all my attention. I could do it just as well at your place as mine."

"Are you sure?" Lizzie asked cautiously. It was a measure of how much she wanted to go that she was even contemplating the idea. "You do know that Roman can be a bit of a handful."

"Pfft." Yvonne waved an airy hand at Lizzie. "He's only a little boy. I've looked after him before. What on earth can go wrong?"

Lizzie sent Adam a text confirming she would be there at six. She somehow managed to get through the rest of the day without screwing anything up too badly, which was something of a miracle in itself. If she left work at four, she'd have plenty of time to get Roman settled. If she were really lucky, he'd be ready for bed by the time Yvonne arrived.

When she picked Roman up from Gabby's she checked out Coretta's house, but there was still no sign of her. The car that had been parked in her short driveway was also missing. Roman was chatty and full of energy while he skipped along the sidewalk with Doofus dragging along behind him. Lizzie told him about Yvonne coming over, which cheered him up even more because he knew she'd bring him sweet treats.

After feeding Roman and settling him down with his Legos, Lizzie took a quick shower, leaving the doors open so that she could still hear her son talking away to himself. She put on her only set of matching underwear, her best jeans, and a floaty, flowery, off-one-shoulder top her mother had bought her for Christmas last year, and that she'd never worn.

Her heart was jumping around like a wild horse and she didn't dare attempt to put on makeup. She'd probably take her eye out with the mascara wand or end up with clown mouth.

Just as she was explaining to Roman for the twentieth time that Doofus didn't need to brush his teeth, the doorbell rang, and she went down to let Yvonne in.

"Aunty Von!" Roman rushed over to hug Yvonne. "Cake? Please?"

"Of course." Yvonne bent to return the hug and patted his cheek. "If it's okay with your mom."

"Sure, but if you have something sweet, Ro, you have to promise that you'll brush your teeth really well, okay?"

"I'll make sure he does." Yvonne put a pink box on the countertop and studied Lizzie. "You look great!"

"Thanks." Lizzie patted her hair, which she'd left down "I wasn't sure what to wear because it's not like we're going on a date or anything. I didn't want to go too fancy, and I don't have anything like that *anyway,* so—"

Lizzie ran out of breath at about the same time that Yvonne politely interrupted her.

"You really do look nice."

Lizzie glanced ruefully down at her jeans. "I look the same as ever. I wish I was good at doing my hair and putting on makeup, but I suck at it."

"You don't really need it," Yvonne said. "You have very distinct coloring."

"I have wishy-washy red hair, blue eyes, and pale skin that doesn't tan, ever," Lizzie said firmly. "And that's okay. I was too nervous to even attempt anything special tonight."

"I could do your makeup for you," Yvonne suggested. "I have a really steady hand."

Lizzie glanced down at Roman who had gone back to his Legos. "How long will it take? I have to be there at six."

"Five minutes at most, and who wants to be on time?" Yvonne encouraged her. "The light's better in here. Get your stuff, and I'll make you even *more* beautiful, and Adam will be struck dumb."

"I'm trying to encourage him to talk more, so that's not really the effect I'm going for," Lizzie muttered as she fetched her pathetic makeup bag and put it on the table in front of Yvonne. "My mom bought me all this stuff. I have no idea if it suits me or not."

Yvonne was already busy going through the bag and didn't comment except to point to the chair.

"Sit down and close your eyes."

Lizzie did what she was told and patiently endured the dabbing and patting while Yvonne murmured to herself in French as she worked.

"Voilà!"

Lizzie cautiously opened her eyes and stared into the mirror Yvonne helpfully put in front of her face.

"I still look like me, only better."

"*Bon.*" Yvonne nodded as she packed away the cosmetics. "Now, off you go and have fun!"

Lizzie paused at the door, her gaze on Roman who appeared supremely happy to be left with Yvonne. "I'll text you if I'm going to be later than nine-thirty. I know you like to get to bed early."

"If I feel at all sleepy, I'll let you know." Yvonne blew her a kiss. "Have fun."

Lizzie went down the stairs and out into the warm night air. She hadn't bothered with a coat because her commute was barely five minutes. Ted Baker, Sr., was working in the gas station while his son had dinner. He still lived over the old shop and would help close the place up around nine.

Lizzie noticed that the Lexus pulling out of the gas station was the same color as the one that had been parked outside Coretta's house. She wondered if whomever it belonged to had been out with the old lady for the day and was just filling up before leaving town. She walked farther along Main Street until she reached the corner where it intersected with Morgan, and went into the Red Dragon, which was full of locals enjoying the start of the weekend.

She smiled at Nancy who worked behind the bar.

"Hey, are the Millers here yet?"

Nancy pointed behind her. "They're already seated. Third booth down on the right beside the window."

"Thanks."

As she approached the booth, Lizzie's steps slowed and a knot of uncertainty unfurled low in her stomach. Adam slid out of his seat and stood looking down at her, his face inscrutable. Why the heck had he asked her to come if he was going to stare at her like that? For a second, Lizzie considered bolting back to the safety of her apartment.

"Hey." Lizzie offered Adam a quick impersonal smile before she scooted along the old leatherette seat. "Hi, Daisy. Hi, Jackson."

Adam sat beside her and the booth suddenly felt very small. "I'm glad you agreed to come." He nodded over at Daisy. "I was already getting sick of being a gooseberry with these two lovebirds."

"Hey, that's not fair," Daisy protested. "We can't help it." She kissed Jackson's cheek and grinned at Lizzie. "Thanks for coming. Adam's turning into a really grumpy old man these days. Perhaps you can help lighten him up?"

"I'll do my best." Lizzie fought to keep a straight face. "Although he never usually laughs at my jokes."

"He'd need a sense of humor before he could do that."

Daisy winked at her brother who didn't look at all bothered by all the teasing. He stretched one long arm along the back of the seat, his callused fingers perilously close to Lizzie's bare shoulder, and picked up his beer in his other hand to toast Daisy.

Deborah, one of the servers, came over and handed Lizzie a menu. "Hey, you. How's it going? Still working at Yvonne's?"

"I love it there," Lizzie said as she ordered herself a beer. "What's everyone having to eat?"

"I think that's Deb's line tonight, Lizzie," Jackson joked. "You get to sit back and relax."

He was enjoying himself. Daisy was always good company. The happiness she'd found with Jackson shone through her, making Adam feel old and way too crabby.

He remembered how that was—how love made you feel invincible—even when it was all a lie. Not that he would ever say that to Daisy or trample on her happiness, but he'd learned the hard way that love couldn't always save you.

Lizzie was a little tense. As the evening wore on, she relaxed more until she was leaning in toward his body, accepting his presence, and the shelter of his arm almost around the back of her shoulders. He wanted to pull her tight against him, thigh-to-thigh, shoulder-to-shoulder. Hell, he wanted her to straddle his lap so that he could put his hands all over her. . . .

"So, how's Spot doing?"

Lizzie's question penetrated his heated imaginings and he turned to look at her.

"He's doing good. Seems to like his new name as well."

"You don't have to call him that, you know."

"Why not?" Adam shrugged. "It's as good a name as any."

"Roman will be thrilled," Lizzie said. "He even drew you a picture. I offered to bring it with me, but he wants to give it to you himself." She paused. "You could come over to dinner one night, if you'd like, and pick it up."

"That would be nice." It was his turn to hesitate. "Although as my mom's just about to arrive, I'm not sure what my schedule will be like over the next two weeks."

"There's no rush. It will keep."

"To be honest, if Leanne and Dad run true to form, she won't last two weeks because they'll have a fight within the first twenty-four hours, and she'll be straight back on the plane." He grimaced. "I can't say I'm looking forward to reliving their shouting matches."

She put her hand on his thigh, her whole body flowing toward him, sympathy in every line, and he leapt to attention. "That's terrible."

"We'll see how it goes." He glanced at his phone. "What time do you need to be back?"

Her smile faltered, and she withdrew into herself. "If you need to go, I'm more than happy to leave right now."

"That's not what I meant." Jeez, sometimes he hated his own social awkwardness. "I was thinking that maybe we could ditch the lovebirds and have coffee together."

"Do you want to come back to my place and have coffee there?" Lizzie asked. "Yvonne's watching Roman and she likes to turn in early."

"That would be nice," Adam agreed, aware that he was treading on dangerous ground, but unable to stop himself. Being with Lizzie, *talking* to her, made him feel more like a regular human being. "If Roman's awake he can show me the picture."

"If he's awake, I won't be very happy," Lizzie said with mock severity. "He's terrible at getting up if he hasn't slept well. I don't have a lot of time in the morning to coax him into a better mood."

"I'm the same," Adam admitted. "Louisa always used to say—" He stopped speaking.

"That you were a terrible grouch in the morning." Lizzie finished his thought, speaking of Louisa with an ease he envied. "That's because she was an early bird like me. I remember how often you almost missed the school bus."

"Yeah, I was pretty bad." Adam found a smile somewhere. He glanced over at Daisy and Jackson who were engrossed in their own little bubble of happiness. "We might as well go. I don't think they'll miss us, do you?"

He leaned over and waved a hand in Daisy's face. "I'm going to walk Lizzie home, okay? I'll see you back at the ranch."

Daisy and Jackson sprang apart and managed to wish

Lizzie good-bye before returning to gaze into each other's eyes.

As they exited the bar, Adam took Lizzie's hand as they strolled down the boardwalk, past the fountain of the town's founder, and toward the gas station. It was still warm with very little breeze to bother them. Being with Lizzie, watching her smile and interact with other people, made him feel like he'd been missing out on something—that his self-imposed exile had been a mistake.

"Let me find the key." Lizzie slowed as they approached the lower door. She shoved a hand in the pocket of her tight jeans and did a little shimmy that made everything male in Adam sit up and pay attention. "I should never have worn my best jeans."

"You look nice," Adam blurted out like an awkward teenager.

"Thanks." She offered him a smile. "So do you."

She put the key in the lock and half turned, her attention now over his shoulder. "There's that car again."

"Which car?" Adam looked, too.

"The Lexus." Lizzie shrugged. "Don't mind me. I'm probably being paranoid." She opened the lower door and he stepped into complete darkness, bumping up against her. He instinctively steadied her and didn't want to let go.

"Adam . . ."

He kissed her, and she sighed into his mouth. He was lost in her taste as he eased her back against the wall. She stood on tiptoe and wound her arms around his neck. It still wasn't enough. He lifted her until her booted feet rested on his ass and the bulge behind his fly fitted perfectly against the center seam of her jeans.

He couldn't help rocking his hips while the kiss went on

and on, turning into something so life-giving that he forgot himself and lost his mind in Lizzie.

"God . . ." Lizzie moaned into Adam's mouth as he moved against her, his big body pressing her against the wall. Her breasts were flattened against his broad chest and her thighs clasped his hips. As he continued to thrust, the hardness of his jeans-covered shaft set her off on an unintentional and totally unexpected climax. She bucked and shuddered against him in a moment of complete surrender.

Wrenching her mouth away, she shoved at his chest.

"I have to—let me *down*."

He immediately complied. She ran up the stairs as if her life depended on it, unlocked the door, and burst into the apartment, scaring Yvonne who was sitting on the couch.

"*Mon Dieu!*" Yvonne shot to her feet, her hand on her bosom. "Are you okay?"

"Bathroom!" Lizzie croaked and ran on by. She locked the door and stared at herself in the mirror, aware of her wide eyes, well-kissed lips, and the lingering buzz of her unexpected sexual high. "God, I'm so *pathetic!*"

She washed her flushed face and took some deep breaths. If Adam had any sense, he'd let himself out again downstairs, and not come up.

"Come . . ." Lizzie whispered. "Shut *up,* Lizzie!"

After another stern talking to herself, she left the bathroom, checked that Roman was asleep, and went back into the kitchen where Adam was, of course, standing at the counter talking to Yvonne.

"Are you okay?" Yvonne asked. "Did you eat something weird?"

"I'm good," Lizzie said. "I just needed—" She waved a vague hand in the direction of the bathroom. "Thanks so much for babysitting. Was Roman okay?"

After one last quizzical glance, Yvonne picked up her bag and stowed her laptop inside. "He was great. I made sure he brushed his teeth, read him a story, and he went straight to sleep."

"Thanks again," Lizzie said, all too aware of Adam's quiet presence and unwilling to even acknowledge him until she got herself together. As if that was ever going to happen when he was around. She walked over to open the door as Yvonne said good-bye to Adam. "I'll see you tomorrow at work."

Yvonne kissed her cheek and went on down the stairs. Lizzie closed the door and reluctantly turned back to Adam who was regarding her steadily, one eyebrow raised.

"I'm sorry," she said.

"Sorry for what, exactly?"

Heat rose in her cheeks. "I think you know."

He leaned one hip against the countertop and slowly shook his head. "Did I scare you?"

"*No*."

A crease appeared between his brows. "Then why did you run away?"

Lizzie stared at him, her brain scurrying around like a cage full of rabid mice. "It was . . . personal."

"You needed to use the bathroom?"

"That wasn't it." Lizzie decided to be brave. "You made me, I mean . . . *I* climaxed."

His silence this time was so long that Lizzie only remembered to breathe again when she felt giddy.

"I—" It was his turn to be lost for words. "I didn't mean to do that."

"Of course you didn't," Lizzie fervently agreed with him. "It was on me. Now, can we just forget about it, have some coffee, and then you can leave?"

He slowly rubbed his hand over his unshaven jaw and mouth, which made Lizzie's newly reawakened lady parts perk up even more.

"That's kind of a . . . hard thing to forget."

Lizzie marched over to the door and held it wide open. "Then maybe the sooner you leave, the sooner you'll get over it?" She smiled sweetly. "If you like, I could push you down the stairs so you'll land on your head and forget about it completely."

He didn't move an inch, his curious gaze fastened on her. "Do you do that a lot?"

Lizzie folded her arms over her chest. "Not that it's any of your business, but no, I don't. It was a first for me. I can't believe I was stupid enough to mention it to you."

He nodded, finally straightened up, and walked toward the door, stopping only when he was nose to nose with her.

"What?" Lizzie refused to drop her gaze.

He smiled, took her hand, and pressed it against the still-hard bulge in his jeans. "Well, at least you got off." He let go of her and kissed her on the nose. "The only place I'm heading for is a cold shower. 'Night, Lizzie."

She watched him leave, one hand covering her mouth in case she gave in to the urge to call him back and offer to help him out with his little problem. Not that it was little. . . . Her body was very keen on the idea, but her mind was not ready to go there—yet.

With a groan, she flung herself down on the couch. *What was happening to her?* Hadn't she learned anything from her brief fling with Ray? Sexual attraction didn't last, and wanting sex just because you hadn't had any for years was never a good reason to jump into bed with someone. There were other more reliable ways to get sexual satisfaction that currently resided in her bedroom drawer. The fact that she'd come so easily for Adam Miller should be a warning, not a source for celebration.

Chapter Nine

If he took any more cold showers his skin would fall off. Adam stared grimly at the new calves Ben and he were unloading. The smell of shit, the bawling cattle, and the sudden rain weren't making him feel any better. He counted the calves as they emerged down the ramp into the prepared field, and closed up the back of the trailer.

"We're good."

Ben, who had been stacking hay and feed cakes, and making sure the plumbing worked on the water trough, nodded. "They should be fine here for a couple of days until we decide where to put them."

"Might as well keep them here and get them fixed and branded." Adam wiped the sweat from his brow, and Ben grimaced.

"Dude, you've just wiped cow shit all over your face."

Adam had already worked that out from the smell. "It's good for the skin."

"Ha!" Ben grinned at him. "Don't you have to get back and go pick up Mom?"

"I thought I'd go like this." Adam looked down at his damp mud-splattered jeans, chaps, and boots.

They walked toward the gate, the calves moving as one to huddle beneath the shelter in the corner of the field.

"If you don't want her here, that's one way of making sure she won't even get in the car with you," Ben remarked as he padlocked the gate behind them. "Although why you and Daisy are so fired up about it, I don't know."

"Probably because I remember what it was like better than you do, and Daisy was abandoned when she was five," Adam said dryly.

"True." Ben mounted up on his horse and Adam did the same. "I don't claim to remember much. I just woke up one day and she was gone."

Adam adjusted his Stetson to keep out as much of the drizzle as possible. He was grateful for the much-needed rain, but it sure as hell was echoing his dismal mood. He'd unintentionally helped Lizzie climax and immediately been shown the door. Even as he thought about it, his body stirred.

But they hadn't talked about any of it—the kissing, the "were they in a relationship?" thing, the unexpected surge of desire he had every time Lizzie so much as smiled in his direction. That last one was on him. If Lizzie had wanted more, she could've asked. Instead, she'd acted like it was a mortal insult and hustled him out of her apartment.

But then she had a kid, and maybe she'd been thinking more clearly than he was at that moment with all the blood from his brain still residing in his dick. He could've said something. He could've tried to talk to her about his complicated feelings, but kissing her, being with her, was so new and raw that he was afraid to admit anything out loud in case he messed up. Touching her in the darkness of the hallway, letting her touch him without the complication of words, had seemed way safer.

"Hey, dreamer."

Adam turned to Ben who was riding alongside him.

"I was just trying to figure out where the main herd is,

and how far we'd need to take the new cattle out to join them," Adam said.

"Sure you were." Ben rolled his eyes. "Thinking about cattle always makes you look like a man trying to defuse a ticking bomb."

"Are you still going to help BB Morgan out with that tracking and survivalist course he's running up at Morgan Ranch?" Adam asked, aware that it was a diversionary tactic, but totally okay with it.

"Yeah, I am, but what's that got to do with you?"

"I'm just asking." Adam shrugged. "I'm always interested in what my siblings are up to."

"And total shit at sharing what you're doing," Ben countered.

Adam stared out between his horse's ears. "I'm not up to anything except working out how to deal with Leanne if she upsets Dad or Daisy while she's here."

That had always been his job. Watching out for his siblings, protecting them from the parental arguments, and literally stepping in between his mom and dad if things got too lively. The fact that his brothers weren't worried about Leanne coming back meant that he must have done a good job back in the day even though he'd hated every second of it.

"Maybe it will all be fine," Ben said.

"Maybe it will." Admiring his brother's positivity, Adam gathered his reins and pointed toward the ranch. "Race you home. Last one in takes care of the horses."

"Hi!" Lizzie smiled at the suited businessman occupying one of the outdoor tables at the café. "Welcome to Yvonne's. What can I get for you?"

"Hey." He smiled back. "This is a great little place. Kind of a hidden gem."

"Morgantown? Yes, it is. I love it here." Lizzie found her pen and notepad. "Can I start you off with a drink while you check out the menu?"

"I'll have a cappuccino, please. A large one." He checked the menu. "I think I need a few moments to decide what I want."

"We have a couple of specials if you're interested." Lizzie pointed at the blackboard on the door. "The fish tacos are great, and so is the smoked salmon quiche."

"Thanks." He set his cell phone on the table next to him. "You have good reception here."

"We're lucky." Lizzie went to deal with a family who had just arrived at the only vacant table and handed them some menus. While they were sorting themselves out, she made the cappuccino and took it out with a glass of water.

"Here you go."

"Thanks." He moved the glass of water as far away from his cell phone as he possibly could. "I have been known to spill stuff. Have you lived here long?"

"My parents came here when I was about five, so I consider myself a local." Lizzie flipped through the pages of her pad to find a clean page. "It's a great place to grow up. Did you decide on lunch?"

"I suppose that in such a small town, everyone knows everyone's business. I think that would drive me crazy."

"I suppose it depends what you've got to hide," Lizzie joked.

He picked up his menu and handed it to her. "I'll have the smoked salmon quiche and a salad on the side, please. No dressing."

"Got it." Lizzie jotted down the order. "Would you like the quiche warm or cold?"

"Warm might be nice." He grinned at her. "Although it's pretty hot out here already. Do any of these old buildings have air-conditioning?"

"Most of them."

"Do you live in town or out on one of the ranches?"

"In town. It makes my commute a lot easier."

Lizzie got on with her other tasks. She hadn't heard from Adam, but as Leanne was due to arrive today, she suspected he might be busy worrying about other things. Which was fine by her. The longer it took for her to see him again, the better. In a year or two she might be able to face him without blushing.

She delivered the quiche and salad and received a distracted thank-you as the guy was busy typing on his phone. She checked on him occasionally, between other customers, topped off his water, and removed his empty plate.

When he beckoned her over, she approached with a smile.

"Can I get you anything else? Or would you like the check?"

"Check, please."

Lizzie went and prepared the check and brought it back to his table.

He sat back and regarded her as she placed the billfold in front of him "I've got to stay here tonight since I'm meeting a client. Can you direct me to the Hayes Hotel?"

Lizzie pointed. "It's literally just down the street. You can park behind it."

"Cool. My name's Mike by the way." He slipped his credit card into the billfold. "How long does this place stay open?"

"We close at six." Lizzie picked up the folder. "I'll get this right back to you."

"Does the hotel have a restaurant?"

"Yes, it's really good." She paused. "There's also the Red Dragon Bar, which does less fancy food, and Gina's, which is mainly pizza."

"Which do you like best?"

"It depends on how I feel, and how much money I want to spend," Lizzie quipped.

"How about if I was paying?"

She raised her eyebrows. "Then it would be up to you."

He grinned at her. "Come on, you know what I mean. I can't be the first guy who's asked you out after being so well taken care of over lunch?"

"You certainly aren't," Lizzie agreed. "But I generally don't go out with customers I've just met."

"Generally? So you only go out with local boys?"

Inwardly, Lizzie sighed. She hated it when a man wouldn't take a hint. "I'll just go run your card."

She went back into the shop where Angelo was dealing with a fresh batch of roasted coffee beans.

"Can you hang with me here for a minute?" Lizzie asked her fellow server. "I've got one of those persistent customers who wants to take me out to dinner, and doesn't seem to understand the word *no*."

"Sure." Angelo took a quick survey of the room and flexed his considerable muscles. "Where is he?"

"Outside." Lizzie groaned. "Correction. He's coming in the door right now."

She busied herself dealing with the credit card machine, handed the man the slip of paper to sign, and returned his card.

"Here you go."

He made a face. "I guess I screwed up, huh?"

Lizzie focused on resetting the register.

"It's hard to tell these days whether it's okay to make the

approach. Are you married? You don't wear a ring," he commented. "Do you have a boyfriend?"

Just as Lizzie was about to reply, Angelo suddenly appeared at her shoulder. "None of that is any of your business, is it, sir?" He gestured at the check. "How about you sign that, go on your way, and have a nice day."

The man shrugged as he pocketed his card. "There's no need to call for backup, honey. You don't get anything unless you ask." He looked pointedly at Lizzie. "Have a great day, now."

She only let out her breath when he disappeared out the door.

"I hate guys like that," Angelo muttered. "They give the rest of us a bad name." He patted Lizzie's back. "Are you okay? Do you want me to walk you home after your shift?"

"I think I'll be okay, but thanks for the offer." Lizzie smiled up at him. "I've got to pick up Roman at four. If the guy is stupid enough to follow me, and finds out I've got a kid, he'll probably run a mile."

"Not every guy hates kids, Lizzie." Angelo checked and changed the filters on the coffee. "I'd love to have a family one day."

"And you'll make a great dad," Lizzie agreed as she put the signed check in the register drawer and made a face. "Dude, he didn't even give me a tip!"

Adam drove into a spot at the airport parking lot. He made sure he had the ticket, and some idea of where he'd parked, before he walked over to the small regional terminal. He'd showered and changed into another pair of jeans, a blue T-shirt, and his second-best boots. His working boots were always caked in mud and his spurs were stuck fast on them so he tended not to wear them off the ranch.

He'd been joking with Daisy, but he really didn't have a clue what his mother might look like now. More than twenty years was a long time not to see someone. He wasn't sure she'd recognize him either, as he'd tripled his weight and added a foot to his height.

He stood near the back of the small arrivals hall, his superior height for once an advantage, and scanned the passengers coming through the exit. He recognized her immediately; her eyes were the same brown as Ben's, and her hair was still auburn. His stomach twisted and he found himself unable to move forward. So much to unpack in that small unassuming figure, so many things she'd missed in his life—in his siblings' lives.

An unexpected wave of anger coursed through him. Did she care what she'd done? Why had she suddenly decided to descend on them and wreck their lives all over again? And even worse, why was his father okay with it?

For a second, he considered turning around and walking away before he managed to stuff his unwanted and completely unexpected reaction back down his tight throat. His dad wanted to see her. After everything that had gone down, the least he could do was walk over there and be pleasant. He'd survived way worse than this. He went toward her while she turned a slow circle attempting to orientate herself, and waited to see if she'd recognize him.

"Adam?" She pressed her fingers to her mouth. "Good Lord, it is you!" She reached up and cupped his chin. She was petite like Daisy. "You're as tall and broad as my father."

"I suppose I should say welcome home." Adam took charge of her luggage. "Are you good to go?"

"Yes, thank you. Did you park up?"

He nodded as they exited into the warm afternoon air and glaring sunshine. She winced and put on her sunglasses.

"I'd forgotten how bright it gets out here."

Adam led her across the road to the parking lot, stowed her bags in the back of his truck, and waited as she settled herself into the passenger seat. He checked his phone and sent a quick text to Ben to let him know they'd be back in about an hour.

She glanced over at him as he backed out of the parking space. "I appreciate you coming to get me. I told your father I could've gotten a taxi."

"It's not a problem." Adam maneuvered his ticket into the slot, paid for the parking, and waited until the barrier lifted to release them. Dealing with the normal stuff, and not directly looking at her, gave him a chance to recover from his unexpectedly emotional reaction to simply seeing her. "It's only an hour away."

"But I'm taking you away from your work."

"Ben's taking up the slack today." He checked the navigation and made sure he got in the correct lane as he exited the airport. It was a fairly straight route back to Bridgeport and out to the ranch.

She set her purse on her knee and opened it, bringing out her phone. "I'd better let everyone know I've arrived safely."

Adam badly wanted to ask whom she meant, but he still wasn't sure he wanted to know. She texted with one finger at a rate Roman could probably manage. Had she married again? He had no idea.

"That's better. Would you like a mint?"

"No, thanks."

Adam kept his gaze on the road, and made sure the air-conditioning was set at a high level. Out here in the open, there was no shade and the glare off the road onto the glass windscreen was intense.

"I was sorry to hear about what happened to Louisa," Leanne said.

Adam risked a sideways glance at her, his fingers tightening on the steering wheel.

"She was such a lovely girl."

"Yeah, she was."

"I wrote to her parents. I knew them quite well before I left Morgan Valley."

"They never mentioned you wrote."

"Why would they?" She looked at him thoughtfully. "I have to assume from your expression and your tone that your father didn't give you the letter I wrote to *you*."

"Why wouldn't he do that?" Adam parried.

"Because he's a very stubborn man who has probably never forgiven me for leaving him." She sighed. "It's okay, Adam. I know you don't want me here. I'm not stupid."

There was a lot he wanted to say to that, but he was driving, and he didn't want to end up in an argument. He hated it when people got angry and said shit they didn't mean. Keeping his cool, stepping back from any attempt she made to rile him up, was the way to go. She wanted closure? He'd give it to her with the minimum amount of participation possible.

She waited for a moment, and then sat back in her seat and closed her eyes, her expression resigned. Adam should've felt like the victor of their first encounter, but for some reason he didn't. She wasn't rubbing anything in his face; she wasn't being brash and defiant as if nothing had happened. She wasn't giving him anything to grab hold of and run with. Did he want her to? Did he want an excuse to let some of that good and righteous anger simmering deep in his gut out?

He continued to sneak glances at her as she dozed, noticing the good quality of her clothing and the fancy leather purse she was carrying. Whatever she'd gone on to become, she looked nothing like the mother he'd once known in her jeans and shirts, her red hair braided down her back. She didn't look ill either, but that didn't mean that she wasn't. Louisa hadn't looked ill until after the chemo and radiation treatments. . . .

Had Leanne really written to him? She was right that it would've been just like his dad to hold back any mail from his estranged wife. But it had hurt him when he'd heard nothing from her, and it had stuck with him like another layer of resentment.

She let out a little snore, and Adam returned his focus on the road. The sooner he got her to the hotel, the sooner she'd be off his hands and become his father's problem.

Lizzie jumped when her doorbell rang and contemplated not answering it. She'd picked up Roman from Gabby's and noticed the gold Lexus was parked at Coretta's again. There was no sign of the woman herself, but Lizzie felt like she needed to be on her guard the whole way home.

She walked down the stairs to the lower level, stood on tiptoe to check out who was calling, and opened the door.

"Hey."

Adam regarded her steadily and her cheeks heated.

"What's up?" Lizzie asked.

"I was in town, dropping Leanne off at the hotel. I thought I'd check in on you."

"Come on up." Lizzie waved him through the door. "We can have that coffee." She immediately wished she hadn't referenced their last embarrassing meeting.

"Thanks." He paused at the top of the stairs and looked down at her. "Is everything okay?"

"Well—"

Adam kept talking, his voice low. "You looked kind of apprehensive when you opened the door. I want to reassure you that if I did anything you didn't like last time I was here then just tell me."

She stared down at his boots. "I *liked* what happened. I'm just embarrassed."

"There's no reason to be. We all have needs." He cleared his throat. "I suppose we should talk."

"No!" Even the thought of that sent Lizzie into a panic. "How about we don't?"

"I thought all women liked to talk things through." Adam frowned.

"Not this one." Lizzie looked up at him. "And the reason I looked weird when I opened the door is because there was some guy at the café today who was a creeper. I was worried that he'd found out where I live."

Adam went still. "Who was it?"

"Nobody you know." She patted his rigid arm. "It's okay; it happens. Yvonne gets it worse because of her French accent."

"What did he do?"

"He just asked me out, and wasn't too happy when I turned him down." She tried to make Adam move into the apartment, but he stood his ground. "Come on, it's all good. Nothing happened."

"Some men suck," Adam muttered as he reluctantly yielded to the pressure and came inside. "You call me if he shows up again, okay?"

"I can defend *myself,* you know. I took BB Morgan's women's defense class twice," Lizzie pointed out.

"I'm sure you can, but—"

She put her hand flat on his chest. "But nothing. Everything is fine. Now come and say hi to Roman, and I'll get you that coffee."

Roman had already spotted Adam, and was making a beeline for him, his expression full of excitement.

"Adam! Come and see!" He grabbed Adam's hand and dragged him over to the refrigerator. "Spot!"

"Yeah?" Lizzie's lips twitched as Adam leaned in close to look at Roman's drawing, which was pinned to the refrigerator door with a magnet. "That looks just like him. Good job, buddy."

"It's for *you!*" Roman jumped up and down. "Isn't it, Mom?"

"Yup." Lizzie nodded at her son. "You can carefully take it down, and give it to Adam, okay?"

Adam lifted the little boy up and accepted the drawing with suitable gravity, studying it once more before setting it on the countertop beside his keys.

"Thanks. I'll show Spot when I get home."

Roman nodded. "He'll like it."

"I'm sure he will. I'll pin it up in his stall." Adam pointed at the three stick figures under the large spiky sun who were all holding hands. "Is that you and your mom?"

"Yes." Roman nodded vigorously. "And you." He peered at the drawing and jabbed it with his finger. "The big fat one."

Lizzie made the coffee and brought it over to the couch where Adam had settled himself as Roman went back to the table to continue drawing.

"How did it go with Leanne?" Lizzie asked as he took an appreciative sip of his coffee.

"It went okay." He stared into space for quite a while. "She was very pleasant to me."

"You sound surprised."

He half smiled. "When she lived at the ranch, she was so full of energy, quick to anger, and quicker to laugh—you just never knew which it would be—and now she's so serene."

"She's over twenty years older."

"Yeah, I get that, but she just seems like a completely different person altogether." He drank more coffee. "She said she wrote to me after Louisa died."

Lizzie waited, but he didn't say anything more, so she risked a question. "I guess you didn't get that letter?"

"Nope. I asked her if she thought Dad might have kept it from me, and she said it was highly likely." He paused. "The thing is, she didn't say it like she hated him or anything, more that it was simply something he would do."

"Is she right?"

"Yeah. It's totally something he would do." Adam sighed. "After she left, he had a big bonfire out back. He literally burned everything she hadn't taken away with her—bedsheets, towels, rugs, clothes. Anything she'd touched went up in flames."

Lizzie winced. She could just imagine Jeff Miller doing that.

"Leanne said that she'd also written to Carlos and Ines." Adam continued talking. "I said they'd never mentioned it, but after I dropped her off—just before I came here, I checked in with Ines and she confirmed that they'd had a lovely letter of condolence from her." He shrugged. "So if she was right about that, maybe she did write to me after all."

"You could always ask your dad," Lizzie suggested.

"Maybe I will." Adam met her gaze, his own conflicted.

"But maybe I'll wait to see how he and Leanne get on with each other when we all meet for dinner tonight."

Lizzie jumped up to refill his coffee, pausing to admire Roman's latest drawing, and offer him more milk.

When she returned, Adam was checking his phone.

"Is everything okay?" Lizzie asked as she set the mug in front of him.

"Yeah, I'm just making sure everyone turns up at the hotel at seven for dinner with Leanne."

"That should be an interesting evening," Lizzie said tactfully.

"Which is why I suggested we hold it at the hotel. Hopefully, if anyone starts fighting, we'll only have to pay damages to the Hayes family," Adam replied. "I'm hoping everyone will be on their best behavior."

"Good luck with that." Lizzie toasted him with her mug.

"Maybe I should hire some security." His swift smile took her by surprise. He rarely made the gesture, which was a shame because it really was a thing of beauty. "I bet you wish you could be there."

"Not really," Lizzie confessed. "I've never got my head around the dynamics of big families. There are so many unknown pitfalls to fall into."

"True. I suspect you'll see Leanne at the café if she stays around." He checked his cell again. "I'd better get back home. I need to change."

She waited as he drank his second cup of coffee in three gulps. "Let me know how it goes, okay?"

He took his mug through to the kitchen and then returned to crouch beside Roman at the table.

"Thanks for the picture, little buddy. It's awesome." He ruffled Roman's hair. "I'll see you soon, okay?"

Roman leaned forward, grabbed Adam's ears, stared into his eyes, and kissed him smack on the mouth. "Bye, Adam."

Lizzie went to open the front door as Adam put on his Stetson and followed her out onto the landing.

"Thanks for the coffee."

"You're welcome," Lizzie said, glad that the awkwardness between them had disappeared, and that she'd avoided getting into a deep conversation about anything. He had enough on his plate with his mom right now, and she . . . well, she wasn't sure what she was doing kissing him in the first place.

He angled his head and kissed her gently on the mouth. "Thanks for listening to me."

She smiled. He kissed her again as if he couldn't quite help himself, before straightening up, his intent gaze on her face.

"I'll be in touch."

"Okay."

She shut the door behind him and leaned against it, her gaze fixed on Roman who was busy drawing and humming to himself. She really should tell Adam to stop kissing her. But she didn't want to. It was as simple and as complicated as that.

Chapter Ten

Adam put his hand on his father's shoulder and held him back as his other siblings walked into the Hayes Hotel chattering like a bunch of starlings.

"Are you okay to do this, Dad?"

"Of course I am. I'm looking forward to it." His father frowned at him. "There's no need to baby me, son."

"I'm just checking in," Adam replied. "She was very pleasant on the ride over here."

He walked to the door and held it open for his dad to pass into the Victorian-themed lobby of the Hayes Historic Hotel, which had once been Morgantown's premier saloon and brothel. Tom Hayes, the owner, was behind the mahogany-fronted reception desk dressed in his usual three-piece suit.

"Hey, Jeff. I set you guys up in a room down the hall on the right. Someone will be down to welcome you in a second. I thought you might enjoy some privacy."

"Thanks, Tom." Adam's father offered him a gruff nod. "Appreciate it." He glanced up at Adam as they turned the corner. "Better than the whole of the dining room listening in, and our family business being all over the valley."

"Yeah." Adam saw a crowd of his siblings and went

toward them. "Go on in, guys. Tom's sending someone to take drink and dinner orders shortly."

He braced himself as he went through the door, but there was no sign of Leanne yet. He wondered if she was as nervous as they were, and concluded that facing six kids and an ex-husband was probably a way worse way to end your day than his had been. He'd gotten to kiss Lizzie Taylor. Again.

Daisy didn't look too happy so he walked over to stand by her. She hadn't made an effort to change out of her usual jeans and the T-shirt advertising her flower shop on Main Street.

"You doing okay?" Adam asked.

"Not really." Daisy blew out a long breath. "I just don't know what I'm supposed to say, or how I'm supposed to act."

"I think we all feel like that." Adam glanced around at his four brothers who were all unnaturally quiet and wearing their Sunday best. "She wasn't like I remembered her."

"I don't really know her," Daisy confessed. "My own *mother*. I wish Auntie Rae was here to help smooth things along."

"Don't we all," Adam murmured. His father's sister had taken on the task of bringing up his kids, and had done an amazing job of it. "I think she decided this was too big for her to handle."

There was a stir at the door and Leanne appeared. She wore a pantsuit in a soft gray color with a bronze silk blouse that caught the light.

Adam's dad stood up and walked toward her while everyone else held their breath.

He took her hand in a double clasp. "Leanne. You're looking well."

"So are you, Jeff." Her smile reminded Adam of Daisy's. "Thank you so much for letting me come visit with you."

"I could hardly stop you, could I?" Adam winced, but Leanne didn't seem to take offense at his father's abrupt manner. "It's a free country."

Ben, who was the peacemaker in the family, stepped forward and offered Leanne a welcoming smile.

"Hi, I'm—"

"Ben." Leanne smiled and touched her hair. "You were the only one with my hair color. It's lovely to see you again."

Ben put an arm around her shoulders and turned her to face his siblings. "That's Kaiden on the end, Danny in the middle, and Evan on the right."

All three men came forward to offer Leanne awkward hugs. When she turned toward Adam, he took Daisy's hand.

"You've already met me. This is Daisy."

Leanne's face softened, and she took a step toward them. "Oh my gosh, Daisy, you're so *beautiful*."

Daisy made no effort to leave Adam's side as she nodded. "Hi."

Leanne's hand fell to her side and she swallowed hard before brightly addressing her ex. "This place hasn't changed much."

"No need to. It's fine as it is." Jeff took her elbow and led her over to a chair by the fire. "Now what would you like to drink?"

Sometime later, Adam went out to use the bathroom and to check in with Tom about clearing away the dinner plates. He was awaiting Tom's return from the kitchen when a man strolled out of the dining room and came over to him.

"This is a really nice place."

"So I hear." Adam nodded. "It certainly has a great bar and restaurant."

"You're local?" the guy asked.

"Yeah. My family just came in for dinner."

"Nice. Do you ever go to that café in town? Yvonne's?"

"It's a great place for breakfast if you don't want to eat here," Adam replied.

"Cool, I'll definitely give it a try if I'm up early enough." The man nodded. "Thanks. Good to talk to you."

He walked over to the comfortable couches set out in the lobby and took out his phone.

Tom joined Adam who had kept his gaze on the unknown man.

"Who's that?" Adam asked quietly.

"Now you know I can't give away that kind of information, Adam."

"I just wondered who he was meeting." Adam shrugged. "It's a small town."

"Then feel free to drop by tomorrow and spy on him to your heart's content." Tom slapped him on the back. "Now, shall we go and sort out dessert?"

When Adam got back to his family, Leanne and his dad were still talking intently, but there was no sign of either of them getting upset or mad. It was really weird. He'd half been expecting to have to separate the pair like he'd done when he was twelve. Occasionally, his dad would beckon imperiously to one of his siblings, and they'd be included in the conversation, but mainly it was just them. He guessed they had a lot to catch up on.

Daisy came over to him. "Where did you go? I got dragged in to talk to her."

"How was it?" Adam asked.

"She was . . . okay. She asked me about the flower shop,

about my company, *and* about Jackson." Daisy frowned. "She seemed really well informed for someone who hasn't been here for twenty-plus years."

"I had the same thought," Adam said. "I wonder whether Auntie Rae's been in touch with her all along."

"It's possible. Rae was the one who said Leanne wanted to come back."

"Exactly." His dad waved at him, and he got up. "I guess it's my turn for a grilling. Wish me luck."

Daisy gave him a thumbs-up and helped herself to another glass of wine.

Adam took the seat between his parents. "How's it going?"

"Leanne said she's already spoken to you about Louisa," his dad said.

"She mentioned it on the ride home." Adam nodded. "She said she'd written to me."

"Ah, well." Jeff rubbed a hand over his jaw and looked remarkably uncomfortable. "I might not have passed that letter on. I thought you were upset enough."

"I did say to Jeff that if he thought my letter was inappropriate, he should keep it to himself and give it to you later," Leanne said.

"There's no need to be making up excuses for me now, Leanne. I was wrong not to give it to the boy." Adam's father met his gaze. "I'm sorry about that."

Adam tried to think of the number of apologies he'd received from his father in his lifetime, and couldn't get beyond two. Jeff wasn't the sort of guy who spent much time mulling over his past or his decisions.

"It's okay, Dad," Adam said and turned to Leanne. "Who told you Louisa had died?"

Leanne blinked and shared a quick covert glance with his father. "Rae told me."

"Not Dad?"

"Were we speaking to each other by then?" Jeff asked. "I can't remember."

Adam sat up straighter. "Hang on a minute. Are you saying that you've been in contact before this?"

"Why wouldn't we be?" His dad looked affronted. "We had stuff to discuss."

"Like *what?*"

"You kids, for one thing."

Adam met his father's indignant gaze. "You wouldn't allow us to speak her name, and you were going around *chatting* to her?"

"Hardly that," Leanne intervened, her voice still calm. "We exchanged the occasional message through our solicitors while the divorce was going through. Didn't we, Jeff?"

"Yeah, that's it." His father sat back. "Now, how about you tell your mother what's been going on in your life?"

Still not convinced his father was being entirely straight with him, and determined to get the truth later, Adam returned his attention to Leanne.

"I've been working on the ranch with Dad. That's about it."

"You didn't go away to college?"

"I thought about it, but Louisa didn't want to go, and I didn't want to leave her for three years."

He was glad he'd made that decision. At the time, it had been hard. But if he'd taken one of the football scholarships offered to him, he might have come home too late to marry Louisa at all. . . .

"Do you like being a rancher?" Leanne asked.

"Yeah, I do." Adam really thought about it for the first time. "I suppose it's in my blood."

"Then you're in the right place." She leaned over and patted his knee. "Jeff says you're seeing Lizzie Taylor now . . . ?"

"Not exactly." Adam shifted away from her touch. "She's been having some issues with a family member. I've just been helping her out."

"You were always good friends. She's a sweet girl," Leanne commented. "I hear she has a little boy now."

"Yeah, Roman. He's three or four I think. He's a nice kid."

"Do we know the father?"

"Lizzie knows, and that's all that matters, isn't it?" Adam held his mother's gaze for a moment. "She's a great mother."

"She is," Jeff agreed. "She brought Roman up to the ranch last week. He had a great time running around." He touched Leanne's elbow. "You'll have to come out and see the ranch tomorrow. Adam can pick you up."

"We've got quite a lot on tomorrow, Dad—" Adam started to speak, and his father interrupted him.

"It can wait. Adam will pick you up around nine, if that's okay?"

Lizzie checked her messages and found one from Gabby that she'd missed, which made her immediately pick up her phone.

"Hey, so what's this about Coretta?" Lizzie got straight to the point.

"Well, she's got some guy visiting her."

"Like a boyfriend?"

"*No,* he turns up in his fancy gold car and then leaves again. He's a youngish guy with a nice smile."

Lizzie tensed. "Brown hair, brown eyes, wears chinos and golf logo shirts? Drives a gold Lexus?"

"That's the one."

"He came into the café today and kind of asked me out."

"*What?*" Gabby whistled. "If he's got something to do with Coretta, she *must* have told him about you. It's all she ever talks about these days."

"Exactly." Lizzie thought for a moment. "He said he was staying at the Hayes tonight. Maybe I'll drop Roman over to you a little bit earlier tomorrow morning and see if I can interrupt his breakfast."

"It sure sounds like he has some explaining to do," Gabby agreed. "I'll see you around eight-fifteen, then."

Lizzie ended the call and plugged her phone into the charger on the countertop. What did it say about her that her first instinct was to call Adam and ask for his advice? Why had she started to depend on him so quickly?

"Because despite everything, you trust him." Lizzie spoke the words out loud into the quietness of her apartment. "You always have."

Adam was meeting his mom tonight. He had enough to worry about without her dropping her unconfirmed suspicions on him. She lingered by the phone. If she just sent him a text asking how it had gone, that wouldn't be overstepping any boundaries, would it?

She typed fast before her doubts overcame her.

Hope it all went okay with Leanne.

She stared hopefully at the phone but there was no sign of a reply. He was probably busy. She decided to get an early night and set the apartment to rights before changing into her pj's and coming back into the kitchen to get a glass of water.

Her cell lit up as she went past it and she backed up fast.

It went okay. Might pop in with Leanne early tomorrow morning at the café if you're around?

Lizzie considered.

Are you picking her up at the Hayes? If so, can I meet you there around eight thirty?

Sure. I'll let her know I'll be a bit early. See you then.

In typical Adam fashion, he didn't waste words or ask questions, which suited her just fine.

Will do. x

That would give her time to pop her head into the dining room of the hotel to ascertain if gold Lexus guy was the same guy who had hit on her in the café, and maybe have a few words with him. . . .

When Lizzie came into the lobby, Adam was leaning up against the registration desk talking to Tucker Hayes, the eldest son and general manager of the hotel. Tucker was a calm guy with a ready smile and an amazing ability to do twelve things at once.

As Adam had his back to her, Lizzie had a chance to appreciate his finest qualities and the way he filled out a pair of Wranglers. As if sensing her gaze, he turned around, his gray gaze fixing on her as he slowly straightened and came over to talk to her.

"Hey."

"Hi! Are you bringing Leanne to the café for breakfast?"

"I thought I might." He kept his gaze on her. "What's wrong?"

She sighed. He was way too perceptive sometimes. "I'm not sure. I might be making a huge mistake, but it's just not sitting right with me."

"What isn't?"

She appreciated his calm reply more than she could say.

"Okay, so yesterday there was that guy at the café—"

He frowned. "The one who hit on you?"

"Yes, that one. Gabby says she thinks he's a friend of Coretta's, which means he must have known who I am. So why would he be interested in me, let alone ask me out?"

"That's a great question."

"The thing is, I think he might be staying here," Lizzie said. "I thought I'd come over and check if he was having breakfast in the dining room."

"Is he about my age, and a bit too smartly dressed for around here?" Adam asked.

"Yes, why?"

"I think I met him last night. He came over to talk to me—asked me whether Yvonne's was a good place to eat."

They both turned toward the dining room where Tucker was coming out with a tray full of plates and walked toward him.

"Okay if we take a quick look in here?" Adam asked.

"If you promise not to start anything." Tucker eyed them both dubiously. "What's up?"

Lizzie scanned the dining room, but there was no sign of their man. "Maybe he decided to take your advice and went to Yvonne's after all."

"If he did"—Adam's expression was grim—"we'll find him there."

"Find who where?"

Lizzie turned to find Leanne standing behind her. She wore pressed jeans and cowboy boots, a T-shirt, and a blue fleece. She looked nothing like the frazzled woman Lizzie remembered picking up her sons from school in her old truck.

"Hey, I'm Lizzie." She stuck out her hand.

"I remember you!" Leanne's smile was all Daisy. "You and Adam always had your heads together when I came to pick him up from school."

She glanced back at Adam who was looking grim. "Is something going on I should know about?"

Adam turned his mother in the direction of the door. "Nothing for you to worry about. Shall we go and have breakfast at Yvonne's? I think you'll love it there."

Lizzie made small talk with Leanne as they approached the café, and then excused herself to get ready for work while Adam talked his mother through the menu. By the time she returned, Adam was ready to order. Lizzie served him and a whole line of caffeine-deprived customers while keeping an eye on the door.

Eventually, Mr. Lexus came in wearing running gear, which explained his nonappearance at the hotel, and jogged up to the register.

"Hey, beautiful, can I have an egg white muffin with a vegetarian patty, and a green smoothie?"

Not sure whether she was impressed or horrified by his ability to forget his behavior of the day before, Lizzie took the order. She met Adam's gaze and nodded slightly as she went into the kitchen to relay the food order to Yvonne.

When she came out, she wasn't surprised to find that Adam had moved to stand beside her customer.

"I see you decided to take my advice."

Mr. Lexus smiled up at him. "Yeah, thanks for that."

"You haven't been here before?" Adam inquired and Lizzie tensed.

"Well . . ." Mr. Lexus looked past Adam directly at Lizzie. "I *might* have dropped by yesterday."

"So, why pretend you hadn't?" Adam asked.

The other guy sighed. "Look, I'm just doing my job, okay? There's no need for the interrogation."

"As in what job? Spying?" Lizzie joined the conversation.

"I'm a private investigator." He handed them both a card. "And, no, I can't tell you anything more than that, and yeah, I'm leaving town soon so you probably won't see me again."

"You're meeting Coretta Smith?" Lizzie asked.

"I can't confirm that." He turned toward the counter as Yvonne delivered his smoothie and breakfast muffin. "Thanks. I think I'll take these to go."

Before Lizzie could think of a polite way to stop him, he was off, the shop door closing behind him. Adam made as if to follow him and Lizzie grabbed hold of his arm.

"Don't."

A muscle twitched in his jaw. "I just want to ask him what the hell is going on."

"I think it's obvious, don't you? Coretta is trying to find evidence against me," Lizzie said. "Although, why that guy approached you, I have no idea."

"I do," Adam said grimly. "She's trying to make you look bad."

"Which is probably why he flirted with me, just to see how easily I'd go out with anyone." Lizzie shuddered. "That's just *gross*."

"Yeah." Adam briefly squeezed her shoulder. "I have

to take Leanne up to the ranch, but text me if anything happens, okay?"

"Will do." Lizzie nodded. "I still don't understand why Coretta is so obsessed with bringing me down. You'd think she'd be pleased that Roman is growing up in a great place surrounded by love. And the worse thing is that I can't even talk to her about this. She just hates me."

Even as she finished speaking, she found herself wrapped in Adam's arms, her head resting just under his chin.

"It's okay, Lizzie," he murmured against her hair. "You've got this."

He stepped back and looked down at her. "Call me, okay?"

She nodded as he went back to sit with his mother and she checked in on her customers. She had a bad feeling that whatever Adam believed, they hadn't seen the end of Coretta's obsession yet.

"You're worried about Lizzie, aren't you?"

Adam glanced sideways at Leanne as they traveled up toward the ranch. She'd put her sunglasses on so he couldn't see much of her face.

"Yeah."

"Is there anything I can do to help?"

"I doubt it, but thanks for asking." Adam returned his attention to the road.

"I used to know Coretta Smith quite well. I could go talk to her."

Adam considered that as they made the final turn up to the ranch. "You'd best speak to Lizzie."

"Maybe I will." Leanne picked up her purse and released

her seat belt as Adam came to a stop. "Can we just sit here for a minute?"

"In the truck?" Adam focused on her fully for the first time.

She let out her breath. "I'm just trying to get my head around being here. Your father was adamant that I'd never set foot on his land again."

It sounded like the kind of thing his dad would say, so Adam kept quiet.

"It's changed quite a bit, but the house is basically the same," Leanne added.

"You know Dad," Adam said. "Ranch first, house last."

"I know." Her smile was rueful. "I remember when I needed a new washing machine to cope with the clothes for the eight of us, and he refused to buy one. For almost a year, I had to take everything to Ruth Morgan's place, and do all the laundry there."

"I don't remember that," Adam said slowly.

"I'd do it when you were all at school. Thank God for Ruth," Leanne said. "She found me here one day crying my eyes out, trying to hand wash fifteen pairs of filthy Wranglers, and offered her help."

Adam wasn't sure he was comfortable hearing about his father being an ass from the woman who had left him, but he didn't doubt she was telling the truth. His father was a stubborn man. He had a sudden memory of his mom endlessly folding laundry and the washing machine working every single day.

"The only reason I got a new washer was because Ruth shamed Jeff into it by calling him out after church one day." Leanne half smiled. "It wasn't a new one, but it did the job. I was ecstatic."

"Daisy and Kaiden both earn an income outside the ranch, and Evan and Danny contribute as well," Adam said in his most neutral voice. He refused to get drawn into a discussion about what had gone down between his parents. If she was playing on his sympathy and wanted him to take her side, she was way out of luck. "They help out a lot these days."

"That's wonderful." Leanne took a deep breath. "I think I'm okay to get out now."

"Then hang tight, and I'll come round and help you down. It's muddy out there." Adam opened his door. Despite his decision not to engage, he couldn't help but feel some compassion for her obvious uncertainty. "Dad stayed home especially to welcome you."

Chapter Eleven

"How did it go?" Daisy asked as she sat down beside Adam at the kitchen table where he was just finished sorting clean silverware from the dishwasher. She'd chosen not to stay home to see her mother, and had gone into town to open up her shop as usual. It was now late in the evening and everything had quieted down.

"Leanne's visit?" Adam grimaced. "It went well. Dad stayed with her all morning showing her around the house and outbuildings, and then took her out for a ride in the afternoon, just the two of them."

"Dad took a whole day off just to spend with Leanne?"

"Yeah." Adam met Daisy's surprised gaze. "It was quite a sight. They seem to be getting on really well together."

Daisy frowned. "And she's kind of nice to everyone, too."

"You say that like it's a bad thing," Adam teased her. "Maybe she is nice."

"She left us, Adam." Daisy didn't sound convinced. "She walked out that door without a care in the world."

"Hardly that," Adam objected. "I was there, remember? Dad basically threw her out. He even picked her up and dumped her in the seat of her truck when she kept arguing with him." He paused. "She didn't want to go, Daisy. She was begging him to listen to her, and he just . . . wouldn't."

"You make it sound like Dad was the bad guy in all this."

For the first time in years, Adam reluctantly let himself consider her words. If he couldn't be honest with Daisy, who loved him and would never judge him, he might as well stop talking entirely.

"Dad certainly wasn't blameless. Watching Leanne walk around the house today made me think about when she was here. I don't remember a second when she wasn't working. Sometimes she'd fall asleep at the dinner table. I'd find her there after Dad had taken himself off to bed."

He recalled awkwardly trying to wake her, and how she'd hug him close, and thank him with a kiss on his forehead before getting up and making her way to bed.

"Adam." Daisy folded her arms over her chest. "She. Left. Us."

"I know." Adam shoved a hand through his short hair. "And I'm glad we had Dad, because he's been a great father, but that doesn't mean he was a great husband."

"It sounds like Leanne has won you over without even trying," Daisy commented.

It was Adam's turn to take a deep breath and meet his sister's gaze. She had no idea how much his opinion on what had happened had changed. "Maybe no one has to win, Daiz. Maybe we all lost something when Leanne decided to leave."

Lizzie curled up on her couch and checked her cell phone. There was nothing from Adam or Gabby, just a note from her mother checking Roman's clothing size, which meant Lizzie should be expecting a parcel soon. Even though her parents had moved to Las Vegas, they were still connected to their grandson. They were due to visit in two weeks to take him on vacation. She replied to her mom, and then went to check if Roman was asleep.

She lingered in the doorway, studying his innocent face. Why Coretta didn't want a relationship with Roman was a mystery. Did she really think Lizzie was such a terrible mother? Even the idea of it made her heart ache. She walked slowly back into the kitchen. Should she bypass Coretta, who obviously had issues, and try and have a conversation with Ray?

Not for her own sake, but for Roman's? Ray wasn't a bad guy; he'd just not wanted to face the responsibility of being a father. She could hear Yvonne's and Nancy's voices in her head as clear as day reminding her that Ray *was* a bad father, period. There were a lot of divorced people who managed to co-parent their children by putting their own hurt aside. There were also a lot of parents who couldn't hack it. . . .

She also had no way of contacting Ray except through the TV station he worked for, which she guessed wouldn't go down well . . . *Hi, I'm just wondering if you want to see your son? Love Lizzie. P.S. Please RSVP!*

Lizzie snorted and went to make herself a cup of hot chocolate. The private investigator guy's car hadn't been at Coretta's when she'd picked up Roman. She hoped he'd kept his word and left town. What would Coretta do with the information he'd gathered for her? Try again with CPS? Do something worse?

Lizzie didn't even want to think about it. The threat to her and her son felt way too real to ignore, but she couldn't fight if she didn't know her opponent's next move. She sat back on the couch, sipping her drink, and scrolling through the books on her tablet. She needed something fun to read that would take her out of herself for an hour before she went to bed.

Her cell buzzed and she checked the message, which was from Adam.

Any news?

She found herself smiling like an idiot.

Nope. All quiet here. How did the visit go?

Good.

No fights?

No, it was weird. I felt kind of sorry for her.

Why?

She obviously found it hard to come back and she let slip a few details I'd forgotten about how often Dad went off to compete in the rodeo and left her with all of us kids and the ranch to run.

Lizzie winced. It was hard enough being a single parent to one kid let alone six. She typed her reply.

I can sympathize.

Daisy thinks I've gone to the dark side. I'm not sure I believe there are clear-cut lines anymore, you know?

Recalling her earlier thoughts about Ray, Lizzie could only agree.

She's here for two weeks, right? Maybe you'll get a chance to talk some of this through with her.

Yeah, maybe.

Lizzie held her breath as Adam continued typing.

Shouldn't you be in bed?

She smiled foolishly at the phone.

I'm already in my pj's and I'll be off to bed soon. Why are you still up?

Just thinking things through and trying to sort out the payroll.

I could help you with that.

The thinking or the payroll?

The thinking is on you, but I do bookkeeping for some of the ranches and businesses around here. I'm slowly working toward my accounting degree.

Cool. I might come back to you on that.

Lizzie waited, aware that her hot chocolate was cooling rapidly, but unwilling to miss anything Adam had to say.

What kind of pj's?

She looked down at her crossed legs. Pink cupcakes and kitties, and just a cami on top.

Bra?

Lizzie fought a laugh. Adam Miller, are you sexting me?

Might be if I knew what that meant. :)

No bra. No panties either. She held her breath and awaited his reply, aware that her body was waking up as well. Shame you aren't here.

He took a while to reply. Yeah.

Fair's fair, what are you wearing? Lizzie asked.

T-shirt, and jeans that are now too tight, thanks to you.

She'd forgotten his dry sense of humor and reveled in it now. Sorry.

No need to be. I'll take a cold shower and I'll be fine.

She imagined him undressing and then lathering soap all over his big powerful body and almost whimpered with lust. There was no longer any point in denying it. She wanted to see Adam naked.

You okay?

She must have taken too long to reply, which was mainly because she was panting with desire. They were supposed to be friends. That was it. Her fingers typed out a reply anyway.

Just imagining stuff.

Me, too. And now I really need that shower.

Lizzie got a grip and typed again. I'll speak to you tomorrow, okay?

Yeah. Sleep well, Lizzie.

She restrained herself from telling him that she'd sleep much better if he was beside her, and that they wouldn't actually be doing much sleeping. . . . He wasn't hers, and she was currently in the middle of a nasty battle with her son's family that she didn't fully understand and didn't want. It wouldn't be fair to drag him into that.

You too. x.

She waited a whole minute to see if he'd text back, but there was nothing, which was good. Maybe he had really needed that shower after all. . . .

* * *

Adam brought his coffee over to the kitchen table where his dad was digging into a plate of pancakes, bacon, and maple syrup. It was still early, and they were the only two members of the family up, which was fairly typical. He hadn't slept well, his mind full of images of Lizzie smiling down at him as she straddled his hips, her hair falling over her shoulders to tickle his skin. . . .

He was so screwed.

"What needs doing today?" Adam asked as he loaded his own plate with a side of pancakes to go with his eggs. He thought about reminding his dad about his cholesterol levels, and decided not to ruin the day before it started.

"Those new calves you got?"

"What about them?" Adam sipped his coffee.

"Vet's coming out to see them this morning."

"Why?" Adam picked up his fork. "The paperwork was all in order."

"I heard from Roy up at Morgan Ranch that the batch he just got weren't all vaccinated, and as we bought from the same supplier, I want to be sure they're okay before I add them to the herd."

"Makes sense. Do you want me to hang around here and help you deal with it, or can you do it yourself?"

"I'm not planning on being here all day." His dad kept his attention on his food. "Someone needs to be here when the vet shows up."

"Where are you planning on being then?" Adam asked, although he'd kind of guessed the answer.

"I'm taking Leanne to visit with Ruth Morgan."

"I could've done that," Adam pointed out. "Or I'm sure

one of the Morgan boys would have come into town to pick her up."

"I wanted to do it myself." His dad finally raised his head and looked at Adam.

"You seem to be getting on great," Adam commented.

"We are."

"Like you hadn't been separated for years after a horrible and acrimonious divorce."

"Are you getting at me, son?" His father glared at him. "What Leanne and I decide to do together has nothing to do with you."

"Except that it does—seeing as Leanne is my mother, the woman who left us for all those years without a word of explanation." Adam refused to back down.

"It's still none of your damn business." Jeff pushed his plate away. "And, as far as I'm aware, you might be my son, but I'm still your boss. I'm telling you to stay close to home for when the vet arrives so we can sort out this damn paperwork."

"I hear you," Adam said evenly. "I just don't get it. For years we weren't even allowed to mention Leanne's name and now, suddenly, you're okay with everything?"

"People change, Adam."

"I get that, but—"

"Just because you like staying in the past, doesn't mean I have to."

"Hang on a minute." Adam glared at his father. "How did this suddenly become about me? We're talking about you and Leanne."

"I'm talking about people letting go of stuff and moving on. Something you can't seem to manage, Adam." His dad stood and took his plate over to the dishwasher.

"Maybe instead of reading me a lecture, you should look at some of your own behavior."

"Like what exactly?"

"Like missing your chance with Miss Lizzie because she's not Louisa."

"They've never been the same," Adam protested. "And I'm not—"

Jeff waved his protests away. "Yes, you are. Well, I'll tell you this for nothing." He pointed his finger at Adam. "Watching you wallow in your own misery taught me a lesson about how to deal better with Leanne."

Adam had nothing to say to that so he just grimly stared at his father, one eyebrow raised.

"Talking to the other person really helps, you know. You should try it sometime."

"Wow. *Really*? You finally worked that out?" Adam abandoned his breakfast and rose to his feet. "Shame you didn't think about that years ago when Mom was begging you to listen to her, and you were too busy screaming at her to get off your property."

Adam rammed in his chair, walked out of the kitchen, put on his boots, and headed to the barn. Mucking out the stalls should help him weather his impulse to strangle his own father. What the hell had that all been about? Jeff Miller was the last person in the world who should be allowed to talk shit about anyone.

He'd *created* the situation by not being there for his wife, and now he had the nerve to tell Adam he was a changed man?

Adam's breath condensed in the still-cold air as he raised his head to study the outline of the Sierra Nevadas and the sun rising over them. He didn't like the way things were changing around him. He felt . . . unsure, like the foundations of everything he'd believed in were being challenged. His father was talking to his mother. Lizzie was becoming more than a friend. Louisa's parents were moving on, and his baby sister was talking about getting married.

And, he might as well admit it, he was angry with all of it. Like some rift had been breached deep inside him and now, despite his best efforts, he couldn't stop the red-hot lava seeping through the hairline cracks. Which was so damn stupid, he didn't even know how to deal with it. He had no right to be angry about anything.

He concentrated on the outline of the mountains, glad of that constant in his life and the sense of continuity and history. Did he want everything to stay the same? Maybe his dad was on to something. . . . But what was he afraid of? Why was he resisting so hard?

His cell buzzed. He took it out of his pocket and squinted at the screen before silently cursing and heading back to the house at a run. His dad was just coming out of the back door, his mouth open as if ready to argue again. Adam paused to speak to him.

"Carlos isn't doing good. I'm going over to see if I can help. Tell Ben to watch out for the vet, okay?"

"Will do." Jeff slapped him on the back. "Give them my best, won't you? And let me know how it goes."

It took less than ten minutes for Adam to reach the Cortez ranch. He parked to the side of the barn and went into the house, calling out to Ines as he heel-and-toed his work boots off.

She appeared at the bedroom door and beckoned to him. "He won't wake up! I've tried and tried."

She stepped aside so Adam could get past her.

"Did you call nine-one-one?" Adam asked as he approached the bed.

"No, I—"

"Can you do that now?" Adam said gently as he searched for a pulse.

Like all ranchers, he'd taken his fair share of first-aid classes and knew the basics. He held his breath and focused on the faint flicker of life pumping beneath his fingers. Still holding Carlos's wrist, he used his left hand to send a text to Dr. Tio in town.

The doctor responded immediately and Adam put the phone to his ear.

"What's up, Adam?"

"I'm at the Cortez place. Ines couldn't wake Carlos up. I'm with him now. His pulse is weak and so is his breathing."

"Okay. Did you call nine-one-one?"

"Ines's doing that now, but I thought you might be closer." Adam hesitated. "Is there anything in particular I should be doing right now?"

"Just make sure his airway is clear, and keep an eye on him. I'm already on my way. Call me if anything changes."

Adam set his cell phone on the bedside table and returned his attention to Carlos who appeared to be breathing more easily. Mindful of the doctor's instructions, he checked his airway, and kept a firm grip on Carlos's wrist.

Ines came back in, her expression distraught. "I called them. I left the front door slightly open so that anyone can get in."

"Great. Dr. Tio's on his way right now," Adam said. "Come and sit by Carlos. He'll want to see you when he wakes up."

Ines brought a chair over and sat down. She reached out her rosary bead–wrapped fingers to touch Carlos and started to pray.

It wasn't long before Adam heard the roar of Dr. Tio's truck. He placed Carlos's hand in Ines's and went to meet him.

"Hey."

Dr. Tio was about Adam's age and had moved to Morgantown from Texas when the new medical center had opened up. His friendly manner and up-to-date expertise had endeared him to everyone except Adam's father who didn't like being told to regulate anything, including his cholesterol.

Adam lowered his voice. "He's alive, but his pulse is faint and inconsistent, and his breathing is shallow. He still hasn't regained full consciousness."

"Thanks for the update." Dr. Tio hefted his medical bag. "I'll talk to the nine-one-one guys as they get closer and decide how we're going to deal with this."

"Got it." Adam stepped back to allow the doctor into the bedroom. He stayed at the doorway as Dr. Tio spoke gently to Ines, and commenced his primary examination.

"Adam?"

He looked over at the doctor. "Yeah?"

"Can you get the big blue padded bag out of the back seat of my truck? It's heavy, so be careful bringing it in."

"Sure." Glad of something to do to calm his jittery nerves, Adam strode out into the yard, opened the back of Dr. Tio's truck, and located the square bag without any problem.

He brought it back inside and set it on the floor beside the doctor, withdrawing to his useless position holding up the wall. He'd hated that when Louisa was alive—all the waiting around, and not being able to do a damned thing to help her get through the chemo and other stuff. The smell of antiseptic and a hint of latex from the gloves reached him and he wanted to gag.

Dr. Tio unzipped the blue bag, brought out a portable ECG unit, and plugged it in at the wall socket.

"Just want to get some stats to share with the emergency techs." He reassured Ines. "I think we'll have to take him into hospital to make sure he's in a stable condition."

Ines sighed. "Are you sure he can't stay here? He hates hospitals."

"I know he does." Dr. Tio patted her hand, his voice sympathetic. "But I'd really like to work out what's going on. I'm afraid I can't do that locally. You can go in the ambulance to get him settled in."

"Then I'd better pack some clothes." Ines straightened up. "Adam, could you fetch my suitcase down from the hall closet?"

"Of course I can." Adam followed her out. It was the same case she'd taken with her when Louisa had been in hospital all those years ago. He guessed she didn't travel much. "Here you go."

"Thank you." Ines patted his cheek. "You're a very kind man."

"Would you like me to come with you?" Adam offered.

"That's very sweet of you, but as I don't know what they are going to do, how long it will take for him to be admitted, or whether they'll move him to the cancer hospital, I'd rather not waste your day."

"It wouldn't be a waste, Ines."

Her eyes filled with tears and he struggled to keep his own composure.

"If you come back and you need to visit Carlos at any time, just call me, and I'll take you," Adam said gruffly.

"I think I'll stay put in the hospital until he's able to come home." She attempted a smile. "Do you think you could keep an eye on the ranch while we're gone?"

"I'll do that gladly." Adam nodded. "Maybe you'll be home sooner than you think."

After checking with Ben that the vet had come and given all the new calves a clean bill of health, Adam locked up the Cortez house, made a quick round of the premises, and went on into town. It was almost lunchtime, and after his abandoned breakfast, and his harrowing morning, he was more than ready to eat something.

Carlos had regained consciousness just before the ambulance arrived, which had pleased Dr. Tio, but not stopped him from sending his patient off for further tests. As he'd privately confided to Adam after Ines and Carlos had gone, it was possible that Carlos was just tired of fighting, and wouldn't survive long enough to attempt the experimental treatment offered by the pioneering Californian hospital.

Adam hadn't wanted to hear that, and was still attempting to block it out of his head when he texted Lizzie to see if she was free for a late lunch. He parked behind the café and waited until she appeared at the back door before he got down from his truck.

She came toward him, her expression worried.

"Are you okay?"

"I'm good. They took Carlos to the hospital. He's not doing well."

She pressed her fingers to her lips. "Oh God, I'm so

sorry." She touched his arm. "Do you want to come back to my place and just chill? I can make you a sandwich if you're hungry."

"That sounds great." Adam cleared his throat. "If you're sure."

"Of course. I'll just tell Yvonne I'll be back in an hour." She ran back into the café and emerged soon afterward with one of the café's pink boxes in her hand. "Yvonne wanted you to have these."

"That's nice of her." Adam gestured at his truck. "Do you want to drive or walk?"

"Let's walk. It's only five minutes away."

As she was holding the cake box, Adam didn't take her hand, but locked his truck, and walked alongside her down Main Street toward the gas station. She unlocked the downstairs door, and he followed her inside and up the stairs. Her place smelled like lemons and was strangely quiet without the presence of Roman.

She put the box down on the counter and turned toward him.

"What happened?"

"Ines called me. She said she couldn't wake Carlos up." He took his hat off and shoved a hand through his hair. "I went over there to see what was going on."

"Is he okay?"

"He's still alive, but it's not looking good." Adam met her gaze. "When I saw him lying there, I thought he was dead. I made myself check his pulse. . . ." He ran out of words and gazed helplessly at her. "I thought he'd be dead like Louisa."

With a soft sound, Lizzie reached for him, and he buried his face in the crook of her neck and just breathed her in. He stayed like that as she stroked his hair and murmured something soothing that he couldn't quite catch, but that somehow made things better.

With a groan, he raised his head and sought her mouth, wrapping her in his arms with a fierce need that swiftly overpowered him. She let him kiss her, but he gradually became aware that she was pulling away, her expression gravc.

He made himself stop and held her at arm's length, still reluctant to let her go completely, but conscious that she was asking for distance between them.

"I'm sorry, Lizzie. I'm behaving like an ass."

"No, you're not." She met his gaze head-on. "I just don't want there to be any misunderstanding between us right now."

"In what way?" Adam frowned.

"That you're going to do something with me that you're going to regret later on."

Her softly spoken words froze him to the core. He released her like she was a hot coal. The flash of hurt in her eyes made him feel like a coward. He took a deep, shuddering breath and stepped back.

"You're right."

"Okay," Lizzie said breathlessly. "Let's do this. I'll make the sandwiches, and we'll talk after we've eaten."

Adam looked toward the door, the misery in his eyes making Lizzie swallow hard. "Unless you want me to go."

"*No*." She met his gaze. "No more walking out on me either. I want you to *eat* something."

He sat at the counter and watched her somberly as she made them both a chicken sandwich and brewed some coffee. She was aware of time ticking by, and the sense that if she didn't get things right with Adam now, he'd walk away, and this time he would never come back.

"Here you go." She put the plate in front of him and sat down herself. "If you eat it all up, I'll let you have that éclair from Yvonne."

"I'm not five, you know."

Relieved that he was finally speaking again, Lizzie smiled at him. "Sorry, it's a mom thing."

He ate his whole sandwich in six bites, and she offered him another one, which he declined. While she finished hers, he made the coffee, and sat sipping from his mug and contemplating the view from her kitchen window. After a swift glance at the kitchen clock, Lizzie drank her coffee in scalding gulps and hurried to put the dishes in the sink.

"I can help you wash up," Adam offered.

He still looked like he wanted to get away. For a second, Lizzie contemplated letting him before she reminded herself that she was tired of that particular dynamic.

"Can we leave it?" She walked over to the couch and patted the seat beside her. "Will you talk to me?"

He came over and sat down, his expression unreadable. Lizzie took a deep breath and faced him.

"I don't want you to think that you can't kiss me."

He stayed quiet, his attention fully on her. "Okay."

"If you want to, that is," she qualified.

"You know I do."

"Good, so maybe we should establish some rules?" Lizzie asked hopefully.

"Last time I tried to talk to you about this you told me to stop."

"Which was a mistake," Lizzie admitted. "I was . . . afraid that I was attracted to you. I didn't know what to do about it."

"Afraid?"

"We've just become friends again. I didn't want to mess that up."

He nodded, his gray gaze fixed on her face. "I felt the same."

"And I have Roman, which complicates things even further."

"That I also understand." He paused. "I wouldn't ever do anything to hurt him, or you."

"I know that." She grabbed his hand. "You're a good person."

"I don't feel like one right now." He sighed, his thumb caressing her palm.

Lizzie leaned in and deliberately kissed him right on his frowning mouth. "As I said, I like it when you kiss me."

His free hand came around her neck and stayed there. "So, you're saying we should take it slow?"

"Yes." She smiled into his eyes. "See? You are smart." She kissed him again. This time he let her into his mouth and she sighed with pleasure. "Adam . . ."

"What?" he said hoarsely.

"That's so good."

The next moment he lifted her to sit on his lap and his arms came around her. "This okay?"

"Perfectly okay." She slid her hand under the fabric of his shirt and he shivered. "How about this?"

"Also good." He bent his head to kiss her again.

Ten minutes later, she had his shirt practically unbuttoned, and he had his hand up her skirt.

"I thought you said slow," he groaned as she attempted to pull his shirt out of his jeans without dealing with his belt.

She risked a frantic glance at the clock behind his head and made an executive decision. "Don't move."

"What—"

She urged him back until he was against the arm of the sofa and pushed his knees apart, her fingers busy unbuckling his belt and dealing with the straining button of his jeans. She unzipped him and studied his white cotton boxers before carefully peeling them back to reveal the glories within.

"Oh . . ." She sighed and licked her lips. "It's so nice when everything is exactly in proportion."

"Lizzie—" Adam made a desperate grab at her shoulder as she lowered her head, cupped his balls, and took him into her mouth. "God—that's—"

He forgot how words worked as she sucked him deep. He wanted to close his eyes against the pleasure, but he also wanted to watch. His fingers clenched around a handful of her hair, and his hips rocked forward urging her on.

"Lizzie." It seemed to be the only word he knew right now. He wasn't sure if he was pleading with her to stop, or to never stop as pleasure grew at the base of his spine. He was so close to coming. "I need—"

His climax roared over him with a crash, leaving him temporarily at the mercy of his own desires and totally unhinged from reality. It was glorious, it was terrifying, and now he was afraid to open his eyes and come down to earth.

With one last kiss, Lizzie clambered off his lap and disappeared into the bathroom leaving him dazed and alone, his jeans and underwear pulled down under his ass, and his dick humming a happy tune.

By the time she emerged smelling of lavender and mint, he was standing by the couch attempting to restore himself to order.

"Bathroom's free," she said unnecessarily.

He nodded, and stumbled down the hallway, locking the door behind him. He stared wide-eyed at his reflection in the mirror. He looked like a very startled, but very satisfied man, which was kind of exactly how he felt.

He cleaned up and made sure he was presentable before returning to the kitchen where Lizzie had already washed up the plates, and was rinsing out the coffee carafe. She looked up when he came in and pointed at the clock.

"I have to get back soon. Do you want to take the rest of the éclairs with you?"

"Lizzie . . ." Adam came around the counter and took the dishcloth out of her hand.

"What?" She at least had the grace to blush.

"That was *slow?*"

She bit her lip, her smile dying. "Did I mess up? Was it terrible? I'm *really* out of practice. And, *God*, I didn't ask you if it was *okay*. I just—"

"It was . . . great." Adam hastened to reassure her. "I just wasn't expecting—"

She interrupted him. "I thought I owed you one."

"For what?"

"You know." She blushed even harder. "Last week."

"That's an insult to my skill set and a challenge." Adam cupped her chin so that she had to look up at him. "Next time, it'll be your turn. I promise you."

"Really?" Her eyes brightened. "You mean you're okay with everything? I didn't ruin it?"

He kissed her and then kissed her again just to make sure she was paying attention. Not talking seemed to work better than trying to explain and tying himself in knots.

Her phone buzzed an alarm, and she eased away from him to turn it off.

"I've got to get back." She sighed. "Will you let me know how Carlos is doing, and whether Ines needs anything dealt with at the ranch?"

"Will do." He found his hat, checked he had his keys,

and followed Lizzie down the stairs where she unlocked the lower door.

They walked out together into the glare of the bright sunlight and he adjusted the angle of his Stetson against the sun.

"I won't come back to the café with you," Adam said. "I've got to get home and help Ben, seeing as Dad's gone AWOL."

"Where is he?" Lizzie asked.

"With Leanne up at the Morgans' place."

"Oh."

"Exactly." He grimaced. "He told me to keep my nose out of his business."

"I'm sorry, Adam. This must be really hard on you." Lizzie went up on tiptoe and kissed his cheek. "I really do have to run, but call me if you need me, okay?"

He watched her walk away from him, her hair glinting copper in the sunlight, and tried not to remember what she'd been doing to him ten minutes earlier. He wondered whether he looked as mind-blown as he felt. No one had touched him that intimately for years. . . .

He wished he could call her back and take her to bed.

Yeah. He wanted to do that. There was no point in pretending anymore. He waited for the usual twinge of guilt to hit and had to search hard for it. Change was happening. Lizzie wanted him to take it slow, and for the first time in a long while he was willing to go along with her suggestion.

He turned to leave and caught movement close to his right side. A gold Lexus slid out of the parking spot directly opposite Lizzie's front door. The driver waved at Adam before he disappeared down the street.

"Damn," Adam muttered.

Whatever the private investigator was doing with the information, Lizzie and him coming out of her apartment together at lunchtime wasn't a good look. The guy had his cell phone in his hand and had probably taken pictures. Adam considered whether he should let Lizzie know right away in person. He concluded he'd do better to text her the information and get back home before his brother killed him.

Chapter Twelve

"That's a real shame about Carlos," Yvonne commented. "He was so lovely when we met him, and so happy to chat with Rio in Portuguese."

"He is a nice guy." Lizzie untied her apron strings and tossed the apron into the laundry pile before rolling her shoulders. "Adam said he's doing okay. He's in the hospital for further observation, although Ines would rather he was at home."

"I bet she would." Yvonne checked her tablet and started writing out her list for the morning. The rest of the staff had gone home. Lizzie had stayed late to cover Angelo's dental appointment. "I know Rio's dad hates all the hospital appointments—although he's rich enough to make the medical profession come bowing and scraping to his door."

"How's he doing?" Lizzie asked.

"Hanging in there." Yvonne grimaced. "Hopefully for a long time."

Lizzie already knew that Rio had no wish to take over his father's business empire. He had agreed to be on the board and look for a successor to his father, but that was as far as his willingness to help out went.

"I don't know what to do about the Cortez ranch

now," Yvonne mused. "Rio wanted to go back and take a second look, but I don't want to cause Ines and Carlos any extra stress."

"I think selling the ranch would help them a lot, but maybe wait until we know how things go with Carlos before you move forward?" Lizzie suggested.

"That's what I planned to tell Rio." Yvonne nodded. "It's not like we need the place tomorrow or anything."

"Good thinking." Lizzie yawned so hard, her jaw cracked.

"Lizzie."

"What?" Lizzie turned to find Yvonne staring at her.

"Your neck."

She unconsciously raised her hand to touch the side of her throat. "What is it?"

Yvonne fought a smile. "You tell me. Looks like someone or something tried to take a bite out of you."

Lizzie rushed to the back of the kitchen where there was a mirror, and studied the slight bruise on her neck.

"Oh, crap. Has that been there *all afternoon?*" Lizzie breathed through her nose. "Why didn't Angelo *tell* me?"

"Maybe he didn't notice it. I only saw it when you stretched." Yvonne said. "Is that what you were doing on your lunch break?"

"I . . ." Lizzie sat down at the table. "I did something to Adam."

"Was this before or after he nuzzled your neck so hard, he bit you?"

"Possibly during." Lizzie confessed. "Seeing as I didn't even notice."

"*You're having sex with Adam Miller?*"

"Not exactly."

Yvonne blinked at her. "What exactly does that mean?"

"We haven't actually done the deed yet. We've decided to take things slow."

"Okay," Yvonne said cautiously. "That's . . . good, right?"

"Yes. I think it is." Lizzie realized she meant the words. "I've got Roman to think of, and this stupid thing with Coretta, and Adam . . ." She paused. "Well, we all know that Adam lost his one true love, and that he's never really recovered from it."

"He looks like he's recovering just fine now," Yvonne commented dryly. "I've seen the way he looks at you."

"We used to be good friends. I think he trusts me more than most people," Lizzie agreed.

"I just don't want you to get hurt," Yvonne said earnestly. "From what you've told me, you and Adam have a history, and have spent more years ignoring each other than anything else."

"It's okay. I get that." Lizzie nodded. "I'm making sure we communicate better this time. We're definitely both older and wiser."

"With all this going on, have you had time to think about taking on the role of manager here?" Yvonne asked.

"I'd love to do it," Lizzie said, which made her boss leap in the air and do a fist pump.

"Yay! That's great!" Yvonne grinned at her. "As soon as Rio and I get settled, I'll make a more formal offer and we can take it from there."

"Cool." Lizzie smiled back. "I'm actually looking forward to it." She checked the time and took off her apron. "Am I good to go?"

"Yes, you're fine." Yvonne glanced around the empty kitchen. "I'm going to make a start of Nate and Della's wedding cake before I go to bed."

Lizzie hung her apron up on its hook, and turned to her boss. "You work too hard."

"This isn't really work." Yvonne smiled. "I *love* making wedding cakes, especially when I know the people involved.

And this one isn't that complicated. Della didn't want a big wedding and neither did Nate, so it won't take long."

"Is Rio going to be here for that?" Lizzie asked as she found her keys and checked that she had her cell phone. "It's in two weeks, right? Just about the time my parents get here and take Roman off for his Disney vacation."

"Yes, two weeks, which is why I want to get the basics done now. Cakes always work better if they can sit and settle for a while."

"The problem with your cakes is that everyone wants to eat them immediately," Lizzie joked. She blew Yvonne a kiss. "See you in the morning."

"Looking forward to it already," Yvonne sang back.

Lizzie was still smiling as she left the café and walked back along Main Street toward Gabby's house. Her smile disappeared when she saw the gold Lexus parked in Coretta's driveway again.

Even worse, as she drew level with the house, the car window went down and Mike, the annoying P.I., grinned at her.

"Hey, you. How's it going?"

"I thought you were leaving town," Lizzie said pointedly.

"I am, but I got some good pictures of you and lover boy today to pass on, so I'm glad I stuck around."

"Pictures of me doing what exactly?" Lizzie demanded. "Isn't it illegal to spy on people or something?"

"Not to my knowledge." Mike pretended to frown. "You were on a public street kissing, so I didn't invade your privacy or anything."

Lizzie stared him down, aware of a kernel of panic growing in her stomach. "You are an obnoxious human being."

He shrugged. "I'm just doing the job I've been paid to do, ma'am."

"And you seem to get such a lot of pleasure out of it."

"Well, that's true, because mainly I get to catch cheating spouses in the act, and I kind of like bringing liars to justice, you know? But you . . ." He met her gaze. "You're something different."

Lizzie put her nose in the air and continued up the path to Gabby's house while Lexus Mike headed toward the highway. She could only hope he'd really be gone this time.

Gabby opened the door and Lizzie walked with her into the kitchen. The three boys were outside playing happily together, and Gabby urged her to sit down.

"I've fed him so there's no need to rush off. Would you like some iced tea?"

"That would be great." Lizzie found her cell and checked her messages. There was one from Adam mentioning that he'd seen Mike outside her apartment, which at least meant she didn't have to text him to warn him herself.

"What's up?" Gabby asked as she put the tall glass of tea in front of Lizzie.

"Just Coretta stuff," Lizzie said glumly. "They're trying to drag Adam into this mess now. I still don't know what the heck is going on and I'm sick of it."

"Could you talk to someone else in Ray's family?" Gabby asked.

"They all blocked me when Ray told them I'd deliberately gotten myself pregnant to secure my financial future."

"He *said* that?" Gabby bristled.

"Well, not in those words. He was way less complimentary. I think the term *gold digger* was mentioned at least once."

Gabby rolled her eyes. "He's a piece of work."

"Tell me about it." Lizzie sighed. After the high of accepting Yvonne's offer to manage the café, the low of Mike and Coretta was even harder to deal with. "At least Coretta won't be able to sabotage my new job. Yvonne won't listen to her."

"You're going to manage the café?" Gabby asked. "That's awesome!"

"Thanks," Lizzie said. "I won't exactly be living the high life, but at least I'll have regular hours, an interesting job, and bigger paychecks."

"You go, girl." Gabby clinked her glass against Lizzie's. "What's going on with Adam?"

"We're sort of, kind of, maybe seeing each other," Lizzie said.

"Okay." Gabby gazed at her. "And you're sort of kind of okay with that?"

"Yes. Very much so." Lizzie finished her tea. "He's a good man." She rose from her seat and looked out toward the backyard. "Now, I'll go and fetch Roman and leave you in peace."

"Hardly that." Gabby chuckled. "Unless you want to take the other two rascals with you."

Adam did his rounds at the Cortez ranch, and then spent the rest of the day out with Ben rounding up the sparse number of cattle Carlos had kept and bringing them closer to the ranch. He heard from Ines that Carlos was stable and breathed a little easier. There was no word on whether they'd be moving Carlos to the specialist hospital yet.

He took off his boots and jacket and washed his hands in the mudroom at home before going through into the kitchen where he was brought up short by the sight of Leanne cooking at the stove.

"Hi, Adam." She smiled at him. She was wearing jeans and a flowery blouse over a pink T-shirt, and had taken off her shoes to reveal yellow striped socks that Adam thought might belong to his father. "Ruth gave me a huge leg of pork. Jeff decided I should come and cook it for you all for dinner tonight."

"Did he?" Adam wasn't sure how he felt about seeing her there. The kitchen was usually his domain and roast dinners were his specialty. "I could've done it."

"So I hear. But it just seemed like a nice way to thank you all for being so kind to me."

Adam still wasn't feeling particularly kindly toward her when she was messing up his head so he didn't say anything.

"There's iced tea in the refrigerator and coffee brewing," Leanne called out to him as she spooned hot spitting fat over roasting potatoes and returned the pan to the oven. "I hope I made them right."

Adam helped himself to coffee and sat at the table while Leanne fussed around with the pots on the stovetop. Eventually, she came to sit opposite him, her cheeks flushed from the heat. With her hair less styled and her clothing informal, she looked more like the mother Adam remembered.

She flapped a hand in front of her face. "Phew, I'd forgotten how hot you have to get everything when you roast pork."

Adam nodded and sipped his coffee, letting the jolt of caffeine seep through his tired bones. Ben had gone to have a shower, but Adam had needed coffee first.

"Ruth Morgan looked well," Leanne commented.

"Yeah, she's a strong woman."

"She always was." Leanne got the pitcher of tea out and set it on the table. "One of my role models."

It was on the tip of Adam's tongue to ask her why she hadn't stuck it out like Ruth had, but he kept his mouth shut.

"You don't say much." Leanne looked up at him.

"Nothing to say," Adam demurred.

"That's not it. You've got plenty you want to say to me." She half smiled. "I can see it in your eyes."

He shrugged. "No point in stirring things up when you've just come to visit, is there?"

"But I came because I wanted to set some things straight." She fidgeted with her glass. "Ben, Kaiden, Evan, and Danny have been more than willing to listen to me, but Daisy's never available, and you"—she eyed him cautiously—"just don't choose to engage."

"As I said, I'm not one to get into unnecessary fights."

"But why do you assume we'd end up fighting?" Leanne asked.

"Because maybe I don't think walking out on your kids and husband when things get tough is okay."

Leanne looked at him for a long moment. "You weren't a kid when this happened, Adam. You saw how things were, the way your father was never around—the way he spoke to me, and ignored all my pleas for help—the way he always put himself and the goddamn ranch first. At times, you were the only one who stood up for me. What happened to that boy?"

"Maybe that boy grew up to become a man who values people who stick around."

Leanne sat up straighter. "How much did Jeff really stick around, Adam? How long before he drafted Rae in to do all the jobs he hated so he could go back to doing exactly what he wanted? And this time he didn't even have to attempt to explain himself or apologize because Rae already knew what he was like and took on the task willingly."

"He stopped doing the rodeo."

"He stopped because he injured his back," Leanne said patiently. "That was one of the reasons that everything came to a head. He was on strong painkillers, and he wasn't happy, so everyone else suffered."

An unpleasant memory opened up in Adam's head of his father shouting at his mother that he was fit to ride and work when he obviously wasn't. Adam had stepped up then, doing as much of his father's work as he could manage before and after school. His grades had plummeted, and he'd almost lost his place on the football team because he'd never been available for practice.

"Ruth Morgan stayed put when her son and grandsons walked out," Adam said stubbornly. "She was all alone. You had us."

"I know I did." She sighed. "It was the hardest decision I ever had to make, Adam, but I thought . . ." She paused for so long, Adam almost forgot how to breathe. "I *thought* that a few days without me would bring Jeff to his senses, make him realize what he was throwing away, and ask me to come back." Her smile was sad. "Stupid of me, right? Because at that point in his life your father never apologized for anything, and never accepted any of the blame."

She set her glass on the table. "I waited to hear from him for months until he set his lawyer on me, and I finally got the message."

Adam contemplated his coffee. He couldn't deny the sincerity in her voice or continue to pretend that life with his dad had been easy.

"Where did you go after that?" he asked grudgingly.

"I hung around for three months in Bridgeport until Jeff barred me from visiting the ranch or seeing any of you. I went to stay with my brother Patrick in New York. I was a complete wreck and having him in my corner was so helpful. He handled a lot of the legal stuff for me while I lay in my bed and cried my eyes out."

"Daisy cried a lot, too."

For a long time, Leanne didn't speak. When Adam glanced over at her there were tears falling down her cheeks, and she was frantically dabbing at them with a tissue.

He shot to his feet. "I need to take a shower. I'll be back to set the table, okay?"

She nodded but didn't look directly at him as she attempted to control her emotions. He couldn't deal with her right now.

Except, when he reached the door and looked back, her head was down, and he couldn't quite bring himself to leave either. Sharing the buried anger inside him was kind of addictive, but the shame he felt when his words hit home wasn't acceptable either. He walked back to the table and awkwardly squeezed her shoulder before retreating again.

He went into his bedroom and stared at the photo of him and Louisa on their wedding day. He knew how he'd felt when Louisa had left him. She hadn't chosen to go, but, from what Leanne had said, she hadn't really wanted to go either. He sat on the side of his bed and rubbed his hands over his face. Jeez . . . why was life so *complicated?* It had been much easier to hate his mother and love his father without all this gray stuff in the middle.

It had been much easier to mourn his wife and close himself off, too. Opening himself up to Lizzie and his mother was a risk he still wasn't sure he was willing to take. He was so mixed-up—the stupid, childish longing to believe his mother loved him while he kept making excuses for the inexcusable behavior of his father . . . His fear he might get things wrong again, and that the vein of anger and resentment running through everything he did right now was going to boil over.

Despite his best efforts, the women in his life were still managing to get inside his shell and shake him up. He let out a breath. It was way past time for him to shut all his shit down and find his balance again. But right now, how he was going to achieve that without running for the hills and shutting out the whole world was beyond him.

Chapter Thirteen

"It's good of you to come out to the Cortez ranch with me." Adam glanced over at Lizzie who was sitting beside him in his truck. She'd left her hair loose and was wearing a dress and looked very relaxed.

"I'm happy to help out." She glanced out over the sunburned hills. "It was nice of Ines to let Rio and Yvonne see the ranch again while she's still with Carlos. I can deal with the house while you take on the barn and fields."

"You sure aren't dressed to tackle anything too dirty," Adam commented.

"I've got my jeans and a T-shirt in my bag," Lizzie protested. "And I'm wearing my cowboy boots." She lifted one shapely leg to show Adam. "I'm ready to go if you are."

After seeing her thigh, Adam was ready to go, but not quite in the way she'd intended.

"Roman's coming with Yvonne, right?" He made himself concentrate on the basics.

"Yes, they'll be about an hour behind us. Ro loves Rio." She tucked a strand of flyaway hair behind her ear. "He can't decide whether he wants to be a bull rider or a dinosaur."

"A dinosaur what? Keeper? Archaeologist?"

"No, a real dinosaur." Lizzie laughed and Adam couldn't help but smile back at her. "It's either a stegosaurus or a T. rex. Of course."

"Of course," Adam agreed as he checked the time on the dashboard. He pulled off the road into the shade of the trees just before the gates of the Cortez ranch.

"What are you doing?" Lizzie asked as he drew to a stop.

"Making the best use of my time." He pointed at her chest. "Take off your seat belt."

"Okay." She did as he asked and he patted his knee.

"Now come here and be kissed." He picked her up and sat her in his lap. "That's better."

He kissed her slowly, but with great attention to detail, until she moaned his name and put her hands all over him. He liked that. He liked it a lot. She slid her hand down the back of his collar and scratched his neck, making him shudder and draw her even closer.

"Not enough room," he muttered eventually, as he caressed her soft ass, his thumb toying with the lace edge at the top of her panties.

"For what?" she asked.

To answer, he set her back in the passenger seat and strode around the truck to open her door. She looked deliciously rumpled and flushed, which made his dick even harder.

"Sit sideways."

She raised an eyebrow. "My, you're bossy today."

"Please?"

She turned toward him and he immediately stepped between her thighs, spreading them wide and offering him exactly the view he wanted. With her sitting in the truck and him standing outside she was at the perfect height.

"I love it when you wear a dress," he murmured, as he ran his hands up her thighs until his thumbs met in the center right over her already-damp panties. "May I touch you?"

"Yes." Her reply was breathy and so full of need that Adam couldn't wait to get started. "Please."

He bent his head and kissed his way up her inner thigh, his fingers hooking underneath the thin fabric of her panties. "Can I take these off?"

"As long as you don't lose them." She helped him dispose of the final barrier to her most private flesh.

"Mmm . . ." Adam murmured as he stowed her panties in his pocket. "I can't wait to taste you properly." He dipped his head and used the tip of his tongue in a gentle slow caress that made her buck against him. She reached for him, and knocked his Stetson off, which didn't bother him at all.

He cupped her sweet ass in the palm of his hand, tilting her hips toward him. His finger probed her wetness, and he licked and played with her swelling bud.

"Adam . . ." She breathed his name, her fingers tightening against his scalp, and undulated her hips. "That's so good."

He lifted her against his mouth and delved even deeper until her breath was coming in short gasps, and she was grinding herself against him. He forgot about breathing as he felt the first tremor of her climax, and held still to experience it more fully. He thrust three fingers deep inside her, which set off another wave of climaxes that made him shake with need. He loved this, loved pleasuring her, and wanted so much more. . . .

Lizzie closed her eyes tightly as she came again and just held on to Adam like a lifeline. As the last tremor faded she looked down at him, and scraped her fingernails over his scalp, allowing him to move back.

"Sorry."

He shrugged. "It's all good." And slowly he rubbed a hand over his mouth with the air of a man who had enjoyed what he'd tasted. "We'd better be getting on."

"Okay." After experiencing such intense emotions, Lizzie felt dazed and ready for a nap. "Are you sure I can't—?"

He retrieved his hat from the ground and dusted it off against his thigh before placing it back on his head.

"I'm good." He got into the truck. Lizzie couldn't help but notice he was still aroused.

He saw her looking and gave her a crooked smile. "Next time let's try this together, yeah?"

"God, *yes,*" Lizzie agreed fervently. "That would be wonderful."

"Slow and steady, remember?" Adam said. Before he drove off he turned to give her one last leisurely kiss, which made her really wish the being together part would start immediately.

Eventually, the familiar ranch house came into view. Adam pulled into the space between the barn and the fenced-in paddocks.

"The house isn't locked up. You can just go right on in through the mudroom if you want to get started." He was suddenly all business.

"Okay. I have a fair idea of where Ines keeps everything so I should be good to go," Lizzie replied.

"Great." Adam got out of the truck and headed for the barn. "I'll deal with the horses and check back with you in half an hour."

He strode away without a backward glance and Lizzie made her way into the house. The first thing she saw was the big portrait of Louisa and Adam on their wedding day that hung over the fireplace. Her steps slowed as she considered it. Was that why Adam had stopped to touch her before they reached the ranch where his wife had grown up? If he'd really wanted a bed, there were plenty of empty ones here.

Even as she had the thought, she realized that Adam would never do anything to sully the Cortez family or his memories of Louisa. Not that she would've been happy about him touching her here either, but it would've been nice if he'd been up-front and honest about it. She wrapped her arms around herself and shivered, her previous happiness disappearing. Maybe he hadn't consciously thought about the place being off-limits . . .

A breeze drifted through the back door she'd left open. And maybe she should have asked him for her panties back.

She went into the kitchen, checked the solar power was working properly, and filled a bucket with hot water and dishwashing liquid. The energy she could have used between the sheets with Adam was easily converted into a ferocious desire for hard work. Her cell buzzed, and she checked it to see a message from Yvonne saying they'd be there in just over half an hour.

She debated changing into her jeans and T-shirt, but she had no desire to go outside and encounter Adam until she got a hold of her strange mood. She knew she wasn't being quite fair to him, but her emotions refused to fall into line. She opted to borrow one of Ines's aprons, and left it at that.

By the time Yvonne and Roman arrived, the house had been vacuumed and polished to perfection. Lizzie busied herself talking to her son as Yvonne explained that Rio was out in the barn with Adam discussing potential improvements to the ranch.

"I brought us a picnic lunch." Yvonne placed the basket on the kitchen table. "Ines told us to take our time exploring the ranch before we made our minds up."

"It is a lovely place." Lizzie found plates and silverware and put them beside the basket. "I was best friends with Louisa Cortez, so I practically grew up here."

"Did your parents have a ranch?"

"No, my dad was the manager of Morgantown Bank before it merged with three other banks. He took early retirement rather than retrain and move to a different location. I don't think he's ever regretted it."

Lizzie set out the plates and invited Roman to sit down, but he was too busy making friends with one of Ines's many stray cats. Lizzie let him be after reminding him to be careful around the new animal. The last thing she needed was another visit to the emergency clinic with her son going into the CPS report.

She stiffened when she heard voices and Rio and Adam came through from the mudroom. It occurred to her that she had no means of transport home until her friends had finished their business. Rio grinned at her. He wore his usual all-black PBR garb except his hat was white straw as a concession to the sun.

"Hi, Ms. Lizzie, and how are you today?"

"I'm great, thanks." She smiled back, determinedly keeping her gaze from turning on Adam. "I hope Roman behaved himself in your truck."

"He was absolutely fine, but sad that Carlos and Ines wouldn't be here. It was kind of them to let us visit without them being present."

"Very kind." Yvonne came up behind Rio and took his hand. "What do you think?"

"It's possible it might work. Adam says there are plenty

of ways to modify and increase the buildings to deal with my bull-breeding plans."

He had a slight Brazilian accent that made his words flow like mellow honey, which Lizzie always enjoyed.

"Yeah." Adam spoke for the first time. "My brother Kaiden's great at that kind of carpentry, and Danny knows all the best construction guys in town. You should talk to them and get some idea of the costs involved."

"I'll definitely do that." Rio nodded. "Thanks."

"Well, before you go out again, why don't we have lunch?" Yvonne suggested with a twinkle in her eye. "I *think* Roman is hungry."

"Yes!" Roman had abandoned the cat and was now jumping up and down beside the table. "Please!"

Adam glanced over at Lizzie as they drove back to Morgantown. She was unusually quiet, her expression thoughtful, and her gaze directed outside the vehicle away from him. Roman had stayed with Yvonne at the ranch to keep her company after Rio had taken one of the horses out to study the extent of the land.

"Everything okay?" He ventured the question as they neared the outskirts of town.

"Yes, thank you." She smiled briefly at him. "Do you think Rio's going to buy the ranch?"

"It certainly looks possible," Adam agreed. "The good thing is that we know Rio won't mess Carlos and Ines around. He can well afford it."

"That's true." Lizzie paused. "From what Yvonne said, they'd have no problem if Carlos and Ines wanted to stay on at the ranch either."

"I don't think Carlos is going to come back," Adam said simply.

Lizzie didn't reply. When he stole a glance at her, he realized she was close to tears, and silently cursed. He was good at that—making women cry.

"I could be wrong," he added hastily. "I'm only repeating what Dr. Tio—"

"If Dr. Tio said he was that far gone, I believe him." Lizzie surreptitiously wiped a tear from her cheek. "Poor Ines."

It was Adam's turn to stay silent. He knew all about losing a spouse. He'd only had three short years with Louisa. Carlos and Ines had been married for thirty-five.

"As I said, I think if Ines wants to stay at the ranch, Rio would welcome her as family," Adam added awkwardly.

"He's a good man," Lizzie agreed.

"Yeah." Adam drew to a stop in front of Lizzie's apartment and she immediately went for the door handle. "Hey, what's the rush?"

"I've got a lot to catch up on seeing as I was out all day."

"You don't want me to come up?" Adam asked.

She got out of his truck. He rushed to release his seat belt and jump down before she got away from him.

"What's wrong?"

She fished out her key, avoiding his gaze. "Nothing."

Adam wasn't that stupid. "Did I do something to upset you?"

"No, I'm just . . . tired."

"Tired of me?" He felt like someone had hit him with a tire iron.

"No, I . . ." She hesitated. "Can I have my panties back?"

"Jeez, I forgot all about them." Adam reached into his pocket and took out the scrunched-up lingerie. "You've been walking around all afternoon bare-ass naked?"

She shrugged. "I was busy."

"If you'd told me that—" Adam breathed out hard.

She cut him off. "You wouldn't have done anything about it, would you?" She offered him a peck on the cheek. "Thanks for a lovely day."

"Hold up," Adam said, his fingers closing gently on her elbow. "What's that supposed to mean?"

She met his gaze. "It's okay, I get it. So how about we end this conversation, and I'll speak to you tomorrow?"

"How about we don't, and we finish it now?" Adam countered. "I don't understand what's going on."

"Which is fine, because it's probably just me being paranoid." Lizzie sighed. "Which also means it's better if I don't say anything and get us into an unnecessary fight."

"Lizzie, I'm not doing this shit again. We're not kids anymore." Adam held her gaze. "Just *tell* me."

"You could've touched me at the Cortez ranch," Lizzie blurted out. "There was no one there. But you didn't, and now you think you'll get me into bed at my place."

"Why would I think that?" Adam felt like he was floundering around in a snowstorm. "I wouldn't assume anything."

"See?" Lizzie shoved her hair behind her ear. "This is pointless."

"I did touch you up at the Cortez ranch." Adam kept talking, desperate to keep her beside him. "It was awesome. I stopped because we'd decided to take things slow. And, I knew that in less than an hour your kid, Rio, and Yvonne were going to descend on us. You know when you went down on me so fast because you had to get back to work? It was like that."

"Okay." Lizzie nodded. "I accept what you are saying. I'm sorry for doubting your motives."

"*What* goddamn motives?" Adam wasn't moving until they sorted it out. "And for the record, I don't believe you accept what I'm saying, either."

She squared up to him. "I thought you didn't want to come near me at the ranch because it was Louisa's home. You disappeared on me superfast when we had an actual empty house with beds."

"I—" He stared down at her. *Had* that been a factor? Was there some element of truth in what she'd picked up from him when they'd parked at the ranch? He put his hand on her shoulder. "Lizzie, if that was part of my thinking, I really wasn't aware of it, but I can't lie. Having sex with you in the Cortez house would've felt wrong somehow."

"Yeah, I know." Her shoulders sagged. "I really do get it." She smiled up at him. "Can I go now? I really do have a lot to do before Roman gets home."

"As long as we're good," Adam replied.

"We are. I'm just tired and worried about Carlos." She put her key in the lock. "I'll talk to you tomorrow."

"Okay."

Adam waited until she disappeared inside and then returned to his truck. On the one hand, he was pleased with himself for making sure he and Lizzie were straight about things, but on the other hand . . . Was he still so tied up with Louisa that he'd automatically dropped Lizzie like a hot potato after he'd reached the ranch? He could've found a place to make love to her if he'd really tried. Hell, he could've made love to her in the truck if he'd had some protection.

But as soon as he'd reached the ranch, he'd been compelled to walk away from her with a load of excuses that the more he thought about them, the less convincing they sounded. Touching her like that had shaken him, releasing such a need in him that he'd *had* to walk away to preserve the illusion that he still had a choice.

Adam started the engine. So he hadn't been honest with Lizzie after all, had he?

* * *

Lizzie stood motionless in her kitchen listening to the roar of Adam's truck as he drove away. Sometimes, she really did complicate things without even trying. She should've kept quiet. Adam probably thought she was way too sensitive. Despite his explanation, she still couldn't shake the conviction that at some level she was right.

"Have sex . . ." She spoke the words out loud. That's what Adam was looking forward to—not making love like he had with Louisa—just the sex.

Was that it? Was that what was bugging her? Was she in some strange competition with her best friend who'd been dead for over ten years? That was a horrible thought. Lizzie walked over to the sink and contemplated the pile of dishes she'd left there that morning when she'd gone off so happily with Adam to the Cortez ranch.

"There you go again, Lizzie, obsessing over nothing. He never promised you forever. Just having sex is *fine*."

She filled the coffeepot with water and put in a new filter and freshly ground beans. At least Adam had tried to deal with the issue rather than walk away from her. She supposed that was progress. . . .

But if she hadn't said anything, he'd probably be with her right now, in her freshly made bed, naked and having sex. She sighed and turned on the faucet. When was she going to start to believe she was worthy of being loved? She was getting way too old to hide behind her childhood fears.

Growing up with parents who were so engrossed with each other had sometimes made her feel unwanted, as if she was an intruder in their happiness. They had never said as much, and hadn't treated her badly, but once her mother had let slip that they hadn't really wanted children, and

Lizzie had never forgotten it. The fact that they were such perfect grandparents for Roman because they could be involved with his life only when they chose to be hadn't been lost on her.

Wasn't it time that she asked for what she needed and assumed she'd get it? Trouble was, logic was one thing, and emotion was something else entirely. She knew her parents loved her; complaining about how they showed it would get her nowhere. And they really did love Roman and had been nothing but helpful to her all through his life.

Washing the dishes and getting something in the oven for Roman to eat when he got home was probably her just reward for overthinking everything. If she wanted Adam to be straight with her, she'd have to offer him the same deal.

Chapter Fourteen

Lizzie yawned discreetly behind her hand as she leaned up against the wall at the café. Ro had been restless and had ended up climbing into her bed around three in the morning when they'd both finally managed to get some sleep. There was no one waiting to be served as the morning rush had ended, and she was anticipating the brunch people.

"Lizzie?" Yvonne came out of the kitchen carrying her tablet. "Can you look over this menu for Nate and Della's wedding, and tell me if I've covered all the basics?"

"Sure." Lizzie took the tablet and scanned the list. She often provided a second set of eyes for Yvonne. "How many guests?"

"Fifty, I think, with a few more at the evening party. They wanted to keep everything fairly simple and at minimum cost."

"This looks great," Lizzie said. "The only thing that might run short is the dessert part. You know what a sweet tooth the Turner family have."

"True." Yvonne made an annotation on the list. "They thrive on sugar. Are you going to the wedding?"

"Yes, how about you?"

"I'm going early to help Avery with the wedding setup

at Morgan Ranch. Because it's all buffet food, I think I'll be able to sit back and enjoy the rest of the day."

"I can help if you like," Lizzie offered. "My parents are taking Roman to Disneyland for a vacation so I'll be footloose and fancy-free."

"That would be wonderful," Yvonne said. "How long will Roman be away?"

"Just under two weeks." Lizzie grimaced. "I was a bit worried it was too long, but Ro's so comfortable with my parents, I think he'll be okay. It's the longest he's ever been away from me."

"He'll do fine." Yvonne patted her shoulder. "And think of all that free time you'll have to spend with Adam!"

Lizzie didn't have a problem with that. He'd texted her first thing that morning, and suggested lunch, which had immediately made her day better. One thing she liked about Adam Miller was his straightforward, no bullshit, personality. In his mind they'd disagreed, they'd reached a settlement, and now he was marching onward.

"Yvonne, do you ever compare Rio to your first husband?" The question popped out of her mouth before she could stop it.

"Frequently. Rio is everything my first husband was not."

"Do you think it's normal for people to compare their previous partners to their current ones?"

"Yes, of course," Yvonne said. "Don't you do it?"

"Not really," Lizzie confessed. "So maybe I'm worrying about nothing."

Yvonne closed her tablet. "Is this something to do with Adam?"

"Kind of." Lizzie rearranged the pens beside the register. "I know how much he loved Louisa. I saw them together, and now . . ."

"She's gone, and you feel like you can't live up to her?" Yvonne asked gently.

"Yes. That." Lizzie met her gaze. "Does that make me sound horrible?"

"Not at all." Yvonne paused. "It makes you sound human, but you don't have to be the second Louisa in Adam's life; you *can* be the first Lizzie."

"If that can ever be good enough for Adam," Lizzie said.

"Louisa died a long time ago," Yvonne reminded her. "Not only was she your best friend who would never wish ill on you, but, from what I've heard about her, I bet she'd be thrilled if you can get Adam out of his funk."

"Maybe." Lizzie wasn't quite convinced, but she did feel a little better. The door opened and Ruth and January Morgan came in. January was carrying her son Chase William who was struggling to get down.

"He's walking, and now he wants to go everywhere by himself." January set her son on the ground but kept a firm hand on the back of his denim overalls. "He's a daredevil just like his uncle Blue."

Lizzie smiled down at the little boy who had a shock of blond hair and the familiar piercing blue Morgan eyes.

"How about we get you all something to eat and drink, and then, maybe, he'll settle down?" Lizzie suggested and took out her notepad and pencil. When she became manager, she might suggest to Yvonne that all the servers moved to using tablets where they could also cash the guests out.

Adam was coming into town around two, so she'd take her lunch then, and he could join her at the café.

It got busy from eleven onward, and Lizzie didn't have much time to think let alone worry about Adam as she served her customers. It was a warm day and the air-conditioning was working at full blast to keep up with the dazzling heat from the sun.

Lizzie had just helped herself to a cold drink and was fanning herself with a menu as she emerged from the kitchen when she stopped dead.

"Ah, there you are, Elizabeth."

Resplendent in a cream linen pants suit with gold jewelry, and perfectly coiffed hair, Ray's mother looked remarkably out of place in the friendly coffee shop.

"Mrs. Smith." Lizzie acknowledged her and stayed exactly where she was.

Miranda looked around the shop as if she'd been dumped in a field full of cows. "Is there anywhere we can talk?"

"I'm working."

"Do you take lunch?"

Angelo tapped Lizzie's arm. "I'm here if you want to start your lunch early."

Normally, she would've thanked him for his consideration, but now she just wished he hadn't made the offer in front of Miranda.

Lizzie led the way to the back of the shop and indicated that her visitor should take a seat at the table. Miranda sat down, elegantly crossing one leg over the other to reveal gold sandals and perfectly manicured red toenails.

"You look well, Elizabeth."

"Thank you." Lizzie wasn't willing to give an inch, and simply waited Ray's mother out.

"You are probably wondering why I'm here."

"Not really," Lizzie replied. "We get lots of through traffic."

"I came to see Coretta."

"Ah." Lizzie crossed her arms over her chest. "Has she been bothering you? I had to ask the sheriff to talk to her."

"So I hear." Mrs. Smith paused. "Although one might assume her concerns might have been taken more seriously."

"She called CPS on me. I'd say she'd been taken seriously." Lizzie kept her tone pleasant. "Any news on that, by the way? I'd like to know if I have a case against her for defamation of character and, I dunno, outright lying."

"She's an elderly lady, and she's not quite 'well.'"

"I am aware of that."

Mrs. Smith set her purse on the table and produced an envelope. "She sent me photographs."

"Of what, exactly? My son enjoying himself at day care or spending quality time with his mother?" Lizzie met Mrs. Smith's gaze. "What do you want?"

"I merely thought—"

Lizzie wasn't done. "You never merely do anything, Miranda. Why are you here?"

Miranda took out the pictures and fanned them out on the table. "He looks a lot like Ray did as a child."

"To me, he resembles his Polish grandfather for whom he was named."

Miranda looked up. "You've become very . . . *hostile,* Elizabeth."

"Hostile?" Lizzie smiled. "Not at all. I have a great life and a beautiful son. What more could I want? I'm happy, Miranda, I really am."

Miranda gathered up the photographs and put them away. "As to that—I've been wondering whether we were a little too hasty in refusing to meet your sweet little boy."

Lizzie had to let that pile of crap sink in before she could form a reasonable reply. "*We?* I don't remember trying to stop you, your son, *or* your family from having access to my child. You told me I was a classless gold digger who had tried to entrap Ray into marriage. *You* refused to have anything to do with Roman or me."

"I was upset." Miranda looked down at her perfect fingernails. "Your pregnancy came out of nowhere. We'd never even been introduced. I instinctively supported my son as any mother would."

Lizzie sat back and considered her companion. "Just out of curiosity, did he claim I was lying about the whole thing?" One look at Miranda's face told her everything she needed to know. "Of course he did." Lizzie nodded. "Your son has a problem accepting responsibility for anything, doesn't he?"

"That's hardly fair. He's matured into a fine man."

"Good for him." Lizzie raised her eyebrows. "Are we done yet? I'm meeting someone for lunch."

"Done?" Miranda looked shocked. "I haven't even told you what I'd like to propose."

"Maybe I'm not interested in hearing anything you have to say," Lizzie said sweetly. "Originally, I was devastated that your family wanted nothing to do with Roman, but as time's gone by, I've realized that maybe it was a blessing in disguise."

She rose to her feet and pushed her chair in. "You lost your chance, Miranda, and you're the loser in this because Roman is the most amazing kid in the entire world."

Turning toward the door, she saw that Adam had just come in, and was staring in her direction. She stalked over to him and kept walking.

"I need to get out of here."

"Okay." He obediently turned around and followed her out, his searching gaze fixed on her face. "Are you all right?"

"No, I am *not* all right!" Lizzie seethed. "How *dare* she . . ."

Adam took Lizzie's hand and steered her across the road toward her apartment, aware that she was trembling, and keen to get her to a safe place where she could vent. The moment she reached her kitchen, she spun around to face him and he instinctively backed up a step.

"That was Ray's mom."

"Ah," Adam said. He'd never seen her this angry before, and was more than willing to let her do all the talking.

"Coretta's been sending photos of Roman to her, and now she suddenly turns up saying *she might have been a bit hasty* in casting us out from the family." Lizzie took a rapid turn around the room.

"Well, she's right about that," Adam agreed. "Did she say what she wanted to do about it?"

"No, because by that point—after she'd all but agreed that Ray suggested the child might not be his—I wasn't really in the mood to be pleasant to her."

Inwardly Adam cringed. "I thought you wanted Roman to get to know his family."

"I did! I do!" Lizzie said. "But seeing her sitting there suddenly being all nice about Roman just stuck in my craw."

"I understand that, but—"

Lizzie rounded on him. "Whose side are you on?"

"Yours, of course," Adam said patiently. "And, when you calm down you'll realize that—"

"Did you just tell me to calm down?"

There was a dangerous glint in Lizzie's eyes that made Adam scramble to back up and rephrase. "I *meant* that when you look at this logically, it might be an opportunity to allow Ray's family some limited access to Roman, which is, after all, what you originally wanted."

He held his breath as she studied him.

"Okay, you might have a point." Lizzie conceded and took another turn around the room. "She's not going to go away now, is she?"

"Probably not," Adam said. "I'm happy to sit in with you if you want to meet her again."

"Thanks." Lizzie groaned and pushed her hair away from her face. "Why did she have to turn up right now when CPS are investigating me?"

"Coretta probably clued her in," Adam suggested. "And if she did see pictures of Roman, she probably realized what she was missing."

"He is pretty darn cute." Lizzie flopped down on the couch, her anger leaving her as suddenly as it had risen, and raised her arms above her head. "I'm going to have to talk to her again, aren't I?"

Adam sat beside her and put her feet in his lap. "It might be a good idea." He rubbed his hand over the arch of her foot. "I really will come with you if you need me."

"Thanks. You're certainly a lot calmer than I am."

"I don't have a son to protect," Adam said gruffly. "But if I did, I'd want his mother to be just like you."

"Oh, Adam . . ."

Lizzie launched herself at him, knocking off his hat, and wrapped her arms around his neck, burying her face under his chin. He gathered her close and just held her, rocking her back and forth as she cried.

Eventually, she drew back and swallowed hard, her blue eyes still full of tears. "I'm sorry. I hate getting mad. Whenever I do I immediately start crying afterward."

"It's okay." He reached over to the countertop, grabbed a tissue from the box, and handed it to her. "You had a right to be upset."

"Not with you." She blew her nose. "I was so calm in front of Miranda that I couldn't keep it together any longer when I saw you."

"I'm a tough guy. I can take it."

She leaned in and kissed him. "Thank you for talking me down from the ledge."

"You would've gotten there by yourself eventually." He kissed her back. "You're no fool."

He had his arm around her waist, and, as she didn't seem inclined to move, he kept it there. She placed her palm against his chest over his heart.

"I will have to talk to her again."

"Yeah."

"I'd like you to be there, but I'm worried that if she sees you with me, she might get the wrong idea."

"What wrong idea?" Adam asked slowly.

"That we're a couple or something."

He frowned. "I thought we were a couple." He tried not to feel hurt. "Aren't we?"

"I didn't want to assume—" Lizzie sighed. "Oh God, now I've messed up again and hurt your feelings."

"No, I just thought we were going out." He looked into her eyes. "I want that. Don't you?"

"Yes." She didn't hesitate to answer, and some part of his soul quieted down. "I'd love that."

He kissed her. "Then consider it settled. We're a couple. If you want me to come and support you when you talk to Mrs. Smith, I'll be there. Just let me know the when and where."

Lizzie scrambled out of Adam's lap and disposed of her tissue before running to the bathroom where she spent a few minutes splashing cold water on her flushed face. She needed to get back to work, and she refused to let Miranda ruin her day.

When she came out of the bathroom, Adam was in the kitchen. He'd rolled up his shirtsleeves and was cooking something on the stove.

"Get some plates out, will you? I'm making us scrambled eggs."

Tears threatened again at his calm demeanor and the mere fact that he'd thought to feed her when she was at her most vulnerable. She pushed her feelings down and went to open the correct cupboard.

"I've made some toast if you want it." Adam served the eggs, which were perfectly fluffy and sprinkled with cheese and fresh chives she kept on her kitchen windowsill.

"Thank you." She stared at the eggs for a moment, wondering if she could manage to eat after her tumultuous morning. Her stomach growled. She picked up her fork and attempted the first mouthful.

"That's . . . really good," Lizzie said.

"Glad you like it." He got the toast and put it on a plate between them and then put the pan in the sink. "There wasn't much in the refrigerator, but most people like eggs."

"I always forget you like to cook."

"After Mom left, someone had to do it." He shrugged. "I didn't think it was fair that Auntie Rae had to do everything." He lapsed into silence, his gaze elsewhere, and then abruptly started speaking again.

"Leanne said Dad prevented her from coming back to the ranch or having any contact with us."

"It does sound like the kind of thing he might do," Lizzie said cautiously. "He's got a bit of a temper."

"A *bit?* He hates admitting he's wrong about anything and Mom walking out on him must have blown his brain."

He forked up more eggs and chewed for a while. "I made her cry."

"Who? Leanne?"

"Yeah, she was telling me about how she eventually gave up hoping Dad would come to his senses, went to her brother's place in New York, and cried for days. I said Daisy cried too, and she got all upset." He groaned. "I'm crap at this emotional stuff."

Lizzie reached out and patted his arm. "You're not. You've been wonderful to me today."

"I think after Louisa died I just . . . stopped trying. It doesn't come easily anymore," he confessed.

"You're trying now," Lizzie said encouragingly. "And I for one appreciate it."

"Thanks." He finished his eggs, ate another piece of toast, and started cleaning up. "Do you want coffee?"

"No, I'll get that back at work, but make some for yourself if you want." Lizzie lingered over the last bite of eggs, enjoying not only the food, but also the fact that it had been made for her with such care.

She set about drying the items as Adam washed them, and then put them away. She was more at peace than she had anticipated, mainly because of the quiet stalwart presence of Adam beside her.

"Thank you." She went on tiptoe and kissed his cheek. "For everything."

He shrugged. "You're welcome." He glanced over at the kitchen clock. "Do you need to get back? I can finish up here for you."

"I think I'm ready to go now." Lizzie patted her hair. "Do I look like I've been crying?"

He regarded her seriously, his gray eyes scanning her face. "You look beautiful."

Lizzie felt herself blushing and swatted him with the dish towel. "Get along with you."

She busied herself finding her keys and cell phone as Adam reclaimed his Stetson and rolled down his sleeves. If he kept being this nice, she might finally have to acknowledge that her feelings for him were deepening every day, and then where would she be? She set the question firmly aside. Her current focus had to be on Miranda and whatever the Smith family were intending to throw at her next.

After filling up the bed of his truck with lumber and bags of feed, Adam went back home, his thoughts busy with what was going on with Lizzie. He wanted to go up to the Smith family and tell them to leave her alone, but it wasn't his place to do so. The best he could do was offer his support and hope she'd take it.

At least she'd finally agreed that they were going out. . . . Adam smiled to himself. That was progress for each of them. They must be the most reluctant couple ever.

He stopped his truck close to the barn, opened the tailgate, and looked around. As usual there was no one there when you needed them. He shouldered the heavy grain and feed sacks and took them through to the store himself, and then went to look for some help.

He found Ben finishing his lunch in the kitchen.

"Hey, can you help me unload some lumber?"

"Sure." Ben set his plate in the sink and wiped halfheartedly at his bearded chin. "I didn't hear you come in."

With Ben helping, Adam easily stacked the wood under the shelter of the barn roof.

"What's this for?" Ben asked as he laid the final piece down.

"New fencing for the paddock, and if I've got any left, a new chicken house." Adam wiped sweat from his brow. "Kaiden's doing the carpentry. I'm just the labor." He looked around. "Where is everyone? It's really quiet."

"Leanne took Dad out to lunch in town. They're meeting Danny and Evan there. I think she was hoping to get Daisy to come along, too."

"Great." Adam started back toward the house. "How long is she staying again?"

"I think she mentioned something about extending her visit," Ben commented, which made Adam stop and turn around.

"*What?*"

Ben shrugged. "She and Dad are getting on really well. I guess they want to keep talking to each other."

Adam started walking again and went into the mudroom to take off his boots and wash his hands.

"Why are you so against her?" Ben asked as he dried his own hands. "I've talked to her quite a lot, and most of what she says about Dad makes total sense."

"I know it does." Adam went into the kitchen. "I just don't know what her end game is here."

"Why does she have to have one?" Ben raised his eyebrows. "Maybe she just wants to be at peace with her past with the man, who if you ask me, made some pretty stupid decisions."

Adam helped himself to coffee. It was a valid question. Why *was* he so reluctant to embrace his mother's side of the story?

"Don't you feel like you're betraying Dad by believing her?" Adam asked.

"No, why should I?" Ben leaned up against the countertop opposite. He was about an inch shorter than Adam but just as wide. "I'm old enough to realize there can be two different sides to anything. Mom made some mistakes, but Dad didn't have to react the way he did."

"It feels disloyal," Adam repeated.

"Then that's on you." Ben got some lemonade from the refrigerator. "Maybe you just don't want to accept that even people you love can make bad decisions."

"I know all about that," Adam replied, his mind immediately recalling several arguments he'd had with Louisa about her treatment options. "You can't make people do what you want even if it is the right thing."

"Exactly." Ben stared at him meaningfully. "Maybe you should let go of your stubborn streak and see that neither Dad or Mom is perfect." He sipped his drink. "Leanne's not a bad person, Adam."

"I never said she was." Adam defended himself. "And I *have* talked to her."

Ben looked over at the door. "Looks like Dad's back. I wonder if he brought Leanne with him?"

"She might as well move back in at this rate," Adam muttered as he finished his coffee.

His dad came in alone and stopped at the kitchen door to stare at his two oldest sons, his brows snapping together.

"Why aren't you two out working?"

"We were just unloading some timber," Adam replied. "Did you have a good lunch?"

"We went to that new pizza place. It was excellent. Leanne made me have a smaller pizza and a big salad. It wasn't too bad at all."

Adam exchanged a startled look with Ben. None of them had managed to make their dad alter his eating habits since Dr. Tio had recommended some changes.

"Good for you," Ben said. "Did Daisy come?"

"Yes, she did. She didn't say much to her mother, though."

"Leanne left when she was five. What do you expect?" Adam said evenly.

"I expect my children to make an effort to move on," his dad said. "If I can do it, then so can you guys!"

"You were an adult when you chose to separate from Leanne," Adam pointed out. "Daisy was a child who wasn't consulted in the matter. She woke up one morning to find her mother gone, and her father making a bonfire in the yard while he hurled his wife's possessions into the flames."

"That wasn't my finest moment, despite what she did." His dad grimaced. "I regret that."

"Well, I suppose that's something." Ben stirred and walked toward the door. He wasn't the kind of guy to hang around during an argument. "I'll go saddle up. I'll meet you at the barn, Adam."

"Okay." Adam continued studying his father who was helping himself to coffee. He waited until Ben left to continue the conversation. "Is it true that you banned Leanne from coming back to the ranch and seeing us?"

"As I just said, Adam. I didn't behave well back then. I was furious when she pulled that stunt on me and walked out. I thought I had reason to get her out of my life, and I was determined to make her pay for it." He sighed. "I was an absolute fool."

"Yeah, you were." Adam stood and put his mug in the dishwasher. "You also told us that she'd run off for good, not that she was staying in Bridgeport, waiting for you to come to your senses and beg her to come back."

"She tried to come back a couple of times to see you all," his dad said. "I wouldn't let her stay—threatened to shoot out her tires if she came by again."

"Wow, you really made sure she couldn't see her own kids, didn't you?" Adam slammed the dishwasher door shut. "What a hero."

"I was the opposite of that, and you damn well know it. I lost the best thing in my life."

"No, you *gave* it away, which is even worse. She didn't goddamn die on you." Adam faced his father. "You just decided to mess up everyone's lives because you were too stubborn to admit you were wrong."

He walked toward the door, aware that he was angry and unwilling to let his father see how much he was affected by his open admission of, not just his guilt, but also his appalling behavior.

"You disappearing on me again, son?"

"Yeah, I am, before I say something I'll regret," Adam replied.

His dad held his gaze. "I can take it, Adam. I probably deserve it, too." He sighed. "Just let it out. You'll feel much better."

"I'm good." Adam was at the door before his father spoke again.

"Except you're not good. You never allow yourself to get angry at anything anymore."

"What's wrong with that?" Adam demanded, guilt churning in his gut.

"It's not natural."

"Maybe not to you, but maybe growing up with a father who lost it over the smallest thing made me realize I *never* wanted to be like that." Adam pushed open the door. "I've got to get back to work."

Chapter Fifteen

When Lizzie went down the stairs the next morning, she wasn't surprised to see that a note had been pushed under her door. She picked it up, avoiding Roman's questions, and kept walking toward Gabby's. As soon as Roman's attention wandered, she opened it up one-handed, and read it through.

I would appreciate it if you would meet me today at 1 P.M. at Henry Parker's law firm in town. I hope this is a mutually acceptable neutral place. Miranda Smith.

Law firm? A stab of alarm hit Lizzie's stomach. Why on earth would Miranda want to meet her there? She glanced down at Roman's happy face as he skipped along holding her hand, and tried to imagine what might happen next. She had a sense that if she didn't cooperate, Miranda would simply keep trying. She'd been the same back when she'd insisted that Lizzie had no part in her family. An iron will cloaked in a smiling, sweet exterior.

Lizzie reminded herself that she wasn't the same scared woman who'd allowed the Smith family to railroad her four years ago. Having Roman and learning to care for him had made her a different person entirely. She dropped Roman off at Gabby's and told her about Miranda just in case the woman tried to get in and see her grandson.

For once she was glad that it was a busy day at the café with several busloads of tourists passing through as well as the locals to deal with. Yvonne had also made several special occasion cakes that needed to be boxed up and delivered. Ten minutes before her lunch break began, Lizzie rushed into the bathroom to make sure she looked presentable before setting off down the street toward the only law office in town.

Lizzie went through the old-fashioned stained-glass front door. Henry's granddaughter, Chloe, who was home from law school temping for the summer, greeted her with a warm smile.

"Hey! What's up?"

"Nothing much," Lizzie lied and kept smiling. "I'm supposed to be meeting a Mrs. Smith here?"

"Yeah, that's right. She's in with Grandpa already. You can just go through." Chloe waved toward the inner door. "Would you like something to drink?"

"I'm good, thanks."

Lizzie gathered her courage and went through into Henry Parker's office, which faced the rear of the building and overlooked a small garden from when the office had been a private home. The last time she'd been here had been to help her parents with their wills.

"Miss Lizzie!" Henry, who was a stout, short man with white hair and a goatee, stood and held out his hand. "How kind of you to come by."

Lizzie went forward to shake his hand. She turned to Miranda who was seated in front of the desk, looking very glamorous in a pink dress with matching accessories.

"Mrs. Smith."

"Elizabeth." Miranda smiled at her. "So good of you to come so that we can sort out this silly misunderstanding." She gestured to Henry who had resumed his seat behind the desk. "I've been explaining everything to Mr. Parker."

"Explaining what?" Lizzie asked mildly.

"That your sweet little boy is my grandson."

Henry cleared his throat and wagged his finger at Lizzie. "I wish you'd told me about this earlier, young lady, because I could've gotten it all sorted out for you."

"I'm still not sure what you're getting at." Lizzie said, playing dumb just for the heck of it. "Sorted out what?"

"I understand that the father of your child hasn't played much of a part in your son's life," Henry said tactfully.

"That's correct." Lizzie nodded. "He ran away when I told him I was pregnant, tried to pretend he wasn't the father, and blocked me from contacting him."

Henry winced and Miranda was quick to intervene.

"He was . . . conflicted and he panicked. And, as you didn't pursue the matter through the courts, Elizabeth, we *did* start to wonder whether he'd been right all along, and that you'd managed to get the real father to pay up."

Lizzie's first reaction was to start screaming, but she tamped down her frustration and pictured Roman's innocent little face.

"Ray is the father of my son." Lizzie said the words slowly and clearly. "After you blocked me, I decided I'd rather not have anything to do with you, and managed by myself."

"Would you both be prepared to provide DNA samples to establish whether Ray is indeed the father of Roman?" Henry asked.

"Fine by me," Lizzie said.

"I am willing to do that as well," Miranda conceded.

"Well, that's a start." Henry nodded. "Perhaps, Mrs. Smith, you might wait for the results before you make any further decisions?"

"Decisions about what?" Lizzie asked.

"Well, I assume from what she's been sharing with me, that Mrs. Smith would like to have some kind of relationship with her potential grandchild. Is that correct?" Henry looked at Miranda.

"Yes."

Lizzie had to bite her lip not to shout out the instant denial that rose in her throat. She reminded herself that she'd always wanted Roman to have the option to know his father's family, and that she had to negotiate in good faith. She still wasn't prepared to sit there and let Miranda dictate all the terms.

"Surely that's up to me?" Lizzie asked sweetly.

"Coretta said you *wanted* Roman to know his family," Miranda said.

"Coretta chose not to take advantage of that option. Why would I assume any of you would want to do so?"

Miranda sighed. "There you go again, being all prickly. I don't know what's happened to you over the past four years. You used to be such a sweet, friendly, girl."

"Maybe I had to bring up a child with no support from the father?" Lizzie wasn't going to roll over that easily. "Maybe working two jobs, counting every penny, and having to rely on my parents way too much had an effect on me?"

Miranda looked at Henry and raised her eyebrows "Now you understand why I came to you."

"You forget that I've known Lizzie all her life," Henry said gently. "I have nothing but admiration for her, and how well she's brought up her son."

"*Oh*." Miranda picked up her purse. "Perhaps you'll let

me know how to obtain a DNA sample and we can talk again." She stood and offered them both a brusque nod and a brittle smile. "Thank you for your time."

After the door shut behind Miranda, Henry let out a whistle.

"She's not very fond of you, is she?"

"Nope, which is why I'm suspicious about her interest in my son," Lizzie agreed.

"You'd be surprised how many grandparents want to have a part of their grandchildren's lives even if they don't like the parents." Henry sat back and regarded Lizzie thoughtfully. "Getting older and realizing they're missing out on the next generation can have quite an effect."

Lizzie sighed. "I'm trying to think about what's best for Roman here, but it's hard when they were so awful to me when I found out I was pregnant."

"I understand," Henry nodded. "You're one hundred percent certain that Ray Smith is the father of your son?"

"Yes." Lizzie met his gaze head-on. "But I'll do the DNA test anyway."

"Good for you." Henry wrote something on his notepad. "I think Dr. Tio can take care of that for you down at the clinic." He winked at her. "I'll put the charge on Mrs. Smith's bill."

Lizzie managed a smile and stood up. "I'd better get back to work. Thank you, Henry."

"Now, if you need any legal advice, you come and see me whenever you like, my dear," Henry said. "At no charge."

"That's really kind of you," Lizzie said.

He frowned. "I don't think she's the type to give up easily. I'm expecting to hear from her again. I'll keep you informed, so don't you worry about that, either."

She went around the desk and kissed the top of his head. "Thank you."

"You're welcome. Now off you go, and give my regards to Ms. Yvonne."

Lizzie left the office and walked slowly back to work. The sun was a bright ball in the clear blue sky and beamed relentlessly down on her uncovered head. She paused at the back of the café and found some shade so that she could text Adam.

He didn't immediately reply, and she went back inside enjoying both the air-conditioning and the smell of roasting coffee. She helped herself to a sandwich from the industrial-size refrigerator and sat at the table to eat while the last fifteen minutes of her lunch hour ticked down. For once she was completely alone in the large kitchen.

She'd pop into the clinic and get the test done on Roman after she picked him up from Gabby's. It was a relatively simple thing to do, and didn't involve taking blood, which would freak Roman out. All Dr. Tio would need to do was take a swab from the inside of Roman's cheek.

Her cell buzzed with a reply from Adam.

Do you need me to come over this evening?

She smiled foolishly at her phone as she typed her reply.

No, I'm okay. I'm taking Ro to get a DNA test.

Her phone rang and she transferred it from the table to her ear.

"What?"

Adam's voice sounded even growlier on the phone. "Who wants his DNA?"

"Miranda. She apparently wants to be a grandmother now."

There was a long silence confirming Lizzie's suspicions

that the phone probably wasn't Adam's best method of communication.

"Are you okay about this?" he finally asked

"I think so. At least they won't be able to sling that 'Roman's not Ray's son because you slept around' crap at me anymore."

"Hmmph." She waited again for him to form a new sentence. "Once they've proved Ray is the father what happens next?"

"As I said, I don't know yet," Lizzie reminded him. "I assume Miranda will want to visit with Roman or something."

"You'd better make sure you know exactly what she wants before you let her see him."

"I'm not stupid, Adam. Henry's offered me free legal advice for as long as I need it."

"Henry Parker?" Adam asked.

"The only lawyer in town, yes."

"That's good." He sighed. "You really doing okay?"

She considered that, pausing almost as long as he did before she answered him. "In a weird way, I'm glad I'm finally reaching some kind of resolution about this matter. I want Roman to know his family. If they can overcome their dislike of me to offer him their support, then I suppose that's a good thing."

"You're a strong woman, Lizzie Taylor."

"Thank you." She swallowed hard. "I'm just doing my best for Roman."

"You sure you don't want me to come and see you tonight?" he asked abruptly.

"No, because I'll probably cry all over you again, and you'll get fed up with me."

"I won't."

"You might," Lizzie replied. "And I don't want Roman

to see me upset." She hesitated. "When you're with me, I can be my real self, you know?"

"There's no weakness in crying, Lizzie," Adam said. "Sometimes you just need to let it out." He paused. "Let me come over. I can just hold you."

Lizzie blinked back the tears forming in her eyes, and focused hard on the back door of the kitchen. "I'm okay, really. Why don't you come by this weekend? We can take Roman out for ice cream or something."

His silence this time was so long that she thought she'd lost the connection.

"Okay, I'll do that, but call me if anything happens."

"I will." Lizzie clutched her phone hard. "Thank you. I'll speak to you soon."

She ended the call and just sat staring into space, carefully gathering her defenses again. She wanted to drive up to Miller Ranch, grab hold of Adam, strip him naked, and hide under the covers with him. But she also wanted to be strong—to be the woman she'd had to become rather than relying on someone else.

"Wow, Lizzie, that's a pretty specific fantasy you've got going on there about Adam Miller's bod," she murmured. "Like you have plans for all that glorious naked flesh. But you've got to get through this yourself. It's not fair to drag Adam into your mess."

"Talking to yourself again, my friend?"

Lizzie spun around to see Yvonne advancing toward her, two trays balanced in her hand. She hastily pinned on a smile.

"Just giving myself a little pep talk."

"You okay?" Yvonne studied her carefully.

"I'm just"—Lizzie waved her arms around—"getting by, doing my best, being an independent woman, and definitely not letting you down."

"I don't feel let down."

"Yay me!" Lizzie gave a halfhearted fist pump. "I'm just sorting through a few things with Roman's father's side of the family. Once all that is straightened out then things will be great."

She'd recently told Yvonne the whole story about Ray just in case Miranda decided to have a word with her employer.

"Ray Smith is Ro's father, correct?" Yvonne set down the trays and leaned against the edge of the table. "Was that his mother who came into the café yesterday?"

"Yes. She's not very fond of me."

"Then she's a fool," Yvonne said firmly. "Does she want to see Roman?"

"I think so."

"Well, about time, too." Yvonne checked the clock. "Are you okay to start now? I've got to go over the wedding menu with Della again today. She's due here in five minutes."

"I'm good." Lizzie put her cell away and went to find her apron. "Give Della my best, won't you?"

Adam picked at his food as he fought the urge to ignore Lizzie's earlier call and just turn up at her place. He was damn sure that she was upset. Everything inside him wanted to get out there and help her.

"Cat got your tongue?"

He looked up at his father who was seated at the head of the table where they were all having dinner and raised an eyebrow.

"What?"

"Food not to your liking, seeing as your mother spent all afternoon cooking it for you?"

Adam put down his fork, glancing toward Leanne who sat at the foot of the table. She was looking down at her plate, her smile disappearing.

"The food is great. I just—"

"Want to act like a spoiled brat." His father spoke over him. "Trust you to spoil a nice meal."

"Jeff—" Leanne spoke up.

Adam fixed his gaze on his father. He was in no mood to pussyfoot around his father's deliberate attempts to rile him up.

"You've spoiled plenty of meals with your bad temper and unexplained disappearances. I remember Mom sitting here in tears waiting for you to show up when you'd decided to hoof it off to another rodeo."

"I'm not *like* that anymore." His father banged his knife on the table for emphasis. "I stopped all that shit after Leanne left, and you damn well know it."

"You were still pretty mean." Adam kept talking. He had no idea why. It was like that insane urge to press on a bruise until it hurt again.

"I was a parent! Did you expect me to coddle you all?" His father glared fiercely around the table. "I wanted to prepare you for the fact that life is hard, and that you don't get a free pass."

"I think we all got that," Kaiden said dryly. "And have the scars to prove it."

"If you got a whipping from me you sure as hell deserved it," his dad snapped. "And by the time you were sixteen you were all taller than me, and I had to stop."

"Thanks for nothing," Ben muttered.

"And why are you coming after me?" his dad demanded. "Adam's the one being disrespectful to his mother."

"Jeff." Leanne spoke up again.

"What?" He frowned at her.

"If you start this, I'm going back to the hotel."

"Start what?" he protested. "I'm just getting your son to show you some respect."

"Respect is earned." Leanne didn't shy away from her ex-husband's ire. "I don't have to sit here and watch you lose your temper anymore, and I don't intend to do so."

Adam held his breath as his father stared at Leanne.

"I apologize," Jeff said gruffly.

"Apologize to Adam. He's the one you've been getting at all evening."

Adam braced himself as his dad looked over at him.

"She's right. I'm sorry, son."

"That's . . . okay," Adam said slowly.

"I'm just trying to make things right here and you're not helping!" Jeff stated.

"For a moment, I almost got misty-eyed there." Ben looked over at Adam. "But Dad just has to keep talking, doesn't he?"

"While we're on the subject of Dad apologizing," Daisy piped up, "could you clarify something for me?"

"What is it *now?*" Jeff demanded.

"Leanne said that she sent birthday and Christmas cards every year. None of us ever received them."

"Goddammit!"

Adam flinched as his dad shot to his feet and marched out of the room. They all sat there listening to the faint sounds of his cursing, and a lot of banging before he reappeared with an old-fashioned trunk, and dumped it onto the floor beside the table. A cloud of dust flew up and Daisy coughed.

"Here you go." Their father opened the trunk.

Leanne pressed a hand to her throat. "You kept *everything?*"

"I took the money out and used it to get the kids

presents," Jeff admitted. "I didn't have much cash for such things."

Daisy left her seat and went over to the case, her eyes wide. "Oh my goodness! There are hundreds of letters in here."

"I couldn't bring myself to throw them away." Jeff looked over at Leanne. "I read every single one of them."

Daisy sank to her knees and plunged her hands into the trunk, gathering up a handful of letters. "How *could* you have done this?" Her voice faltered. "I thought Leanne didn't care about any of us. I *hated* her for it."

Knowing Daisy had idolized her father after Leanne left, Adam could hardly bear to look at the hurt in her eyes, or see his father's reaction to that condemnation.

Jeff rubbed an awkward hand over his jaw. "I thought you'd all do better without the memories. That if you saw this stuff you might think she was coming home, and get upset all over again. I couldn't deal with all the crying and hoping when I was working so hard just to get by."

Daisy started sorting out the letters into piles and Kaiden went to help her. Adam held back, watching the interaction between his parents who were now standing close together and if he wasn't mistaken, holding hands.

It was weird seeing them like that. He wasn't sure if he liked it, but with all the recent revelations about his father's choices, he was making some massive adjustments about the past. Had he misjudged them both? Had he made completely the wrong call back in the day? He had a sense that there was a lot more information to come out before things were straightened out. Years of misunderstandings was a long tail to unravel.

"Adam?" Daisy called out to him. "Do you want yours?" She held up a pile of letters.

"Can you stick them in my room?" Adam replied. "I've got to go and check on the barn."

He went out into the mudroom, found his boots and hat, and walked out into the still-warm evening. The sun had dipped down below the Sierras and the lush pink and purple shades of twilight were already spreading across the foothills and paddocks, creeping ever closer to enfold the barn and house.

Adam fed the barn cats and dogs and made sure all the horses were watered and comfortable for the night. Doing something—anything—other than wishing he was with Lizzie—was better than sitting around moping, or worrying what this visit from Leanne had done to his family.

"Adam?"

He looked up to see his mother standing at the entrance of the barn. She looked worn-out, which didn't surprise Adam knowing how exhausting it was to deal with his father when he got angry. He set down his shovel and went toward her.

"Can you take me back to the hotel?" She wrapped her arms around herself. "I don't want to be stuck in a truck with your father arguing his case with me."

"Sure." He nodded, the words of comfort she needed sticking in his throat. "I'll just wash up and get my keys."

He didn't need to go back into the main house as his jacket and keys were in the mudroom. He walked out to his truck and opened the passenger door so that Leanne could climb on board.

"Thank you for doing this," Leanne said as they set off.

"You're welcome."

"Everyone else was knee-deep in letters. It was just too much to ask them to step away and take me back. I couldn't even deal with all their excitement because I was too mad at Jeff for concealing them from you in the first place."

"From what he said, he thought he was causing us less heartbreak," Adam commented without inflection. "He hated it when Daisy cried, or we asked too many questions."

It suddenly occurred to him that he'd become more like his father than he'd realized—shying away from emotion, rebuffing attempts to get close to him. The only thing he didn't do was snap at everyone. But even that was changing.

"Which is why I ended up leaving him in the first place." Leanne sighed. "He's not a bad man. He just struggles with anything emotional, or with expressing his feelings."

Yeah. He and his dad were like twins. . . . They reached the county road and Adam got out to open the gate, drive through, and then close it behind him.

He focused on driving, aware that Leanne was busy texting someone. She caught one of his glances and set her phone back down.

"I'm texting my other daughter."

Adam almost veered off the road. "Not Daisy?"

"No, your half sister, Eileen. She was a bit of a surprise." She smiled. "I married again. My husband, Declan, died three years ago after a series of heart attacks."

"I'm sorry." Adam contemplated this amazing information. "I had no idea. Is she your only kid?"

"Yes. Declan was quite a bit older than me, and we agreed that one miracle was enough. She's sixteen and staying with her half sister in New York."

"Does she know about all this?"

"About the fact that I have six other children? Yes, I told her after her father died." She paused. "He asked me not to tell her until then because he thought she might go haring across the country to try and meet you all. That's one of the reasons why it's taken me so long to get back in contact with your father."

"She already sounds like one of us," Adam commented.

"She looks most like Ben, and has auburn hair like me and my mother. She's very strong-willed."

"Does Dad know?" Adam wasn't normally one to pry, but he couldn't help himself.

"We've discussed it. I sent him pictures when she was born. He met Declan once as well."

Yet again Adam marveled at all the stuff his father had never mentioned. "He didn't tell us anything. As far as we knew, you were dead."

"I know." She sighed. "He probably thought it was for the best."

"Maybe the best for him," Adam agreed. "Less emotion to deal with."

For the first time, anger stirred in his gut against his father. They could've seen Leanne, met her new husband and daughter. It might have been hard to deal with, but at least they would've known she was alive and doing okay.

"Don't be too hard on your father," Leanne said softly.

"I'm not sure how you can say that after how he behaved toward you." Adam slowed down as they turned toward Morgantown.

"I had to let go of all my anger. If I hadn't have done so I would've become a very bitter person. I was also lucky because I had my brother supporting me. He helped me find a new job, paid for me to go to college in my spare time, and stuck by me." She chuckled. "He even introduced me to Declan, although I don't think he quite anticipated the effect *that* would have."

Adam considered her words as he approached the Hayes Hotel. He feared he was more like his dad than his mother, closing himself off after a tragedy rather than letting it go and moving on. He pulled into the parking lot behind the hotel and turned off the engine.

"I'm glad you had your brother and found Declan," he said gruffly. "You deserved to be happy."

Leanne reached for his hand. "What a lovely thing to say." She choked up. "I never expected you, of all people to understand, and . . . *forgive* me."

She grabbed her purse and got out of the truck. "Don't worry about coming in with me. I'm fine. Tell your father to call me tomorrow."

She slammed the door and left him sitting there in the darkness.

Did he forgive her? *Could* he?

He could call Lizzie and see if she wanted to see him. . . .

He stared at the lighted windows of the hotel. Lizzie didn't need to hear him going on about his mother and father. She had enough problems of her own. And to be honest, the way he was currently feeling about his past actions was a raw wound he wasn't ready to share with anyone yet. He didn't like himself, his certainties and stubbornness no longer a feature, but a hulking roadblock. How on earth could he burden Lizzie with all that?

Chapter Sixteen

"Come on, Ro. This will just take a minute."

If Lizzie hadn't been so worried about the results of Roman's DNA test and busy helping Yvonne get the catering done for Nate and Della's wedding she might have noticed Adam's weekly absence far more. He texted her regularly to check in, and had apologized about not seeing them the previous weekend because of some problem up at the ranch.

As she was expecting her parents to turn up any day, she'd also been busy cleaning her apartment, and making sure Roman had all the necessary clothes washed and packed for his trip to Disneyland. He was so excited about going that he'd been exhausting to deal with all week. After he left, she suspected she'd need a week off just to sleep and recover.

"Look! It's Adam!" Roman tugged on her hand as the man of her dreams came out of the medical center. He wore his usual Stetson, jeans, boots, and shirt over T-shirt combo. "Adam! It's *me!*"

Adam turned and waited as Lizzie let Roman run over and climb him like a monkey. His smile was slow to emerge, making Lizzie study him closely as she approached. He looked worn-out.

"Hey." He spoke to Roman first. "I hear you're going to see Mickey."

"Yes!" Roman nodded. "Soon! Mom's not coming, though."

Adam finally looked at Lizzie, which wasn't reassuring. "I'm sure she's devastated."

"She is." Roman nodded. "She loves Mickey." He stared earnestly at Adam. "Are you sad, too?"

"Yup," Adam said. "But I'll try and get over it." He settled Roman securely on his shoulder. "Have you guys got time for ice cream?"

"Sure," Lizzie said easily. "I was just going to check if Dr. Tio had any results yet, but it can wait a while."

"How about I take Ro to get an ice cream and you meet us there?" Adam suggested. "We're only going as far as Gina's."

"Okay." Lizzie was grateful for his consideration. "I won't be long." She fumbled in her pocket for some money, but Adam waved it away.

"I've got this. What flavor do you want?"

She considered saying cowboy, but the wary look in his eyes wasn't encouraging her to flirt. "Ask Ro. He knows what I like."

She watched them move off and turned back to the medical center. There had been no sign of Miranda around town, but if the DNA results were in from both parties, Lizzie guessed she might be hearing from her soon.

Lizzie asked the nurse to send a copy of the results through to Henry at his law office. She walked back to where Adam and Roman were sitting in the shade of one of Gina's umbrellas, eating ice cream.

"He said you liked mint chocolate chip." Adam handed her a dripping cone.

"Thanks, I do." She licked hastily at the melting ice

cream, aware of Adam's intense gaze lingering on her mouth. "That's really good. What did you get, Ro?"

"Bubblegum." He was already halfway down his small cone. "I said thank you."

"He did," Adam agreed. He'd taken his ice cream in a cup and wasn't getting all sticky like she and Roman were.

"Adam's got banilla bean," Roman said.

"Vanilla," Lizzie automatically corrected him.

"Vanilla vean." Roman parroted solemnly back at her, and she fought a smile.

"He's way too clever for his own good," Adam commented as he finished his ice cream and stood up. "I'm going to get more wipes."

"Thanks," she called after him. "Although I think we're both going to need a shower at this rate."

He returned with a sheaf of napkins. Lizzie tidied herself and Roman up as best she could.

"I think we're going to need to wash properly," Lizzie said. "Do you want to come up and talk to me, or are you in a rush?"

Roman clambered into his lap and put his hands on Adam's face. "Come and see my new picture of Spot on the moon."

Adam gingerly set Roman on his feet. "Seeing as I'm now as sticky as you are, I'd love to."

Adam followed Lizzie up the stairs and washed his hands and face in the kitchen sink while she cleaned Roman off in the bathroom. After being shown the latest picture of his horse, Adam accepted some iced tea and leaned against the counter while Lizzie set Roman up at the table with his latest Lego creation.

She looked tired, which wasn't surprising seeing as her

life was pretty complicated right now. He regretted staying away from her, but he'd needed the distance for himself. He still hadn't read the cards and letters Daisy had left for him in his bedroom. He didn't have the nerve. He didn't want to stir the simmering anger that still burned low in his gut.

Lizzie came over, kicked off her sandals, and set them by the door.

"It was crazy busy at the café today. I barely got to sit down."

"Then sit down now." He pulled out the stool next to him and patted it. "You look exhausted."

She took the seat and silently handed him a piece of paper. He read the results and nodded.

"Okay, nothing you didn't already know here. What's the next step?"

"That's up to Miranda." She took the paper back, folded it in half, and then in half again. "I suspect she'll be contacting me fairly soon." She looked over at Roman who was humming to himself as he built a spaceship. "He deserves to know all his family."

"Yeah, I get that." Conscious of how many years he'd lost of Leanne's life, and his new knowledge of his half sister, Adam could only agree. "But only on your terms."

"Don't worry. I'll be careful."

He took her hand. "I know you will."

"Ro's the most precious thing in my world." Her voice quivered, and he squeezed her fingers hard. "I'll do anything to keep him safe." After a moment she cleared her throat. "Have you heard anything from Ines and Carlos?"

It was his turn to pause and search for the right words. "He's not doing too well. The experimental treatment place won't work for him now."

"Poor Carlos," she said softly. "Is he able to come home?"

"I think that's what both he and Ines would like. I talked to Rio this morning. He offered to fly him back on the company jet."

"That was good of him," Lizzie said.

"He's a nice guy." Adam sipped his coffee.

"And is Leanne still here?" Lizzie asked. "I thought I saw her with Daisy the other day."

"Yeah. She's staying a while longer. She and Dad have a lot of ground to cover."

"That must be . . . hard for you." Lizzie said diplomatically.

"She married again. Apparently I have a sixteen-year-old half sister called Eileen."

Lizzie blinked at him. "*What?*"

"I know. It was quite a shock for all of us—apart from Dad, who apparently knew already." He grimaced. "I'm kind of annoyed with him right now."

"I'm not surprised," Lizzie agreed. She was petting his arm and he didn't want her to stop. "I suppose he thought it would be better if you didn't have to deal with all those things."

"*He* didn't want to deal with them," Adam stated. "He never gave us the opportunity to make a decision about anything. The least he could've done was tell us the truth when we turned eighteen and allowed us to make up our own minds."

"I agree." Lizzie nodded. "I'd already decided that whenever Roman asked me about his father, I'd tell him the truth."

"The thing is . . ." Adam hesitated. "I've always seen my dad as a hero, bringing up six kids, managing the ranch full-time, never speaking about the wife who ran out on him, and it's not true. *None* of it is true."

He was relieved when she just heard him out rather than rushing to comment either way.

"Life can be pretty sucky sometimes, can't it?" Lizzie said softly. "My mom always used to say there are three sides to every story—yours, mine, and the truth."

Adam finished his drink and slowly wiped his mouth. "Leanne says she's staying for another two weeks, and then she has to go back to New York."

"She'll be here for Nate and Della's wedding then." Lizzie picked up his glass and put it in the sink. "I wonder if my parents remember her? They're due here at the end of the week."

"Leanne certainly knows Nate's parents. She used to know everybody." He straightened up and retrieved his hat. "Are you going to the wedding?"

"Yes, I'm going to help Yvonne set up the buffet, and I'm free for the rest of the day."

"Then will you hang out with me?"

She smiled at him. "In public? Like we're a couple?"

Adam nodded. "Exactly."

She turned around and hugged him hard. "I'd love to do that."

He bent to kiss the top of her head and then put on his Stetson. "It's a date."

Adam had hardly been gone five minutes before Lizzie's cell phone rang. She checked the number and answered.

"Hello?"

"Hi, Lizzie, it's Chloe. I know it's late, but do you have a minute to pop down to the office? Mrs. Smith is here, and Grandpa thinks you should be here, too."

"I'll have to bring Roman with me." Lizzie cast a

distracted glance toward her oblivious son. "And I really don't want Mrs. Smith to meet him just yet."

"Don't worry. I'll take him out with me so you won't be disturbed," Chloe reassured her. "I've met him at kids' Bible study during church, so I won't be a stranger."

"Okay, I'll be there in a few minutes."

Lizzie ended the call and rushed to find her sandals. "We've got to go out again, Ro. I'm really sorry."

"It's okay." He slid off his chair and grabbed Doofus. "We like going out."

As Ro had already met Chloe, he was quite happy to go down to Yvonne's with her to have cake. Lizzie watched them walk down the street and braced herself to meet Miranda again.

She went through to Henry's office where Miranda was sitting in the same chair as last time. The only difference was her outfit was blue, and her expression even less pleasant, if that were possible.

"Hi, Henry." Lizzie smiled at the lawyer. "Afternoon, Mrs. Smith."

"Sit down, my dear." He smiled back at her. "Mrs. Smith has received the DNA results and accepts that Ray is the father of your son."

"Yay me," Lizzie said and looked directly at Miranda. "Would you like to apologize now?"

"As I said before, Elizabeth. If you had only followed *through* when you were pregnant, and not left us all believing you'd found the real father, all of this silliness could've been avoided."

Lizzie opened and shut her mouth twice, but still couldn't find the right words. She glanced over at Henry and raised her eyebrows.

"What Mrs. Smith is trying to say, Lizzie, is that she is prepared to acknowledge her grandson. She wishes to make some kind of arrangement with you to allow her to get to know him."

"Okay." Lizzie nodded. "What exactly do you have in mind?"

"One weekend a month would be enough to start with," Miranda said briskly. "I have an apartment in San Francisco. We can meet there, and he can stay overnight."

"That's *so* not happening," Lizzie said. "He's barely four, and he doesn't know you at all. I suggest you come here once a month and spend the afternoon with both of us until he gets used to you being around."

"That would be highly inconvenient for me."

"And it would be highly inconvenient for *me* to give up my entire weekend transporting Ro to San Francisco. It's way too expensive. I am also not prepared to leave him in your company overnight yet."

"Ladies . . ." Henry attempted to intervene.

"I will send a chauffeur for him." Miranda carried on talking.

"That's not good enough," Lizzie countered. "He's too young to be stuck in a car with a complete stranger for three or four hours."

"I'll fly him out."

"And expect him to be on a plane by himself?" Lizzie wasn't backing down. "That's not okay. If you want to see Roman, you're going to have to agree to come here and build up a relationship with him in an environment that he is familiar with before you get to take him anywhere without me."

Miranda turned to Henry. "I'm assuming you will be acting as Elizabeth's lawyer in this matter?"

"If she needs a lawyer, absolutely." Henry nodded.

"Hold on." Lizzie frowned. "What are you saying?"

"I was hoping we could resolve this amicably." Miranda rose to her feet. "But if you want to make this difficult, Elizabeth, I will consult my *own* lawyer, and make sure that my family are given access to their blood as they deserve."

"Two weeks ago you refused to believe Roman existed, and now you think you can bully me into agreeing to your terms?" Lizzie asked. "Come on, Miranda, let's be reasonable here. I *want* you to get to know your grandson. What the heck is *wrong* with you?"

Miranda ignored Lizzie and kept her gaze on Henry. "I will be in touch. Thank you for your time and attention."

She went out, slamming the door behind her as Lizzie stared helplessly at Henry.

"Can she really take me to court about this?"

"Unfortunately, yes, in California she can." Henry grimaced. "Now that we have established Roman's parentage, she can use the evidence in court to gain access to him."

"That's so not fair," Lizzie gasped. "She and Ray have done nothing to help or support me, and suddenly she gets to see my son just because she feels like it?"

"If she does take you to court, her previous neglect of you, and her son's lack of financial payments toward his own child, will certainly not reflect well on them. You are still Roman's mother, and the courts tend to favor the full-time caregiver." Henry sighed. "But you must prepare yourself for the fact that the court *might* allow her visitation rights."

"Not on her terms," Lizzie responded.

"We can offer our own solutions to such issues, and we will be heard. It's not as if she can throw any mud at you in return now, is it?"

Lizzie bit her lip. "CPS came to see me a couple of weeks ago. I think Coretta set them on me."

"Oh dear." Henry frowned. "Did they file a negative report against you?"

"Not that I know of. But I got the sense that they wouldn't be telling me anything anyway." Lizzie paused. "And there's been a private investigator following me around as well. I'm beginning to wonder whether that was Miranda's doing."

"You're suggesting it's possible she has been gathering evidence to use against you?" Henry frowned. "Which means she probably didn't intend to negotiate with you in good faith after all."

"Bingo," Lizzie said.

Henry rose and came around his desk to pat Lizzie on the shoulder. "Don't despair, my dear. We still have plenty of ammunition to fight back with. You are well-known and loved in this town. I'm certain we can gather lots of character witnesses to support your side of the story."

"But I don't want to fight," Lizzie whispered. "I just want my son to be happy."

"I am afraid that if you want to keep Mrs. Smith in line you're going to have to," Henry said gently.

Lizzie took Roman home in something of a daze as she tried to grapple with what had just happened in the lawyer's office. Had she been too unwilling to compromise with Miranda? If she'd agreed to her terms, would the specter of a court case not be hanging over her? But she couldn't have allowed Ro to go to San Francisco alone with a woman he'd never met. Miranda must have known that. Maybe she'd only said it to provoke a negative response from Lizzie as justification for taking her to court.

Her cell buzzed, and she took it out of her pocket, relieved to see that it was only her mom calling.

"Hey, where are you?"

"We're about fifty miles away. Your father has decided he's too tired to drive any farther so we'll see you in the morning. Is everything all right?"

Lizzie looked down at Roman's head. He was going on his first vacation with her parents, and they were all looking forward to it immensely. This wasn't the time to worry her mom about Miranda Smith. She could tell them all about it when they returned from their trip.

"Everything's good, Mom," Lizzie replied cheerfully. "We're both looking forward to seeing you very much."

Chapter Seventeen

Lizzie's mom, Angela, had not only brought new clothes for Ro, but for Lizzie, too, which meant she had a new dress to wear for the Turner wedding. It was strange having time to get ready and put on her makeup without being constantly interrupted by her son. She'd waved him off with her parents that morning, and was expecting him back in just under two weeks.

He'd seemed happy to go, his focus entirely on everything Disney. Lizzie had no doubt that if he did get tired and miss her, her mom would step up and give him all the comfort he needed. She'd already made sure to arrange several video calls so she could see how he was doing.

Her mom had met Adam briefly, and had cast speculative glances at Lizzie for the rest of the day until Lizzie had caved and told her they were going out together. After the usual mom-type warnings, Angela had been thrilled. She remembered Adam and the rest of his family from his high school days. Lizzie had also told her about Carlos's illness and the possible sale of the Cortez ranch.

Her cell buzzed, and she put down her mascara wand to check the message from Yvonne.

I'll pick you up in fifteen minutes, okay?

Lizzie sent her a smiley face and concentrated on finishing her makeup and arranging her hair up on the top of her head in an unstructured bun that allowed tendrils to frame her face.

She was ready to go when Yvonne arrived in Rio's pickup truck, which was huge enough to get all the essentials up to Morgan Ranch where the small wedding was being held.

"You look so pretty!" Yvonne said. "New dress?"

"My mom gave it to me." Lizzie did a little twirl, which allowed the chiffon overskirt to take flight around her. "Don't worry. I'll put an apron on before I start setting out the food."

"You'd better." Yvonne got back into the truck and Lizzie joined her. "It's not going to take us long to get set up. Avery's got most of the details covered. It's a relatively small wedding for Morgan Ranch to handle these days."

"She's a very efficient wedding coordinator," Lizzie agreed. "I'm going to watch her at work and see if I can learn anything to bring to managing the café."

"Good idea." Yvonne expertly backed up the truck. "The wedding starts at one so we've got plenty of time."

Half an hour before the outdoor ceremony was about to start, Lizzie ran into the bathroom at the Morgan ranch guest center. She took off her apron, made sure her dress was splatter-free, and reapplied her lipstick. Nate Turner and his best man were already pacing the hallways, and the guests were starting to arrive. There was no sign of the bride, but according to Avery everything was on schedule.

Lizzie checked her cell, but there was nothing from her parents. There was a message from Adam saying he'd just arrived and was wondering where she was. She gave one last pat to her hair and went outside into the bright sunlight, shading her eyes against the glare.

She spotted him immediately leaning up against the corner of the building. He was looking down at the wedding marquee, arms folded, white straw Stetson tipped low over his eyes, booted feet crossed at the ankles. She paused to admire his broad shoulders in his newly pressed blue check shirt, and appreciate his height and strength. He looked as solid and dependable as the Sierra Nevada mountain range and just as climbable.

Lizzie sucked in a breath. If she wasn't careful, she was going to fall in love with him. . . . And then where would she be?

He turned as if suddenly aware of her scrutiny, and looked her up and down, a smile illuminating the harsh contours of his face.

"Lizzie. You look beautiful."

"So do you."

He tugged at the neck of his shirt. "Ben put too much starch in it."

She walked around to look at him, and felt the stiff collar. "As soon as the ceremony is over, you can let it all hang out."

"I can't wait." His fingers trailed down from her shoulder to her hand. "You look good in that shade of blue."

"My mom said it's lilac, but I think it's more mauve." Lizzie smoothed her skirts. "What do you think?"

"Let's stick with blue," Adam said firmly, and placed her hand in the crook of his elbow. "Shall we get a seat?"

"Where's the rest of your family?" Lizzie asked as he maneuvered around the vases of fresh flowers and into the actual marquee.

"I have no idea. They're coming together. I had to go

and make sure the livestock at the Cortez place was okay, so I came on by myself."

He found two seats and waited for her to take hers before sitting beside her.

Lizzie pointed at his boots. "Are they new?"

"Yeah." He regarded his pointed toe, which was imprinted with black and white skulls. "My family bought them for me last Christmas. This is the first time I've dared put them on."

"They're awesome." Lizzie looked up as Nate Turner and his best man came striding down the aisle. Nate looked his usually calm self and was smiling and waving at the guests as he went past.

"No nerves there," Adam commented. "I was a nervous wreck when I married Louisa."

"I remember," Lizzie said. "At one point, I thought we'd be waving you two off to Vegas before your families would agree to letting you get married."

"They came around eventually," Adam agreed, and lapsed into silence again.

Lizzie saw Avery approaching, a clipboard in her hand, and an earpiece with a mic she was currently speaking into. She waved at Lizzie as she went by and kept going toward the entrance of the guest center. Lizzie wondered if Della and her family had arrived. From what she remembered, Della's father was dead so her mother was going to walk her up the aisle.

A whole bunch of Morgans and Millers filled up the two rows in front of Lizzie and Adam. They spent a few minutes catching up before being asked to stand to welcome the bride. When he stood, Adam took hold of Lizzie's hand and held it, his callused thumb rubbing circles around her palm.

A guitar started playing way off to the right and Adam went still.

"That sounds just like Travis Whitley," he murmured.

"Who's that?" Lizzie asked.

"Just one of the best country and western singers of this generation." Adam looked over the top of her head toward the small stage setup. "Jeez . . . that *is* Travis Whitley! How the hell did he end up singing at Nate Turner's wedding?"

"You'll have to ask Nate after the service," Lizzie suggested. She had no idea when Adam had developed a taste for country music. "Which, by the way, is just about to begin."

Della appeared, wearing a short full-skirted white dress with a hat and veil that looked like she came straight out of the 1950s. Her smile was for Nate alone, and Lizzie had to stifle the urge to cry.

A handkerchief appeared under her nose and she took it gratefully.

"I knew you'd cry," Adam murmured in her ear. "You always do."

"Thank you." Lizzie dabbed at her tears, gently blew her nose, and settled down to watch the wedding.

He'd told her that she looked beautiful, and she'd waved it off with a smile. But she really had taken his breath away. The softness of the silky dress and her pale, auburn curls made her look like she might fly away at any second. He didn't want her to leave him, and was determined to keep her firmly anchored to his side.

He hadn't been to a wedding for ages. Seeing his old school friend Nate get married had reminded him so much of his own wedding day. He and Louisa had been ridiculously young and so in love that they'd rushed through the whole thing just to get it done so that they could get on with their life together.

If he'd known their time together was going to be so short, he would've savored those vows, made sure she knew he meant them, enjoyed the moment more. But hindsight was a marvelous thing and he couldn't change jack about what had happened in the past. But he *could* put that knowledge to good use with Lizzie.

He went to look for her and found her on the edge of the small dance floor tapping her foot to the music. She'd always loved music. He remembered her and Louisa making up elaborate dance routines to all their favorite songs while they were supposedly watching him at football practice.

He really wished he could dance. . . .

His father was out there with Leanne, and they were laughing and chatting like old friends. The Morgan twins, HW and Ry, were dancing, too, swapping their partners like professionals.

A slower song came on just as Lizzie looked hopefully up at him. He resigned himself to his fate.

"Would you like to dance?" He nodded in the direction of the dance floor.

"You don't dance," Lizzie said. "You never did."

"I think I can manage this one." He tugged on her hand and pulled her gently into his arms. "I'll try not to step on your toes."

She laughed, and wrapped her arms around his neck, aligning herself against him, her head fitting nicely against his shoulder. He let out a long sigh as his body recognized hers and flowed to close the gap between them. The actual song made no impression on him because he was too busy enjoying having Lizzie in his arms. She felt right there—as if suddenly all the pieces of their particular puzzle made sense.

"This is nice," Lizzie murmured eventually.

"Mmm." He breathed in the essence of her and kissed the top of her head. If it was up to him, he could stay there all night, swaying with her and holding her close. Unfortunately, he caught his brother Ben's eye who gave him an enthusiastic thumbs-up. Changing direction, Adam steered Lizzie off the dance floor and into the lengthening shadows between the old barn and the new guest center. The smell of warm straw mingled with the sweetness of the wedding flowers in the sultry night air.

"Lizzie?" Adam put his finger under her chin, raising her gaze to meet his. "May I kiss you?"

"Yes, please." she whispered, and went up on tiptoe to wrap one hand around his neck. Not that she needed to keep hold of him. He had no intention of going anywhere for quite a while. He licked a line along the seam of her lips, and she opened her mouth, letting him deep inside. She shivered, and pressed closer as he luxuriated in kissing her, relearning her taste, the things she liked, and the things she loved, as his hands roamed unhurriedly over her body.

Time was a precious thing to him these days and he wasn't going to waste a second of it.

Eventually, Lizzie drew back, her gaze serious, her mouth already lush from his kisses, which made him want even more.

"Would you like to come home with me?" Lizzie asked.

He must have hesitated for a second too long because she attempted to retract her offer. "Sorry, that was presumptuous of me. I didn't think—"

He kissed her again, this time quickly and urgently. "I'd love to."

"Okay." She smiled. "I just need to tell Yvonne that you're giving me a ride home, and get my things."

He nodded. "I'll meet you in the lower parking lot, okay?"

After texting Ben, Adam walked down to the overflow lot below the barn. He knew that if he went home with Lizzie, they might have sex. Was he prepared for that? His body, long starved of physical affection, was totally on board with it. His conscience? Not quite so much.

None of which was Lizzie's fault. It was all on him. He unlocked his truck and stuck the keys in the ignition before returning to stand outside. It was almost dark and pinpricks of starlight were appearing in the vastness of the sky, reminding him that his life and losses were a very small part in a very big universe.

He firmly reminded himself that they didn't have to have sex. Lizzie was his friend, and they were perfectly capable of having a reasonable discussion about the matter without either of them getting offended. He shouldn't get too cocky. Lizzie might not want him that way either. There really was no pressure on either of them.

Her apartment was still warm from the heat of the sun and strangely quiet without the presence of Roman. Adam took off his hat and stepped into the kitchen, which was striped with silver shadows from the full moon. Lizzie shut and locked the door behind them.

She came toward him and smiled. "Would you like coffee? I—"

He reached out, pulled her into his arms, and kissed her, making her gasp his name. He needed to taste her, feel her, and *be* with her.

"Adam . . ." She moaned as he kissed his way down her throat, one hand cupping her rounded ass. "God—"

He picked her up and walked through to her bedroom, which was also bathed in moonlight, and laid her gently on the bed. At least a dozen frilly cushions slid off the other side of the bed and onto the rug. Holding her gaze, he stripped, flinging his clothes to the floor until he was buck naked.

"Oh . . ." She sighed and licked her lips. "You are so perfect."

"Yeah?" He climbed onto the bottom of the bed and set his hands on her ankles. "Not half as perfect as you are." He kissed his way up to her knees and crouched between them, easing her thighs apart to reveal the soft blue lace of her panties.

She smelled like she wanted him, and it made him dizzy with need.

"I need to taste you," he said hoarsely, and hooked a finger into her panties, drawing them down her legs to join his clothes on the floor. He parted her with his thumbs and set his mouth on her most intimate flesh, licking and teasing her as she bucked against his hand. He swirled the tip of his tongue around her swollen bud until it throbbed, and plunged two fingers deep inside her.

She moaned his name, her hand tangling in his hair, her nails digging into his scalp as she climaxed against his mouth. He stayed where he was lapping at her, crooning to her, as she slowly came down from her sexual high.

So much for sensibly talking it out and taking his time. . . .

But he might not have time. They could both be dead tomorrow.

Adam eased himself forward until he could kiss Lizzie's mouth, and helped her out of her dress and bra. He cupped her breasts, tracing the hard calluses of his fingers over her already-tight nipples until her breath shortened, and he sucked her into his mouth. As he moved over her, his dick pressed against her stomach, sliding through his own slick need.

"Do you want me?" Adam murmured against her throat as he came up for air.

"Yes." She pointed toward her bedside drawer. "There are condoms in there."

He was up and moving, switching on the lamp before she'd even finished speaking, and jerked open the drawer only to stop short.

"You sure about that?"

Lizzie sat bolt upright, her blush spreading down from her cheeks to her bosom. "Not *that* drawer!"

He considered the pink vibrator he'd revealed in the drawer. "I'm bigger."

"Don't even go there!" She flapped a hand at him. "Try the second drawer."

"And better." He smiled at her as he did what she asked. "I can outlast any batteries. I'll prove it to you, okay?"

"You will not." She flopped back down on the pillows and covered her eyes. "Because I'm about to die of embarrassment."

"Don't do that," Adam said as he opened the foil packet and covered himself. "And there's nothing to be ashamed of. My right hand's gotten a good workout over the years."

Lizzie made an inarticulate sound as he knelt between her spread thighs and readied himself.

"Lizzie."

She peered at him through her fingers, her eyes widening as he eased the first inch of his cock inside her, and he made himself slow down.

"You *are* big," Lizzie breathed.

"Yeah." He held still, waiting for permission to keep going. "Just like the rest of me." He rocked his hips and she took more, her brow furrowed as if she was working on a complicated math problem.

"You good?" Adam managed the words through clenched teeth as his body responded to the intimate clasp of hers.

"Mmm." She grabbed hold of his shoulders, changing the angle. He slid deep, making her gasp. "Oh."

He held still as she climaxed, resisting the urge to thrust, counting backward in his head, imagining cold showers and ice floes, which didn't help with the heat of her, or with the power of her demanding flesh.

He was fully inside her now; her breasts were against his chest and her feet were climbing the sides of his thighs. He let himself enjoy being held so completely in the cradle of her body and the shelter of her arms.

"Adam?" she whispered, and he reluctantly opened his eyes.

"Yeah?"

"Are *you* okay?"

He stared down into her beautiful face. How to tell her that he was more okay than he'd been in years? Perhaps, knowing his conversational limitations, the best way to get that across was to show her.

He rolled his hips, gathering her in his arms, and then retreated until he found a rhythm that satisfied them both. He kissed her mouth, her throat, his teeth grazing her skin as the need to move faster, harder, to claim every inch of her roared through him.

"Ah . . . God." Adam climaxed, and collapsed over Lizzie like a felled tree. "That was . . ."

It was her turn to smooth his hair and whisper nonsense in his ear until he slowly recovered his senses and rolled onto his back. He stared up at the ceiling, one hand behind his head, and let himself luxuriate in the slow buzz of his satisfied body.

Eventually, he turned to Lizzie, who was watching him carefully. Did she think he was going to get up and leave her even now? He wrapped an arm around her shoulders and urged her closer until she was half across his body.

"Did I squash you?"

"I'm still breathing." She kissed his chest, her fingers moving through the dark hair. "Do you have to rush off, or can you stay and sleep for a while?"

He heard it then, that note of uncertainty, like she was still on the outside looking in.

"I'm not going anywhere." He kissed her slowly. "If you're okay with that." He glanced ruefully at the mattress. "I do take up a lot of space."

"Don't worry. I'm used to Roman coming in here. He's a terrible cover hog."

"Too hot for covers," Adam commented. "I'm just going to use the bathroom, and I'll be right back."

A while later, Lizzie woke up to a strange buzzing sound in her ear. It took her a few moments to realize she was draped over Adam like a blanket, and that he was gently snoring. She smiled against his muscled chest and breathed him in. Even without his clothes, he still smelled of leather, hay, and the great outdoors, as if they were so much a part of who he was that they never left him.

She got up to use the bathroom and, out of habit, stuck her head into Roman's bedroom even though she knew he wasn't there. She went through to the kitchen to get a drink of water, and paused by the window to look down at the quiet moonlit town. Without the traffic, it looked very much as it must have done over a hundred years ago when it was founded. She half expected a posse to come around the corner and swagger up to the old saloon in Hayes Hotel.

Adam Miller was in her bed, and she still couldn't quite believe he was there. . . .

But neither of them could claim that this time had been a mistake, or an aberration, or a moment of shared grief. She'd asked, he'd agreed, and she wouldn't regret that. Except that now she couldn't pretend she hadn't developed feelings for him. Did he feel the same? *Could* he? Some small part of her was afraid to ask. The last time she'd been this close to him he'd walked away, and hardly spoken to her for years.

With a sigh, Lizzie went back into the bedroom, pausing at the door to appreciate the sight of a naked Adam stretched out on her sheets. She wanted to be with him, to touch him and have him touch her.

She climbed in beside him, and he moved over to accommodate her, curling his big, hard body around her back, his arms around her hips and breasts.

"Mmm . . ." He murmured in his sleep. "Nice."

She smiled to herself as his touch became more purposeful, and deliberately pressed her butt back against his groin.

"God, Louisa, honey, you'll wear me out."

Lizzie froze and then gently eased herself out of his arms. She grabbed her robe again and went through into the kitchen. She was sitting on the couch, her arms wrapped tightly around her knees, when she sensed him come into the room.

She waited in silence as he crouched on the floor in front of her, his gaze steady.

"I didn't mean to say that."

She tried to tell him that it didn't matter. Somehow the words stuck in her throat, and she could only look helplessly back at him.

He wrapped a hand around her ankle. "Lizzie, I was half asleep. I just—" He sighed. "Didn't think."

This time she managed an awkward nod.

"It's the first time I've ever spent the night with someone other than Louisa." Adam kept talking, his voice roughened with sleep. "I woke up feeling great, and my mind just . . . took me back to her."

"Of course it did," Lizzie said woodenly.

"I'm sorry."

"Was that what you were thinking the whole time?" Lizzie couldn't believe she'd actually spoken her worst fear out loud. "Were you imagining I was Louisa?"

"*No.*" He met her gaze head-on, his gray eyes clear. "I knew it was you. I wanted *you.*"

She let that sink in, wondered desperately if it was enough, and if she could believe him and live with it.

"Come back to bed." Adam stroked his strong fingers over her skin. "Let me prove it to you. I'll keep my goddamn eyes open the whole time I swear it. *Please.*"

"You don't have to convince me of anything, okay?" Lizzie finally found the strength to answer him. "You don't have to stay either, if you don't want to."

She got up, gathered her robe around her, and went through to her bedroom where she spent a moment folding his clothes before hanging her dress in the closet.

"Lizzie, I don't want to go."

She closed her eyes and didn't turn around to where he stood at the door. Instead, she placed his clothing carefully on the top of her chest of drawers. Could she accept that he'd always love Louisa, and that she could never have that? Could she accept what he was offering her right now? Friendship, support, *sex?*

She contemplated telling him to leave. But, she couldn't bear the thought of actually doing it, which left her at the acceptance phase. Stripping off her robe, she walked over to Adam, took his hand, and led him toward her bed. He sank down onto the mattress, drew her into his lap, and wrapped his arms around her, his whole body shaking.

"Lizzie," he said, low and fierce. "Please."

She rested her cheek against his broad shoulder. She didn't want to fight with him right now.

Adam kissed Lizzie, gathering fistfuls of her hair to hold her mouth pinned against his. Waking up properly, realizing what the hell he'd said, had propelled him out of bed to find her, and make her understand. He kissed her again, his hands roaming her body, pressing her against him, making sure she felt every urgent inch of his need.

She sighed into his mouth, and relaxed against him, all the tension evaporating, which made his desire even more rampant. He needed her to see him, feel him, and want *him.* The moment when she'd left him alone in the bed had sucked all the air out of his lungs. She'd made him come alive again, and he didn't want to go back down into the pit.

"Lizzie . . ." He murmured her name again as he one-handedly opened a condom wrapper and hurriedly covered himself. "Let me . . ."

She went up on her knees, her thighs spread. He gently lowered her down onto his shaft, loving the way her breasts slid past his face, and into his waiting hands. He cupped them, stroking her nipples with his thumbs as she shivered and rocked over him.

She nipped his lip, and he opened his mouth for her, letting her dictate the pace of their lovemaking, willing to do so much more if she'd just forgive him. He spread his fingers over her ass, helping her move on him until he curled his hand over her hip, and played with her bud, driving her ever higher.

She closed her eyes when she climaxed, but he kept looking at her, enthralled at the expression of bliss on her face as she threw back her head and squeezed his cock so hard he prayed it wouldn't break. Eventually, he couldn't resist rolling her onto her back, hooking her knees over his elbows, and rocking into her until he forgot his own name, let alone hers.

Damn, it was scary feeling like this, but it was better than feeling nothing at all. He thrust deep and held still.

"Lizzie, look at me."

She slowly opened her eyes and he held her gaze before pushing into her one last time and climaxing. He let her see her power over him, his weakness, and his complete vulnerability while he came deep inside her. She didn't look away, and he was glad of it.

This time, he managed not to collapse over her, but eased away to deal with the protection, and then came back to bed. She was already half asleep as he took her in his arms, her body pliant and supple with pleasure.

"I don't suppose you have any duct tape around here do you?" Adam asked softly.

"No, why? You're not thinking of tying me up, or anything kinky, are you?"

"Not tonight." He paused to kiss the top of her head. "I was thinking more of my big mouth."

She reached back to pat his cheek. "It's okay. I'd rather you put your mouth to other uses."

"Good to know." With a sigh of deep thankfulness, Adam let out a long, contented sigh and nuzzled her neck. "Sleep tight, Lizzie. Thanks for everything."

* * *

Adam paused, boots in hand at the door of the mudroom. He'd parked his truck away from the house so as not to disturb anyone, and was now intent on getting to his bedroom without anyone seeing him. The last thing he needed right now was an interrogation from one of his brothers. It was almost four in the morning, and he'd have to get up by six. But he needed to sleep in his own bed, to think about the night he'd just shared with Lizzie, to come to terms with it in his own way.

He was just about to move off when he heard a low laugh, and froze as the door of his father's bedroom started to open. He backed up until he was deep in the shadows, and watched openmouthed as Leanne came creeping out, her disheveled hair down around her shoulders, and a big smile on her face. Adam's dad followed her out, wearing only his boxers, and whispered something that made her chuckle and swat his rear.

They went into the kitchen, giving Adam the opportunity to run in the other direction. He lay down on his bed and put his hands over his eyes, feeling like a horrified teenager wishing he hadn't seen what his parents had obviously been up to.

Whatever his relationship with his mother, he suspected that he hadn't seen the last of her and, that even when she left, she'd definitely be back. Rolling over, he determinedly closed his eyes. If he could deal with having a new sexual relationship with Lizzie, he could—

"Nope," Adam muttered. "Actually, I can't deal with that yet, so I'm just going to pretend I didn't see a thing."

Chapter Eighteen

When Lizzie woke up there was a note from Adam on her pillow explaining that he had to get back to the ranch for his morning chores, and that he'd call her later. Seeing as it was Sunday, and she didn't have to work, she contemplated the unusual notion of staying in bed for a while.

Her body ached in some unusual places, and the idea of a hot, uninterrupted bath without Roman's bubbles and shrieking was highly motivational. She got up and made the bed, making sure she didn't lose Adam's note in the pillows. His handwriting was as bold and strong as he was, and he wasn't one to waste words on silly declarations of love.

She left the note on the kitchen countertop, put on the coffeemaker, and took her bath in luxurious silence. By the time she'd washed her hair, dressed, and had her coffee, her mom had texted to say they were settled in Anaheim, and that Roman was raring to go and explore the park.

Lizzie contemplated what to do with her day. She could just sit at home, read a book, and laze around on the couch. The idea of having all that time to herself felt quite decadent. She fixed herself two croissants and ate every bit.

Her cell buzzed. She unplugged it from the charger and read the text message from Yvonne.

Sorry to disrupt your Sunday, but thought you might like to know that Rio's flying into the Morgan ranch airstrip with Carlos and Ines. He'll be here in about two hours.

Lizzie texted back. If you like, I can go up there and make sure everything's dusted down and ready to receive them.

Are you sure you're okay to do that? I'm at Morgan Ranch dealing with a celebratory anniversary lunch involving lots of cake. I can't get away until three at the earliest. Rio kind of sprung this on me. LOL.

I'm happy to help out. Have you told Adam? Lizzie asked.

I haven't, but I will. I'll probably see you there later, okay? Text me if you need anything, or ask Rio. x.

Lizzie immediately went to her freezer, pulled out frozen lasagna, and a loaf of Yvonne's bread, and set them on the countertop. Ines probably wouldn't want to be cooking the moment she arrived back home. Lizzie also found a half gallon of milk and added that to the pile.

It was already warm so she decided to stick to her denim skirt and T-shirt. She added sturdy cowboy boots to avoid the worst the ranch had to offer. She braided her hair, lamenting the loss of her wedding curls, and found her battered cowboy hat to shade her face from the sun.

Her old car was hot from sitting in the sun at the back of the building. She left the windows down as she backed out of her parking space. Because her landlord was a mechanic, and a really decent guy, her car drove way better than it looked.

She put in an old CD and sang along to various songs, as she drove up to the Cortez ranch. She smiled, remembering Adam's starstruck face when he'd come face-to-face with his idol Travis Whitley and been offered a cordial handshake and an autograph.

The gates were already unlocked so she drove through them without stopping. When she pulled up in front of the house, Adam's truck was already there. For a moment, she stayed in the car, suddenly shy about seeing him again.

Would he be pleased to see her? Or would he have retreated back to that place where she couldn't reach him?

Even as she pondered her next move, Adam came out of the barn and looked over at her car. His slow smile did something weird to her heart, making her gulp in air as he approached her vehicle.

"Hey."

She scrambled to get out of the car. "Hey, yourself. Did Yvonne text you?"

"She did, but I'd already heard from Rio and Ines." He paused. "What brings you out here?"

Lizzie's smile faltered. "Don't worry. I'm not stalking you or anything. Yvonne can't get here until three. I offered to give the house a quick clean and guessed that Ines might need something for dinner, so I brought her lasagna." She went around to the trunk of her car, avoiding where he was standing, and opened it with a jerk. "There's no need to hang around. I won't get in your way."

"Lizzie."

She avoided his gaze as she struggled to get a hold of the largest of the boxes. A second later, he'd whisked it out of her grasp and was walking toward the house. She grabbed the remaining items and followed him inside, putting everything down on the kitchen table. She turned and collided with a wall of warm, muscled man, and had to grab hold of his T-shirt.

He bent his head and kissed her with a thoroughness that made her go all quiet inside. When he finally raised his head, he framed her face with his large hands and looked down at her.

"What's wrong?"

"You didn't look particularly pleased to see me," Lizzie blurted out.

"I was just surprised." He leaned in to kiss her throat, making her shiver as his teeth grazed her skin. "I was going to text you to see if you'd like to come out and help. I thought you'd think I was being too pushy. That you'd probably be sick of the sight of me."

"Pushy?" Lizzie queried. "If there is an opposite of pushy that would be you. I was worried that you'd changed your mind about being with me at all."

"I'm not a stupid, grieving twenty-one-year-old anymore, and I'm not planning on going anywhere." Adam cleared his throat. "I'd like you to believe that."

"I'm just . . . not used to guys choosing to hang around," Lizzie confessed.

"I can see why." Adam gathered her close again. "How about we promise to try and keep talking to each other like reasonable human beings? I'm going to say stupid shit sometimes, and maybe you will, too, but if we're communicating . . . ? We can sort it out."

"I'd like that," Lizzie agreed.

"Then problem solved." He kissed her nose. "I've got to get on. Rio said he's about an hour away."

Adam lifted Carlos out of the back of Rio's truck and smiled down at him. Even swaddled in blankets, the man barely weighed more than Roman. His face had sunk in on itself, revealing high cheekbones under the tautness of his skin.

"Nearly home," Adam said.

"*Graças a Deus,*" Carlos whispered. "Thank God."

"Do you want to go straight to bed? Or do you want to sit in your chair?" Adam asked as he bent his head to get through the door.

"Bed, please. I'm exhausted." Carlos tried to smile at Ines, Rio, and Lizzie who had gathered around him. "*Obrigado.*"

Rio patted his shoulder. "*Va com Deus,* my friend. Take care. I'll speak to you when you feel more up to it."

Ines went ahead of Adam to open the door into the bedroom. "You can put him here. Lizzie said she changed the sheets."

Adam gently set Carlos down, helped Ines arrange the pillows behind his head, and pulled up the cotton sheet. The older man was already half asleep when they tiptoed out of the room.

"Thank you." Ines patted Adam's arm. "Everyone is being so kind."

"Carlos deserves it."

Adam walked back into the kitchen where Rio and Lizzie were sitting at the table having coffee. Rio immediately stood up and for the first time Adam really took in that he was wearing a smart, probably custom-made suit, and well-polished shoes. He looked like an all-high-powered businessman, nothing like a world champion bull rider.

"I'm going to collect the pilot and crew. They're staying over at Hayes Hotel until tomorrow when they'll take me on to Boston." Rio smiled at Ines. "I'll call you tomorrow to see how Carlos is doing."

"That would be lovely." Ines came around the table to

give Rio a big hug. She murmured something in Portuguese that made him blush.

Adam waited as Rio said his final good-byes before walking him to his truck, and shook his hand.

"Thanks for bringing Carlos home."

Rio shrugged as he opened the driver's door. "It was the least I could do. He's dying, Adam. His last wish was to come back to the place he loved."

Adam fought a sudden and completely unexpected wave of emotion. Opening himself up to his feelings was way harder than he had anticipated. "Yeah. I guessed as much. Did they say how much time he has left?"

"Days, weeks, not long. But both he and Ines have made their peace with it."

Adam had never made his peace with Louisa's death. He wondered if he ever would.

"They are still happy for me to buy the ranch." Rio carried on talking. "The only question I have, Is that okay with you? Because technically, as Louisa's husband, you could block the sale quite easily."

Adam considered that. He was fairly certain that Rio would not only deal honorably with Carlos, but that he would provide Ines with enough capital to see her through to the end of her own life in great style and comfort. That was way more important than anything else.

"I think it's up to Carlos and Ines," Adam said finally. "It wouldn't be easy trying to help out my dad and run this place. I've been doing that for the past few weeks, and it's been a real stretch."

"Ines is going to stay here with us," Rio said. "Both Yvonne and I are very fond of her. I promise that we will treat her as part of our family."

"That's great." Adam nodded as his feelings threatened to choke him again. "She deserves to be loved."

"Then all is good." Rio patted his arm. "I'll speak to you soon, my friend."

Adam stood for a long moment watching Rio's truck drive away before he retraced his steps into the house.

Ines and Lizzie were chatting as they sat at the kitchen table drinking coffee. Adam paused in the doorway to study them, and to make sure Lizzie wouldn't notice how emotional he was.

She glanced up and immediately came over to his side, taking his hand in hers. So much for fooling her.

"Would you like some coffee, Adam? Ines is going to put the lasagna I brought in the oven. She asked if we'd both like to stay and have dinner with her."

He found a smile somewhere and gently disengaged his hand from hers. "That sounds great."

He sat quietly, letting Ines and Lizzie do most of the talking, checked in on Carlos, and sent a text to Dr. Tio to let him know his patient was back in town. When the lasagna was ready, he ate a large portion of it, drank his iced tea, and managed to reply to every question Ines asked him about the ranch and his family without betraying any apparent interest in Lizzie.

Eventually, Lizzie checked the time and turned to Ines. "I'm going to have to go soon—unless you want me to stay the night and help out with Carlos?"

"I'd rather do that myself." Ines hugged her. "You have been so kind and helpful." She smiled at Adam. "Hasn't she?"

"She's a good person," Adam confirmed.

Lizzie wasn't looking at him as she searched for her purse and car keys and his gut knotted. He waited until Ines went to check on Carlos and stood up.

"You okay?"

"I'm good." She gathered up her stuff. "I promised Ro I'd FaceTime with him tonight, so I've got to be home in half an hour."

"Would you like me to come over after I've finished up here?" Adam asked.

"If it fits in with your plans, sure."

He regarded her steadily. "Are you mad at me?"

She held his gaze. "I thought you said we were a couple?"

"We are."

"Then why don't you want Ines to know that? You've spent the whole afternoon avoiding talking about me or touching me."

Adam went quiet. "That's different."

"In what way?" Lizzie kept her voice low and pleasant.

"Because she's got a lot on her plate right now. I don't think she needs to hear—"

"Her son-in-law is seeing another woman?"

"Yeah. That. Exactly," Adam said, fisting his hand at his side. "I will tell her. I just want to find the best time to do it."

To his surprise, Lizzie just chuckled and shook her head. "Sometimes men are so dense." She walked over and kissed his cheek. "Come over if you like. I'd love to see you."

She disappeared out of the door, leaving him puzzling over her last comments. At least she hadn't gotten mad at him. That was progress.

Ines came in and helped herself to more coffee. "Carlos has taken his pain pills. He'll sleep for at least eight hours. Dr. Tio has arranged for someone to come and help me bathe him if I need it."

"I could do that," Adam offered.

She sat next to him and patted his hand. "I know you could, but you've already been through this once with Louisa. I don't expect you to do it again."

"At least I'd know what I was doing this time," Adam murmured. "Just call me if you need me for anything, okay? Dad understands."

"I will." Her smile was sweet. "It was so kind of Rio to bring Carlos home. I will never forget it."

"Are you still okay with Rio buying the ranch?" Adam asked.

"Yes." She nodded decisively. "I think he will take great care of the place and love it as much as Carlos and I have." She looked closely at him. "Are *you* okay with it? I know we talked about you buying us out early, but—"

"I'm good with whatever you want," Adam said firmly. "I have no right to anything here."

Ines cupped his cheek. "You are still our heir."

"It's all good." Adam stirred uneasily in his seat. "We don't need to talk about that right now."

"As you wish." Ines sat back and sipped her coffee. "We should talk about somcthing more pleasant. Lizzie Taylor is such a lovely young woman, isn't she?"

Adam nodded cautiously. "Yes."

Ines smiled at him. "It's all right, Adam. I'm not going to shout at you."

"For what?"

"Falling in love with Lizzie."

Adam opened and closed his mouth, and then just stared at her until she chuckled.

"Oh my goodness, do you think I'm blind? You can't keep your eyes off her." Her expression sobered, and she again reached for his hand. "It's all right, Adam. Louisa would be the first person cheering you on. She loved

Lizzie and she loved you. She'd never have wanted you to spend the rest of your life alone."

Adam swallowed hard. "Thank you," he said gruffly. "I wasn't sure—"

"Whether I'd notice?" Ines rolled her eyes. "I've seen you in love before, Adam Miller. It's hard to mistake the signs."

"We're definitely seeing each other," Adam confirmed. "As to the rest of it . . ." His voice trailed off. *Was* he in love with Lizzie? "We'll see how it goes."

Lizzie checked her phone, and when she saw the text from Adam, she looked out of her window to discover his truck had pulled into the parking lot behind her apartment. She ran down the stairs to open the lower door and waited for him to emerge from the darkness.

"Hey." She smiled at him as he approached. "Come on in."

He followed her up the stairs and into the kitchen where she immediately put on a fresh pot of coffee.

"How was Carlos when you left?" Lizzie asked as she spooned in the coffee and turned the machine on.

Adam didn't say anything. She turned to face him, one eyebrow raised, to find he was looking at her as if he'd never seen her before.

"Is everything okay?"

He blinked and slowly rubbed his hand over his stubbled chin and mouth. "Yeah."

"You sure?"

He set his Stetson down on the countertop and took off his jacket. "Yeah."

"Wow, you're chatty tonight." Lizzie found cream in the refrigerator and set out two clean mugs. "Roman's having a great time, by the way."

"That's good to hear." He paused. "Are you missing him?"

"A lot," Lizzie confessed. "It's the first time he's ever been away from me for this long."

"Ines said she knew," Adam said.

"That we were dating?" Lizzie asked. "That's definitely the impression I got from all the hints she was dropping." She met his gaze. "Did she say something to you then?"

"She told me she was okay with it."

"Good." Lizzie contemplated his unsmiling face. "Do you have a problem with her knowing or something? Because you sure don't look happy right now."

"I'm . . . glad that it's out in the open."

"You still don't sound convinced." Lizzie turned and checked the coffee just to avoid looking at him.

"I'm sorry, I've just got a lot of my mind." Adam sighed. "Rio asked me if I was still okay with him buying the ranch even though Carlos doesn't need the money for the cancer specialist."

Lizzie still wasn't convinced he was being straight with her about what Ines had said, but she understood his other worries. To be honest, she wasn't sure she wanted a discussion about how *either* of them were feeling right now about their new relationship.

"And are you okay about it?" Lizzie asked.

"I can't run two ranches. Keeping the Cortez ranch would be selfish in many ways. Rio and Yvonne will take great care of Ines when Carlos is gone and, not to be crass, but I'm still in their will. Rio's got the money to keep the place looking nice and running well right now."

Adam looked down at his boots as though he was inspecting them for dirt. "But, yeah, it was still hard to let it go—emotionally I mean. Because of Louisa."

Lizzie stared at him openmouthed. "Did you just voluntarily express your innermost feelings to me?"

He raised his head. "I suppose I did." A reluctant smile touched his hard mouth. "I think I need to sit down."

Lizzie went over and put her hands on his broad shoulders. "It's not like the ranch is going to strangers. You can still visit."

"Louisa and I spent so much time there even before we were married," Adam said. "Carlos was always way nicer to me than my own dad, and Ines was just the kind of mom I was missing."

"They were very kind to me, too," Lizzie agreed.

"Of course, you were there almost as much as I was." Adam looked down at her. "Probably more, seeing as I was never invited to the sleepovers."

She kissed his cheek. "We spent most of the time talking about you."

"*Really?*" He smiled properly for the first time.

"Well, Louisa did. I was too busy wondering what on earth she saw in you." Lizzie gasped as he lifted her off her feet and tossed her over his shoulder without even breaking a sweat. "What are you *doing?*"

"Taking you to bed."

"What about the coffee?"

"It can wait."

"Adam Miller . . ."

He gently patted her butt. "Consider it payback for all the sass."

"Sass?"

"You know what I'm talking about, Miss Sweet Cheeks."

Lizzie smiled against his back as he dumped her on her bed, and tried to look like she was full of remorse.

"My vibrator is way less bossy than you are."

"Yeah?" He took off his belt, slowly unzipped his jeans to display the growing bulge in his cotton boxers, and knelt in front of her on the bed. "But can you do this to it?"

Lizzie rolled her eyes as he hooked a finger in the top of his boxers and urged her even closer. His breath hitched as she dropped a kiss on his hard shaft.

"I *could,* but it wouldn't taste as good as you do."

With a groan, he braced one hand on the headboard behind her and leaned into her touch.

"Nothing else to say?" Lizzie demanded as she slowly licked him like an ice cream cone.

"Not with my most precious possession in your sights, no," Adam murmured.

"Good." Lizzie winked, and then sucked him deep into her mouth until he stopped talking completely.

Chapter Nineteen

"Ms. Taylor?"

"Yes, right here."

Lizzie looked up as a delivery guy came up to the counter, and offered her a slim, sealed envelope she had to sign for.

"Thanks."

"You're welcome. Have a great day."

Seeing as there was no one in the café who needed her immediate attention, Lizzie went back into the kitchen to open the envelope and read the single sheet.

"Wow." She breathed out slowly through her nose. "Miranda doesn't waste any time, does she?"

Yvonne looked up from frosting a cake. "What's she done now?"

"It's from the Mono County family court. She's petitioning for visitation rights. We will be assigned a court mediator to see if we can come to an agreement." Lizzie stared blindly out at the back window.

"May I ask you something?"

"Of course." Lizzie turned automatically back to Yvonne.

"What does Ray think of all this?"

"I don't know. I assume that he's in on it otherwise

Miranda wouldn't have gotten his consent to do the DNA test."

"She could've gotten the DNA some other way," Yvonne suggested.

Lizzie sat down at the table opposite her friend and put the letter in her apron pocket. "Are you suggesting I contact him myself? What good would that do?"

"Well, if he doesn't know what's going on, he might like to. If he *does,* maybe you'll be able to have a more reasonable conversation with him than with his mother."

"I'm not sure about that," Lizzie said doubtfully. "God knows what will come out of my mouth if I actually get to see him again. And I don't know how to contact him anyway."

"Henry might have that information. If he's acting as your lawyer, he might be able to make the connection for you."

"I hadn't thought of that." Lizzie contemplated Yvonne admiringly.

Her friend shrugged. "I've been dealing with the courts for years because of my ex. I know way more about the legal systems in France and the USA than I ever wanted to."

"That's a great idea. I'll go and talk to Henry during my lunch break," Lizzie said, her spirits marginally rising. "If he has Ray's address, I'll ask him to contact him for me."

"You can go now, if you want to. There's no one around." Yvonne went back to her frosting. "The rain will keep the tourists and the locals away from the café for at least the next hour or so."

Lizzie wiped her mouth with her napkin and smiled over at Adam. Her hair was tied back in a ponytail and she wore a red T-shirt with her usual jeans. "Henry says he'll reply on my behalf, and set up the initial meeting, which will probably be at the Bridgeport courthouse. If it isn't there, it'll be at Mammoth."

Adam considered her carefully. He'd brought her out for dinner at the Red Dragon, and although she was acting as though she didn't have a care in the world he wasn't totally convinced.

"You'll have to take time off work," Adam said neutrally.

"I know." She grimaced. "Which sucks because Yvonne and I were hoping I could start being more managerial as soon as possible."

"I'm sure she'll understand." He sipped his beer. "Did Henry say anything else?"

"Not really." She lowered her gaze to her food and started picking at the chicken. "I did ask him to confirm whether Ray is also petitioning for his rights, or whether it's just Miranda."

Adam eased back in his seat, one hand grasping his beer bottle. "If Ray doesn't know, aren't you risking drawing his attention to you and Roman?"

"It was his DNA, Adam. Either Miranda obtained that without his consent, or he knows perfectly well what's going on, and is prepared to let his mommy handle it for him."

Adam winced. "Neither scenario makes him look good."

"True." Lizzie dipped one of her fries in the ketchup and licked it clean, which almost diverted Adam's attention from what she was and wasn't telling him. "He's a minor celebrity so maybe he just wants to stay as far away from this as possible."

"Is he married?" Adam asked.

"Almost." Lizzie blushed. "I know he just got engaged because I occasionally Google his ass just to keep track of him."

"Does he have other kids?"

"Not that I know of." Lizzie ate another fry and then licked her lips. "Mmm . . . Bella is *such* a good cook."

The thought of Lizzie contacting Ray, let alone talking to him, made Adam uncomfortable. He sternly reminded himself he had no right to feel like that, and that what Lizzie needed right now was for him to support her as a friend. She was perfectly capable of dealing with her own shit. It was hard to remain noncommittal when he wanted to snatch her up and growl at any other man who dared try to mess with her again.

"Henry's going to contact him, so it's not like I have to get involved. I bet Ray won't want to have anything to do with me."

"But if he wants to see Roman, you're going to have to see him at some point," Adam reminded her.

"I suppose so." She grimaced. "The thing is, I have to deal with this. I *want* Roman to get to know the other side of his family, but on *my* terms. They don't know him, and I'm not going to let him be scared or afraid. If I don't turn up at the hearing, they'll be doing all the arguing, and I'll be on the back foot before we even start."

It all sounded very reasonable but Adam still didn't like it. He glanced up as the door into the bar opened, and Leanne came in with his father.

"Jeez, no," Adam muttered.

"What's up?" Lizzie turned around and spotted Leanne. "Do you want me to call them over?"

"No, thanks. I'm not into double dating with my folks." He slid farther into the booth until he was against the wall, and Lizzie followed his example. "The other night, when I got home late? I caught them in bed together."

Lizzie's mouth formed a perfect O. "Like *literally?*"

"No, thank God, or I would've gone blind. Leanne was creeping out of Dad's bedroom."

"Maybe they'd just been chatting?" Lizzie said hopefully.

"Nope. They were way too flushed, happy, and handsy for that." Adam shuddered.

"But doesn't Leanne have a life and family back in New York?" Lizzie asked.

"So she says."

"Then maybe it was just a fling for old times' sake."

Adam blinked hard. "Stop making it worse."

"I think it's nice." Lizzie pushed her plate away and put her silverware neatly on top with her balled-up paper napkin.

"*Nice?*" Adam stared at her. "Lizzie, they fought so hard, they nearly burned the ranch down, they traumatized the entire family, and now they get to have sex and *enjoy* it?"

"You sound very judgmental, Adam."

"I think I have a right to be. This is my parents we're talking about." He folded his arms over his chest.

"They are still human beings with needs." She stared right back at him, her voice calm. "Maybe Leanne will decide to come back here for good."

Adam almost choked on his beer.

"Nothing to say about that?" Lizzie asked.

He shook his head, still coughing.

"Okay, then let's move on." She drank the rest of her beer. "I'm going to check in on Ines and Carlos tomorrow after work. Yvonne's made them at least twenty different dinners and I'm going to stock up their freezer."

"I'll be there tomorrow as well." Adam finally found his voice again. "Maybe after you're done, you'd like to come and have dinner up at the ranch with me."

"With you and all your family?"

"Yeah." He studied her apprehensive face. "Is that a problem?"

"No, it's just like you're making a public declaration of us being together."

He reached over to take her hand. "We *are* together, right?"

She nodded, her smile returning until it blossomed into something that made his world so much brighter.

"There you are."

Adam glanced over to his right and found that his father was standing right by the booth.

"Hey." He hastily released Lizzie's hand. "What's up?"

"Leanne and I are having dinner here. Thought we'd join you."

"That would be great," Adam said heartily. "But Lizzie and I are just about done, so—"

"I haven't had dessert yet," Lizzie piped up. "We could stay for a while."

As his father turned to call Leanne over, Adam raised an irate eyebrow at Lizzie.

"Dessert? You never eat the stuff."

"Yes, I do." She smiled sweetly back at him. "Bella makes her own ice cream and it's fantastic in a sundae."

"Right, which means now I've got to look Leanne in the eye after hearing . . . that."

"How do you think you were born, Adam?" Lizzie asked. "If Jeff and Leanne hadn't—"

He leaned over and put his finger on her lips, but as she kissed it and sucked it into her mouth, his reaction was totally physical, and not quite what he'd intended at all.

"Hi, Lizzie!" Leanne took the seat next to Lizzie, which meant that Adam was doomed to look at her, which might be marginally better than looking at his father, who was in a remarkably good mood these days. "How are things at the café, and how's your darling little boy?"

As Lizzie started chatting it gave Adam a much-needed moment to gather his resources before he had to deal with his father. Could Lizzie be right? Was Leanne contemplating a move back to Morgan Valley?

Eventually, even Lizzie ran out of reasons to hang around with his parents, and said she had to leave to go speak to Roman on the phone. Adam was just about to announce that he was going with her when his mother put her hand on his arm.

"Could you stay a minute, Adam? We wanted to talk to you about something."

His gaze instantly swung toward Lizzie, almost begging her to give him an out, but she simply smiled and eased out of the seat.

"Come over when you're ready, Adam, or I'll see you tomorrow." She blew him an air kiss and disappeared on him.

He reluctantly turned back to his parents who were now sitting side by side.

"What's up?"

"Well, firstly, I made Jeff go down to Henry's office yesterday and draw up a proper will," Leanne said.

"Okay." Adam searched their faces. "That's a good thing to do."

"I'm leaving the ranch directly to you, Adam, not to Leanne first," Jeff said abruptly.

"I don't need his money," Leanne added. "Declan left me very well off. I own property overlooking Central Park, which will hold its value very well."

"I bet." Adam focused on his father. "What about the others?"

Jeff shrugged. "That's up to you. I'll be dead."

"What Jeff means"—Leanne hastened to intervene—"is that if you wish to share the ranch with your siblings then you can do that yourself without any interference from me."

"Why can't you just leave it to all of us equally?" Adam asked.

"Because I've seen what happens when someone dies," Jeff commented. "If there's no will, some of the kids don't want to live on a ranch, but want the money, and the ones working the ranch end up getting the place sold out from under them."

"Our family isn't like that," Adam protested.

"You never know who they're going to end up with, or where they'll end up living," Jeff said ominously. "Better to keep it safe in one pair of hands when you pass it on. Then it's your call."

"Have you told Ben and the rest of them about this yet?"

"Nope. Wanted to tell you first."

Adam let out a breath. "I don't think they're going to like it."

"I don't care what they like. It's my decision and I'm sticking by it." Jeff scowled at Adam. "If you don't want the place on those terms just spit it out right now, and I'll change my will and leave it to Ben."

"Jeff . . ." Leanne patted her ex-husband's arm. "How about you let Adam think about it overnight, and get back to you tomorrow?"

"Before I agree to anything, we have to run this by the whole family," Adam said firmly. "It's only fair to hear what everyone has to say."

Leanne smiled at him and then at Jeff. "I think that's a great idea. We can do it after dinner tomorrow evening."

Adam's father grumbled under his breath, but reluctantly agreed to their request. He wandered off to get another beer, leaving Adam alone with Leanne.

"Just so you know, you are all mentioned in *my* will, Adam. None of your siblings will ever be short of money, or not have the ability to buy a home."

"You must've done pretty well for yourself in New York," Adam replied.

Leanne chuckled. "Well, to be honest, after I got married again I didn't do much other than manage Declan's family trust fund and sit on a lot of fancy boards."

"Family trust?"

"Yes." She held his gaze. "Which is why you don't have to worry."

"Won't all that money go to your daughter and to any other kids he might have?"

"Most of it will go to Eileen and her half sister, but there's plenty left over. When I met Declan he was volunteering at the soup kitchen Patrick and I helped out in. I had no idea who he was, or what he did for a living. I just thought he was a really decent guy." She sighed. "His son from his first marriage had developed a drug problem and despite all their efforts ended up on the streets. He died of an overdose at twenty-three, which was why Declan was always willing to put his money, and his time, into helping the homeless."

"He sounds like a good guy." Slightly ashamed of his cynicism, Adam attempted to make things right again.

"He was the best man I've ever met." Leanne's smile faltered. "I loved him very much." She busied herself finding a tissue in her purse. "All I'm trying to say is that you shouldn't feel bad about taking on the ranch."

"I decided not to block the sale of the Cortez ranch. Rio Martinez is going to buy it." Adam tried to offer her something personal in return.

"It must have been hard for you to let it go," she said gently. "I kept all kinds of things from our ranch for years until it dawned on me that all my memories, all that really mattered, were branded deep in my heart and in my head." She pressed her fist to her chest. "Rae somehow managed to get my brother's address, and send me pictures of you all growing up. Even though I wasn't there, I at least got to see a glimpse of you."

"I wish—" Impulsively, Adam leaned forward and then stopped talking as his dad rejoined them. He stood up instead. "Look, I've got to go. I'll see you both later."

"Off to see Lizzie?" His dad winked at him and Adam wanted to die. "She's a lovely girl. You should ask her up to the ranch, let her stay the night. I wouldn't mind."

"Dad . . ." Adam knew he sounded like a scandalized teen, but he couldn't help himself. "Knock it off, okay?"

His dad waggled his eyebrows and sat down next to Leanne. "You never know who you'll meet in our kitchen in the middle of the night these days."

"Jeff Miller!" Leanne nudged him in the side. "Adam's right. Knock it off."

As his parents laughed their asses off, Adam was already halfway out the door and he wasn't looking back.

Chapter Twenty

Lizzie walked into Henry's office and smiled at Chloe. "Is he in?"

"Yes, and he's expecting you."

Lizzie went through into the rear office and was brought up short by the sight of Miranda conversing amicably with Henry.

"Hi!" She stayed by the door. "Do you want me to wait outside?"

"No, come in!" Henry waved her forward. "Mrs. Smith has something she wishes to say to you."

"Okay." Lizzie came in and sat down, her gaze fixed on Miranda who was smiling at her. "What's up?"

"I wanted to have one last chat with you before it all becomes official," Miranda said.

Lizzie didn't reply, and waited for Miranda to continue.

"I think we both agree that it would be nice for Roman to know his father's side of the family."

"Correct." Lizzie wasn't going to argue with that.

"So, if it is simply a matter of money—"

"Hold up," Lizzie interrupted. "When did money come into this?"

"It's obvious that you aren't doing too well, financially," Miranda said. "I mean you have two jobs, one of which must be quite demeaning seeing as I understand you are working toward an accounting degree."

"What's demeaning about being a waitress?" Lizzie asked mildly. "I get great tips, I love my boss and my commute."

"You said that you couldn't afford to let Roman travel to meet me. What if you had the money to accompany him?"

"As in, we'd both come and meet you in San Francisco?"

"No, that you would travel together, and then you would do whatever you wanted to do in the city while I spent some time with my grandson." Miranda looked at her expectantly.

"You'd pay for that?" Lizzie asked just to make sure she was hearing right and tried to be fair.

"Yes."

"I can see that being a possibility in the future after Roman has gotten to know you sufficiently well, but any meetings between you would need to start here in Morgantown where he feels secure."

Miranda opened her purse and got out her checkbook. "How much would it take to change your mind on that?"

"It's not *about* money, Miranda. It's about *Roman,*" Lizzie said patiently. "He needs to feel safe, and introducing a whole new set of people into his life needs to be done carefully."

"Two thousand dollars a month?" Miranda uncapped her pen. "Until he's old enough to come by himself?"

"*No.*" Lizzie cast a frustrated glance over at Henry who'd been listening quietly to their exchange. "Can you please explain to her that I don't want her money?"

"Lizzie's got a point, Mrs. Smith. Money can't buy love. If you truly wish to have a relationship with your grandchild, listen to his mother who knows him best."

"She's just saying that to make it difficult for me to see him," Miranda objected. "She's just using the child to get back at me."

"I'm offering you the opportunity to meet your grandchild in a secure setting in his own home," Lizzie replied. "That's it."

Miranda put away her checkbook and pen and spoke directly to Henry. "If this is the way she wants to behave, I suppose we will have to go to court after all."

Lizzie also looked at Henry. "If *she* thinks she can bribe me to give up my son then perhaps she's right." She stood up. "I have to get back to work. Thank you for your time, Henry, and keep in touch."

She walked back to work, dodging the packs of tourists, and skipping across the street between two heavy trucks. Why couldn't Miranda see that money wasn't the issue? Was she so used to getting her own way by throwing cash at something that the notion someone didn't want it was too much of a shock for her to accept?

Lizzie shook her head as she pushed open the door into the café, releasing the aroma of roasting coffee. Someone had her priorities all wrong, and for once she didn't think it was her.

"Henry says it will take ages to hear anything from the court," Lizzie relayed the information to Adam as he drove her toward his home after their visit to the Cortez ranch later that same day. "He also said Miranda and I can keep trying to talk things out before the courts get involved."

"Makes sense." Adam had his attention on the road. "Do you think she's willing to hear what you have to say?"

"Not if she thinks I can be bought." Lizzie sighed. "But

I really don't want her sharing all that information from CPS and her private investigator, and dragging you into it."

"No need to drag me. I'm already in. I'll do anything it takes to make sure you and Roman are safe and protected."

Lizzie glanced over at his stern profile. There was no one else she'd rather have at her back than Adam Miller.

"Thank you. I'd rather you were kept out of it altogether as Miranda would be smearing your reputation as well as mine. You don't deserve that. I'm surprised she hasn't suggested Roman is your kid yet."

"The DNA says differently," Adam reminded her. "And how would she know you and I have been friends for years? She doesn't live here."

"But Coretta does," Lizzie said gloomily. "And I bet she remembers all the town gossip back to the Stone Age. I suppose that seeing as I've only ever had sex with two people, she'd have a fifty percent chance of being right."

Adam suddenly pulled the truck over to the side of the road and put the foot brake on.

"What happened?" Lizzie said. "Did we get a puncture?"

He turned to her and whipped off his sunglasses, his expression grim. "What did you just say?"

"Which bit?"

"About only having sex with two people."

She blinked at him. "What about it?"

A muscle twitched in his jaw. "That time . . . after Louisa died . . ."

"Was my first time, yes."

He turned away and stared out over the pasture before exhaling and dropping his head toward the steering wheel and banging it twice.

"I didn't know."

She shrugged. "We didn't exactly talk much at the time."

"But, jeez, Lizzie, I'm a big guy. I must've *hurt* you,

I must've—" She reached out to touch his arm, and he flinched away from her. "Don't be goddamn nice to me. I don't fricking deserve it."

"It wasn't great, Adam, but if you think about it, none of that night was great. It was all about pain, and loss, and . . ." She hesitated, aware that he was no longer able to look at her. "It was still *you*, my best friend, and . . . I was okay about that."

"No wonder you didn't have sex for over ten years," Adam muttered.

"I didn't have sex because I didn't meet a man who made me want to have sex," Lizzie said patiently. "I'm not going to let you take the blame for everything that went on in my life."

This time when she tried to take his hand, he let her. "I didn't mention it to make it a big deal." She paused. "I thought you knew."

"I should've." He sighed. "Just another thing I blocked out in my selfishness and grief."

"It's okay." Lizzie squeezed his fingers. "It was a long time ago, and we're both different people now."

He framed her face in his hands. "I'm sorry."

"It's *okay*." She returned his stare. "It really is."

"I don't deserve you," he said roughly.

"Who does?"

With an inarticulate sound he bent to kiss her, and she wrapped one hand around his neck to keep him right where she wanted him.

"I can't change what happened, what I did," Adam murmured against her mouth. "But I swear that I'll never hurt you like that again."

He released her, and brought the truck back onto the pavement, his expression dire. He stretched out his right hand and placed it on her thigh, anchoring her against the rocking of the truck. Lizzie slowly let out her breath, aware that they'd somehow managed to find their way through yet another block in their personal road.

She hadn't lied when she'd told him she hadn't minded him being the first man she had sex with. That night was still something of a blur to both of them. She only remembered the urgency, the desperate need to be close, and to somehow offer him a haven to bury his pain and share their grief together.

"Lizzie?"

"Yes?" She turned toward him.

"When's Roman coming home?"

Glad that he seemed to have moved on, she replied, "In about six days. Why?"

"I was just wondering how much time we have left." His smile was wry.

Lizzie sighed. "Yes, I *had* thought about that."

"My dad said you're welcome to stay over at our place," Adam said. "I'm only telling you before he drops it on you during dinner."

"That's what he wanted to talk to you about yesterday?"

Adam had come over to see her last night, spent ten minutes chatting to Roman on the video link, and then had gone home, his gaze so distracted that she had let him leave without a murmur.

"That was just his parting shot. He and Leanne wanted me to know they've left me the ranch outright."

"That's good, right?" Lizzie asked cautiously.

"I said I wanted to talk it through with my siblings first."

There was an inflexible note in Adam's voice that Lizzie knew rather well.

"They won't be that surprised, will they? I mean you've always been your father's right-hand man. You deal with the majority of the work now, and only Ben works alongside you full-time."

"That's true. Kaiden has the carpentry business, and Danny and Evan work part-time in construction. Daisy has that whole Silicon Valley thing going on, so I don't think I need to worry about her."

He turned into the road leading up to the ranch, and got out to open and then close the gate. "I still want to hear everyone's opinions, though." He paused. "It feels kind of grabby."

"I don't think they'll see it like that at all. They'll all be pleased the ranch is in safe hands."

He gave her a sidelong glance. "We'll see, won't we?"

Lizzie was welcomed warmly by the Millers, and ate her dinner sitting next to Adam who always lightened up when surrounded by his family. He loved them very much and it showed. Lizzie had never been loved like that. What would it be like if Adam included her in this circle? She suspected she'd never feel alone again.

Her parents had treated her more like a valued guest in their home than a living, breathing part of the family. They'd never gotten angry with her, or overinvolved in anything she experienced because they'd been too involved and happy with each other to have any emotion left over. Sometimes she felt like she'd grown up in a vacuum of benign neglect.

Even when she'd ended up pregnant and alone, they'd not chastised her, but had offered all the practical and financial help she'd needed to survive. She was extremely grateful for what they'd done. They'd been amazing. Perhaps she needed to finally understand that love came in all shapes and sizes, and that they'd simply been doing their best.

"So, seeing as Adam's being a pain in the rear about

this, I suppose I'd better tell you that I've left the ranch to him in my will," Jeff Miller suddenly stated. "Anyone have a problem with that?"

Lizzie winced as all the Millers sitting around the table went silent. Maybe being in a family who expressed their innermost feelings over the dinner table wasn't much fun, either. Should she sneak out and let them get on with it? But she had no way to get home without stealing someone's truck, and she wasn't that desperate.

"What the hell are you talking about?" Ben asked slowly.

"Leanne and I went to see Henry. I rewrote my will, taking her completely out of it, and I left the ranch to Adam." Jeff elaborated on his original statement.

"What about the rest of us?" Ben's gaze shifted between his parents and Adam.

"Leanne's got pots of money now, and you're all beneficiaries." Jeff shrugged. "You won't starve."

Lizzie winced and put her hand on Adam's rigid thigh.

"Jeff thought it would be better to leave the ranch to Adam, and then let him make the decisions about how he wants to share it with you all," Leanne added.

"I trust Adam." Kaiden spoke up. Danny and Evan nodded. "I don't think he's going to do us wrong."

Daisy turned toward her oldest brother. "And I trust him, too. I don't need money from this place, anyway. I have my own. Jackson and I are going to live on the Gardin ranch once everything's sorted out."

Adam finally stirred. "I won't go ahead with this unless all of you are on board." He turned to Ben who had gone silent. "You're the person most affected by this. What do you think?"

"I'm happy to go along with the majority," Ben said. "I'm working with BB Morgan on his new venture right now, so I'll have my own income soon."

Adam nodded and turned back to his father. Lizzie kept looking at Ben and saw the hurt in his eyes. Whatever he was saying, he obviously didn't quite believe it. She was very fond of Ben. There was a gentleness and strength to him that had helped her in the past and she'd never forgotten it.

When Adam had fallen in love with Louisa, Ben, who was only a year younger than his brother, had often tagged along with the three friends to make up a fourth. He'd never complained, and for a fifteen-year-old boy had taken great care to make Lizzie feel valued and appreciated when she'd been feeling like an outsider again. After Louisa died, and Adam had stopped speaking to Lizzie entirely, Ben hadn't. He'd kept her informed about all the Millers without making it obvious that he was trying to make up for his brother's behavior.

"If I do take the place on, I'll do my best to buy out any of you who want me to," Adam stated. "I know I'll technically own it all, but I'm not going to operate like that. If you want out, you tell me, and we'll come to some arrangement."

Jeff snorted. "You don't need to do that, son. I might as well divide the place in six, and the hell with it."

"You can do whatever you want." Adam stared his father down. "But if you trust me with the ranch, I'll do it my way."

"Seeing as I'll be dead, you can do what the hell you want." Jeff cackled. "Now, how about some dessert? Leanne made pie."

Later, after the meal, Lizzie helped Adam clean up the kitchen. He was very quiet, which made her want to chat to cover the silence. He'd made the effort to seek out each of his siblings individually and talk to them about his dad's decision. From what Lizzie had seen, everyone had been okay with him taking the place on except Ben who looked miserable whenever no one was talking to him.

"I think we're done." Adam folded the dishcloth. "Do you want me to take you home, or would you like to stay the night?"

"I don't want to intrude." Lizzie leaned back against the countertop and searched his face. She had to be careful. Her yearning to be part of such an amazing, giving family was way too visible right now. "What would you prefer?"

His smile was pained. "I'd like you to stay, but that's because I've had a hell of a day, and I'd just like to hold you."

"I don't have a problem with that." Lizzie went over and wrapped her arms around his waist. "Holding is good."

"And maybe a few other things once I get you naked." His voice deepened as he bent to kiss her forehead.

"As long as that doesn't involve running around your *house* naked, I'm good."

He shuddered. "I'll leave that to my parents." He took her hand. "Come on. I have my own bathroom. You won't have to see anyone but me, and I'll make certain I lock the door."

She met his gaze. "Are you sure about this?"

"Because this was Louisa's place?" He studied her for a long moment. "I'm okay with it, if you are."

She knew what a big deal it was for him to say that even if he didn't. Her love for him deepened even more. But she simply nodded and followed him into his bedroom only to be confronted by the big picture of him and Louisa on their wedding day.

He hesitated. "Do you want me to put that away?"

"No, of course not," Lizzie rallied. "Louisa loved us both. She's still part of our lives and is in our hearts."

"That's . . . very generous of you," Adam said.

"It's the truth. Now if the photo starts spinning in midair, and there's a lot of weird screaming, we'll know I was wrong."

Adam's slow chuckle was so endearing that she almost buckled at the knees, and instead sat on the end of his huge bed. He followed her down, pinning her beneath his large body with her wrists easily held in one of his hands over her head.

"Sassy."

"So you keep saying." She nuzzled his lower lip as he nudged her thighs apart with one of his knees and lowered himself over her; the hardness behind his fly was positioned just where she wanted him, minus a few more clothes. "You're just a big bully."

"Yeah?" He kissed her until she couldn't breathe, and then, with one expert move, rolled them both over until she was the one straddling him. "Better?"

"Much better." She grinned down at him. "Now if I only had something to tie you up with."

"I'm not quite ready for that, yet." He eased his hands free of hers and brought them over his head to grip the headboard. "Will this do?"

"Yes, after I've stripped you naked."

She took her time revealing his glories, the heavy slab of muscle over his chest and shoulders, the visible ridges of his abs, and the dusting of dark hair that narrowed as it went down his stomach to his groin. He didn't complain about her slowness, the only evidence of his impatience in the rising curve of his shaft and his harried breathing.

She took her panties off and settled over his stomach, her thighs gripping his hips, and moaned with pleasure at the rigid heat and slickness now pressed against her softness.

"You're leaving your dress on?" he asked hoarsely.

"No." She smiled sweetly at him.

"Can I help you take it off?"

"No, again." She pointed at him. "Keep your hands up there, okay?"

He licked his lips; his heavy-lidded gaze focused on her face as she lifted her arms and took off her dress.

"No bra?"

"I don't always need one." Lizzie glanced ruefully down at her small boobs. "I have to wear one at work, but other than that? I try not to."

"Good to know," Adam said fervently. "May I touch you?"

"Not quite yet." Lizzie leaned forward until her naked breasts brushed his chest. She wrapped her arms around his neck and kissed him slowly and thoroughly, rocking her hips into the rhythm of her tongue until he groaned her name. She felt way too vulnerable right now, like her skin was supersensitive, and that the slightest hint of uncertainty would destroy the moment.

"Lizzie, I need a condom," he murmured against her lips. "Where are they?"

"Bathroom cupboard."

He grimaced as she peeled herself off him, ran into the bathroom, and came back with the whole box. She helped him ease the condom on, and then raised herself over him, and slid home, gasping as he filled her.

He shifted on the bed, spreading himself more widely so that she sank right down on him. "You still want me to hold onto the headboard, or can I touch you now?"

"Touch me." Lizzie deliberately squeezed her internal muscles and his eyes almost popped out of his skull. He was hers for a little while and she was determined to enjoy it. "Touch me a lot."

* * *

Much later, after they'd changed positions a couple of times, used up half the box of condoms, and even dozed off for a while, Adam lay on his back, Lizzie curled up against his side. Her thigh rode his stomach and her hair was tickling his chest. He hadn't felt this content for years. . . .

"You still awake?" Lizzie whispered.

"Yeah, just thinking too hard."

"I know how you feel." She spread her fingers over his chest. "I've spent way too many hours of my life recently worrying about Miranda and the Smith family."

"I was just thinking about something Carlos said to me today," Adam admitted. "He said he wasn't going to do any more treatments. I get what he's saying, but it's going to be hard to watch him fade away."

"I can imagine," Lizzie replied.

"I had to watch Louisa go through the same thing." He paused, and then let out his thoughts into the intimate darkness and to Lizzie. "But with her, it felt even worse because there were some treatments she could've tried, and she chose not to."

"I remember her talking about that," Lizzie said.

"It's a shame neither of us could convince her to at least try," Adam said. "It made me angry sometimes, and then I hated myself for feeling that way when she was going through so much. But I wanted her to stay with me—to fight for us—and sometimes I felt like she'd accepted her fate, and that I was irrelevant."

"She wanted to stay with you." Lizzie stroked his chest. "But near the end she started to believe that she might make it through the pregnancy, and that she'd be leaving you your child."

Adam almost stopped breathing.

"I don't understand."

"Some of the new treatments would have affected the baby. She wasn't convinced they would work anyway, so she decided she'd rather give your child a fighting chance." She looked up at him, her brow creased. "You guys must have discussed this, right?"

Adam carefully sat up and set Lizzie away from him. He turned to his side, put his feet on the ground, and buried his face in his hands.

"What's wrong?" Lizzie touched his shoulder.

"I didn't know she was pregnant."

His words fell into the silence like shards of ice.

"Adam . . . how could you not *know?*" Lizzie rushed to put the light on. "What are you saying?"

He went into the bathroom and grabbed his robe before coming back to Lizzie who had already started scrambling into her clothes. It was too much—too goddamn much. He faced her, arms folded over his chest, aware that he was shaking, and unable to stop the long-held fury in his soul from finally consuming him and everything around him.

Lizzie rushed toward him, her hand outstretched. "I'm so *sorry*. I had no idea that Louisa—"

"I don't believe you."

"Okay." Lizzie went still, her breathing almost as loud as his.

"Why would Louisa tell you something like that, and not tell me?"

"I don't *know*. I'm *really* sorry." Lizzie spread her hands wide. "Maybe—"

"Maybe she didn't say it, and you're just making shit up."

"Look, I realize this is obviously something of a shock to you, but that's hardly fair. She told me in confidence, and—"

"It's a fucking lie!"

Lizzie winced as he raised his voice.

"I don't know what you *think* she said, or what you've

imagined, in some weird attempt to make me feel even worse about all the shit that's currently going on in my life. Isn't it bad enough that I took your virginity and didn't even realize it? Do you feel compelled to tell me *all* this crap? Because I don't goddamn want to hear it right now!"

His angry words echoed around the room, leaving behind a void of vibrating silence.

Lizzie took a deep breath, nodded, and headed for the door, pausing only to look over her shoulder.

"Maybe when you calm down, and think this through, you'll come and talk to me about it, okay?" she said carefully.

"There's nothing to talk about."

She raised her chin. "You're basically calling me a liar?"

Even through his haze of anger he caught the hitch in her voice, the *hurt* he was inflicting, and still couldn't reach her through his own howling pain.

"Yeah, I guess I am."

"About *both* things?"

He didn't answer her. He couldn't.

"Wow, thanks." She unlocked the door. "I've had enough of the men in my life not trusting me. Don't bother to call, Adam. I've managed without you in my life for fourteen years. It won't be that hard to shut you out again."

She closed the door quietly behind herself. Adam sank down to the floor as fear and rage fought for control of his head.

"Louisa . . ." he whispered. "What the hell did you do?"

Lizzie walked out into the kitchen gulping for air, and desperate to get away before she started bawling in earnest. She came to a halt and realized that her car was at the Cortez ranch. She glanced down at her inadequate sandals and made a decision. There was no way she was going back in that room and ask bloody Adam Miller for anything ever again. It felt like her heart was literally going to burst with pain.

She paused in the mudroom, borrowed a small fleece to put over her dress, and let herself out into the inky blackness. She was halfway down the drive when a truck came idling up behind her. Setting her teeth, she kept walking. Maybe if she were lucky, he'd do them both a favor and mow her down.

"Lizzie, where the hell are you going?" She only looked over her shoulder when she realized it wasn't Adam, but Ben hanging out of the driver's window. "Get in."

She wasn't stupid. It was at least two miles to get back to Morgantown and her feet were already killing her. Ben glanced over as she got into the passenger seat.

"Are you okay?"

She shook her head, aware of the heat of a tear trickling down her cheek.

"Did Adam . . . hurt you?" He cleared his throat. "I heard you two guys fighting."

"No. He just broke my heart." Lizzie dissolved into wrenching sobs. "Can you take me home, Ben? Please?"

It took a long time for Adam to stumble to his feet, wash his face in the bathroom, and get some clothes on. He walked out into the kitchen, expecting Lizzie to be sitting there, but there was no sign of her. He checked the other rooms, his fear rising as he searched for her. Her car was at the Cortez ranch and she had no other way of getting home.

Had she taken a horse? He couldn't imagine her doing so, but she'd been desperate to get away from him, and who could blame her? For the first time in his life he'd fricking lost it big-time. He put on his boots, grabbed his jacket, and headed out toward the barn, his steps slowing as a truck came up the ranch drive.

He waited until it came to a stop, and then walked over as Ben got out of the driver's side to face him.

"She was walking home," Ben said abruptly. "I picked her up and made sure she got there safely."

"Thanks. I . . ." Adam shoved a hand through his disordered hair.

"She was sobbing so hard, I had to put her key in the door and help her up the stairs. What the *hell* did you do to her?"

Like Adam, Ben rarely lost his temper, but he was obviously spoiling for a fight now. "What's *wrong* with you, Adam? Why do you have to destroy everything good in your life? Like how dare you be happy, and have someone who loves you?"

"It's not—" Adam didn't even know why he was bothering to interrupt. He had nothing useful to say.

Ben shook his head. "Do you know how lucky you are to have been loved twice? Have you any idea how much I'd like a woman to look at me the way Louisa looked at you, how Lizzie *does?*"

"It's not that simple." Adam stumbled over the words, but Ben still wasn't done.

"I remember when Lizzie brought you home after Louisa's funeral, soaked to the skin, covered in mud, Dad's pistol in your pocket. She practically goddamn carried you up here. She was exhausted, and scared, and so desperate for you to live that she would've done *anything* for you."

Adam winced. "She did."

"And this is how you repay her?" Ben snapped. "Years of silence because you're too much of a coward to say thanks for saving my life? Finally getting with her only to ditch her again because she's not your sainted Louisa?"

Adam looked away from his brother's furious gaze. There was so much he wanted to say, but the words were ashes in his mouth. How could he defend himself when Ben was right about so many things?

He could only repeat himself like a fool. "It's not that simple."

"Yeah, it is. But you're just like Dad, Adam, too damned stubborn to realize it."

Ben slammed the driver's door before heading for the house without another word or a backward glance. Adam could only watch him leave.

Chapter Twenty-One

The silence in her apartment was the only thing that mattered right now. On her return from the ranch, Lizzie had crawled into bed and stayed there, curled up in a ball of hurt so visceral that she'd been afraid to move in case she shattered. When it became too light to ignore the fact that she was going to be late for work, she managed to send a text to Yvonne pleading illness, and went back to sleep.

When she woke up properly the second time, it was the next day, and she had to get up to pee. One look in the bathroom mirror was enough to confirm that her makeup was all over her face, and that her eyes were puffed up from crying so hard. She took a shower and put on her pajamas, stuffing the dress she'd worn with such anticipation over to Adam's place into the laundry basket to deal with later. Not that she'd ever be able to wear it again.

She moved slowly, as if someone had physically hurt her, wincing at the brightness of the sun, and craving cold water and coffee in equal measures. When she checked her phone, there was a message from her mom with an attached picture of Roman whizzing around in a teacup and grinning, which almost made her cry. She focused on his face. He was the most important thing in her life. Nothing else mattered except keeping him safe.

There was also a message from Ben just checking in with her, which made her swallow hard. It was the second time he'd brought her home in tears from his family ranch. She was grateful for both his compassion and his silence. She brewed some coffee, nuked a couple of frozen chocolate croissants in the microwave, and sat down at the counter. It was hard to choke down the food, but she made herself do it. It wasn't the time to give up or give in. Her son needed her even if no one else did.

At some point, she'd have to think about what had happened with Adam, but she wasn't ready to face it quite yet. When Ray had walked out on her, she'd learned to take small steps and to take care of her physical health first. That required her to eat, drink, take showers, stand up straight, and show the world her happiest face.

"Smile even though your heart is breaking . . ." Lizzie muttered through her teeth as she determinedly chewed another mouthful of croissant. Even that thought made her want to cry again, but she wasn't going to let that happen. She'd unwrap the hurt slowly and gingerly when she was ready to deal with it, and not before.

After finishing her brunch, she washed up her plate and mug and set them to drain. With Roman away, her apartment stayed remarkably clean so there was very little for her to do to keep her mind off what had occurred. She worried her lower lip. Should she go to work? She'd already missed a day and it was halfway through a second one. What if Miranda appeared? In her current vulnerable state one wrong word from Ray's mother might tip her over the edge. She hated crying in public.

Late that afternoon when her doorbell rang, she was almost glad for the opportunity to do something. She went down the stairs, only slowing as she approached the door to check out her visitor through the peephole. She opened the door and Yvonne came in on a cloud of roasted coffee and caramel.

"How are you feeling? Did you eat something weird up at the Millers' the other day?" Yvonne suddenly stopped talking and took a closer look at her face. "*Mon Dieu*—is Roman *okay*? Are you—?"

"I'm . . . *going* to be okay." Lizzie beckoned for Yvonne to follow her up the stairs. "I was just wondering whether I should come into work this afternoon."

"Not when you look as if you've been crying for a week. You'll scare all my customers away." Yvonne shut the door and came into the kitchen. "What happened?"

Lizzie shrugged. "Adam dumped me." Her voice shook, and she tried to smile. "So, as I said, I'll be fine. It's not the first time he's acted like a complete ass."

Yvonne grabbed her hand and marched her over to the couch. "Tell me."

"I'm not sure what you want me to say." Lizzie attempted to weasel out of confession time. "We had a fight. He got mad about something I said. I walked out and told him not to contact me again. The usual."

"But you're in love with him," Yvonne said simply.

"I'm *not* . . ." Lizzie glared at her as a tear ran down her cheek. "Why did you have to go and say that?"

"Because it's the truth. I've never seen you look happier than you have the last month or so." Yvonne hesitated. "Are you sure this isn't fixable? I mean Adam obviously has a temper, but maybe he's sorry for what he said, and wants to make things right with you?"

"He won't be sorry, and he won't be apologizing to me," Lizzie replied. "He thinks I lied to him, and worse, he thinks

I lied to him about something Louisa told me because he can't believe he didn't know everything about her."

Yvonne grimaced. "And since she isn't here to tell him the truth, I suppose he can't accept it."

"Exactly." Lizzie's voice wobbled. "And I'm not going to chase after him, Yvonne. Either he works it out himself, and comes back to tell me he was wrong, or we're done."

From the moment he'd called her a liar that thought had been crystalizing in her head. She'd let the Smith family assume that her lack of pursuing them meant she'd lied about Ray being Roman's father. She wasn't going to explain or defend herself to Adam. If he wanted the truth, it was out there. Whether he had the balls to discover it, or would prefer to cling to his beliefs, wasn't up to her.

Lizzie sat down on the couch beside Yvonne and curled her feet up under her.

"Louisa was pregnant before she died. Apparently, she didn't tell Adam because he thought they'd agreed to wait to have kids until they were twenty-five. I only knew about it because I caught her puking her guts up when she came to see me one day. I figured it was the cancer drugs. She made me promise not to tell anyone." Lizzie sighed. "She had this mad idea that if she could just hang in there for a few months longer, she'd be able to give Adam a baby to remember her by. I told her it was too risky, but she was determined."

Yvonne nodded sympathetically.

"I assumed she must have told Adam because he stopped trying to make her take any new drugs." Lizzie grimaced. "I didn't realize he'd just given up fighting because he was aware that her time was so limited."

"That must have been very difficult for both of them," Yvonne said.

"The other night we were talking about Carlos's treatment.

Adam compared him to Louisa, and I"—Lizzie paused—"put my great big foot in it, and reminded him that Louisa hadn't tried the newest drugs because she was trying to protect their baby."

"And Adam didn't know." Yvonne pressed her fingers to her mouth. "Dear Lord, the poor man."

"He blamed me. He called *me* a liar—as if I was just saying it to make his life worse."

"Shock makes people react in different ways." Yvonne nodded. "I'm not saying he was right to blame you—he certainly wasn't—but I can almost understand him going on the defensive rather than letting it sink in."

"Which is what I tried to say to him. He must've been feeling *awful*." Lizzie nodded. "I said I'd be happy to talk it through when he calmed down, but he wasn't having any of it." She swallowed hard. "He looked at me as if he hated me. I just couldn't deal with that again."

"I'm so sorry, Lizzie." Yvonne patted her hand. "But maybe, when Adam's calmed down and thought things through, he'll—"

"He'll do nothing." Lizzie cut across her friend. "Even if he realizes he was at fault, he'll still blame me. He'll hide up there on that ranch and let another dozen years go by without apologizing to my face. I've seen it all before, and I'm not holding my breath."

"But he's in love with you, too," Yvonne persisted. "Maybe this time he'll get things right and realize what he's about to lose."

"He's already met and married the love of his life, Yvonne. Even if he does love me, I'll never measure up to how he felt about Louisa." Lizzie finally allowed her tears to fall. "I've just got to learn to live with that."

* * *

"What the hell is wrong with you today?"

Adam's dad pointed his fork at him across the kitchen table. Adam had spent the day working hard on the far reaches of the ranch and was physically exhausted. He just wished his mind would stop circling around the drain of Lizzie's comments about Louisa.

"And where's Lizzie? Did you make her get up and go home last night? I told her it was okay if she stayed."

Adam finally met his father's gaze. "She decided she wanted to leave."

"It's okay, Dad." Ben spoke up. "I took her home."

"You did?" His father's attention swung toward Ben. "Why?"

Ben shrugged. "I was awake tending that sick calf. I made sure she got home safely."

"How's the calf?"

"On the mend."

Adam glanced at Ben who had avoided talking to him all day and was obviously still mad. Would he tell their father about the argument? In the mood he was in, Adam wasn't quite certain.

"Leanne's leaving for New York in a few days," Jeff said as he set his silverware down on the plate.

"But I'm planning to come back soon." Leanne smiled at her children. "If that's okay with all of you?"

She received a lot of positive replies. Even Daisy was smiling at her. Adam wasn't in the mood to be nice so he kept quiet. Of course, his dad picked up on it.

"Jeez, son, your face is sour enough to curdle milk. Can't you even try and be happy for us?"

"Happy for what?" Adam asked levelly. "That you're getting on okay? That you've forgiven her? That's great." He turned to Leanne. "Good for you."

"What exactly do you mean by that?" His dad wasn't letting things go tonight.

"I said I'm glad that Leanne got what she wanted."

"What do you think I want, Adam?" Leanne asked quietly.

"Forgiveness?" Adam shrugged. "How the hell would I know?"

"The only person doing the forgiveness around here is Leanne." His dad interrupted him. "I treated her like shit."

Adam noticed all his siblings were now nodding, and that Kaiden was giving him the universal throat-cutting gesture to shut up now. But he was tired of deception. Tired of all of it.

"I saw you, Leanne." Adam leaned forward and stared directly into his mother's eyes. "In town. Meeting that guy."

"What are you talking about?" Jeff demanded. "What guy?"

Leanne didn't look away. "I assume you're talking about before I left the first time?"

"Yeah. I saw you kiss, hug, and cry all over him."

"And what did you do about that, Adam?" she asked softly.

"I . . . left a note in our mailbox telling Dad everything. The next day he threw you out."

The silence around the table was now deafening

"That was you?" His dad was now looking at him, a frown on his face.

"Yeah." Adam shifted in his seat. "I thought you should know. I was too scared to tell you to your face."

"Why didn't you ask me about it?" Leanne asked.

"I was already mad at you for fighting with Dad. But I thought *he* was the bad guy, and then I saw you with that man, and I guess I felt betrayed," Adam replied.

"Did you think I was having an affair and that was why

Jeff threw me out?" Leanne asked. "That it was because of you?"

Adam could only nod as his throat closed up with anguish like he was a teenager again, and being forced to relive the whole thing.

"That was my brother, Patrick, Adam. You'd never met him because he and your dad didn't get along. He'd come to see me because he was in San Francisco, and he knew I was close to giving up," Leanne said gently. "Jeff threw me out because we had one too many arguments. That time I let him because I knew Patrick was in town, and that he would help me. I wanted to give your father a shock."

Adam turned to his father for confirmation and found him nodding along.

"I thought the note was from one of the town's busy-bodies. I threw it in the trash. Your mom's right. It had nothing to do with why she finally left that day."

Adam slowly stood up and walked out, aware that a cornerstone of his beliefs was nothing but hot air. His guilt about precipitating his mother's departure was fake. His fear of her returning and never acknowledging that she'd been having an affair on the side was built on a complete misunderstanding of the facts. One he could've easily cleared up if he'd had the guts to talk to his mother at the time.

He stopped moving.

His *anger* with her . . . anger that had spilled out to encompass Lizzie was completely unwarranted.

He walked out to the barn, let himself into Spot's stall, and buried his face against the horse's neck. He inhaled the warm, peppery scent of the gelding's skin and closed his eyes.

Nothing was right in his world. All he wanted to do was find Lizzie, tell her what had happened, and let her comfort him. Not that she would want to see him. He'd called her a liar and she'd walked away from him.

Adam got the grooming tools from the tack room, his attention straying to the drawing of Spot that Roman had given him he'd put up on the wall. He reached up and traced the three figures in the picture who were holding hands and smiling.

He'd ruined that relationship, too.

He took his time grooming Spot, the task soothing his mind even as his already-tired body protested each movement. Apart from the occasional sounds of horses moving in their stalls, or the rustling of smaller critters and birds in the hay and bedding the barn was quiet.

Adam contemplated going back into the house but couldn't face it. Maybe he'd take Spot out for a ride and come back when everyone had gone to bed. He let out a frustrated breath. There he went again. Running away from everything. He really was pathetic.

"Adam? You in here?"

He straightened up as his father's bellow reached him at the bottom of the barn where Spot's stall was located. Gathering up the grooming tools, he made sure the lock was secured, and stepped out into the glare of the overhead lights.

"I'm here." Ignoring his dad's piercing stare, Adam walked up to the tack room and put everything away in its correct place. Unfortunately, his father followed him and blocked his exit through the door. It was also obvious that he was still spitting mad.

"Did you really think your mother was doing the dirty on me?"

Adam winced. "Do we have to talk about that? I've already admitted I made a mistake."

"No, you haven't. You just walked away like you usually

do whenever anything gets hard. How about apologizing to your mother? How about that?"

Adam made himself meet his dad's irate gaze. "I'll apologize to her when I come back in, okay?"

"Which will be when—tomorrow? Or will you put it off until she's gone again?"

Adam set his jaw. "I'll come back in right now and apologize if you'll just get off my back, okay?"

"You do that." His father scowled at him. "Don't you think I would've known if your mother was seeing someone else? I'm not stupid. Whatever else happened between us, she never needed to look to another guy for sex."

"Thanks for that visual," Adam muttered. "Way to go, Dad."

"It's the truth. People have needs, Adam. Even you."

"I do know that." Adam raised an eyebrow. "How about this? I'll walk back to the house and apologize to the whole family for being a dick if you just promise to shut up about your sex life?"

"Jealous, son?" His father winked at him, his good humor apparently restored.

"Yeah, that's it." Adam snapped off the light and followed his father out.

"You've got to move on, Adam."

Jeez, his dad was still talking.

"I'm trying to."

"Lizzie is a wonderful girl. Don't mess this up, okay?"

"Too late. I already have," Adam muttered.

"Then fix it!" His dad punched his arm. "Don't be a jerk! If I can sort this stuff out with Leanne after all these years, then you can definitely make things right with Lizzie. She's a lot less argumentative than your mother."

"You'd be surprised. She can hold her ground with the best of them."

"Which is why she's the ideal person for a stubborn man like you," his dad replied.

Adam glanced down at his father as they walked back to the house. "Is this supposed to be some kind of helpful pep talk? Because, man, you really suck at it."

"Leanne wanted to come out, but I told her I'd handle it this time."

"You should've listened to her," Adam said.

"No." His dad stopped walking and looked up at him. "You're a stubborn ass, like me. I understand you. I know how hard it is for you to admit a fault and sort your life out." He jabbed Adam in the chest to emphasize every word. "Don't make the same mistakes I did and waste years of your life hating on someone who didn't deserve it. Got it?"

"I hear you, Dad." Adam rubbed his chest.

"Good. Now, come on in and make things right with your mother."

Three days after she went back to work. Lizzie finally received a text from Adam asking if she'd be willing to talk to him. She deleted it without replying, her focus on her new responsibilities and Roman's upcoming return. He didn't text again and she wasn't sure if that made her happy or sad. In fact, she was determined not to even think about him.

Of course the next day he came into the café with his mother and Daisy. She realized she was *so* not over him that she couldn't even look at him let alone serve him. Heading out into the kitchen, she grabbed hold of Angelo.

"Can you deal with the Millers?"

Angelo nodded. "Sure." She'd already told him that she and Adam weren't dating anymore so he totally got it. "If he asks about you, what shall I say?"

"Just tell him I'm on my break." She grimaced. "At some point, I'm going to have to deal with him, but this is the first time I've seen him, and it's . . . *hard.*"

"No worries. I've got this." Angelo patted her shoulder. "You hang out in here and handle the food orders. I'll manage the tables until they leave."

After about half an hour, Lizzie took a peek out of the kitchen into the café, and silently groaned. It was getting way too busy for Angelo to handle alone, and she was supposed to be the manager. She'd have to suck it up and deal.

Putting on her apron, she went out with a smile on her face, and started taking orders from the outside tables, and anyone who wasn't near the Millers. Angelo worked out her strategy and focused his attention on the cluster of guests around them. Just to steel herself, Lizzie cast the occasional glance over at the back of Adam's head, but it didn't help. She just felt his anger and betrayal washing over her all over again.

When a line formed at the counter, she switched jobs and dealt with those patrons. Eventually, she turned back with someone's take-out cappuccino to discover Adam had come up to pay the bill.

She took it off him and busied herself making change, avoiding his gaze.

"Thanks so much." She dumped the money in his hand and immediately turned away.

"Lizzie."

She forced herself to look over her shoulder, concentrating her attention on one of the buttons of his green shirt.

"What's up? Did I get the change wrong?"

He sighed and lowered his voice. "Look—I owe you an apology, and this isn't the best place to get into it. Will you let me come over?"

Her heart thudded so hard in her chest that she wondered if he could hear it.

"I don't think that's a good idea." She fiddled with the coffee machine, wiping down the steamers.

"We can't just leave things as they are."

"There's no 'we,' Adam. We're done. Over. Finished."

"I get that, but you did say you'd talk to me."

So he really did think they were done. . . . Lizzie finally found the courage to look him in the eye. "Why would you want to talk to a liar? If you want the truth, there are plenty of other people you can ask whom you trust, so just for once, leave me out of it, okay?"

She deliberately shut him out, looked past him to the next person in the line, and smiled brightly. "Hey, welcome to Yvonne's. What can I get for you today?"

Adam returned to the table, the coins clenched in his fist, his frustration close to boiling over. She didn't want to talk to him. She thought things were over between them, and she didn't want to see him alone ever again.

"Are you okay, Adam?" Daisy asked tentatively.

He took his seat and sipped the remains of his coffee, which was now cold, his gaze fixed on Lizzie as she interacted with her customers. Her smile was forced, and he knew she was way more emotional about what had just happened between them than she was letting on. He'd called her a liar, and it had obviously hurt her badly.

"How did it go with Lizzie?" Daisy asked.

"How do you think?" Adam replied, his stomach twisting. "She doesn't want to talk to me."

"Perhaps she needs more time," Leanne added. "She looks pretty upset."

"That's on me." Adam sighed. "She won't even talk things through."

"Well, this is hardly the place for a heart-to-heart."

"I mentioned that, but she doesn't want me going around to her place anymore either."

Leanne patted his hand. "Give her time. It's a small town; you're bound to bump into her, and things will eventually get better."

"It took him fourteen years to come around last time, Leanne, so I wouldn't hold your breath." Daisy murmured.

Adam shot Daisy a wounded look as she sided with their mother. "Thanks, sis."

"He's so like Dad." Daisy was still talking to Leanne. "So stubborn!"

Being compared to his father was the last thing Adam needed to hear at this point. He couldn't stop staring at Lizzie, drinking in the sight of her beautiful face, and the soft curls of her flyaway hair. She was a lot tougher than she looked. He should remember that.

The trouble was—he was still conflicted over what she'd told him. Until he got the chance to sort out what Louisa had supposedly told her, he wasn't in a good place to fix anything between *them*. But she wasn't going to talk to him about Louisa again. He knew that in his soul. Now that he'd calmed down, he also couldn't believe Lizzie had lied to him.

His heart plummeted to his boots. Maybe she was right, and there was no solution, and this was the end.

His whole being rebelled at the thought of never seeing her again, never being with her, never holding her . . . so what could he do? Adam frantically searched his memory. Would the medical center still have Louisa's records? Would they even release them to him? Somehow he doubted it.

Or could he simply do what Lizzie had asked him, and take her words as truth?

Leanne nudged him. “Adam, as I’m leaving tomorrow, do you think you could take me up to see Ines and Carlos before I go?”

Adam stared at his mother as if she was a genius. If anyone knew the state of Louisa’s mind, it had to be her parents. “Sure. I’ll take you right after we finish lunch.”

He stood up and followed Daisy and Leanne to the door, thanking Angelo as they passed him. He paused to hold the door for some guy to come into the café and did a double take. There was something terribly familiar about his black, curly hair and smile.

Adam stayed where he was as the man walked confidently up to the counter where Lizzie was staring at him as if she’d seen a ghost. If Adam wasn’t mistaken, she almost had. He took an instinctive step toward Lizzie and then another one. Why the hell was Ray Smith back in town, and what exactly did he want with Lizzie?

Chapter Twenty-Two

"Lizzie!" Ray Smith held out his hand. "How are you *doing?*"

She instinctively shook his hand, mesmerized by the evenness of his tan, and the startling whiteness of his teeth. He looked just like he did on TV and totally out of place in a small-town café. The occupants were starting to murmur as if they were aware that there was a celebrity in their midst. As Ray hosted the local sports news broadcast, they were all probably familiar with his handsome face.

She became aware that Adam was striding purposefully toward her and fixed her gaze on Ray.

"As you can see, I'm working right now. If you don't want to eat or drink, maybe you could come back later?"

Ray checked his very fancy gold watch. "What time's your lunch?"

Angelo nudged Lizzie, his enthralled gaze fixed on Ray. "Take as long as you like. I can manage. Becka's here in five."

Ignoring Adam, Lizzie motioned for Ray to follow her out to the kitchen, and shut the door firmly behind him. Yvonne had taken the two kitchen helpers up to Morgan Ranch to set up an evening dinner celebration so the place was empty. Ray looked around the large industrial kitchen and whistled.

"Wow, this isn't what I was expecting. Looks almost professional."

"It *is* professional, and I'm the manager." Lizzie stated. "Now, how can I help you?"

He gestured at one of the tables. "Can we sit down?"

"Sure."

After all the torment with Adam, Lizzie found looking at Ray relatively straightforward, which was something of a pleasant surprise.

"Okay." Ray folded his hands together on the table. "I just got off the phone with my mother, and she said that your son was also my son."

"Correct." Lizzie nodded.

"It was a bit of a shock when she suggested I do the DNA thing after all these years. She told me back in the day you'd stopped bothering her, and she just assumed you'd found the real dad."

"And you believed her." Lizzie didn't make it a question.

He grimaced. "I was . . . just about to start my new career, and I was selfish enough to want her to be right."

"So, you didn't bother to follow up with me."

"You didn't come after me through the courts even though you must have known I was earning a lot of money. I kind of assumed you'd changed your mind." He winced. "Wow. When I say it out loud, it sounds awful."

"Yes, it does." Lizzie gave him a pointed smile. "I didn't come after you because I had more pride. I was lucky enough to have parents who were willing to financially support me. I work two jobs, Ray, and I get by just fine."

"Mom said she offered you money to let her see her grandson."

"Yes, she tried to buy access to him. I wasn't very happy with her terms. Did she mention that?"

"She did." He sighed. "Why she thought you'd be happy to let him come to San Francisco by himself I'll never know."

"I offered to allow her some supervised time with Roman here in Morgantown until he gets to know her better. That wasn't good enough. She started flashing her checkbook around, and then petitioned the courts for visitation rights."

Ray looked furtively around the empty kitchen, and then returned his gaze to Lizzie. "The thing is . . . I'd rather do this without the courts getting involved."

"Why's that?" Lizzie asked sweetly.

"Because it's a waste of time when we can come to a satisfactory financial arrangement with basic visiting rights without my mother interfering."

"How are we going to do that?" Lizzie regarded him warily.

"Well, firstly, I'd start paying child support, backdated to his birth. Secondly, I'd appreciate it if you'd allow my mom to come to Morgantown maybe once every two weeks to get to know Roman at your place."

Lizzie regarded him until he started fidgeting.

"Why this sudden change of heart, Ray?"

"I told you. Mom really wants to get to know Roman. She just went about it all the wrong way."

"What about you?"

It was his turn to look puzzled. "What about me?"

"Do *you* want to see your son?"

He looked down at his linked hands. "Look, I'm getting married in three months' time."

"Okay." Lizzie paused, but he didn't elaborate. "What's that got to do with anything?"

"I really love Kim."

"That's great." Again, Lizzie waited for enlightenment.

"Doesn't that bother you?" Ray asked.

"Why would it?"

"Because you loved me, and had my baby."

Lizzie sighed. "Ray, we had a one-night stand and my contraception failed. It was hardly a torrid love affair."

"*Yeah,* but—"

Lizzie held up a finger. "Hold on a minute. Are you worried that I'm going to turn up and cause a *scene?*"

"Maybe," he muttered, doing everything to avoid looking at her, which reminded her vividly of the day she'd told him she was pregnant.

"*That's* why you're willing to offer me money, and set up your mom's visits?"

"Yeah. Pretty much."

"Do I *look* like I've been pining over you for the last four years?" Lizzie asked.

"It's hard to tell." He considered her carefully. "Some women are really good at keeping it together. I know I'm something of a catch, and you *are* a few years older than me, and must be wondering if you'll ever find someone as great as I am."

Despite all her worries, Lizzie's mouth kicked up at the corner at the absurdity of his self-absorption.

"If I confess that I was never in love with you, and that I've barely given you a thought in years, will you change your mind and rescind your generous offer?"

"Of course not." Ray looked affronted. "I just want to make sure that there are no skeletons in my closet going forward—that if I run for political office no one can come around here and dig up dirt about me."

"The Senator's Secret Love Child?" Lizzie made bunny ears with her fingers. "Wow, you are thinking far ahead." She gazed at him with grudging respect. "I never thought you had it in you."

"Well, Kimberly's family is very well-known in political circles," Ray said modestly. "And they think I've got what it takes."

"Does Kimberly know about Roman?" Lizzie asked softly.

"She's going to have to." He shoved a hand through his immaculately arranged hair. "I can't imagine keeping Mom quiet about this, can you?"

"Maybe you and Kimberly could come and visit Roman together and see how it goes," Lizzie suggested.

"He looks like me," Ray said awkwardly. "I saw the photos Coretta sent to Mom."

"He does," Lizzie said simply. "And even if you don't want to be involved in his life, I think it would be good for him to meet you at least once because he's already asking questions about you."

"He has?" Ray looked startled. "I'll talk to Kim. See what she says, and get back to you on that." He hesitated. "You'd be nice to her, right?"

"You mean you don't want me to tell her how fast you ran away when I told you I was pregnant?"

Ray's expression blanched. "Okay, I was a coward and a fool. I'm a better man than that now, I *promise* you. I'm trying to do the right thing."

The fact that he was doing it purely out of self-interest seemed to escape him, but Lizzie let that go. She didn't particularly want a relationship with him. She just wanted the best for her son.

"Are you okay if I tell Mom to withdraw the court petition, and I'll set my attorney onto sorting out a proper legal agreement just between us?" Ray asked.

"Sounds good to me." Lizzie nodded, and Ray's face lit up.

"Thanks for being so reasonable. Mom said you wouldn't agree to anything."

Lizzie nobly didn't rise to that insult. "Henry Parker is acting for me in this matter. Your mother has all his details. And, Ray? You might want to check in with Coretta. I don't think she's acting like herself."

"I noticed that when I visited with her." He grimaced. "I'll make sure she gets the medical attention she needs."

"Good."

"I'll speak to Mom, and I'll be in touch with you very soon." Ray stood and took her hand, drawing her to her feet. "Thank you."

"You're welcome."

He kissed her cheek. "I'm truly sorry that I acted like such a jerk."

"Yes, you did." She agreed with him. "But we have the most amazing son in the world, so you can't be all bad."

He laughed. "If Roman has your great sense of humor, I'm really looking forward to meeting him and being put in my place."

Lizzie saw him out into the café and gave Angelo a thumbs-up before returning to her seat. She needed a moment of quiet reflection before she went out and started working again. Ray hadn't changed a bit. He was still a self-involved jerk, but his need for a squeaky-clean image was working in her favor.

She didn't need his money, but she could use it to set up a college fund for Roman to widen his choices when he grew older. She could even tolerate Miranda if she got along with her grandson. . . .

"What did he want?"

She looked up to find Adam at the kitchen door and straightened her spine.

"That's none of your business."

"I get that, but I'd still like to know." He hesitated. "I still care about you and Roman. That hasn't changed."

Lizzie considered him. "Then you'll be happy to know that Ray and I sorted everything out, and that we won't be going to court after all."

"That's . . . great."

She couldn't deny the note of genuine relief in his reply.

"Thanks." She stood up. "Now, I really have to get on . . ."

He didn't move away from the door. "I'm sorry I lost my temper with you, Lizzie. You didn't deserve that. I lashed out at the wrong person."

"Okay."

"Will you forgive me?"

She wished he didn't sound so hopeful. "Sure."

"I just . . . can't believe Louisa would've done that."

"I get it. But Louisa was my best friend and she wasn't a saint," Lizzie said. "She was just a person with good points and bad points, and maybe she screwed up on this particular thing because she so desperately wanted to be right. Do you know what would've been nice, Adam?"

"What?"

"If you'd chosen to believe *me,*" Lizzie said simply. "That just for once you'd let go of your idealized portrait of Louisa, and even considered that maybe she could have lied to you instead."

"I—" Adam shook his head, his frustration clearly evident. "I *do* believe you—I *want* to believe you, but—"

"But you just can't quite get there, can you?" Lizzie interrupted him. "It's very clear where your loyalties lie, and it was stupid of me to forget that." She walked up to him and pushed past to open the door. "I've got to get back to work."

* * *

Adam returned to his mother who had been waiting very patiently for him at the table. Daisy had already gone back to her flower shop. With a huge effort, Adam forced his mind away from Lizzie's damning comments, and concentrated on Leanne.

"Do you want to go up to the Cortez ranch now?"

"Yes, please. I texted Ines, and she says it's fine to come over." Leanne touched his arm. "Are you okay?"

"Not really." Adam held the door open and followed her out onto the raised, wooden sidewalk. "Lizzie's still pissed with me."

Leanne didn't say anything as they walked back to his truck and he boosted her up into the passenger seat.

Adam didn't immediately start the engine. "Lizzie said I always put Louisa first—that I've put her up on some kind of pedestal where she can do no wrong."

"Is she right?" Leanne asked softly.

"I don't know anymore," Adam confessed. "I feel like all the certainties I built my life on are currently crashing to the ground."

Leanne nodded. "Sometimes that's a good thing, because then you have to climb out of the rubble, pick yourself up, and start again. I know I did."

Leanne's words stuck in his head as he drove up to the Cortez ranch. Was that what he needed? For his whole world to come crashing down again? He'd lived through that once with Louisa, and it had made him even more cautious about building a new life. But had he gotten it wrong? Was he still stuck down there hiding in the foundations of his first life and clinging to the rubble?

Louisa hadn't been a saint. They'd argued all the time

about having kids. The more he thought about it, the more he realized that her wanting to leave him with their baby made a horrible kind of sense. He'd tried to get that across to Lizzie, but somehow he'd failed, maybe because he still didn't want to say the words out loud and make them real.

Ines welcomed them warmly. She took them through to see Carlos whose bed had been moved out onto the covered back porch so that he could look out over the pastureland he loved. Adam held back as Leanne went to greet her old friend and sat by his bed holding his hand. Carlos had the same look in his eyes Louisa had at the end—as if he was already untethered to his earthly existence and moving onto another.

Ines touched Adam's shoulder. "I don't think he's got long. Dr. Tio's coming up here every day now."

"Yeah." Adam sighed.

"Come and get some coffee while Leanne talks to Carlos."

"Okay." He went back inside and sat at the familiar kitchen table surrounded by pictures of Louisa growing up into the beautiful vibrant women he'd married.

"Can I ask you something?" Adam looked down and gripped his coffee mug hard. "Did Louisa tell you she was pregnant before she died?"

Ines was silent for so long that Adam ended up having to look at her anyway.

"Yes, she did." Ines met his gaze. "She . . . wouldn't listen to anyone. She was convinced the baby would be fine if she could just hang on for a few more months."

"Why didn't anyone tell me?" Adam asked.

"Because Louisa only told me and Lizzie, and swore us

to secrecy. I'm not even sure she told her doctors until she had no choice." Ines grimaced. "We both knew she was delusional, but the very idea of it made her so happy and hopeful that we even began to wonder whether she'd will herself to live that long just to see it happen."

Ines got to her feet. "I found something the other day when I was clearing out Louisa's bedroom."

Adam followed her through into his wife's old room and caught a hint of the candy perfume she'd loved as a teen. Ines had started to box up the books, soft toys, and horses that had still been on the shelves before Yvonne and Rio came to live at the ranch.

Ines handed him a letter with his name written on it surrounded by hearts. "It was stuck in the back of the drawer of her vanity. I have no idea when she wrote it, but I thought you should have it."

"Thanks." Adam sank down on the side of the bed, which was covered in a unicorn and pony bed set, and turned the letter over several times in his hands.

"I'll leave you to it." Ines smiled, and left, shutting the door behind her.

It took all his willpower to open the seal and pull out the sheets of pink writing paper. It was dated about three months before Louisa's death and written in her familiar loopy handwriting.

Darling Adam, the cancer's not going away. It's moving fast, and you don't want to hear that or talk about it, so I'm writing this so that maybe you'll read it after I'm dead. Cancer sucks. I hate it, but I can't wish it away, and neither can you, which means I'm going to die, and you are going to have to deal with it, dude.

Don't do your Adam thing and get all grumpy and stubborn. Get out there! Find someone new who will love you as much as I do, and GO FOR IT. I will be mad at you if you don't!!!

You deserve to be happy. I love you with all my heart, but so will someone else. Find her and love her as much as you loved me, and I promise not to come back and haunt you!!!!

All my love, Louisa xxxx

p.s. promise me you'll take care of Lizzie? She's going to need a friend xxxx

Adam only realized that he was crying when the first tear hit the paper. He put the letter on the bed, buried his face in his hands, and let go.

Every word she'd written was *so her,* he could picture her standing there, pointing her finger at him and shouting out the words. He'd cut off all her attempts to talk about a future that didn't contain her. He'd never been able to get his head around the sheer *stupidity* of her dying at twenty-one. That it wasn't fair, that it just wasn't *right,* and that at some point someone would tell them there had been a terrible mistake and she was going to be fine.

But it hadn't happened, and Louisa had died in his arms, leaving him with nothing but bitterness toward life, and a personal promise to never let anyone get close to him again.

Which was exactly what she'd known he would do, and warned him about in the letter. . . .

Adam clumsily wiped at his eyes and took a deep, steadying breath. Had the letter turned up right now for a reason? All the women in his life were trying to tell him something. Wasn't it about time he shut up and really listened?

"Mom!" Roman yelled as he hurtled into Lizzie's arms, and she lifted him up for a hug. "I'm back!"

"So I see." She breathed in his scent like oxygen, and kissed the top of his head as she carried him up the stairs. "Did you have a haircut?"

"He did." Her mom came into the kitchen her arms full of bags. "He screamed the place down."

"Sorry." Lizzie made a face. "I would've mentioned that if I'd known you were going to cut his hair."

"Trust me. I didn't intend to." Angela set the bags on the countertop. "He got this huge wad of gum stuck to his skull, and I couldn't get it out."

"Ice didn't work?" Lizzie set Roman on his feet and he immediately grabbed Doofus from his backpack and set off on a tour of the apartment.

"Nope. It was stuck fast."

"He looks so grown up without his curls," Lizzie said wistfully.

"He looks great." That was her dad speaking, who was completely bald. "Couldn't just cut half of it off now, could we?"

Lizzie hugged him and then her mom. "Thanks so much for taking him. Did he drive you completely nuts?"

"He was delightful," her mom said firmly with a look at her husband who shut his mouth. "We had a blast Didn't we, Derek?"

"We sure did. Any coffee around here?" He looked hopefully at Lizzie.

"Sure. Sit down, and I'll make a fresh pot."

While she made the coffee, her mom sorted out

Roman's dirty laundry, and put his clean clothes back in his room. He seemed to have acquired a large quantity of new T-shirts.

Roman came up to her with a bag in his hand. "I got this for Spot." He showed her a gold plastic sheriff's star.

"Don't you think that should go to Nate Turner, the actual sheriff?" Lizzie asked him.

"Nope." Roman shook his head. "It's for Spot and my Adam."

Unwilling to dump too much bad news on her son the moment he got home, Lizzie turned to her parents.

"Ray Smith came down to see me this week."

"The loser who ran out on you?" Her dad frowned. "What did he want?"

"To make amends and to pay child support." Lizzie handed over the coffee and brought her own mug to the couch. "His mom would like to get to know Roman."

"*Would* she?" Angela harrumphed. "Well, it's about time."

Neither of her parents looked thrilled about sharing their grandparent responsibilities, which amused Lizzie greatly.

"She's going to come here and meet Roman, and we'll see how it goes."

"I suppose that's progress, at least for Roman's sake," her father said. "I hope she follows through and doesn't leave the little chap hanging."

"So do I." Lizzie smiled at him. "Ray said he's going to arrange to pay child support through his attorney, so I'll be able to pay you back some of the money you loaned me when Roman was born."

"Don't worry about that," her dad said gruffly. "Keep it and put it in a college fund. We don't need it."

"Thanks, Dad." Lizzie went over and kissed the top of his head. "You're my hero."

She was so out of tears that she could only smile foolishly at her parents. Even if she never found another man to love, she'd always have her family and her son. She reminded herself that she was a very lucky woman.

Chapter Twenty-Three

"Adam!"

Lizzie groaned as Roman spotted the last man she ever wanted to see again and ran straight for him. Adam was coming out of Maureen's shop where they'd been heading to buy Roman an ice cream. Her parents had left for home the day before, and she still hadn't told them or Roman that she and Adam had broken up.

"Hey, dude." Adam picked Roman up and set him on his shoulder. "How was your vacation?"

"It was great!" Roman drew a breath, and then started telling Adam all about it as Lizzie reluctantly went toward them.

"Hey," Adam said.

"Hi." She kept her gaze at his chest level. "Sorry he's bothering you. We just came by to get an ice cream."

"He's not bothering me at all."

His voice sounded hoarse as if he'd picked up a cold. When she risked a glance up at him, he looked like he hadn't slept in days.

"Are you okay?" She blurted out the question before she even realized it.

"I'm . . ." He paused. "I'm not doing too good."

"Are you sick?"

"Sick of being an idiot, yeah."

She didn't have an answer for that, and, as Roman was wiggling to get down, she reached forward to help Adam set him on the ground.

"Thanks." Lizzie grabbed Roman's hand. "See you around."

Roman dug in his heels. "Mom, Spot's present!"

Inwardly, Lizzie sighed. "Can we sort that out next time, Ro? We've got a lot to do today, and Adam's really busy."

"No, he's not!" Roman stamped his foot. He was still a bit out of sorts from his vacation.

Lizzie crouched in front of him. "Don't shout at me, okay? I've told you we have to go. If you still want that ice cream, you'd better listen to me right now and do as I say."

Roman's lip came out. "You're mean."

"Yes, I am."

"Your mom's right, Roman. I do have to go. I only came into town to get some supplies for Ines and some prescriptions. I have to get back real quick."

"Okay." Roman still didn't look happy.

Lizzie straightened and lowered her voice. "Thanks for backing me up."

"You're welcome."

"And give Ines and Carlos my best, won't you?"

She was just about to go into the store when he spoke again. "If you've got time, I think they'd love to see you. Carlos isn't going to live much longer."

She nodded, and went into the shop, her composure even after five minutes of his company completely shot through. The thought of living the next ten years with him around making her feel things she really didn't want to admit to wasn't good.

Maureen came out to see Roman and listened intently

as he started telling her all about his vacation. Lizzie touched her shoulder.

"Can you keep an eye on Roman for a sec? I've just got to do something."

"Sure!" Maureen smiled at her. "Take your time."

Lizzie practically ran down the sidewalk, her gaze fixed on the tall figure heading for Dr. Tio's medical center.

"Hey." She called out to him and he swung around like a gunslinger.

"What's up?" His expression was guarded.

"If we're both going to stay in this town, I think we do need to talk," Lizzie said breathlessly.

He considered her and nodded. "Okay."

"How about I meet you up at the Cortez ranch this afternoon?"

"Fine by me."

He tipped his Stetson, turned, and walked on, leaving her staring at his broad back, and wondering what the heck had possessed her to do such a stupid, impulsive thing. But things couldn't stay like this between them, and this time she wasn't willing to wait another fourteen years just to clear the air.

Lizzie held Carlos's hand and smiled into his brown eyes. "It's so good to see you."

He nodded slightly. "You, too. Like . . . another daughter."

She squeezed his fingers. "You and Ines have always been kind to me and Roman. Thank you. Thank you so much."

His eyes closed, and his breathing altered slightly as whatever the machine was feeding into his vein took effect.

"He'll sleep for a while now."

Lizzie looked over her shoulder to find Adam propping up the door into the house. She wanted to go to him and let him hold her so badly that she had to curl her toes up in an effort not to rush him.

He raised an eyebrow. "Do you want to talk to me?"

"Yes." Well, she didn't want to, but she feared it had to be done. "Somewhere we won't annoy Ines."

He stepped into the quiet house and she followed him.

"Ines is napping. Perpetua, Dr. Tio's nurse, will sit with Carlos for the next hour or so," Adam said. "She'll let us know if anything changes."

He walked into Louisa's old bedroom and Lizzy stopped at the door.

"Where's everything gone?"

"Ines is set on clearing out the place for Yvonne and Rio." Adam shrugged. "She says she's got way too much time on her hands and she likes to be busy." He walked over to the window seat, perched on the edge, and folded his arms over his chest. "Do you want to go first?"

"Sure." Lizzie sat on the mattress and gathered her thoughts. "I just want us to find a place where we can see each other, smile, and get along. If you still want to be friends with Ro? That's also okay. He needs good role models in his life, and Ray Smith isn't likely to be one of them."

"I don't have a problem with any of that."

"Then, that's good." Lizzie blew out a relieved breath. "That's all I have to say, really. Except that maybe one day we can be friends again, too."

He studied his crossed feet. "I don't know."

"Oh, okay." Her faint hope plummeted. "Then let's just stick to the not shouting at each other, and the being pleasant thing. We're both adults. We can manage that."

He slowly raised his gray eyes to meet hers. "Ines told me that Louisa was pregnant."

"I thought we were just going to talk about being friends?" Lizzie desperately parried.

"She said Louisa made you both promise to keep it a secret." He held her gaze. "Even before I spoke to Ines, I'd already realized it was just like something Louisa would do. We fought more about when to have kids than about anything else. I just couldn't admit that even to *myself.* I couldn't admit that *she* might have lied to me, so I took it out on you." He let out a breath. "You were right. I was wrong to call you a liar."

"I'm glad that someone corroborated my story for you." Lizzie tried to stop her voice from wobbling. "But the fact that you didn't believe me the first time is still sticking in my craw."

"I get that." He hesitated. "I was just so shocked, I hit out at the messenger. I'm *sorry,* Lizzie." He got up and started moving restlessly around the room. "Louisa knew I'd mess up after she died. She tried to warn me about closing myself off to possibilities, and I didn't want to hear it. I shut myself off. I was kind of happy in that safe place, because I still had my family, and that perfect image of Louisa, you know? And then you came along again, and . . . *everything* changed, everything shifted. I felt like a man trying to climb out of a steep-sided, gravel pit."

He sighed. "And part of me wanted to stay down that hole where it was safe, and I didn't have to risk anything. Where I could just hold on to the ideal of Louisa, and never get hurt like that again. Where I could hold my anger and resentment deep and let it fester.

"But Leanne came back, and everything I believed about her turned out to be wrong as well. And, even worse, my dad, a man who never lets the truth get in the way of his grievances, suddenly found a way to *talk* to the woman he ran off his ranch. That threw me for a new one, you know?"

Lizzie nodded warily.

"And you—beautiful, courageous, *you*. A woman who has more reason to hate me than anyone showed me how to *love* again. How to *feel,* and every so often, I'd get scared of it—of the emotions, of the sheer need to see you again. I'd try and retreat back to my hole in the ground where I felt safe, where Louisa was always twenty-one, and smiling at me."

He grimaced. "But I can't go back there, Lizzie, because if I do, I'm dying inside. I want to move forward, and yet how can I do that when I've destroyed your trust in me?"

She went to speak, and he held up his hand.

"Don't try and sugarcoat it. You said it earlier. I chose not to believe you when you needed me to. I let you down."

"But you're talking to me now." Lizzie finally found some words. "And what I'm sensing, is that you've done a lot of thinking about what you want."

"Yeah." He grimaced. "I'm trying."

"And what you want is a relationship with me?" Lizzie barely managed to form the words, she was so afraid.

He nodded slowly.

"Even though you think you've blown it."

"Like you said, I just wanted you to know where I was in my thinking." He shrugged and looked down at the floor. "You don't have to do anything about it. We can just be friends if that's all you can deal with."

Lizzie rose to her feet and crossed the rug that lay between them until she was staring down at his bent head.

"What if I chose to forgive you after all?"

He went absolutely still as she put her shaking hand on his rigid shoulder, and raised his head.

"Why would you when I'm the biggest screwup in Morgan Valley?"

"I think that honor goes to Ray Smith." She smoothed

her thumbs over his cheekbones and framed his face. "I like this new Adam Miller. The one who talks to me, and works things out."

"And who loves you." His gray gaze met hers, and she couldn't look away. "Even if you choose to walk away from me right now, I'll always do that." He took a quick breath. "I can't change what I did, but I swear to you that from now on I will *always* put you first, I will always listen to you, and I will never call you a liar ever again."

Lizzie regarded him seriously. "If you ever do *any* of that again, I won't be hanging around to discuss it. I'll be kicking your ass out the door."

He nodded. "And I'll deserve it."

A tap on the door made them jump apart as Ines put her head around the door.

"I think you should both come. Perpetua has already called Dr. Tio."

Adam grabbed hold of Lizzie's hand and walked with her out to the porch where the nurse was holding Carlos's wrist. His face was serene, his lips slightly parted as if he was going to say something. But Adam recognized the rasp in his breathing for what it was, and went over to kiss his father-in-law's cheek.

"*Va com Deus,*" Adam murmured. "And don't worry about Ines. We will take care of her."

He stepped back, allowing Lizzie to offer up her own words, and then relinquished the spot to Ines who sat beside her husband and held his hand in both of hers as she prayed.

Dr. Tio arrived at some point and took up his stance on the other side of the bed, checking the machines. He eventually turned them off and relied on his fingers on Carlos's pulse.

Adam put his arm around Lizzie and endured, as Carlos's breathing faltered, grew fainter, and eventually ended with a final, soft, exhale.

"He's gone." Dr. Tio stood and started speaking in Portuguese to Ines who nodded along, her expression serene, her composure putting Adam to shame.

Dr. Tio glanced over at Adam and Lizzie. "I think Ines wishes to spend some time alone with her husband before Perpetua and I do what needs to be done."

"Then we'll get out of the way," Adam said automatically. "Thanks for everything you've done."

"You're welcome. Maybe you could help Ines and contact everyone who needs to know Carlos has passed?" Dr. Tio looked expectantly at him.

"We can do that." Lizzie spoke up, her hand firmly in Adam's. "We'll be in the kitchen if you need us."

While Lizzie focused on the townsfolk and called Gabby to ask if Roman could stay the night, Adam spoke to Rio, Yvonne, and his father.

No one was surprised to hear the news, but everyone had a story to share. Adam let them talk, knowing from past experience how important it was, how comforting to remember the best of the person who had just passed.

Lizzie brewed a fresh pot of coffee and made sure there was food in the refrigerator for Ines's family who were on their way from Bridgeport to support her. Eventually, Lizzie looked over at Adam who had returned to sit at the kitchen table.

"I don't think we'll need to stay the night. Ines is going to be surrounded by family. Do you need to get back?"

He finished his coffee. "Ben's doing my chores, so no."

She bit her lip. "Would you like to come home with me? Ro's at Gabby's for the night. You look exhausted."

"Yeah, I'd like that." Adam sucked in a breath. "I'd like that very much."

They checked in with Ines who hugged and kissed them good-bye. Adam promised to return the next morning to take care of the livestock.

He followed her back to her apartment in his truck, glad of the chance to be alone, to process what had just happened, and to contemplate what might happen next. The fact that Lizzie had not only heard him out, but had seemed to understand his muddled thinking, was astounding.

By the time he parked, she'd left the lower door open for him and gone in. He stayed where he was by the truck and contemplated the sight of her moving around the upper rooms letting light into the darkness. He took his time climbing the stairs out of that darkness, and emerged into the warm glow of her home and into her arms.

"I love you, Lizzie." He muttered against the top of her head. "I can't believe how dumb I've been."

She raised her head to look at him, her eyes grave. "It's okay."

"It's not, but all I can do right now is move forward and promise you that I'll be a better man."

"Sounds like a plan," she said solemnly.

"Do you think"—he paused—"that you could put up with me again?"

"I think so." She kissed his mouth. "I don't know how I'd get along without you now. You're my rock."

He swallowed hard, swept her up into his arms, and walked through to her bedroom. "I need to be naked with you, right now."

She set about removing his clothing while he did the

same to her until they were entwined together on the bed, skin to skin, chest to breast.

She kissed him very slowly and thoroughly. "Let's just go to sleep, okay?"

He smoothed a hand over her ass. "You sure about that?"

"You look exhausted."

"I'm never tired enough not to want you." He rocked his hips against hers, and she gave a tiny gasp. "And, Lizzie. I need you *so much* right now."

She rolled onto her back, and held out her arms, and he fell on her like a teenage dork, and just loved her until the need to be inside her became too much. She helped him cover his shaft, and he pushed inside her, closing his eyes at the sheer wonder of finally coming home.

"I love you, Lizzie." *Jeez, was he about to cry now? Would she care?*

"And I love you, too."

She bit his ear and came so hard that he completely lost it, forgot about bawling, and joined her. For the first time in days he finally relaxed.

He'd do what was right, and slowly they would build a new life together as best friends, lovers, and parents to her son. He knew it in his soul.

As his eyes finally closed, he pictured Louisa laughing, blowing him kisses, and cheering him on. She'd always been the smart one in their relationship. Mentally, he sent her his love, and knew she'd always be with him, but she'd be the force pushing him forward, and not holding him back. That had all been on him.

"Adam?"

"Hmm?" He slid a hand around Lizzie's shoulders as she snuggled against his side.

"Just an FYI. Roman is terrible at waking up at night and jumping into bed with me."

"Good to know." He smiled into the darkness. "Maybe one day, when we're both okay with me staying over, he'll get a bit of a surprise."

Lizzie's chuckle warmed his heart. As he finally drifted off to sleep, his last thought was of his rapidly expanding future, the amazing woman who'd taken a chance on him again, and the son he'd be gaining.

Light was always preferable to darkness. Thanks to Lizzie, he'd emerged from his own personal hell into a new life full of possibilities. Louisa had been right above love—it changed, it grew. And if he'd learned anything from her, he'd be passing it on to those around him for the rest of his life.

My Big Sister Annie's Lemon and Herb-Roasted Chicken for Adam

1 fresh or defrosted chicken
½ a regular onion
1 bunch fresh sage, rinsed
1 bunch fresh thyme, rinsed
(You can also use fresh parsley, or rosemary, so pick a combination you like.)
1–2 lemons
Olive oil or butter
Sea salt
Splash of white wine
Chicken stock
Corn flour or flour as a thickening agent

Preheat oven to 375 degrees. Make sure chicken is washed and the cavity is clear. Pat skin dry.

Place half an onion and both herbs in the cavity.

Place lemon slices under the skin and squeeze one half of juice over the chicken.

Rub olive oil or butter over the chicken skin.

Zest one lemon and sprinkle zest over the buttered chicken.

Put remaining half lemon or whatever you have left in the cavity.

Sprinkle sea salt over chicken.

Roast in the oven at 375 degrees until chicken is cooked. (Use weight of chicken and check internal temperature to make sure it is done.)

Rest the bird after cooking and remove the excess fat from the roasting pan.

Add white wine to deglaze the remaining liquid and add enough chicken stock to make the gravy.

Thicken gravy with corn flour or flour and serve.

Please turn the page for this bonus novella,

AN UNEXPECTED GIFT,

by Kate Pearce!

Chapter One

Morgantown, Morgan Valley, California

After saying his good-byes, Billy Morgan came out of the feed store and checked that everything he'd loaded in the back of his truck was secure. It was one of the beautiful crisp, clear winter days he loved, with just enough bite in the air to catch at his breath and taste the incoming snow on his tongue. Even though the inclement weather would soon cut off Morgan Valley, winter had always been his favorite season.

He checked the list his mother Ruth had given him, and headed off to Main Street. The smell of coffee from Yvonne's French Café drifted across the road, and he inhaled appreciatively. When he'd completed his errands, he'd pop in and finish off his morning in style. The Morgantown shop owners had draped their old-fashioned storefronts and boardwalks in Christmas lights, which would come on at night, and make the old gold rush town look enchanting.

The place hadn't changed much since he was a kid. He always remembered the day his grandfather had sat him down and told him how his great-grandfather had come all the way from Wales during the California gold rush, and ended up owning a livery stable and saloon in the new settlement before buying himself a ranch on the profits. Having a whole town named after your family was something special, and Billy had sworn to his grandfather that he'd never let his family down.

He grimaced as he went into the post office. He'd sure messed that up. Twenty-three years ago the disappearance of his wife and baby daughter had almost destroyed him, and sent a tremor worthy of an earthquake through the lives of his four sons and his mother, Ruth. It had taken him twenty years to come home, and he was still working at being forgiven.

He sorted out the mail noticing none of it was actually for him, but that his mother had received a whole bunch of Christmas cards. A couple of letters had stuck together, and when he separated them out he discovered one was addressed to his old friend Bella Williams at the Red Dragon Bar.

Being close to the bar, which sat on the corner of Main and Morgan, he walked around into the parking lot and approached the back entrance. The door was open, and Bella and some guy were standing on the threshold. Something about the young guy's stance set everything protective in Billy to attention. He altered his angle of approach and came up behind the man.

"Axel, I asked you to leave." Bella was speaking, her voice calm.

"And I told you to give me my wages or I'll take them myself."

"Jay will be back any second now." Bella raised her chin. She wasn't a tall woman, but after running a bar for twenty-five years she wasn't easily intimidated. "Do you really want to take on a retired Navy SEAL?"

"He's not coming, Bella," Axel said. "I saw him heading out on the county road toward Bridgeport." Axel took a step closer, invading Bella's personal space. "Give me my damned money, bitch!"

Billy gently cleared his throat. "Hey, you."

Axel swung around, his hands curling into fists. "What the hell do you want?"

"I want you to leave." Billy held up his cell. "I just sent a text to Nate Turner and he's coming right now, so maybe you'd better stop menacing women and take a hike."

"Like you'd be able to stop me," Axel sneered.

Billy stepped closer and held the young fool's gaze. "Do you really want to find out if that's true?"

Something in Billy's eyes made Axel pause, which was just as well because Billy had survived a year in prison and was nobody's pushover.

A siren blared on Main Street, and with one last disgusted snarl, Axel ran off into the parking lot, got on his motorbike, and roared away.

Billy instantly went over to Bella. "Are you okay?"

She let out her breath and pressed her hand to her heart before reaching for him. "Thank goodness you came along, Billy. I was getting scared."

"You didn't look it." Billy wrapped an arm around his old school friend and she leaned into him, her whole body trembling. "You'll be okay. It's just the shock."

"I know." She took a deep, shaky breath. "There was something in his eyes that frightened me. Do you think he's on drugs or something?"

"Probably." Billy looked up as Nate Turner, the local sheriff, pulled into the parking lot. "Do you want to talk to Nate, or shall I do it?"

"Why don't you both come inside my kitchen and we can talk there?" Bella suggested. "It's cold out here."

Billy hadn't noticed the chill, but he was used to working outside in all weathers and had grown up on the ranch herding cattle and riding horses. After being incarcerated for a year, he'd yearned for open spaces, and never felt happier than when he was out in the fresh air.

"You go on in." Billy patted her shoulder. "I'll bring Nate."

He waited as Nate got out of his truck and put on his official hat before strolling over to greet him. Nate had been to school with his sons, and was another local boy.

"Hey, Mr. Morgan. What's up?" Nate asked.

"Some guy was threatening Bella Williams."

Nate frowned. "I assume Jay isn't around?"

"If he was, you'd probably be investigating a murder," Billy said dryly. "No one would be stupid enough to misbehave with the mother of a retired Navy SEAL if they knew he was on the premises."

"So it was probably a good thing you were around instead." Nate gestured at the open door. "Is Mrs. Williams in there? Is she okay?"

"Yeah, she's a bit shaken up, but no harm done. She said for us both to come in."

Billy went through the back door and into the large kitchen where Bella dealt with all the culinary needs of the Red Dragon Bar. She was sitting at the kitchen table with a cafetière of coffee and three mugs.

"Morning, Mrs. Williams." Nate touched his hat. "Is it okay if I come in?"

"Of course, take a seat, Nate." Bella smiled, but still looked a little upset. "Did Billy tell you what happened?"

Nate sat at the table and took out his notebook. "He gave me the basics, but I'd like to get your take on it. Did you know the guy who was harassing you?"

"Yes, he's been working here as my assistant for the past three months."

"Great. So you have his name and social security?"

"His name is Axel Jordan. He came with good references from a San Francisco hotel, but I did notice he'd moved around a lot." Bella sighed. "Everything was going okay until last Friday when he didn't turn up on time. It's our busiest day and we were really shorthanded. When he did arrive, he was sullen, uncooperative, and kept messing up the orders."

Bella sipped her coffee and cradled the mug in her hands, her brown gaze distant. "At first I thought he was sickening for something, but it was more than that. Eventually, Jay got mad and told him to go home and only come back when he was willing to put in a day's work for a day's wages."

"And he turned up today?" Nate asked.

"Yes, after three days of nothing and me having to do everything myself." Bella grimaced. "I tried texting him and calling, but he didn't bother to pick up. Today he came seeking his wages for last week. I told him that Jay was the only one who can authorize those payments. He didn't believe me."

"Which is where I came in," Billy said. "He was demanding his wages and threatening to take them if Bella didn't cooperate."

"Do you have his address here?" Nate asked. "I'll go and pay him a visit."

"He rents a room over Ted Baker's garage," Bella said.

Nate got to his feet. "Then if you don't mind, I'll go over there and see if I can head him off at the pass. I'll come back for your full statement later this afternoon."

"Go ahead. I'll be fine." Bella waved him on. "Thanks for coming so quickly."

"Thank Billy," Nate said, smiling at her. "He's the one who texted me."

Billy waited until Nate shut the door behind him, and turned back to Bella. "Are you sure you're okay? Would you like me to call Jay?"

"No, I don't want to worry him. He's gone to an appointment at the VA and I would hate for him to miss it."

"You still look a bit shaken up," Billy said slowly.

"It's not the first time this has happened, but it's never pleasant." She let out a long breath. "Thank you for being there. I really appreciate it."

"You're welcome." He dug out the letter he'd found mixed in with his mail. "I was just coming to deliver this. It was in the wrong box."

She picked up the letter and laughed. "This must be the first time the IRS has ever done something right."

"Fancy that." He joined in her laughter and noticed that she was starting to look a lot better. He hated to bring her back on topic, but he had no choice.

"I'm worried that you're all alone here if Axel comes back."

Bella patted his hand. "I'm not entirely helpless, Billy." Her smile was both charming and wicked. "I know how to shoot a gun. Jay taught me."

"I bet you do, but still . . ." Billy's gaze scanned the kitchen. "What time are you supposed to start serving lunch today?"

"In about two hours." Bella pointed at the walk-in refrigerator. "I prep a lot of stuff so it's ready to go when needed."

"I could stay," Billy said impulsively. "And help out."

"You?" Now she was definitely smiling at him. "Don't you have a huge dude ranch to run or something?"

"Not really," Billy confessed. "My boys seem to have

that in hand. I suspect I'd be more useful right here. I'm a trained chef."

"You *are*?" Bella blinked at him. "Since when?"

"When I decided to stop drinking and get a job, the only place that would hire me on was as a dishwasher in a restaurant. I stuck it out for about two years, and somehow ended up moving on to more useful things like washing and prepping the fruit and veg. Eventually, I took classes at night school and earned my stripes."

Now Bella was looking at him as if she'd never seen him before. "That's amazing."

He literally squirmed in his seat. "Not really. I'd already messed up so badly that there wasn't anywhere else to go but up."

"A lot of people never work that out." She sat back and studied him. "Can you man a grill?"

"With one hand tied behind my back." He held her gaze. "I'll check in with Mom, but I don't think anyone will miss me if I'm not up at the ranch."

She reached over and shook his hand. "Okay then, you're hired."

Bella snuck another glance at Billy Morgan as he put on an apron and went to wash his hands in the big industrial-sized, stainless steel sink. He wore the Morgantown uniform of jeans, a plaid shirt, cowboy boots, and a hat. Now he'd taken off his Stetson and looked quite different. His hair was streaked with silver, as was his short beard.

She'd known him since they were in kindergarten together, which was more than forty years ago. He'd gone on to marry a girl from out of town and had five kids whereas she'd married a local boy and only had Jay before her husband died in a car accident. Both of them were widowers now, and had resumed their friendship when Billy had sweet-talked her into using organic Morgan Ranch beef in her patties and other dishes she created for the bar.

"Okay," he said as he came toward her, his vivid blue gaze meeting hers. "Where do you want me to start?"

For a moment, she couldn't think what to say. After the shock of the morning, seeing him in her kitchen was so unexpected her brain wasn't functioning properly.

"How about I show you where everything is?" Bella suggested. "I know you won't remember it all, but some of it will stick."

He laughed, displaying his nice white teeth and the fine lines around his eyes. "I dunno, Bella. At my age remembering my name is a bit of a challenge."

"You're not that old," she scoffed.

"I was twenty-one when Chase was born, and he insists he's thirty-two now, so that makes me pretty damn old."

"You're a year older than me, and I'm not old," Bella told him firmly. "You've still got all your own hair, your teeth, and no beer belly, so you're doing good."

"You too." His blue eyes twinkled back at her. "Unless that's a wig."

Bella patted her dark hair, which was drawn into a bun on the top of her head. "It's all mine. I can promise you that."

"Yeah?" He smoothed a hand through his own hair. "Do I need one of those stupid hairnets?"

"I think you'll be okay." His hair was still very thick, but he kept it quite short. "Unless you'd like one. I could do with a laugh."

In fact, just being with him was calming her down and making her feel better. He had a soothing effect on everyone, which, considering his history, was somewhat surprising. He definitely wasn't the boy she'd known, but unlike some of the townsfolk who whispered about his past, she wasn't afraid of him. She'd never believed he'd murdered his wife and baby in cold blood, and she'd been proven right.

"Let's start with the pantry." Bella led him into the walk-in storage cupboard. "I used to make all the buns and bread, but thank goodness Yvonne does it for me now." She pointed at the freezer space beyond. "The patties, steaks, and poultry start off in there, and depending on the health and safety requirements, either thaw in the refrigerators or come directly out of there."

"Got it." Billy was right at her shoulder.

Despite removing his cowboy gear, he still smelled of leather, horses, and the outdoors. A day in her hot, steamy kitchen dispatching orders would probably change that. . . . Sometimes she thought she'd never get the smell of fried food out of her pores.

"Where do you keep your eggs?" Billy asked.

"Some of the organic eggs are out on the counter and others, like the omelet mixes and egg white only ones, are in the refrigerator. I make them up earlier and put them in big plastic jugs so they are easier to pour."

"Good thinking." Billy leaned against the countertop and surveyed the huge metal grill plate and industrial-sized extractor fan over it. "I assume most of your food is grilled or fried?"

"Correct. What can I say? It's a bar." She shrugged. "We keep the menu quite simple because most people around here don't like change. Jay made me get a bit more adventurous, and I'm enjoying supplying organic and locally produced meals. Apart from the thinking up new and seasonal recipe ideas, it's kind of fun."

"I worked in a great organic restaurant in San Francisco,"

Billy said. "I'll have to see if I can remember any of their recipes for you."

"That would be awesome." She closed the door into the pantry. "Let me show you the rest of the kitchen and how the orders come up and are sent out."

"Mom?"

Jay Williams limped into the kitchen and pulled up short when he saw Billy washing pans in the sink. His sharp, wary gaze rapidly assessed the situation for any sign of a threat, reminding Billy of his son Blue, who was also retired military.

"Hi, Jay. Your mom was a bit shorthanded today, so I offered to help out."

"That was good of you, Mr. Morgan." Jay sat down at the table. "I didn't know you could cook."

"I get by." Billy shrugged. "It wasn't too busy so we managed just fine."

Bella backed into the kitchen from the bar side of the property and Billy went around to take the tray from her.

"I've got it, Bella. Jay's back, by the way."

Her smile as she turned and saw her son was so glorious it made Billy blink. She loved Jay the same way he loved his boys, but without the complications. It was a pleasure to see.

"Jay! How did it go?"

He shrugged his wide shoulders. "Okay, I think. They don't want to see me for six months, so that's progress."

He'd been invalided out of the Navy SEALs after being blown up by an incendiary device. From what Billy had been told, he'd endured a long and arduous return to fitness.

"That's great!" Bella said. "Did you tell Erin?"

"Yeah, I called her on the way back. She'll be here tomorrow. She had to go back and tell her parents the news." Jay got to his feet. "If you're okay with it, I'm going to take a nap before we open up for the evening."

Bella nodded. "I was just clearing the last of the tables, so we're almost good to go." She paused and tucked a strand of her dark hair behind her ear. "Billy offered to help out today, and he's been awesome."

"That's great." Jay turned to Billy. "Thanks. Let me know if you'd like to make the job permanent, okay?"

Bella laughed. "As if Billy doesn't have enough to do, what with running that huge ranch up there."

"No harm in asking." Jay grinned at his mother and kissed her cheek. "I'll be down as soon as I wake up. Nancy knows how to set up, so don't go and do it all yourself."

Jay left and Bella's smile faded.

"Are you okay?" Billy asked.

She picked up a dish towel and started drying one of the bowls he'd washed. "I try not to be *that mother,* you know? But I wish he were a bit more forthcoming about how he's doing. I hope he tells Erin these things."

"It's hard when your kids start confiding in other people, isn't it?" Billy washed another plate.

"Yes," Bella sighed. "You get so used to soothing their hurts and telling them that everything is going to be all right that when they no longer need that from you, it feels weird."

"I think they still need to hear it occasionally," Billy said. "Even when they think they don't."

"The first year after Jay got injured and came out of the rehab hospital, he was so down, and in so much pain, that I really used to worry he wasn't going to make it," Bella confessed. "Every morning I'd go into his bedroom and just be grateful that he was still alive, and talking—even if he *was* telling me to get out and leave him alone."

"It's hard to see our kids suffer like that." Billy rinsed another plate.

"I think that's why I try not to be too intrusive now." Bella looked over at him. "I'm scared to push him away again even though he's feeling so much better."

"I know just how you feel," Billy said. "I walked out on my boys when they were kids and left them with their grandmother. I got lost in a bottle because I blamed myself for losing Annie and baby Rachel. I lost *myself*. And now I'm back, I worry about giving them advice sometimes because what the heck do I know? Why should they listen to a guy who wasn't there for them?"

Bella patted his cheek. "But at least you came back. That was a brave thing to do."

"I don't know about that." He smiled down at her. "It just seemed to happen."

Bella snorted. "With Ruth Morgan involved, I doubt that. Your mother is a magician. She got all her family back to the ranch and saved it from being sold off."

"Yeah, she is incredible." Billy grinned. "Scary sometimes, but still remarkable. And we were talking about you and Jay, so how come I ended up monopolizing the conversation?"

Bella shrugged. "Because I'd said everything I needed to say, and was interested in what you had to say? You know, one of those conversation things that people have?"

"Oh yeah, one of those give and take things, right?" He let out the water in the sink and quickly rinsed off the rest of the silverware and plates so that he could stack them in the industrial-sized dishwasher. "In my family it comes down to who shouts the loudest, and Blue usually wins that game."

"Jay talks to Blue."

"Which is probably good for both of them." Billy closed the dishwasher and wiped his hands on his apron. "None of us can really understand what it must be like to be in a war." He checked his watch. "Are you going to tell Jay about what happened with Axel?"

Bella made a face. "I suppose I'll have to."

"I think it would be wise," Billy agreed. "Aren't he and Erin moving into a new house up the street after they get married?"

"What's that got to do with it?"

"Won't you be here on your own?" Billy held her gaze. "What if Axel decides to come back and try and break in?"

She shrugged. "Jay's got this place wired up like a bank vault. Nothing can get in."

"Bella . . ." Billy put his hand on her shoulder and she covered it with her own.

"It's okay, *really*. I'll tell him what happened when he comes down, and if he wants to go all Navy SEAL on the guy, it's on you."

"Nate won't let him do that." Billy grinned. "Well, I hope he won't. Do you need help tonight?"

"I think I'm good, but thanks for offering." She went on tiptoe and planted a kiss on his lips. "Thanks so much for everything you've done today. I can't tell you how much I appreciate it."

"You're welcome." He kept his hand on her shoulder. "If you can't get anyone to help out, please call me."

"Like you have time to help me everyday," she gently mocked him.

"I meant what I said earlier. The boys are running the ranch really well, Mom cooks for the family, and there's a chef for the guest dining room. I struggle to find enough to do everyday."

"I think you underestimate yourself." She eased away from him and he immediately missed her presence. "Thanks again, and I promise I'll tell Jay what happened before Nate gets around to it."

Aware that he was being dismissed, and still not quite happy about it, Billy gathered up his belongings and left the bar. As he walked back toward his truck, he rubbed his finger against his lips where Bella's kiss lingered. He couldn't remember the last time a simple kiss had given him such pleasure or made him feel so special.

He'd loved Annie and had never looked at another woman while she'd been with him. After her disappearance, when the guilt and the drink had drowned him, he'd had the odd hookup, but nothing measured up to the sweetness of that first kiss. Billy fished out his truck keys and stared blindly at the parking lot. Until now. He'd wanted to slip his arm around Bella's waist and kiss her back. . . .

With a snort, Billy got into his truck. The sweetness and nostalgia of Christmas were obviously getting to him. Bella was his friend. She'd meant nothing more than a thank-you, and he was a fool to think anything else.

Chapter Two

"I'm not happy about this," Jay muttered as he stared at Bella, arms crossed over his muscled chest.

The evening rush had ended and Bella finally had time to tell him what had happened with Axel. To no one's surprise, Jay wasn't happy.

"What would you have done if Billy Morgan hadn't turned up?" Jay asked.

Bella raised an eyebrow. "I'm not a fool, or a damsel in distress, young man. I *can* take care of myself."

"I *know* that." Jay leaned over to pat her shoulder. "I've seen you knock out a drunk with one of your cast iron pans. But this guy was threatening you in broad daylight. That sucks."

"Nate knows all about it, and he'll swing by every so often to make sure I'm okay," Bella reminded him.

"And that's another thing. Why didn't Nate find this bastard and lock him up already?" Jay demanded.

"Because Axel wasn't at his apartment," Bella explained again. "Nate will keep checking there as well."

"I don't like it," Jay said stubbornly. "This is even more reason why you should move down the street to our new house. Erin wouldn't mind at all."

"Erin is a saint to put up with you. The last thing she needs is your mother moving in as well."

"Hey, she loves you," Jay protested.

"I know she does, and I love her right back, but you two need some privacy right now. You just got married." She mock frowned at him. "In Vegas, without your mother."

Jay groaned. "Don't bring that up right now. I know, we *suck*, okay? I only agreed to it because Erin's parents were behaving like giant assholes about having this massive society wedding, and neither of us wanted that."

"It's okay, I know why you did it." Bella had a plan of her own to execute over Christmas to make sure the family got to celebrate the wedding, but she wasn't giving away anything yet. "I still don't want to live in your new house."

"Mom . . ."

"Look, I'll make sure I lock the doors when I'm alone here—which doesn't happen very often anyway, and I'll keep my phone with me. If I see Axel or his Harley anywhere near here, I'll call Nate."

"Call me," Jay stated.

"No, because I don't want you arrested for murder," Bella countered.

Jay gave a reluctant grin. "You know me too well."

Bella rose and kissed his forehead. "Now, how about you go on home? Erin will be wondering what's happened to you."

"Erin's fast asleep." Jay winked. "She's still dealing with jet lag, but I might think of a few ways to wake her up."

Bella stuck her fingers in her ears. "I can't hear you. La la la!"

Jay was still laughing as she practically pushed him out the door and locked it securely behind him. The fact that her son was enjoying his sex life was great, but not something she *really* needed to hear about.

Bella walked through the silent bar checking and setting the alarms, and then went up the stairs to the large apartment above the bar. What would it be like to have sex with someone again? As she brushed her teeth, she paused to consider the unexpected question that had popped into her head.

She looked okay for her age; she was definitely plump and bosomy, but that never seemed to worry most men. After Ron had died, she'd had the occasional boyfriend, but only rarely had such a relationship led to sex. She missed it. She'd been good at it.

Chuckling at her own boast, Bella made her way into her bedroom. Tomorrow she was going to call Billy Morgan and ask his advice about something. . . .

Not about sex—although when she'd kissed him, she'd got an unexpected kick out of his reaction—but about hosting an event up at the ranch. That the thought of seeing him again made her heart race was odd, but still thrilling. She lay down on her bed and stared up at the ceiling. How would his beard feel under her hand? How would it feel against her *skin*?

With a groan, Bella turned on her side and clicked off the light. She had enough to worry about without involving her old friend Billy Morgan in her romantic fantasies. Just because he'd helped out, didn't mean he was her white knight. Although he did look fantastic on a horse . . .

Billy finished mucking out the stall and wiped his brow. It was weird how his four sons were so good at organizing things on the dude ranch, but often forgot to do the basics. . . . Not that he minded much. He enjoyed spending time with the horses, and was at peace just being around them. He sometimes felt as if he no longer had a stake in the old place, but it was in his blood, and he wasn't planning on walking away any time soon.

He'd offered to take on the cooking for the dude ranch guests, but no one had wanted him to do that. He'd told Ruth to let him know if she needed his help in her kitchen, but she hardly ever let him assist her. He liked to cook, and had enjoyed working in Bella's kitchen more than he had anticipated. But that might have been the company. . . .

"Billy?"

As if he'd conjured her from his thoughts, Bella Williams stood in the middle of his yard smiling at him. Her car was parked close to the ranch house. Today she wore jeans, red cowboy boots, and a thick pink fleece that made her skin glow. He could hardly believe she'd turned fifty. She looked just like the girl he'd known at school.

"Hey!" He walked over to her and held up his hands. "I've been mucking out the stalls so I won't shake your hand just yet. Would you like to come up to the house?"

"I'd love to." She pushed her sunglasses back on top of her head where her long hair was piled up in a messy bun.

He had no idea why she'd appeared or wanted to speak to him, but he wasn't complaining. He led the way into the house through the screen door and heel and toed his boots off in the mudroom.

"Does this visit require you sit in the parlor or the kitchen?" Billy asked Bella, who was unzipping her fleece.

"Kitchen's fine with me. It's my natural habitat."

He walked her through to the kitchen and pulled out a chair for her. "I'll be back in a minute; make yourself at home. Ruth's out looking at the pigs with Roy. I've never met a ranch foreman who loves his pigs more than his horses before."

When he returned, Bella was sitting at the kitchen table

rummaging in her large purse. She looked up as he entered and took out her phone.

He smiled at her. "I'm all clean now so we can shake hands."

"No kisses today?" she joked.

"I'm good either way." He went over to the ancient refrigerator. "Would you like iced tea or something warmer?"

"Coffee if you have it." She mock shivered. "It's getting cold out there."

"Yeah, the Sierra passes are closing up and won't be open until late spring."

He poured them both a mug of coffee from the pot, gathered up some cream, and brought everything over to the table.

"So what can I do for you today?" Billy asked as she stirred cream into her coffee. "Do you need my help in the bar?"

She made a face. "I'm still shorthanded if that's what you mean, but I'm not here to offer you a job." She hesitated. "I didn't want to say anything the other day until I cleared it with Jay, but he and Erin got married last month."

Billy blinked at her. "Really? That's great, isn't it?"

"Well, yes and no, seeing as they did it in Vegas without anyone being present."

He registered the hurt behind her smile and instinctively reached over to take her hand. "That's kind of sucky."

She sighed. "I know why they did it like that, and Jay did FaceTime me just before the ceremony so I could kind of be there with them while they said their vows, but it wasn't the same."

"I wouldn't be very happy if any of my kids did that to me either," Billy confessed. "I'd be happy for *them*, and I'd never say a word, but inside? I'd probably feel hurt as well."

She squeezed his fingers. “Thanks for understanding. Jay knows I’m hurt, and he’s trying to make it up to me, and I’m trying to tell him it doesn’t matter, because it really doesn’t. . . .”

“But it does.” Billy nodded. “It’s okay. I get it.”

“So I thought maybe the best way to get it out in the open was to have a party for them,” Bella continued. “I’d invite Erin’s parents and family, and everyone here, and then we could all enjoy *that* and move on.”

Billy stared at her for a long moment. “I think that’s a great idea.”

“You do?” Her brilliant smile made him catch his breath. “Then that’s what I need to talk to you about. I don’t want to hold it in the bar because Erin’s parents aren’t that kind of people, but I thought they’d love it up here.”

“When were you thinking about doing this?” Billy asked.

“In the next couple of weeks?” She stared at him hopefully. “Or do you shut everything down between Christmas and New Year?”

“We’ll be here, but we’re no longer taking guests over the holidays because it’s too much work.”

“Oh, then never mind.” She bit her lip. “Maybe I can find another venue.”

“Don’t do that yet,” Billy suggested. “I’ll talk to Ruth and Chase and see what we can do. How many guests are you planning on inviting?”

“To stay over? Only Erin’s family. Everyone else is local. I doubt it will be above fifty in total.”

“So it won’t be that much work,” Billy mused almost to himself. “Gustav, the guest chef, is off to Switzerland for a month, which means I’d have to do the cooking.”

“We could do that together.” She raised their joined

hands, kissed his knuckles, and laughed. "Now I'm getting ahead of myself."

"Be my guest," Billy said. "I'll talk to Chase and Ruth, and get back to you."

Confident that Billy would work something out, Bella gave him her cell phone. "Can you put your number in there for me, please?"

"Sure. Maria taught me how to text last year, and now there's no stopping me." He winked at her. "Who knew teenagers could be so useful?"

She stood up, and he walked her back to the mudroom so she could collect her boots and fleece.

"Is it weird having a granddaughter already?" Bella asked impulsively.

"It was something of a surprise to all of us," Billy acknowledged. "Blue most of all. He had no idea he'd become a father at such a young age, but once he found out, he did the right thing and stuck by his responsibilities. We all love Maria very much."

Bella gazed up at him. In the confines of the mudroom they were very close, and his eyes were very blue. "That's because you brought him up right."

His smile disappeared. "Not me. I wandered off in a drunken haze of grief, remember? Everything Blue became is down to Ruth."

She cupped his jaw, amazed at how soft his beard was under her hand. "I think you're undervaluing yourself here."

"Nope, I'm really not."

"Yeah, you are." Her thumb drifted to the corner of his mouth. There was a small scar on his lip. She couldn't look away from his eyes. . . .

Behind her someone cleared their throat, and they jumped apart like guilty teenagers.

"Hey, Dad, I just wanted to run some stock numbers

by you, but I can come back later if you're busy." Chase Morgan stood there, his interested gaze on his father. "Is everything okay?"

Bella grabbed her fleece. She wasn't usually the kind of person who got flustered, but she was definitely blushing. "I was just going. Thanks for the coffee, Billy, and let me know about that other matter. There's no need to come out with me."

"Bella . . ."

Ignoring Billy's outstretched hand, she bolted out the back door, ran down the steps, and got into her car. She pressed one hand to her hot cheek as she started the engine, and carefully backed out. She'd wanted to kiss him again. *Would* have kissed him if Chase Morgan hadn't interrupted them.

After checking the time, Bella drove back to town and parked up close to the village store. Her best friend, Maureen, who owned and operated the shop, looked up as she came through the door.

"Hey! I wasn't expecting to see you until tomorrow at knitting club."

Bella glanced around the store, noting there was someone working at the checkout, and turned back to Maureen. "Have you got a minute?"

"Sure! What's up?" Maureen walked her through into the private part of the store. "You look kind of flustered."

Bella dumped her purse on the table and rushed over to check herself out in the mirror. She scrubbed at both her cheeks.

"Maybe it's hormonal? Yes! That's got to be it! Maybe I'm just all confused right now."

"You're not the only one who's confused." Maureen regarded her warily. "What's going on?"

Bella collapsed beside her old friend on the couch. "I wanted to kiss Billy Morgan."

"So?"

"That's all you've got?" Bella asked.

"Well, he's a good-looking guy, he's a widower, and his son is a multimillionaire. What's not to like?"

"But *I'm* not looking for a man!" Bella said. "I've never wanted to kiss someone like that before."

"Not even your husband?" Maureen looked mildly curious now.

"Of course I wanted to kiss *him*, but this is different!"

"Why?" Maureen shrugged. "He's a man, you're a woman. It's only natural."

"Not for me," Bella said fervently. "What am I going to do?"

Maureen just looked at her as if she was nuts, but maybe she was nuts. "It seems you have two choices here."

"Okay."

"You can kiss Billy Morgan, or you can not kiss him."

"That's not really helping, Maureen," Bella growled. "He's my friend, he lives here, and I can't spend the rest of my life avoiding him if everything goes wrong."

Maureen shrugged. "Then don't avoid him."

"But what if I want to kiss him *again*?"

"You think you'll want to do that?"

"Yes." Bella nodded.

"Then maybe you should listen to your gut and kiss him until you no longer want to kiss him, and have fun with it."

"Fun?" Bella practically levitated off the couch. Sometimes she could see where Nancy, Maureen's daughter, got her outspokenness from. "I don't do fun, and you know it. I was always the sensible one while you and Leanne Miller

were being crazy. I drove you home, let you crash at my house, mopped up your tears."

Maureen grinned at her. "So maybe this is your time to cut loose and be the wild and crazy one?"

"I'm over fifty!" Bella protested.

"And so is Billy, which means it's all quite legal," Maureen pointed out.

Bella sank back on the couch. "He might not want to be kissed either."

"Oh, come off it. You know when a man wants to kiss you. Did he run away screaming?"

"No, he seemed quite interested in the idea."

Maureen patted her shoulder. "Look, I have to get back, but how about you talk it through with Billy? You know that thing we always tell our kids to do when they're having issues with a relationship?"

"Won't he think that's terribly presumptuous?" Bella asked.

"Honey, you're over fifty. Half your life has already been lived, and time is rapidly running out. How about you forget about your manners, and just have an honest conversation with the guy?"

Bella rose from the couch and collected her purse. "I suppose you've got a point, but reminding me of my mortality seems a bit heavy handed."

"Maybe it's the only way to get through to you." Maureen poked her in the ribs. "Now, get along with you, and make sure you call and tell me all the filthy details if you do get it on with that fine figure of a man."

"Glad you're okay with what I'm suggesting." Chase closed his laptop and smiled at Billy. "I'm great with company stocks, but not so good with the bovine version."

Billy shrugged. "You could've asked Roy or Ruth. They are way more knowledgeable than I am."

"But it's your ranch," Chase pointed out.

"You know how I feel about that, son. Sure, it's legally in my name, but Ruth is the heart of this place, and then it'll be handed down to you guys."

Chase frowned. "You underestimate yourself. You grew up here, you're a Morgan, and the land is in your blood."

"And I betrayed and almost destroyed that legacy," Billy reminded his son. "I left Ruth bringing up my kids, and walked away."

"But you came back. That took some guts."

"Yeah." Billy smiled at Chase. "It did. I wasn't sure if you'd let me stay."

He remembered those first few weeks when his two oldest sons had viewed him with suspicion in Chase's case, and outright hostility in Blue's. He'd deserved it, but it had still been hard. The moment he'd stepped foot back on the ranch, he'd found his purpose, and his family again. The fact that they'd let him stay meant the world to him.

"It's your ranch," Chase stated again. He wasn't one to beat around the bush. "Ruth likes to threaten us all with changing her will, but now that you are back, the place, *and* its future, are in your hands."

"And you're all doing a fantastic job of making sure the ranch survives well into the twenty-first century," Billy replied, keen to change the subject. "Now, is there anything else you need to talk to me about, or can I ask *you* something?"

"I'm done." Chase checked his cell phone. "What's up?"

Billy explained what Bella had suggested, and Chase listened intently.

"I don't have a problem with it. Jay's practically family, but run it by Ruth as well."

"I intend to." Billy nodded and went to rise.

"So what's going on with you and Bella?" Chase asked, his gaze still on his cell.

"Nothing at all, why?" Billy was glad he had a beard because he was fairly certain he was blushing.

"Didn't look like nothing," Chase said, a hint of amusement in his voice. "Neither of you even noticed I was there until I practically tapped you on the shoulder."

"That's because I'm old and deaf," Billy countered.

"Who's old and deaf?" Ruth came into the kitchen and stared at Billy and her grandson, one eyebrow raised. "I hope you're not talking about me."

"Never." Chase traced a cross over his heart. "I was talking about Dad getting up close and personal with Bella Williams in our mudroom." He stood up, tucked his laptop under his arm, and winked at Billy. "Have a great day!"

Billy turned to Ruth, who was watching him in some surprise, and tried to look unconcerned.

"I have no idea what he's talking about. The mudroom is pretty small, and we were just standing close together."

"If Chase noticed something was up, then there must have been something going on," Ruth observed. "He's usually oblivious."

"We were just talking." Billy realized he sounded as lame as a teenager now. "She came up here to ask whether we'd be able to host a party to celebrate Jay and Erin getting married."

Ruth got herself some coffee and put on her apron. "When is the wedding?"

"It's already happened. They got married in Vegas last month. Bella wants to host a celebration party here at our ranch in the next couple of weeks. I explained that we were shut down for guests over Christmas, but I thought I'd sound you and Chase out about the possibility of doing it anyway."

"What did Chase say?" Ruth sat down at the table, her blue gaze fixed on Billy's face.

Billy shrugged. "He was fine about the idea."

"How big is this party going to be?"

"Just Erin and Jay's family, and a few locals. You'd only need to offer accommodation if the Hayes family can't put guests up at the hotel."

"Gustav's on vacation."

"So I'll take over the kitchen." Billy held Ruth's gaze. "You won't have to do a thing."

Ruth snorted. "Like I'd ever sit back and let that happen."

"You could, you know," Billy encouraged her.

"Sit back?" Ruth smiled at him. "And then what? Stay on the couch and watch TV all day? I'll rest when I'm dead." She sipped her coffee. "I have no objection to Bella hosting a party for her only son and his bride at our ranch."

"Great. I'll give her a call, and then we can hash out the details." Billy smiled at his mother. "Thanks so much."

"Bella didn't mention she had been to Vegas for the wedding when I saw her at church last week," Ruth murmured.

"That's because she didn't know there was going to be a wedding until it was just about to happen," Billy said. "And then she only got to watch it on a screen."

"If anyone in my immediate family did that to me, I wouldn't be very happy at all," Ruth observed.

"Bella was quite upset, but she doesn't want Jay to know that. It wasn't about her. From what she said, it had something to do with Erin's family being overprotective, and wanting to take charge of the arrangements."

"So you *have* been exchanging confidences with Bella

Williams after all." Ruth chuckled. "Chase was right." She waved a hand at Billy. "Don't worry. I'm not going to say anything; you're a grown man who can take care of himself."

"Exactly." Billy blew his mother a kiss. "Not that there is anything for you to worry about anyway."

"Get along with you. I'm not worried." Ruth winked at him. "I'm enjoying the show."

Chapter Three

Bella wiped a hand across her brow and studied the mountain of plates, pots, pans, and silverware she'd left to pile up while she made sure every diner got fed. She'd originally had one of her servers to help out in the kitchen, but they'd had an unexpected rush of tourists, and she'd had to send him back out front. To make sure she got the food out, she'd decided not to clean up as she went, which was her normal practice.

The thought of doing it all over again in the evening was almost making her weep.

A knock at the back door had her spinning around to see Billy Morgan peering through the glass. She let him in and walked back into the kitchen proper as he took in the chaos.

"Are you okay, Bella?" Billy asked.

She let out her breath as he came toward her. "Barely."

"So I can see." He took off his thick denim jacket and hung it on the back of the door. "I'll start loading the dishwasher."

With a calm efficiency that startled her, he managed to help her bring order to her kitchen in a remarkably short period. By the time the dishwasher was humming and the pots were put back in their places, she'd regained her composure and they were working happily alongside each other.

"What do you need to prep for tonight?" Billy asked as he cleaned down her work surfaces.

She waved a hand at the refrigerator. "Just fruit and veg mainly. The bread's here, the patties are made, and everything else comes out of the freezer."

"So the same as we did the other day?"

"Yes, exactly," she said, smiling at him. "But I'm good now, *really*. Jay will be in soon. He just had to take Erin to pick up her new car in Bridgeport."

Billy put his hands on her shoulders. "How about we do this? You go upstairs, get yourself some lunch, and I'll come find you when Jay gets here?"

"I'm fine," Bella immediately protested.

"Have you eaten anything substantial today?" His blue gaze captured her attention.

"Not really," she admitted.

"Then go and fix yourself something." He gently rocked her back and forth. "Take half an hour. I promise I won't ruin your business in that time."

Despite her tiredness, he'd made her smile, and she really was feeling a bit wobbly.

"Okay, half an hour, and then I'll be down again."

"Great." He turned her to face the exit. "Off you go."

At the door she looked over her shoulder. "Are you sure you know where—?"

"Whatever it is, I'll find it." He pointed his finger at her. "Go."

Bella climbed the stairs to her apartment and let out a relieved sigh as she closed the door. That was possibly the nicest thing any man had done for her in decades—if ever. And all without a lecture or any mansplaining . . .

Okay, so she'd wanted to kiss him again, but this time he deserved it.

Her smile faded. She couldn't go on without a full staff. She'd have to talk to Jay.

Billy set about dealing with the fruit and vegetables until he'd filled the stacks of boxes, and replaced everything in the refrigerator. Noticing there was very little soup left, he set a huge pan of vegetable and lentil soup on the stove to slowly cook through. He glanced at the kitchen clock, noting that an hour had gone past, and that Bella hadn't reappeared. He could only hope she'd fallen asleep.

She was a strong woman who'd prioritized the needs of her customers over the state of her kitchen, and he could only admire her for that. The problem was, one person couldn't do everything. She was wearing herself out.

The back door banged, and Jay came into the kitchen. Billy nodded to him.

"Hey, Bella's just upstairs getting herself some lunch. I volunteered to finish up in here for her. She had quite a day."

Jay glanced at the door that led into the bar. "Is everything okay? I asked two of my waitstaff to help out so Mom wouldn't be alone in the kitchen."

"I think it got busy out there, so Bella sent them back out." Billy wiped his hands on the towel. "I know it isn't any of my business, but I don't think she should be trying to do everything out here."

"It's okay. You're preaching to the choir." Jay sat down at the table with a *thump*. "She's always been reluctant to accept any help out here. I even offered to get a full-time chef and staff so that she could retire, but she was horrified at the idea."

"She sounds just like my mother," Billy said. "Are you okay if I talk to Avery our event coordinator about getting someone to help out more permanently? She usually has really good leads, and great ideas."

"Be my guest." Jay sighed. "I feel like I'm failing her all around right now." He struggled to his feet. "I should go up and make sure she's okay."

"I think she might be taking a nap," Billy said. "She looked worn out."

"Then I'll leave her to it." Jay nodded. "Thanks for helping out again. Are you sure you don't want a job?"

"I'm happy to help out when I can." Billy shrugged. "And I'm cheap."

"A win-win for Mom then." Jay grinned at him. "I'll be back in two hours to check the bar stock and get set up for the evening rush. There are fewer orders for food, so hopefully we'll cope. I'm sure Erin will lend a hand, too."

With a brisk nod, Jay left and Billy made himself a cup of coffee. He'd given up alcohol after ending up in prison, and still attended the regular AA meetings held in the church hall in Morgantown. He'd never really liked the taste of alcohol, and had just used it to drown his own guilt. Fifteen years ago he'd vowed never to touch another drop, and he hadn't.

Even being this close to the bar wasn't making him regret that decision, which gave him a great deal of satisfaction. But he knew himself now—knew how easily a good man could turn to crutches to help himself deal with grief. He finished his coffee and remembered his original reason for turning up at the bar. In the immediate emergency of helping Bella out, he'd completely forgotten to mention the wedding party.

At least he hadn't blabbed anything to Jay, who did seem genuinely concerned about his mother and was definitely trying to help her. Billy glanced up at the ceiling. Should he go up there and see if Bella was awake, or come back later when she was working the evening shift?

The floorboards creaked, and he made up his mind. If she was already up and about, he'd go and speak to her.

Bella yawned so hard she almost dislocated her jaw as she brushed her teeth in the bathroom. The apartment felt more like hers again since Jay had moved up the street, and secretly she quite liked it. After being widowed so young, and Jay being away in the military, she was comfortable in her own space and almost never felt lonely. She'd lived in Morgantown her whole life, knew everyone, and never felt like she had to be alone if she didn't want to be.

She came out of the bathroom and glanced at the clock in the kitchen. She hadn't meant to fall asleep, but her chair had proved too comfortable, and after finishing her sandwich she'd drifted off. . . .

There was a knock at the door, and she went to peer through the peephole, not wholly surprised to see Billy Morgan standing there.

"Hey." He smiled at her when she opened the door. "Just wanted to see that you were okay."

She held the door open. "Come on in."

He hesitated, his Stetson in his hand. "I don't want to be a bother."

"You are not bothering me in the slightest." She turned away. "Come in and at least let me make you a cup of coffee or something for all your hard work."

He followed her inside, wiping his boots on the mat, and shut the door behind him. He took his time walking through to the eat-in kitchen, quietly assessing the place, which amused her greatly.

"When was the last time you came up here?" she asked him as she set the coffeemaker working.

He perched himself on one of the stools set against the countertop. "About thirty-five years ago, I think. I came to pick up Ron for a football game." He smiled at her. "It looks a lot nicer than it did back then."

"Ron's parents weren't much into decorating." Bella smiled. "And there were five of them crammed into two rooms."

"Yeah, it certainly felt quite small to me, having grown up an only child in a big old Victorian ranch house."

"I'm surprised Ruth didn't have a big family."

Billy made a face. "She was young when she had me, and there were . . . complications. We both almost died, and my parents decided one kid was enough to carry on the family name."

"That was a sensible decision, and Ruth sure made up for it with grandkids."

To her surprise Billy didn't look any happier. "Maybe we should've stopped at one as well."

Bella stared at him. "You don't really mean that? I've seen the pride you take in your family. You love them all."

"Sure I do, but Annie . . ." He sighed. "She didn't do so well."

Bella held his gaze. "I knew Annie quite well, and I can tell you that we all asked her why you wouldn't get the snip. She insisted she didn't want you to do that or get her tubes tied."

"I did offer several times," Billy said. "I should've just gone ahead and done it anyway."

"Hindsight is a marvelous thing," Bella said softly.

"We've all done things that we just wish we could go back and erase from our timelines."

"Even you?" He studied her carefully. "I think you and Ron were the happiest couple I knew."

"We were happy, but we still had our differences." It was her turn to sigh. "I'll never forgive myself for letting him drive off the night he died. He'd had a few beers after the football game and decided he'd go pick Jay up from practice. I told him I'd go, and then I got busy, and just let him do it anyway." She looked down at the countertop. "He crashed into a wall on black ice and never got there."

"That was hardly your fault," Billy said gently.

"But it doesn't matter, does it?" She pressed her fist to her heart. "In *here* I feel responsible, and I always will."

He met her gaze. "Yeah."

She tried to smile, aware that she was actually closer to tears. "Thanks for understanding."

His answering smile was wry. "Remember you're talking to the king of regrets here. I let my wife down, walked out on my kids, *and* left my mother to run the ranch for me."

"That's certainly a long list," Bella agreed. "But you're forgetting that Annie made some bad choices as well. Ruth told me Annie tried to stab you with a kitchen knife."

"She was ill." Billy glanced down at his scarred hands. "She didn't know what she was doing."

Bella raised an eyebrow. "She knew enough to run off with another guy, and take your daughter with her without stopping to see if you were bleeding to death."

"That's true, but—"

"And she never came back. In fact she changed her name and went on with her life without you." Bella held his gaze. "You weren't the only one who walked out on their children, Billy."

"Okay, I get that, but—"

"If she *had* stayed, what would you have done?" Bella asked.

"I would've got her the treatment she needed."

"And you would have remained on the ranch looking after your kids, and none of the rest of it would have happened." Bella nodded. "Annie chose to leave, and her actions caused a lot of yours."

"I thought Annie was your friend."

"She was." Bella got two mugs down from the cupboard. "That doesn't mean I didn't see her faults. She wasn't suited to ranch life. She hated it out here, and she wasn't very happy."

Billy took the mug of coffee she poured him. "Seems as if everyone in town knew that except me. I was too busy running the ranch and trying to help out with the boys to have much time to ask the right questions."

"Just like me letting Ron drive when he was drunk because I was too busy doing other things."

"Bella, I appreciate the support," Billy interrupted her. "But stop trying to equate one stupid mistake with a whole catalogue of misdemeanors. I went to *prison*, for God's sake."

"I'm not." She met his gaze head-on. "I'm just saying that we all do things we regret. How we deal with that regret and move forward is more important than wanting to do the impossible, and go back in time to fix it."

"I think we can agree on that." He sipped his coffee. "I'm definitely trying to make it up to my family."

Bella added cream to her coffee and slowly stirred it in. She'd never imagined herself sitting in her kitchen exchanging heartfelt confidences with Billy Morgan of all people. But she'd noticed since his return that he was always making other people feel good about themselves, and had wanted to repay that instinct in kind.

"I forgot to tell you earlier that Chase and Ruth are happy for you to hold your wedding party up at the ranch," Billy said.

Billy had obviously decided the serious conversation was over, and she hastened to reply.

"That's wonderful."

"Maybe you could come up to the ranch one day this week, take a look at the kitchens, and create a menu?" Billy pointed at his chest. "I'm cooking, so don't make it too fancy."

"I don't think I want to do a sit-down dinner or anything," Bella said. "Just a buffet where everyone can serve themselves, and then maybe free-for-all speeches?"

"If you think that's a good idea."

Bella grinned at him. "Don't worry, I'm not going to get drunk and air my grievances at not being at the actual ceremony or anything."

"*You* might not, but what about Erin's parents? Weren't they the whole reason the couple eloped in the first place?"

"You're right." Bella frowned and tapped her spoon on the countertop. "Maybe we should have preapproved speeches instead—although those sometimes go off the rails as well."

"Feed them lots of carbs and limit the alcohol. They'll be too full and too sleepy to cause any problems," Billy advised. "That's what Avery says, and she should know seeing as she's organized hundreds of weddings and celebrations over the years."

"That's a great idea," Bella agreed. "I'm thinking it will only be about fifty people. It's short notice as well."

"Are you going to tell Jay or is it supposed to be a surprise?" Billy asked.

"I was thinking of surprising him. He certainly deserves it."

"Then I'll remind everyone at the ranch to keep quiet about the details." Billy finished his coffee and slid off his stool. "I'd better be getting home. They'll be wondering where I've gotten to."

Bella put down her mug and came around to his side of the counter. "I'm disrupting your life again, aren't I?"

"Trust me, this is much more fun than inoculating cows." He looked down at her, mischief dancing in his blue eyes, and she couldn't look away.

"I'm glad to hear that." She licked her lips and he stared at her mouth. "May I kiss you good-bye?" she asked.

He leaned in offering her his bearded cheek. She put her hand under his chin until their mouths lined up and kissed him full on the lips. It felt so good that she did it again, and with a groan, his lips parted, and she dove inside. He tasted like coffee, leather, and the great outdoors.

His arm came around her hips, locking her against him, and he took control of the kiss, pressing her against the countertop as she settled her hand on the back of his neck. He kissed with the same tender care he showed her in other ways, which made her feel so cherished.

Eventually he drew back and looked down at her for so long, she had to say something.

"Was I that bad? I am out of practice."

"Not at all, I just . . ." He continued to study her. "I just don't know what to do with this."

"With me kissing you?" Bella asked.

"No, with me kissing you back."

Bella smiled at him. "Well, if we both liked it, then

maybe we should try it again sometime?" She held her breath.

He nodded. "I need to think about it. Is that okay?"

She shrugged, even though she was feeling pretty stupid now. So much for following her instincts like Maureen had suggested. She wasn't a kid anymore, and actions had consequences.

"Nothing to think about." She dismissed him with an airy wave of her hand. "Thanks so much for helping out today, Billy. I don't know how I would've coped if you hadn't turned up." She walked toward the hallway to the front door and opened it wide.

He came after her and was still putting his Stetson on when she literally shoved him out the door, saying, "Bye! I'll be in touch about the party."

She shut the door and leaned against it. He'd definitely kissed her back, and if she hadn't been mistaken, other areas of his anatomy had definitely been interested, too. What had she wanted him to do anyway? Toss her over his shoulder and head for the bedroom? A delicious shiver went through her as she contemplated that little fantasy.

Okay, so she wanted more, but she wasn't going to pursue him. Maureen wasn't always right. One thing being an adult had taught her was that patience and perseverance mattered far more than impulse. If Billy Morgan wanted more, then he'd have to work out how to ask for it without any further encouragement from her.

Billy almost fell down the stairs as he exited the top floor of the bar. Not that he wanted to get away from Bella. It was more a case of self-preservation—if he didn't get away he might do something really stupid like bang on her door and demand more. He let out a frustrated breath as he continued out into the parking lot. She'd tasted so good. . . . He missed that kind of physical intimacy so much. He'd tried to be honest though. He really didn't know what he wanted. The thought that Bella Williams liked him that way was still hard for him to get his head around.

Thinking about hard . . . Billy glanced down at his worn jeans. He was way too old to be worrying about embarrassing himself in public. He hadn't expected to react to Bella's kiss so fast, or so physically. With a groan, he checked his cell, and noticed he'd missed several messages from various family members. He'd been away half the day helping Bella, so he wasn't surprised they were all worried.

"Hey, Mr. Morgan."

He looked up to see Nate Turner hanging out the window of his official car in the street alongside him.

"Hey, Nate." Billy tried to look responsible. "Have you caught Axel yet?"

"Nope. He's disappeared. Hopefully back to wherever he came from, but I'm still keeping an eye out."

"Good. If he didn't get his wages, he might need the money."

"Bella has first-rate security at the bar," Nate said. "I went over the place with her and Jay to make sure."

"Yeah, but the bar is a public space, so anyone can get in there," Billy said. "It's never one-hundred percent secure."

"I know that, but I also reckon most people who know Jay wouldn't risk trying to get past him to his mother." Nate nodded. "I'll keep in touch. Have a great day, Mr. Morgan."

"Thanks." Billy found his truck and got inside. The temperature had dropped considerably since he'd arrived around lunchtime to find Bella in a fix. He used the time waiting for the condensation to clear from his windscreen to text his nearest and dearest that he was on his way home.

Quite what he was going to say to them when he got there, he wasn't so sure.

Chapter Four

To Billy's relief when he arrived home he met Avery coming out of the guest center and flagged her down. He really wasn't ready yet to face all the questions his disappearance would have generated. She still worked occasionally for her parents at the only hotel in town, but focused most of her efforts on the ever-increasing list of functions being held at the dude ranch. She was also his son Ry's fiancée, and the nicest, sweetest woman you could ever wish for a son to marry.

"Hey, Mr. Morgan!" She waved enthusiastically at him. He'd asked her to call him Billy, but she usually forgot. "Ry was wondering where you were. Apparently you were supposed to be hanging out with the cattle this afternoon."

Billy grimaced. "Yeah, I got stuck in town helping Bella Williams in the Red Dragon kitchen. I wanted to talk to you about her staffing situation."

"Sure! Come back into my office so we can chat. It's way too cold to be standing out here."

Glad to avoid his mother's kitchen and her questions for a few more minutes, Billy followed Avery into the newest part of the ranch, which housed the guest dining room, state of the art kitchen, and the company offices. She was using her stick today, which meant she was moving more slowly.

"What can I help with?" She perched on the corner of her desk. "Ruth said that Bella had been having some problems keeping staff."

"That's right." Billy sat down in the nearest chair. "I told her I'd ask you if you had anyone in mind who could help out—even temporarily."

"Well, there is someone." Avery reached over and picked up a piece of paper from her desk. "Do you remember Dev Patel, the architect who designed the guest center and the new barn?"

"Yeah, he's great, but why would he want to work in Bella's kitchen?"

"Not him—his sister Sonali," Avery said. "She's been staying in his apartment in town since she finished up her catering degree. She was working up here with Gustav for a while, but now our kitchen is shut down for a month. I'm sure she'd be more than willing to work at Bella's."

"Have you asked her?"

"Not yet, but I know she's been looking for work because she told me Dev's been nagging her to pay her share of the apartment bills." Avery grinned. "Do you want me to give her a call and ask her formally? She's not far from Bella's place, so she could pop over for an interview anytime, and she'd be nice and local."

"That would be great." Billy smiled at Avery. "Bella's going to need someone long term eventually, but if Sonali can help out for a few weeks, that will certainly make things easier for her."

Billy stood up, came over to the desk, and kissed Avery on the cheek. "Thank you."

"You're very welcome." She blushed and tucked a curl of hair behind her ear. "Bella's a really nice person."

"She definitely is," Billy agreed. "We were in kindergarten together."

"Back when dinosaurs roamed the earth?"

"About then." He tried to smile. "We've certainly known each other a long time."

"Is there something wrong?" Avery asked shyly. "I mean, not that there should be, but you just look so sad."

"Nothing for you to worry about, Avery," Billy said. "I'm just trying to come to terms with how relationships can change and surprise you."

"You mean like between you and Bella?"

Billy grimaced. "You've been talking to Ruth and Chase, haven't you?"

"I *have* heard them discussing certain things about you—you know what they are like."

"And what are they saying?"

"Just that you seem to like her—a lot." Avery paused. "Not that they think that's bad, just that they're surprised."

"Not half as surprised as I am," Billy muttered. "I don't know what to do."

"About what?"

"About liking Bella," Billy confessed. "And I do like her."

"Then why don't you ask her out?" Avery looked at him expectantly.

"On a date?"

Avery grinned at him. "Isn't that what you old folks call it?"

"We're hardly likely to be hooking up, being friends with benefits, tindertweeting, or all the other stuff you guys use to knock boots these days," Billy pointed out.

"Good to know." Avery was obviously trying not to laugh. "Take her out to dinner, or bring her up here and cook her dinner." She studied him seriously. "What have you got to lose?"

"Her friendship?" Billy was long past thinking it was weird to be having a heart-to-heart about his current romantic predicament with his son's fiancée. "Neither of us are planning on leaving this town, so if things go wrong, we've got to live with the consequences."

"You're both reasonable people," Avery pointed out. "I don't see either of you making everything into a big drama if things don't work out. You'd both carry on being the nice, sweet people you are."

When Avery said it, it all sounded so reasonable.

"You think she'd like it if I cooked for her?" Billy said slowly.

"What woman wouldn't?" Avery asked. "Especially seeing as Bella spends her whole life cooking for other people."

"It might work. . . ." Billy nodded his head. "I have to get her up here to pick a menu for the wedding party. I could cook her a proper dinner after that."

"And I'd make sure the rest of the family stayed over in the ranch house," Avery promised. "Because otherwise they'd all be over here sticking their noses in your business." She hesitated. "I think you should go for it."

Billy nodded slowly. "Thanks, Avery. Then maybe I will."

Bella got out of Billy's truck and took in the silence and immediate sense of space around her. Spending her days in a busy kitchen made her happy, but coming out here where the skies rolled endlessly above your head and you could hear a pin drop was a whole 'nother world of peace. . . . She'd left Jay in charge of the bar and her newest team member, Sonali Patel, in charge of the evening shift.

Sonali had impressed Bella with her quick ability to understand the menu and serve up the food in a fast and furious manner. It was also midweek, so the volume of customers was lower and more centered on the local fries-and-burger clientele than the more fussy tourists.

Bella checked her phone, but there were no texts either from Jay or Sonali, so she could proceed with her meeting with Billy without a care in the world. Well—apart from the whole wanting to jump his bones thing, and him wanting to think about it. Bella retrieved her purse from the backseat and waited for Billy to come around the truck.

Maybe he had an answer for her tonight, and the meeting wouldn't all be about choosing cake. . . . Bella smiled at her own absurdity. If Billy didn't want to commit to a more complex relationship, then she was fine about it. She liked him just the way he was.

"Hey."

She turned as he came toward her, his smile so full of delight that all she could do was grin foolishly back at him. He hadn't gotten out of the truck when he'd picked her up seeing as he wasn't stopping and they'd spent the journey back exchanging local gossip and family news. He wore a blue checked shirt that matched his eyes, and his usual jeans and cowboy boots.

"Thanks for picking me up," Bella said. "My car needed gas and Jay said he'd get it for me after his shift."

"No problem." He leaned in to give her a quick hug. "I'm just glad you could get away."

She elbowed him in the side. "You knew I could. You're the one who sent that treasure of culinary goodness, Sonali Patel, my way."

"That was all Avery's doing." Billy took Bella's hand and walked her away from the house, toward the guest center. "She said Sonali was looking for something to do."

"Yes, Sonali told me that after she gets some practical experience, she's planning on becoming a personal chef to some Silicon Valley millionaire." Bella chuckled. "I told her she should be talking to Chase."

"She definitely should, but maybe not until you no longer need her." He opened the door into the quiet guest center. "You've been in here before, right?"

"Yes. It's a lovely space." Bella admired the dining room with its huge fireplace and the large windows looking out toward the impressive Sierras. "Perfect for a party."

"Sonali's brother Dev designed it."

"That's right. So she was telling me." Bella followed Billy through into the state of the art kitchen, and sighed with pleasure. "Sometimes I wish my place looked like this."

"Yeah, it's pretty awesome." Billy nodded. "Chase wanted it to be the best, and he's good at getting what he wants."

"He and Jay have a lot in common," Bella murmured as she noticed two places laid at the kitchen countertop. "They just exercised their talents in different ways."

Billy lit the candles and moved the bud vase containing a single rose out of the way. "I know you said you wanted a buffet, but I thought we could work our way through the courses, sampling potential beverages and food as we go."

"Sounds good to me." Bella put her purse on the work top, and hitched herself up to sit in one of the chairs. She'd chosen a long skirt over her cowboy boots with a silky embroidered top with long sleeves. "Is there anything I can do to help?"

Billy returned from hanging up his hat and her coat. "Nope, not a thing. I want you to just sit there and enjoy."

Bella laughed. "It feels odd to be sitting in a kitchen and not working."

For the first time Billy hesitated. "Would you rather sit in the dining room? I can bring everything out there."

"No this is fine. I was just kidding." She wasn't sure why, but he seemed a little nervous. "It's all good."

"Okay." She fought a smile as he tied a flowery apron that she suspected must have belonged to Ruth around his lean waist. "We'll start with six cold appetizers, and take it from there."

Billy watched Bella's face as she sampled each plate, and tried to work out whether she was enjoying the food he'd so carefully chosen and cooked for her. She wore a red knitted skirt and a black flowery top, and her hair was down around her shoulders. He wanted to plunge his hands into her hair, and hold her still as he kissed her lips. . . .

"Mmm . . ." She licked her lips, and everything male in him stood to attention. "This is all so good! Did you make *everything*?"

"Yeah," he admitted. "I did." He wouldn't tell her that it had taken him all day and several trips to the nearest big town to get all the ingredients he required. "I like to cook."

"You've been holding out on me." She pointed her spoon at him, her brown eyes dancing. "You're capable of manning *way* more than a grill."

He shrugged. "I'm just glad you're enjoying yourself."

"If you have desserts, then I'll probably lose it completely."

Billy shot to his feet. "I have desserts." He hurried into the refrigerated section of the kitchen hoping a cold blast of air might restore his equilibrium. But the sight of Bella Williams licking her spoon and moaning over his food was now seared in his brain. He stuck his whole head in the industrial-sized refrigerator and dragged in a few lungfuls of super-cold air. Nope, nothing was going to help.

"I wasn't sure whether you'd want hot desserts because

they're more labor intensive, so I made these seven cold ones. I have mini Pavlovas, banana pudding, baklava, Eton mess, all kinds of sorbets, ice cream, and fancy ice pops." He set the plate down carefully in front of her. "I'm sure Ruth will insist on adding pie regardless, so we'll definitely have something hot."

Not as hot as he currently was . . . He hadn't felt like this since he'd been a horny teenager ogling his high school gym teacher.

"Oh, I *love* Pavlova," Bella breathed. "I never have time to make it at the bar." She picked up the small piped circle and popped it into her mouth, crunching down on the stiff sugar base, the cream, and berries.

A trickle of raspberry juice touched her lip, and Billy instinctively wiped it clean with his fingertip.

Bella grinned at him. "Am I making a mess? I don't care. This is to *die* for. . . ."

He offered her the second one, and she raised an eyebrow. "You like seeing me all messy?"

He could only nod as he presented the treat. She eased it into her mouth, leaving his fingertips pressed against her lips.

"Bella . . ." He might have groaned before he bent his head and kissed the sweet stickiness of her mouth and the lingering sharpness of the berries within.

With a soft sound, she wrapped one hand around the back of his neck and kissed him back.

He forgot everything except the fullness of her body now pressed against his and the tantalizing taste and scent of her. She fitted perfectly against him, and he never wanted to let her go again.

Sitting on the high stool meant Bella was at just the right height for them to be eye to eye. He eased his second hand around her waist and drew her closer to the edge of the chair.

"Is this okay?" he murmured.

"Oh *yes.*" She wiggled even closer until the bulging fly of his jeans pressed against the woolen fabric of her skirt. He wanted to take the skirt off her so badly. . . .

Before he lost all sense of decorum, he forced himself to remember that they were in a public place, and even if Avery barred the door of the ranch house and lay down across the threshold of the guest center, a determined Morgan would find a way to get around her.

"Come with me?" Billy asked.

For an answer, Bella slid off the stool right down his front, almost giving him a heart attack it felt so good. He took her hand, and led her deeper into the building. His only thoughts were he needed a horizontal surface, and a room with a door that locked.

He stumbled into his office, snapped on the lamp, and locked the door behind Bella. There was a couch against the wall, and he drew her down onto it, his mouth glued to hers, his hands now roaming over her body.

"Where are we?" Bella asked between kisses.

"My office." Billy kissed down her throat.

"I didn't know you had an office."

Billy wasn't really into making small talk, but he made the effort, straightening up, and looking right into her eyes. She looked gloriously rumpled and not at all worried.

"We don't have to do anything," Billy said. "We can just sit together and chat."

"Okay." Bella nodded, and then reached out to run her hand down his muscled upper arm. "I don't want to chat."

He smiled at her. "What do you want to do then?"

"Kiss you? Touch you?" She bit her lip. "But only if you are okay about that."

"I can't say I have any objections." Billy tried to keep a straight face. "Seeing as it's a long time since either of us have been in this position, how about we start with a little making out on the couch session?"

Bella couldn't help noticing that Billy Morgan was definitely very happy to be with her, and that he'd obviously gotten over any doubts about kissing her. She liked the idea of taking it slow, though. Leaning in, she kissed him very carefully until he shuddered under her hands. He tasted of good food, and hot, excited man, a combination that was far more addictive than she had realized.

She toyed with the top button of his shirt. "May I?"

"Sure." He grimaced. "Not much to see except a few scars." He held his breath as she undid each button, sucking his stomach in to make her task easier as she yanked the ends of the shirt out of his jeans.

"When did you get this?" She touched the faded outline of a heart tattooed on his tanned skin. "It's the names of all your kids."

"Yeah." He let out a breath that stirred the top of her bent head. "I had it done when I was in prison to remind me not to give up on them again."

She kissed the ragged blue outline, and he shivered, his hand coming to rest in her hair.

"As soon as I got my head on straight, I missed the kids so much," Billy confessed. "After I got out of jail, I sent money home to Mom whenever I had any, and made sure she had some idea where I was. It was the least I could do after causing her all that pain."

"She never gave up on you." Bella raised her gaze to his face. "I'd see her in town and at church, and she always prayed that you would come home."

"Like the prodigal son?" Billy's smile was so wistful it made Bella's heart hurt. "Ruth is amazingly strong."

"She is, but I don't really want to be talking about your mother right now," Bella said. "I thought we were making out."

"We are." He picked her up and settled her on his lap. "Now it's my turn to kiss you."

She didn't argue, and didn't speak for quite a while as he took a leisurely tour of her mouth, his strong hands finding their way up inside her top to tease and cup her breasts. She might have moaned into his mouth as his fingertip grazed her nipple.

She tore her mouth away from his. "What base are we at now?" she gasped.

"It's so long since I even played the game, I can't remember." He paused. "Are you still okay with this?"

She opened her eyes wide. "Did you hear me complaining?"

"Just making sure." His hand settled over her hip. "Can I persuade you out of that top?"

She bit her lip. "I'm not as skinny as I used to be."

"In kindergarten?" He raised an eyebrow. "The last time I accidentally looked up your skirt was when we were climbing the monkey bars at recess."

"Billy Morgan, you didn't!" Bella exclaimed.

"Couldn't help myself." He winked at her. "I went home and told Mom you had dinosaurs on your panties, and that I wanted some just like yours." He chuckled. "She had a few things to say about that."

"I bet."

"And now I'm back to talking about my mom again." Billy sighed. "I'm beginning to feel like a real teenager."

Bella lifted her arms, took off her silky top, and watched his eyes glaze over as her still glorious bosom was revealed.

"Wow . . ." He leaned in and kissed the spot between her breasts. "Beautiful."

"Thank you." As she'd recently remarked to Maureen, her boobs were her best feature, and she wasn't afraid of showing a bit of cleavage occasionally.

Within moments, her bra had gone as well, and then she just leaned back and enjoyed the sensations Billy aroused in her as she squirmed on his lap. By the time she opened her eyes again, she was half lying on the couch with Billy almost on top of her. She grabbed his hand, and guided it between her legs, and he went still.

"You sure about this?"

"Only if you are," Bella said. "No pressure."

His half laugh, half groan did nothing to stop her arousal as he palmed her panties, his thumb zeroing in just where she wanted it. Her whole body tightened and she shuddered through a climax.

"Oh, dear Lord!" She stared up at Billy, who was looking as startled as she felt. "I've never done that before."

"Yeah?" His smile was full of wickedness. "Then maybe I'll have to investigate further, and make sure you can do it again."

He dropped to his knees and kissed his way up past her thighs, and . . .

Bella reached down and grabbed a fistful of his hair as his mouth and fingers descended on her most sensitive parts and took her straight to heaven and another climax. Tears sprang to her eyes because it was just so *good* to be touched after *so long*. . . .

* * *

Billy winced and eased Bella's fingers out of his hair. He knelt up and looked at her, and his heart stuttered. She looked so beautiful lying there, flushed with the emotions he'd aroused in her. He wanted more; he wanted it all.

She sniffed and wiped at something on her cheek, which had him getting off the floor and sitting back on the couch.

"Are you okay, Bella? Did I hurt you?" Billy had to ask.

She scrambled to sit up, drawing her skirt down over her legs, and grabbed for her bra.

"No, it was lovely. It's just that I didn't expect to have all these *feelings*. . . ." She waved a helpless hand in his direction as she struggled into her bra and put her top back on.

"It's okay," Billy said gently. "I get it."

"I feel so *stupid*."

"There's no reason to feel like that." He wanted to give her a hug and tell her that everything would be okay, but he didn't want to touch her and upset her again.

"I've had some relationships since Ron died, and even the occasional bit of sex, but this felt different."

Billy wasn't sure whether to be proud or worried about what she was going to say next.

"It's okay," he repeated. "How about we do this? You go through to the bathroom, and I'll meet you back in the kitchen when you've freshened up. We can have coffee before I drive you home."

Billy opened the door that led into the shared bathroom with the office next door and switched on the light. He currently needed a really cold shower, but that could wait until Bella was feeling okay.

He went through to the kitchen, buttoned up his shirt, and washed himself thoroughly in the sink. He didn't dare tuck his shirt into his jeans again. Bella wasn't the only one who was confused. He'd felt things he hadn't experienced with any other woman other than his late wife. If Bella hadn't said anything, he wondered whether he would've been the one to pull back.

He studied his face in the small mirror above the sink. Did he regret what he'd done? No, he couldn't say that. He'd enjoyed every toe-curling minute. Was he simply too used up to open himself to the possibilities of a real relationship? This didn't feel casual. It felt like a commitment, and as everyone who knew him was aware; Billy Morgan had the ability to betray everyone. Did Bella deserve that? Would she be a fool to take that chance even if he had the nerve to ask her?

Better maybe to be grateful that she had second thoughts, and leave things as they were. . . .

Bella gasped as she looked at her flushed face and disheveled hair in the bathroom mirror. She looked like a very satisfied woman. Her whole body was humming with the sexual energy Billy had released in her, and yet she still felt like crying.

She washed her face and hands several times, and used her fingers to flatten down her hair, as she'd left her purse in the kitchen. Did she have the nerve to walk out there, smile at Billy, and pretend that nothing was wrong—that he hadn't just given her one of the best sexual experiences of her life without even trying?

She touched her reddened cheeks. If she hadn't cried, would he have carried on? How would it have felt to have Billy Morgan inside her? She was the one who'd encouraged him to kiss her and develop their relationship, and she was the one who'd lost her nerve. She had a sense that if she ever got naked and horizontal with Billy, she would no longer have the ability to deny that she cared for him very deeply.

"So much for a casual fling," Bella sighed. "I'm obviously not cut out for that."

She reluctantly left the bathroom and made her way back to the bright lights of the kitchen where Billy was busy cleaning away their meal. He glanced up as she entered and pointed at the coffeemaker.

"Help yourself. I'll join you when I've finished up."

Bella swallowed hard. "I could help if you like?"

"No, I'm good." The smile he offered her was no different than usual, which kind of hurt. "I'm just stacking the dishwasher. How about you fix me some coffee while you're getting yours? Cream's in the refrigerator."

Desperate for something to do with her hands, Bella complied, then sat at the countertop sipping her coffee while Billy worked. He didn't look upset. Maybe he was fine about everything, and she was the only one who'd gotten things out of proportion.

He washed his hands and dried them before coming to pick up his mug of coffee. He didn't sit beside her, but stood on the other side of the countertop, keeping the barrier between them.

Bella waited to see what he was going to say, but he focused on his coffee. Maybe he was waiting for her to speak first, but what the heck was she supposed to say? Sorry? Thank you? Nothing seemed right.

After chugging his coffee with some speed, Billy went into the back of the kitchen, and returned with a pile of paper that he set on the countertop beside Bella.

"Here's a list of everything we tasted, and an approximate cost estimate depending on the quantities. When you get time, look through it, and get it back to me, okay?"

Bella nodded, took the printouts, and stuffed them in her purse. "Thank you."

"You're welcome. Would you like more coffee, or shall I see you home?"

Bella sat beside Billy in his truck as he navigated the ice-covered roads into Morgantown. He talked about the ranch, his kids, and the upcoming wedding celebration in an easy, conversational way that helped ease Bella's excruciating nerves.

When they reached the parking lot behind the bar, he pulled up and cut off the engine.

Bella rushed to open her door. "It's okay. You don't have to get out. I'm fine from here."

"Jay would kill me if I didn't see you right to your door." Billy was already stepping down from his side of the truck. He walked beside Bella to the kitchen door and waited as she fumbled in her purse for her keys. The bar was still open, and the cheerful hum of the jukebox and conversation floated out from the open windows.

Bella found her keys, unlocked the door, and made herself look up into Billy's face.

"I'm sorry."

"Nothing to be sorry about." He smiled. "Let me know about the menu, okay?"

She touched his arm. "I didn't know I was going to feel like that—I . . ."

"Hey, it's all right." He held her gaze, his blue eyes steady, his tone soothing. "As long as you're okay, we're good."

"You're not mad that you didn't get any?" she blurted out, and then winced.

"I'll survive." This time his smile was crooked and way

more genuine. "'Night, Bella. Thanks for coming up to the ranch."

He tipped his hat to her, turned, and walked away, leaving her standing there feeling somewhere between foolish and very, very blessed.

Chapter Five

"Everything okay, Mom?" Jay's head came around the door of her office.

"Oh, hi! You scared me!"

Bella scrambled to hide the tab open on her laptop that held details of the wedding party. She'd received confirmation from Erin's family that they would attend, had sorted out accommodation at Hayes Hotel, and just needed to go over the final catering arrangements with Billy.

For some reason she was dragging her heels on that last matter. . . .

"You look kind of guilty to me," Jay joked. "Are you buying shoes again?"

She laughed. "You know me so well."

He leaned against the doorframe and continued to regard her. "How's Sonali working out for you?"

Bella swiveled her chair around to face him. "She's amazing."

"Good." He nodded. "I'm just off to the suppliers. Do you have a list for the kitchen?"

"Yup." She found it on her desk and handed it over to him. "Same old stuff."

"I haven't heard anyone complaining." Jay obviously wasn't finished. "Are you okay yourself?"

"What's that supposed to mean?" Bella asked.

"You seem a bit down."

"I've just been busy. Even though Sonali's a quick learner, I've still had to go through everything with her."

"You sure that's it?" Jay persisted.

Bella fixed him with her best Mom stare. "If you have something to say, Jay Ronald Williams, why don't you just spit it out?"

He came in and sat down on the only other chair. "I saw you with Billy Morgan at church last Sunday."

Bella raised her chin. "Doing what?"

"Nothing in particular." He hesitated. "It was just the way he was looking down at you—like you were really special to him."

She shrugged. Having a son who'd been a Navy SEAL meant he noticed every tiny detail. "We've known each other since we were kids. We're good friends."

"I know that, but this was something new." He looked at her. "If you want to have a relationship with him, I wouldn't mind."

She raised an eyebrow. "Like I'd be consulting you?"

He smiled. "You'd think I'd be worried you'd forgotten Dad. I wouldn't. I want you to be happy."

"That's very nice of you, but maybe I can't get over your father. Maybe it's *me* who's the problem," Bella said.

"There's no shame in moving forward, Mom," Jay said gently. "I had to learn to let go of the past, and trust Erin."

"I know you did." She smiled at him. "I'm very proud of you both."

"I just want you to know that I love you, and that I'll always have your back whatever you choose to do." He came over to drop a kiss on the top of her head. "Thanks for everything you did for me when I came home from the hospital. You were my rock. I don't tell you that enough."

"Oh, get along with you." She gave him an affectionate smack on the rear. "I've got to get back to the kitchen. Avery found me a great dishwasher as well, so I hardly have to do a thing anymore."

He laughed, and went out leaving her sitting there feeling like crying again. His words had hit home, but she still wasn't sure what she wanted to do with them. She glanced down at her desk, her gaze coming to rest on the menu options Billy had given her.

Whatever she did next, she owed Billy an explanation. They'd been friends for too long to not seek closure. She'd give him a call later and ask him to come round to discuss the details when he was next in town.

"Did you hear back from Bella?" Ruth asked Billy as he sat down to eat his dinner at the crowded family table.

"Yeah. I had a text from her today, actually. I'm going to sort out the details with her this evening after my AA meeting."

Billy was glad he had something to report. After three days of silence he had started to wonder whether Bella would ever speak to him again. And he already missed her company in so many ways. . . .

"Good, because if we are going to pull this party off, we really need to get the supplies in just in case it starts snowing and the roads become impassable." Ruth passed him the jug of iced tea.

"Good point."

"I hear you're going to do all the cooking, Dad." Chase spoke up from the other side of the table.

"Yeah, seeing as Gustav isn't here, I thought I'd pitch in."

"I keep forgetting you can cook," Chase said.

"That's because no one up here seems to require my

help." Billy met his eldest son's gaze, aware that everyone else around the table was now focused on their conversation. Maybe it was because he was heart sore over Bella, or maybe it was just time for some plain speaking. "I offered to run the guest kitchen, but you all shouted me down."

Chase frowned. "Because that's not who you are."

"What exactly am I, then?" Billy asked. "You're the financial wizard, BB takes care of the horses, Ry and HW manage the special programs, and Roy runs the whole goddamn ranch with Ruth."

"That's not fair." Blue Boy, his bluntest son, was quick to get into the conversation. "You gave up those things. You said you didn't want the responsibility."

"I *said* I didn't want to rock the boat," Billy responded. "You know why."

BB glanced around the table at his siblings. "Because you don't deserve any of this, right? Because you walked out on us."

"Yes."

BB shook his head. "You still tiptoe around here like you're a paying guest—like you can't comment on anything in case you offend someone."

Billy just stared at him. "Go on."

Chase stirred. "BB—maybe this isn't the time."

"No." Billy held up his hand. He was just glad his granddaughter Maria wasn't present to hear her father BB's speech because she wouldn't appreciate them arguing. "Let him speak."

BB sighed. "Look, all I'm trying to say is that you don't have to do that. It doesn't matter what you say, we all know this is your place—that you coming back to Morgan Ranch returned its soul. *Tell* us we're crap. Tell us where we're going wrong. We accepted you back a long time ago. We *want* you here."

Billy looked around the table where everyone was nodding along with BB's words. He gripped the table hard to remind himself that he wasn't dreaming as his son's blunt words sunk in.

"It's still your ranch, Dad," BB said quietly. "You're the one who taught us how to love it when we were kids, just like you did. *You're* the reason we all came home."

Billy managed a nod and then turned on his heel and escaped the kitchen before he did something stupid like bawl his eyes out. How had his children managed to grow up so smart despite their parents' bad choices? He got into his truck and drove to town. The need to sit quietly in his AA meeting and process what had just happened consumed him. Perhaps listening to how others had overcome their demons, and still struggled, would reset and restore him.

Bella glanced at the clock as someone knocked on the back door and then checked her cell. There was a text from Billy suggesting he meet with her after she'd finished her shift. It was getting close to that time now. She usually stopped taking orders an hour before the bar closed, and it was almost ten now.

Sonali closed the refrigerator and came over. "I'm done—unless you can think of anything else that needs attending to?"

Bella smiled as she went to open the back door. "No, you've been great. I can't believe you agreed to work for me."

"It's fun! I love learning new things," Sonali said as she took off her apron. "I don't think I'll stay here forever, but I'd rather be cooking than sitting around the apartment feeling sorry for myself with Dev moaning about me not paying rent."

Bella checked it was indeed Billy outside, and opened the door.

"Come on in. I'm just finishing up." She stepped aside as Sonali came back with her hat and coat. "Have you met Sonali, Billy?"

"Yes, we met at the ranch during her interview with Gustav." Billy shook Sonali's hand. "How are you doing? Is Bella treating you okay?"

Sonali grinned. "She's awesome and I'm having a great time." She glanced back at Bella. "I'll see you tomorrow, okay?"

"Are you good walking home, Sonali?" Billy asked.

"Thanks, Mr. Morgan, but it's literally across the street. Dev's probably already standing at the window twitching the drapes to make sure I cross the road properly." Sonali winked. "He takes his big brother duties very seriously."

She crammed her woolen hat on her head, put on her coat, and set off whistling, her hands in her pockets.

Suddenly all too aware that she was now alone with Billy Morgan, Bella went into the kitchen. There was very little left to do, but completing the regular tasks helped her calm down and get used to being around Billy again.

Without asking, he helped out, putting things away and cleaning surfaces. The bar was still packed, and the noise drifted through the kitchen as they completed their tasks.

"I'll just go and tell Jay I'm done and I'll be right with you," Bella said.

"Not a problem."

For some reason Billy looked more solemn than usual, his warm smile absent. Was he expecting her to deliver bad news, or was something else going on?

After saying good night to Jay, she returned to the kitchen and led the way upstairs to her apartment, where she'd left a single light burning in the window. Billy came in behind her and shut the door.

"What a great view of Main Street and the Christmas lights." He went into the kitchen and stared out over the street.

"It's great until the drunks get out," Bella said.

He swung around to look at her. "My AA meeting got out about an hour ago. Hopefully none of them showed up here."

Bella winced. "Sorry that came out wrong—"

"It's okay. It was my lame attempt at a joke." He drew a sheaf of papers out of his coat pocket. "I brought a copy of the menu suggestions in case you'd lost yours."

"I have them right here." Bella put on the coffeemaker. "I marked my choices, and I've written you a check for ten percent as a deposit."

"I think I trust you." His smile this time was sweet. "I even know where you live."

"Don't they say you should never mix business with pleasure?" Bella asked.

"Or attempt to seduce your old friends?" Billy countered.

Bella sighed. "I'm sorry about that."

"Hey, I wasn't talking about you." Billy frowned. "I was talking about *me*."

Bella carefully lined up two mugs and then straightened them again. "Are you by any chance trying to take the blame for what happened between us?"

"Well, seeing as I'm the one who obviously pushed you too far, then, yeah."

She slowly raised her head to look him right in the eye. "You made me climax. Twice. And then when I panicked, you took me home. How in the world are you taking the blame for *that*?" She pointed her spoon at him. "I wanted you to touch me. I *loved* it!"

"Okay," Billy said, holding her gaze. "That's good to know." He held up the papers. "So do you want this copy?"

"Are you *listening* to me?" Bella asked. "What is up with you wanting to be Saint Billy the Perfect of Morgantown all the time?"

He went still. "You sound just like BB."

"What?"

"He just tore me off a strip at dinner for being too scared to accept any ownership of the ranch, or to rock anyone's boat."

"Maybe he has a point." Bella glared at him.

"Maybe he does," Billy sighed. "So here goes. I want to make things right with you. If that means I accept the blame for what happened the other night and we can move forward and still be friends, then I'm good with that."

"Well, at least that's honest."

"I'm trying here." His smile was crooked. "I never want you to feel frightened with me, or worried that I won't stop trying to get in your pants again."

Bella took a deep, steadying breath. "I wasn't frightened of what we did together. I was frightened of how it made me *feel*—emotionally, not physically, if that makes any sense."

He still looked puzzled, so Bella kept talking.

"When you touched me, it was so wonderful, and so special, that I couldn't handle it. It reminded me of how I'd felt with Ron, and that was such a shock that I didn't know how to deal with it. I felt *guilty*. Like I was betraying *him*. Can you understand that?"

He was nodding now. "Yeah, I think I can. I felt like that after Annie left. I was still technically married, but for a long time I had no idea whether she was dead or alive, and

I was in no fit state to be as discriminating as I should've been. Knowing I'd been stupid just added to my guilt, made me drink even more and do even more stupid things."

"Maybe they both ruined us in different ways." Bella tried to smile.

"Not ruined," Billy objected. "Love is never wasted. The trick is moving on from the guilt, and finding new ways to give and receive that love." He hesitated. "It's fine if you're not ready to move on from your relationship with Ron yet."

"Now you're going back to being all reasonable again." Bella sniffed as she poured them both some coffee.

"I can't seem to help myself." Billy chuckled. "I just want the people I care about to be happy. I came so close to losing everyone and everything I loved that I value every precious second in case it's snatched away from me again." He grimaced. "If that makes me a pushover or too nice, I suppose that's how it is."

"You're definitely not a pushover."

"Thanks." He smiled as she handed over his coffee. "But am I too nice?"

"You're a good, strong man." She pressed her hand over her heart. "In here."

"I try to be. That's all I can do." He sipped his coffee. "So can we be friends again?"

Bella considered him for a long moment. "I can't do casual sex."

He blinked at her. "I beg your pardon?"

"That's what I've realized over the years since Ron died." Bella took a deep breath. "The thing is, I don't feel casual about you."

"Sexually or generally?" Billy asked.

"Either," Bella said, then took her courage in both hands.

"It feels to me that if I did sleep with you, then we'd have to be a couple."

"Okay." Billy nodded.

"Doesn't that scare you?"

He sat back and regarded her. "Should it?"

"Well, because of your kids, and the ranch, and your mother—God, your mother—and Annie . . ." She ran out of breath. "What about them?"

"What would they have to do with us being a couple?"

"Because they'd all *know*, and—"

"That would bother you?" He raised an eyebrow. "You'd prefer to keep everything secret?" His eyes were full of sympathy. "I don't think that's possible in a town this size, and if it does bother you, then maybe, as I said, you aren't yet ready to move on."

"I'm trying to be," Bella whispered.

He reached for her hand. "Look, I'm not going anywhere. If you get to a point where we can be a real couple, then come and tell me." He squeezed her fingers. "I mean it. I'll wait. You're worth it."

"Really?" Bella looked into his eyes and saw nothing but understanding and genuine concern in them. "I feel like I'm letting you down somehow."

"You're not. We're not kids anymore. We're old enough to speak our minds, take things slow, and get them *right*. I don't have a problem with that." Billy did his best to try and get through to her. "I just want you to be okay."

He wanted a lot more for her, but a year in jail had taught him all about patience—about how to pace himself, how to shed his past, and look forward to a better future. He'd even learned to forgive himself, which had been the hardest thing of all. Some things in life were worth waiting for, and Bella Williams was definitely one of them.

She was still worrying at her lip, which made him want

to kiss her real bad, but he also sensed she was relaxing a little.

A loud crash reverberated through the floor, and Billy stiffened. “Did you leave anything out in the kitchen?”

“No. But Jay might have gone in there for something, although it’s unlikely that he’d make a mess.” Bella slid off her stool in double-quick time.

“Could it be a raccoon or some kind of animal?” Billy asked.

“It’s possible. It wouldn’t be the first time that’s happened.” Bella was already heading toward the door. Billy caught her elbow.

“Where are you going?”

“To see what’s happening. This is my home, and I’m not letting any raccoon or skunk run wild in my kitchen!”

“Don’t you think Jay can handle it?”

“He might not have heard a thing. It gets really noisy out front on Friday nights.”

Having rarely been in the bar since his return, Billy could only assume she was correct.

“Shall I call Nate?” Billy offered.

“Not yet. I don’t want to look stupid or waste his time. Let’s see what we’re dealing with first.”

Bella went into her office, opened the closet, and started punching numbers in the safe. When the door swung open she grabbed a box and started loading bullets into the chamber of a gun.

“You’re going to *kill it*?” Billy asked. “I was thinking about opening the back door and simply shooing it out.”

“It depends how big it is,” Bella said. “We had a wild pig in here once, and it was as big as a calf and caused so much damage you wouldn’t believe it.”

Just as they reached the front door leading to the stairs, there was a crash of breaking glass and the creaking sound of wood as the downstairs door was kicked in. Bella started forward, and Billy held her back.

"Wait," he whispered close to her ear. "I'm betting that's not a pig. How about we set up a trap?"

Bella nodded. He reached over her shoulder and unlatched the front door, leaving it slightly ajar. Taking her hand, he set off back toward her office where the safe was still open and on display in the moonlight.

"Let's leave it like that. Now, where can we hide, and make sure this particular pig can't get away?"

Chapter Six

Bella directed Billy behind her desk and they crouched down together. She could clearly hear someone coming up the stairs, and it definitely wasn't Jay. Her teeth were chattering so hard she wondered why Billy didn't say something. He was busy texting while she laid the gun on the floor, making sure the safety was still on.

The stumbling footsteps grew louder and were accompanied by a litany of grunts and curses that Bella remembered only too well. She tensed as her former employee, Axel Jordan, swayed against the doorframe, the smell of alcohol coming off him in waves.

"Stupid bitch," he muttered. "Can't even shut the safe properly. Thinks she's so safe with that disabled vet protecting her?"

Beside Bella, Billy's arm was rigid, his whole attention on Axel, and his normal expression obscured by an icy calmness that reminded her of Jay.

Axel stumbled against the desk, knocking piles of paper to the floor, and then leaned down to look into the safe, where the strongbox was clearly visible.

"I'll just take it all." Axel chuckled. "Bastards."

It took Bella a terrified second to notice Billy was on the move. He crawled around the other side of the desk, gathered himself, and leapt on Axel's back, bringing the younger man crashing to the ground.

Bella shot to her feet as Axel attempted to break free, his flailing fist connecting with the side of Billy's head making him jerk backward. With a *whoop*, Axel attempted to shake Billy off, but Bella wasn't going to let that happen.

"Stay right where you are," she yelled as she pointed the gun at Axel, and took up a two-handed shooting stance.

"Like you know how to fire that." Axel gasped as Billy recaptured one of his hands and wrenched it up against his spine.

"You don't think Jay taught me to defend myself?" Bella asked. "Try me."

Billy shoved Axel's head down to the floor again with some force, and he went quiet.

"Do you have any rope?" Billy asked.

"I have panty hose!" Bella laid the gun down on the desk and ran to her bedroom. Her hands were shaking so hard, it was almost impossible to get the darn panty hose out of the packet. Not that she needed to worry about accidentally snagging them . . .

When she got back, Axel was still out of it and Billy had grabbed hold of his other wrist.

"Thanks." He took the black, silky hose. "What a waste."

Bella's knees gave way, and she sank down beside him. "I hardly wear them anymorc. I prefer stay-up stockings or Spanx."

Billy chuckled. "Good to know."

"How can you be so cheerful?" Bella demanded.

"Because we won." Billy turned to look at her properly. "Are you okay?"

She reached out and cupped his cheek, her voice trembling. "I thought he was going to kill you, and then I thought that would be the second man I've loved taken away from me too quickly."

Billy placed his hand over hers. "You've had a terrible shock—"

"Yes, I have, and maybe I'm speaking the truth because there isn't anything left to hide behind when this kind of thing happens," Bella said. "I'd hate to be the kind of person who ignores a wake-up call."

Billy's cell buzzed, making them both jump. He took it out of his pocket and held Bella's gaze.

"It's Nate. I'm going to call him, okay?"

He pressed the screen and put the sheriff on speaker. "Hey, can you come on over to the Red Dragon? I've got Axel Jordan drunk and tied up in Bella's apartment."

"I'm already in the kitchen." Nate sounded his usual laid-back self. "The back door was wide open."

Bella winced. "I guess I forgot to check if it was locked when Sonali went out, and I didn't put the alarm system on because Jay was still in the building."

Billy patted her shoulder. "It's okay." He could hear Nate coming up the stairs and kept talking to him. "Axel smashed through both doors, so you should be able to walk right in."

"So I see," Nate replied. "I'm coming in now."

Billy made sure that Bella's gun was in full view on the desk, and slowly stood up, offering Bella his hand to help her rise as well.

"You're bleeding," Bella gasped.

"Yeah, I think his ring caught me when he walloped me

on the side of the head," Billy hastened to reassure her. "Nothing to worry about."

Nate stood in the doorway and slowly put his weapon away. "Nice job, guys."

"You're welcome," Billy said. "He's drunk and he's still breathing, and that's all you need to know."

"Got it." Nate went down on one knee and shook Axel's shoulder until he groaned. "You're under arrest . . ."

Billy moved over to where Bella was standing, one hand over her mouth, and put his arm around her. "How about we go into the kitchen and make some strong coffee?"

She nodded, and carefully stepped over Nate, who was busy calling for an ambulance and some backup.

Billy hugged her as they walked down the hallway. "You did good."

She shuddered. "I'm not sure about that."

"Yeah, you did. I believed you'd shoot him and more importantly, so did Axel. Your intervention gave me the moment I needed to knock him out once and for all." He led her to the couch. "I'll get the coffee. Do you want to text Jay?"

"I'm surprised he isn't already up here demanding to know what's going on," Bella said.

As if she'd conjured him up with her words, Jay appeared in the doorway, his frantic gaze fastened on Bella, and he rushed over to her side.

"Are you okay? Nate just told me what happened. How the *hell* didn't I notice what was going down." He took Bella's hand in both of his. "Did he hurt you? How did he get in the kitchen? Did you let him in?"

Billy stepped into Jay's line of sight. "Maybe you could ease up on the questions, Jay. Your mom's pretty shaken up right now."

Jay briefly glanced at Billy and then returned his attention to his mother. "That's it. You're coming to live with Erin and me. I can't let you stay here another night."

Bella sat up straight. "No, I'm not going to do that."

"I'm sorry, but I'm not giving you a choice, okay?" Jay stated. "Just pack a few things and come with me right now."

Bella looked over Jay's head right at Billy, and he cleared his throat.

"Bella doesn't want to live with you."

Jay slowly stood and turned to Billy. "Look, I'm grateful that you were here, and Nate says you were the one who tackled Axel, but this isn't really your business, is it?"

"It is if Bella wants it to be." Billy held Jay's gaze. "Your mother is a grown woman. If she wants to stay here maybe you should respect her decision or at least give her the time to come to one herself."

Silence fell as the retired Navy SEAL contemplated Billy long enough to set all the hairs on the back of Billy's neck on edge.

"Mom can't stay here tonight. The locks need fixing."

"Then she can choose what she wants to do." Billy looked at Bella. "Do you want to stay the night with Jay, or come back to the ranch with me?"

Bella rose from her seat and came to stand beside him. "Thanks for the offer, but I think I'll have to stay nearby so I can be here early in the morning when the locksmith arrives."

"Jay could do that," Billy said firmly. "Come home with me."

"Yeah." Jay cleared his throat. "I'll take care of everything. You do what you want, Mom."

Bella's smile was glorious as she placed her hand in Billy's. "Then I'll come with you."

* * *

Bella glanced over at Billy as they drove back to the ranch. She'd taken care of his bloodied head, talked to Nate, and made sure that Jay went home to Erin. The thought that Axel Jordan was now in custody made her feel so much safer.

"You okay?" Billy asked as they drew up in front of the silent ranch house.

"I'm getting there." She smiled at him, and in the darkness he leaned over and gently kissed her mouth. "Won't Ruth mind another guest?"

"I texted them all to let them know we were coming, so hopefully they've all gotten the message and gone to bed." The gentle humor in his voice was balm for her soul. "They're a nosy bunch."

She climbed down from the truck and looked up as a flurry of snow descended through the blackness of the night. "The ranch house looks like a Christmas card with all the lights and the snow."

"So I've been told." Billy took her hand. "Come on in."

The house smelled of Christmas spices and pine, and was lovely and warm. After shedding their coats and boots in the mudroom, they tiptoed up the stairs to the second floor. Billy opened a door and led her into a room with an angled roof that looked out over the barn.

"Chase converted these attic spaces into separate suites. He and January are across the hall."

"It's lovely." Bella gazed out over the snow-covered roofs and fields. "It smells so new and piney."

"It didn't exist when Annie lived here, so it was a good place for me to start afresh."

Bella pointed at the big wooden framed bed. "That's one of Ruth's quilts."

"Yeah, and BB made the headboard." Billy's smile was wry. "You can't get away from them even in here."

"And you wouldn't want to." She walked straight into his arms, and it felt like coming home. "Come on, admit it."

"It's my home," he said simply. "It's who I am."

Bella went to reply and yawned instead, giving him an up-close and personal view of her tonsils that made Billy smile.

"Let's go to bed."

"I don't think I'm going to be good for much more than just sleeping," Bella confessed.

"Then sleep." He kissed the top of her head. "No pressure, remember?"

She used the bathroom and then climbed into the big bed and lay on her back listening as the extraordinary, all-encompassing silence closed around her like a silken glove. She yawned again as Billy joined her wearing a Morgan Ranch T-shirt and pj pants with horses on them.

"Nice." She pointed at the pants.

"Last year's Christmas present from Maria. I have to wear them, or else she'll be upset." He laid his arm along the top of her pillow, inviting her to snuggle in against him, which she did. "Hmmm. That's nice."

She rubbed her cheek against the softness of his T-shirt. The fact that they were both here, and uninjured, suddenly hit her again. She slid her fingers under his shirt, needing to touch his skin.

"It's okay." He stroked her hair. "We're all good."

She lay there and breathed him in, enjoyed the rise and fall of his chest, and the way he held her as if she was made of spun sugar. She must have dozed off because she came to plastered all over his front, her inner thigh pressed against the heat and hardness of his need.

His hand was planted firmly on her butt, his fingers flexing.

"Billy?" she whispered into the darkness.

"Yeah?"

"I'm awake now."

His low chuckle reverberated against her skin. "I can see that."

"Will you kiss me?"

He slid a hand into her hair. "Always."

And then it all became so simple. Skin uncovered, kisses everywhere until he rolled her onto her back and entered her in one slow thrust that almost made her cry again. She held on to him, her hands everywhere as he brought her to a new peak of pleasure in his own sweet time.

"Bella . . ." He groaned her name as he came, and collapsed onto the pillow beside her. She stroked the back of his head, and let him stay there until he finally found the energy to roll away.

He reached for her hand, interlocking her fingers with his, and searched her face in the moonlight.

"I should've asked you about contraception."

"I'm past all that nonsense," she reassured him. "I would've mentioned it otherwise."

"And I can confirm that I got a clean bill of health from Dr. Tio last year."

They grinned at each other.

Bella kissed his nose. "So we can just have fun."

"Amen to that." He kissed her back. "Do you think you can sleep now?"

"Yes." She eased onto her side. "Just to let you know, I snore."

"So do I."

"Perfect." She spooned against him, and he wrapped his

arm around her waist. "Good night, Billy, and thanks for everything."

Within two minutes she was fast asleep.

"Dad, did you hear about what happened at the Red Dragon last night? I—"

Billy opened one eye to see Chase coming in through the door, laptop in hand. He pulled up short, a look of horror on his face as he took in the clothes strewn around the floor, and the two naked people in the bed.

"Dear God, I'm so sorry, I didn't realize—"

"What's going on?" BB put his head around the door and did a double take. "Jeez, Dad, gross. Lock the door next time, okay? You've traumatized Chase."

Chase backed out with all the care of a hostage situation. "So I'll assume you know what happened, and I'll see you at breakfast." He cleared his throat. "You too, Mrs. Williams."

When the door finally shut, Billy looked down at Bella, who had pulled the sheet almost over her head.

"I did tell you they were nosy, didn't I?"

He suddenly realized she was shaking with laughter, and felt much better.

"It could've been worse. It could've been Jay," she spluttered.

"And now I'd be a dead man," Billy murmured. He glanced at the time. "You okay to get up and face the family over breakfast? I've got chores to do, and I bet you'll be wanting to get home."

Bella grabbed his hand. "Thank you."

"For what?"

"All of this." She waved a hand around, and the sheet fell

to her waist. Billy made himself focus on her face, although it was almost impossible. "I'm okay with *everything*."

"Like with us being a couple?"

"Yes." She met his gaze, her brown eyes so warm and full of shyness that he wanted to kiss her. "Especially that." She bit her lip. "I think I'm falling in love with you."

Billy nodded, too choked up right at that moment to do anything else. The fact that he was home, with his family, and now had this unimaginable, unexpected gift of love from a woman he liked, respected, and lusted after was almost too much to comprehend.

"Are you okay?" Bella asked softly.

"Yeah." He swallowed hard. "I'm just counting my blessings."

Everything he'd had and lost, everything he'd ever wanted to achieve with the blessing of this second chance now made sense. Bella made sense of it. Coming home to his old friend completed a circle he hadn't even been aware he was traveling.

He gave in to the temptation to kiss her, and then she touched him, and . . .

"Wait a sec." He eased himself away and went to lock the door before climbing back into bed. "Maybe just for once, the chores can wait."

Chapter Seven

"So what's so important that you had to drag me and Erin out here, Mom?" Jay inquired as Bella maneuvered him into the darkened guest center at the ranch.

"The lights aren't working."

"There are a load of Morgans up here to deal with that kind of thing," Jay protested. "Why—"

"SURPRISE!!"

Billy snapped the lights on to reveal the fifty or so guests Bella had invited to celebrate her son and new daughter-in-law's Vegas wedding. Following Bella's instructions, he immediately shut the door just in case Jay decided to bolt.

"Mom?" That was Erin's delighted voice. "You and Dad are *here*?"

Whatever Jay might have been going to say was lost as his wife ran over to her parents and started hugging them. Jay stared down at Bella, who gave him her best wide-eyed, innocent look.

"You did this?"

She shrugged. "With a little help from my friends." She touched his sleeve. "I wanted to do something special for you both."

He let out his breath and looked around the crowded

room. She knew he wasn't at his happiest in crowds, but hopefully, seeing as he knew everyone who was present, he'd soon relax and enjoy himself.

"It's all good, Mom. Thank you."

"You're welcome, Jay." She gave him a little push in the right direction. "Now go and say hello to Erin's parents while I see how everything's going in the kitchen."

Bella rushed through the swing doors, her hand to her heart. She leaned against the wall and slowly exhaled. "I thought he was going to bolt."

Billy and Sonali looked up from whatever they were doing and stared at her.

"Yeah, there was a moment when I wondered the same thing," Billy said. "Probably not a good idea to spring too many surprises on a retired Navy SEAL."

"Tell me about it." Bella looked around the kitchen. "Now, what can I do to help?"

"Nothing. You're the mother of the groom, and you're the one throwing the party. Go out and be sociable." Billy came over and pointed at the exit.

"I'd much rather be helping in here."

"We're good." Billy held the door open. "Off you go and charm the pants off Erin's parents."

She raised an eyebrow and whispered, "The only pants I want to charm off are yours."

"Good to know." Billy's blue eyes glinted with warm amusement. "But you still need to get out there."

"Will you come and join me?" She stroked the collar of his shirt.

"When the buffet is all set up I'll come and sit with you, okay?"

"I suppose it's the best I can hope for." She sighed. "Maybe I'll go and talk to Chase. He still won't look me in the eye."

Billy grinned. "Not our fault that he's a prude."

"And then there's BB, who keeps winking and grinning at me like he thinks the idea of his father having sex is a big joke."

"BB does think that, but you can ignore him as well." He hesitated. "You might want to talk to Maria. She and I are very close, and I'd love it if you two could be friends."

"I'll do my best." She went on tiptoe and kissed him. "Don't be too long."

Bella made her way out to the dining room and was immediately engulfed in a crowd of friends and family. By the time she'd talked to everyone, Billy and Sonali had already put out trays of appetizers, and Nancy, Jay's second in command, was doing brisk business at the bar.

Bella spotted Billy's granddaughter curled up on one of the big couches in front of the roaring log fire and went over to join her. Maria wore jeans, a black T-shirt with some kind of cartoon character on it, and a black hoodie.

"Are you having a good time?" Bella asked as she sat beside her.

Maria made a face. "Not really. It's all adults here, and Grandpa's busy in the kitchen, so I have no one to really talk to."

"You know, that's my fault," Bella confessed. "I didn't think to include any other kids your age when I was making up the guest lists."

"There aren't any kids out here," Maria pointed out. "That's why I have to go on the bus to Bridgeport for high school."

"That sucks." Bella nodded. "You should taste the food though. Your grandpa is a really good cook."

"I know. He's made me taste every single thing about fifty times, so I'm good." Maria grinned. "He really wanted to make things right for you."

"That's because he's a really nice man."

"And he really, *really* likes you," Maria said. "You know that, right?"

Bella glanced at the teen. "You think so?"

"Dude, he like can't stop talking about you, and his face goes all funny and goofy." Maria shook her head. "It's hilarious."

"Really?" Now Bella sounded like a teenager herself. "I like him, too."

Maria's smile disappeared. "I hope you mean it. Grandpa's life hasn't been easy, and I don't want anyone to hurt him again."

"I wouldn't do that," Bella reassured Maria. "Did he tell you that I've known him since kindergarten? That's a long time to know someone and still like them."

"That's true." Maria nodded. "Ruth said that you always stuck up for him even when some of the people around here were saying he was a murderer."

"As I said, I knew he couldn't have done that. He loved Annie, he really did. It's a real shame she died before he could make things right with her," Bella said. "So are you okay with me and your grandpa being a couple?"

Maria shrugged. "You make him happy. He smiles a lot more, and that makes me happy because now I live with Dad and Jenna I can't take care of him myself all the time."

"He's wonderful." Bella hesitated. "I never thought I'd find someone I could love again."

"That's awesome." Maria offered Bella a high five. "You should tell him."

"Tell me what?"

Bella looked up to see Billy smiling down at them, a tray of canapés in his hand.

Maria groaned. "Jeez, Grandpa, I ate about two million of those things last week! Take them away!"

"I thought you liked them," Billy protested.

"I liked the first couple of hundred." Maria stood up and stretched. "Is there any of that shrimp thing left?"

"Plenty," Billy said as Maria wandered off. "Poor kid got stuck being my number one taster for everything. She was really helpful, but I think I put her off eating for life."

"I think she'll pull through." Bella also rose and directed her gaze over to the buffet table where Maria was piling her plate with food and chatting to her father, Blue. "Are we almost ready to set out the main course?"

"Sonali and I decided we'd do it in about ten minutes. Do you want to make an announcement or something, or have a few speeches?"

"I'd rather not," Bella said. "It all seems to be going really well at the moment. Even Erin's parents are being gracious about the whole wedding fiasco—in fact, I bonded with Erin's mom over our shared wish to have seen Erin in a beautiful wedding dress."

"Good for you." Billy gestured at the tray. "I'm going to put this down on the table. Is there anything I can get for you?"

"I'm good," Bella replied. "I just need to speak to Yvonne about the cake."

"She's in the kitchen right now setting it up." Billy looked down at her. "Is everything okay?"

"It's wonderful." She smiled into his eyes. "Jay's happy and Erin's parents have finally accepted the fact that their daughter hasn't married a potential member of Congress."

She went through to the kitchen and spoke to Yvonne, who had designed, baked, and decorated the most beautiful cake Bella could ever have imagined. They would set it out after the buffet along with champagne and hope that by then, everyone would be too full of good food and benevolent thoughts to do anything but toast the happy couple.

Billy came into the kitchen and caught hold of her hand. "Come and see this."

"Aren't you supposed to be managing a kitchen or something?" Bella asked.

"Sonali, Avery, and Yvonne are in charge. We can goof off for a few minutes."

He took her to put on her coat and they walked out into the crackling stillness of ice and the gentle fall of snow.

"Look up there," Billy said.

"At what?" Bella stopped and raised her face to the inky night sky. Billy stood behind with his arms wrapped around her waist. "Wow, that's a big moon, and the stars are so clear!"

"Now come and look at this." He led her toward the old barn that housed a mixed collection of farm animals and the family horses.

He paused by one of the stalls and unlocked the top half of the stable door. Bella stood on tiptoe and looked inside to see a newborn foal and her mother.

"Oh, my goodness," she whispered. "What a beautiful sight."

"Roy just came in to tell me the mare had foaled before he went off to take a shower." Billy's chuckle warmed the back of her neck. "Luckily for us we also have a vet in the family, and Jenna was right here on the spot. She's probably taking a shower, too."

Bella turned in Billy's arms to face him as he secured the top door again.

"Thank you for showing me such beautiful things."

He angled his head and looked down at her. "You're welcome."

"All of them give me hope," Bella said. "Jay finding himself again and falling in love, Erin, you . . ."

His smile was beautiful. "I give you hope?"

"Yes, that it's possible to find *two* wonderful men in one lifetime, and fall in love with them."

He kissed her very slowly and carefully. "I can't argue with that." He hesitated and looked down at her. "I'd like to ask you something."

"Okay."

He grimaced. "But I'm finding it hard to come up with the right words because I don't want to offend you, or presume too much, or—"

She pressed a finger to his lips. "How about you just ask?"

"You know that I love you, and—"

"I do?" Bella blinked up at him. "I don't think you've actually said it out loud to me before, although I'd kind of *assumed* that was where we were at—"

It was Billy's turn to stop her talking by kissing her. When he finally drew back they were both breathless.

"Will you marry me?" Billy asked. "I know we have some issues here, like where we would live, and whether we'd both be able to keep working if we wanted to, and all that other stuff. Not even to mention Jay's reaction, and Maria's, and the rest of my incredibly supportive, but nosy as hell family."

He ran out of breath and just stared down at her shocked face.

"Did you hear what I said?"

Bella nodded and bit her lip. "I'm just trying to process the first part."

"My proposal of marriage?" Billy asked.

"Yes, that."

"Am I being stupid here?" Billy asked. "Would we be better off staying as we are? I'm happy, you're happy, and we're old enough not to worry about what anyone else thinks about us being together and not actually married."

Bella was still staring at him as if he'd grown another head, and he felt like a complete idiot. "Okay, then maybe we should shelve this discussion until after the holidays when things have calmed down a bit, and we know where we stand."

"Billy."

"Yeah?"

"Could you stop talking for a minute?" Bella asked.

He pressed his lips together and just looked pleadingly down at her. Around them the horses and cattle slumbered in their stalls and the snow continued to fall.

"Yes."

Billy cleared his throat. "Yes, you'd like to marry me?"

She nodded.

A wave of happiness so profound that it consumed his whole body swept over him, and he framed her face in his hands. "Thank God."

Her smile was so beautiful, and so full of trust that he fought back the urge to cry.

"You'll never regret that decision, Bella." His voice trembled with emotion. "I swear that I will do my best to *never* let you down, and I'll always be there for you."

"I know you will." She used her thumb to gently wipe at the corner of his eye. "It's okay. We can work out the details later, or stay engaged until one of us decides to retire. We'll work it out. I *know* we will."

Billy kissed her again and she wrapped her arms around his neck and kissed him back.

"Oh, jeez, not *again*."

That was Chase's horrified voice. Billy buried his face in Bella's shoulder and shook with laughter.

"Grandpa . . ."

And that was Maria. Bella pushed on his chest and he turned around to see his oldest son and granddaughter staring at him with matching expressions of horror on their faces.

"We came out to see the new foal," Maria explained.

"She's right in here." Billy pointed at the stall and stepped back. "Don't go in yet, okay?"

"I know that." Maria rolled her eyes as if she'd lived on the ranch forever. "Why don't you two go in? Chase can keep an eye on me, and Jay *was* looking for Mrs. Williams."

"Then we'd better go," Bella said.

Maria had one last thing to say. "You know, Grandpa, if you keep behaving like this you should do what I suggested and ask Mrs. Williams to marry you."

Billy nodded. "I just did and she said yes."

Chase grinned and slapped Billy on the back. "That's *awesome*! Congratulations. I can't wait to see Jay's face when he finds out about this."

"Then maybe we'd better mention it to him before Chase starts spreading rumors," Billy murmured as Chase and Maria walked away hand in hand. "Are you okay with that?"

"Yes, better to be safe than sorry," Bella agreed, and squeezed his fingers as they retraced their steps through the snow to the guest center.

They paused outside the kitchen door to remove their boots before returning to the warmth of the dining room beyond. Leaving Bella in the kitchen, Billy went and found Jay and persuaded him to step away from the noise, and into the quieter part of the building.

Knowing Jay was a plain speaker, Billy didn't bother with a long, flowery speech.

"I wanted you to know that I asked your mother to marry me, and she said yes."

Jay stared at him, a muscle moving in his cheek. "Okay."

"That's all you've got?" Billy asked.

"She loves you. That's all I need to know." Jay took a step closer to Billy. "And all you need to remember is that if you hurt her I'll come after you, and no one will ever find your body."

"Understood." Billy nodded.

"Then we're good." Jay stuck out his hand. "Welcome to the family."

Bella helped clear away the food and then returned to the dining room to watch Jay and Erin cut the cake. She'd barely had a moment to speak to Billy, but seeing as both he and Jay were still alive and smiling, she assumed everything had gone as well as it could've.

Billy wanted her to marry him . . . and the funny thing was that she wanted it, too. She hadn't expected him to propose so quickly, but as Maureen would probably remind her, they weren't spring chickens so they might as well enjoy their time together. The thought of that—the thought of being with him every day made her so happy she still couldn't quite get her head around it.

She watched him now, as he passed Erin the knife to cut the cake, his blue eyes gleaming, and the harsher lines on his face disappearing beneath his smile. A man who had disappointed others, had paid dearly for his mistakes, and yet had come home to face his demons, and repay his debts. . . . That took courage and humility, qualities she could appreciate and strive to improve in herself.

And what about her? She pictured Ron and imagined him smiling down at her. She truly had been blessed in her life.

"Mom?"

She looked up, startled as Jay called her out to stand beside him and Erin.

"I'd like to thank my mom, Bella, for organizing this amazing party for me and Erin. I'd also like to thank Erin's parents for coming all the way from the East Coast to celebrate with us."

Everyone clapped, cheered, and drank champagne.

"And I'd like to thank Billy and Sonali for providing all the amazing food and Morgan Ranch and their staff for their hospitality," Jay added. "I had *completely* the wrong idea about why Mom was making me come up here to the ranch this evening."

"What did you think she wanted then?" BB called out.

Jay's smile was crooked. "I knew she was up to something, but I thought it had to do with her and Billy Morgan."

"Well, we all know about *that*," BB joked. "It's hardly a secret that they've got the hots for each other."

Jay raised an eyebrow. "As it happens, there is something to announce about that as well, isn't there, Mom?"

Bella tried to frown him down, but Billy stepped forward.

"Bella Williams has agreed to become my wife." He held out his hand to her. "And she's made me the happiest man on this planet."

Bella walked toward him, aware that she was blushing.

None of the Morgans looked particularly surprised by the announcement, and they all looked thrilled. Ruth was dabbing at her eyes and Maria was doing some kind of victory dance.

Billy took her hand in his and faced the guests. "Thank you very much, but tonight is about Erin and Jay, so let's get back to cutting the cake, toasting their good health, and wishing them the very best of everything for the rest of their days."

While everyone got on with that, Billy and Bella ended up in the kitchen, which felt right somehow. Billy grinned as she rolled up her sleeves, pinned up her hair, and set to work.

"I don't think I'm going to persuade you to leave this time, am I?"

"Not a chance. If anyone wants to come and say goodbye they'll know where to find me."

He threw a dishcloth in her direction and she threw it back and they ended up wrestling over it and giggling like two kids.

"This is going to be fun," Billy said.

"What is—us?"

"Yeah, us." He kissed her nose. "I love you, Bella."

"And I love you."

"Will you stay over?"

"At the speed we're cleaning up I'll probably be here all night anyway," Bella joked.

"We'll work things out." Billy looked down at her. "We'll *make* this work."

"Yes, we will." She nodded. "Despite my son and all the Morgans offering us advice."

"They mean well."

"Yes, but sometimes I wish they'd all butt out."

"We could build our own house halfway between your place and mine," Billy suggested.

"Or we could share our time between both places."

They smiled at each other. Whatever happened next, Bella was quite certain that Billy was right and that they would have fun. Maureen would be so proud of her. . . .

Billy's Mini Fruit Pavlovas

For Pavlova

6 egg whites at room temperature
1½ cups white sugar
2 tsp cornstarch
1 Tbsp lemon juice
½ Tbsp vanilla extract

For Cream

1½ cups cold heavy whipping cream

For Topping/Decor

4 to 5 cups fresh fruits (berries are my favorite)

Instructions

1. Using stand mixer, beat 6 egg whites on high speed for 1 minute until soft peaks form. With mixer on, gradually add 1½ cups of sugar and beat 10 minutes on high speed or until stiff peaks form. (Should be smooth and glossy.)
2. Use a spatula to quickly fold in lemon juice and vanilla extract, and then fold in cornstarch until blended.
3. Pipe meringue onto parchment paper and indent the center with a spoon. Bake at 225 degrees F for 1 hour and 15 minutes, then turn oven off. Without opening the door, leave for 30 minutes more. Outside of meringue should be dry and crisp to the tap.
4. Allow to cool. Can be stored for 3 to 5 days in airtight container. Or topped with whipped cream (follow instructions on carton) and fruit and eaten immediately!

For more recipes,
check out my Web site at
www.themorgansranch.com.